TO Jarret: th___ ___ ___ ___

my dream. ___

to bless yo___

all of your battles.

Joshua's
BATTLE

Best Wishes

Joe Johnson

Joshua's
BATTLE

JOE JOHNSON

ARCHWAY
PUBLISHING

This is a work of fiction. All of the characters, names, incidents, organizations, and dialogue in this novel are either the products of the author's imagination or are used fictitiously.

Archway Publishing books may be ordered through booksellers or by contacting:

Archway Publishing
1663 Liberty Drive
Bloomington, IN 47403
www.archwaypublishing.com
1-(888)-242-5904

Because of the dynamic nature of the Internet, any web addresses or links contained in this book may have changed since publication and may no longer be valid. The views expressed in this work are solely those of the author and do not necessarily reflect the views of the publisher, and the publisher hereby disclaims any responsibility for them.

Any people depicted in stock imagery provided by Thinkstock are models, and such images are being used for illustrative purposes only. Certain stock imagery © Thinkstock.

ISBN: 978-1-4808-0536-1 (sc)
ISBN: 978-1-4808-0537-8 (e)

Library of Congress Control Number: 2014902097

Printed in the United States of America

Archway Publishing rev. date: 03/04/2014

Acknowledgements

I BELIEVE THAT IF GOD GIVES you a vision, he will also give you the provision. I thank God for both the vision and the provision. The most important part of God's provision is the people he's placed in my life.

For the past twenty-two years, my wife Adrienne has been my motivation and inspiration. Thank you for loving and lifting me to greater heights. To my daughter Jayla, thank you for always seeing the best in me and becoming an incredible example of what faith, love, and perseverance can accomplish. To my son Bill, thank you for your unconditional love. To my mother, Mattie Johnson, thank you for your strength and courage and always believing in me. To my sister, Dr. Vivian Johnson, thanks for always bringing out the best in me. To my brother Jim, thanks for the lessons, and to my sister Rose Marie, thanks for being first. Thanks to Kristy Green and the wonderful grandchildren, Taylor, Will, and Ethan. To my sister-in–law Pearline Greene, thanks for the encouragement, and Greg Greene, thanks for the many golf matches that rejuvenated me.

To my family and friends, who supported and encouraged me through it all, I thank God for you. To my editor, Barbara Mohr, thanks for the red pen and sharp eye. Thanks to Mona Spencer for providing your gracious edits.

Thanks to my colleagues for tolerating the repeated mention of my upcoming novel.

Through this incredible journey, I've learned that being a writer is about much more than writing. It's about taking risks and stepping into the unknown and embracing the magic of creativity. It's about sharing and trusting a vision that only you can see.

So many friends have blessed me by providing words of encouragement that kept me pursuing this dream. Although your name may not be reflected on these pages, you are forever in my heart.

My hope is that this book entertains, motivates, and inspires you as much as it has me.

No one will be able to stand against you all the days of your life. As I was with Moses, so I will be with you; I will never leave you nor forsake you. Joshua 1:5 New International Version (NIV)

Prologue

JOSHUA JERICHO BATTLE PULLED HIS SCARF and coat tighter around his neck and increased his pace to the parking garage. The night air had the unmistakable chill of a November winter in Detroit. The frozen gusts off the Detroit River were creating icy bolts of wind that pierced his exposed skin. The flashing overhead sign on the Comerica Bank building read minus -15. He could hear the snow crunching underfoot, as the old clock on the First Baptist Church chimed 11:00. JJ Battle was working late for the first time in two years since he decided to give up his flourishing criminal law practice. He had forgotten how good it felt being one of the best criminal defense attorneys in the city, and he could feel the tug of excitement as he headed to the car. He loved the adrenaline rush he felt from working on a major case. There was no one on the street, and his car was the only car in the parking garage. He quickly strode to his car, searching for his keys. He was tired, yet exhilarated. It was the satisfaction of successfully finishing a tough project. He reached his car and pushed the remote to unlock the door. As he reached to open the door, the window shattered. He stared in disbelief, contemplating a windowless drive home in freezing temperatures. He heard a dull thud and saw a small hole appear in the metal of his door. He turned quickly, seeing a bright flash followed by a hiss of air and the plaster of the garage pillar exploding. He hit the ground, hurriedly crawling to the passenger side of the car. Twice more he heard the dull thud of two more bullets crashing into the side of the Lincoln. Instinctively he opened the door, using the car as a shield. He reached inside the car, fumbling with his keys. His hand shook as he finally managed to get the key in the ignition and the car started. He slid into the car, oblivious to the shattered glass littering the floor and seat. From the floor, he put the car in gear, mashing the accelerator to the floor as he gripped the steering wheel. He clipped the wall of the garage as the car sped wildly forward in the direction of the exit. Nearing the closed gate, he kept going; smashing the security bar before it could rise, splintering wood in his path. As he exited the garage, he pulled himself onto the seat, driving as fast as the ice and snow covered streets would allow. The big Lincoln fishtailed and slid until the weight took hold on the icy pavement. He slid into the turn on Congress Street, oblivious to traffic, accelerating onto the ramp of the Lodge freeway. He could hear a persistent thump, thump, thump, and guessed that a tire was flat. He didn't care. He continued on, exiting to Woodward Avenue barely negotiating the off ramp. For the first time, he checked his rear view mirror, uncertain if they were following him. Consumed by fear, he made a series of lefts and right turns, driving as fast as the conditions would allow. When he did not see any cars in his rear view mirror, he slowed to assess what had happened. The shooter was a professional. That much was certain. No amateur or carjacker uses a high-powered rifle with a silencer. No, they preferred handguns at close range. This was a sniper who had been waiting. Whoever was responsible did not follow to finish the job. He quickly thought of the possible suspects and drew a blank. He had been away from criminal defense for two years and had long since settled those old scores. He began to breathe deeply and forced himself to relax and consider all of the possibilities. He ruled out a robber or a carjacker. They preferred the element of surprise and enjoyed placing their victims in fear. This was different. He struggled to think of likely suspects. He couldn't think of anyone who was capable of, or motivated to, do such a thing. Someone wanted him dead or scared. Finally, as his frustration was making him panic, it came to him. His heart pounded against the sub-zero temperatures of the dark winter night. It came to him, chilling him deep inside his soul. He didn't know how or why, but he knew who. There was only one man who could set these crazy events in motion. There was no one else. This man would change his life forever. **BOBBY BOOGALOO BENNETT.**

Chapter 1

BOBBY BOOGALOO BENNETT WAS A PLAYER, a hustler and a lover. There was nothing in his past to suggest that he was a violent man, although he was now being charged with a violent crime. Looking at him, he was the unlikeliest of lovers. He was overweight, short, balding, and practically illiterate. But he possessed what women affectionately referred to as charm. It was ghetto "charm." His mother supplied him with his nickname, Boogaloo, which was for the 1980's dance she made him perform to entertain her friends. Boogaloo was always ready to oblige. Even as a child, he loved the attention and affections of women, and they loved him. It was a gift. Whatever it was that Boogaloo possessed, it was successful. He made a living from wining, cajoling, and romancing single mothers in the projects and collecting their welfare checks for his efforts. Boogaloo was a regular in the projects, especially on the first of the month when the checks arrived. He would make his rounds collecting the checks and then doling out whatever money he deemed the women needed to survive.

Judging by his new Cadillac and clothes, he had many admirers. Their love and adulation for Boogaloo suggested he had talents and charms that were not obvious to everyone. He maintained his lucrative enterprise through equal portions of skill and fear. But, lately, Boogaloo had developed another, more lucrative, hustle to go with his vast project harem. He was now involved in a complex real estate scheme.

He had elevated his skills to include swindling the poor and elderly out of their property by deceit and intimidation. He would convince the neighborhood property owners that the impending development for the upcoming Super Bowl meant that the city would take their property by eminent domain. For many of the uneducated in the community, eminent domain might as well have been the kiss of death. To them it meant there was no way they could keep their property from the hands of the government.

Boogaloo offered them hope, even if it was false hope. He agreed to pay them in cash for the equity in their property and in exchange; they would sign a quitclaim deed to Boogaloo for their interest in their property. Then, they would pay him rent and remain in their homes. He convinced them that they could stay in their homes for as long as they liked; they just had to continue paying rent. It all sounded good, until Boogaloo's checks started to bounce, and nobody was paid.

Boogaloo was legendary for his ability to maintain a harmonious harem, until one of the flock, Betty Ross, decided to listen to her girlfriend and contemplated leaving Boogaloo. This was an unprecedented defection, and it required Boogaloo to administer swift and meaningful reinforcement, which he did with shocking and sensational consequences. Boogaloo's case gained national attention - not just for its legal and social significance, but also for the sheer audacity of his flamboyance. He was totally unrepentant as he granted repeated interviews, against the advice of his previous lawyer.

The facts were simple and straightforward. Betty's best friend, Brianna Tuller, had been encouraging Betty to leave Boogaloo for some time. It was her opinion, shared by many, that Betty deserved better than Boogaloo. They repeatedly told her that she could do badly by herself, that she didn't need Boogaloo to bring her down. Finally, all of the encouragement had some effect. Betty had planned to leave Bobby and take their kids. They had planned to hide Betty at a friend's house until she could find different living arrangements.

The plan had worked for about a week, with Boogaloo unsure of Betty's whereabouts. The first of the month arrived and Boogaloo was on the prowl for the monthly welfare checks. As luck or fate would have it, while he was looking for Betty and the kids, Brianna came by Betty's apartment to get the rest of Betty's clothes. Boogaloo hid behind the door, waiting, expecting Betty, when Brianna entered.

"Where's Betty?" He asked. His voice was loud with anger and impatience.

"I don't know." Brianna answered with a mix of fear and bravado.

"Then what are you doing here?"

"I came by looking for Betty myself."

"Brianna, don't play with me. I don't have time for this. Then why did you have a key?"

"If you would have treated her better, she wouldn't have left," she answered as she moved closer to the door.

"I told you before, stay out of my business," Boogaloo answered positioning himself between Brianna and the door. "Tell me where she is or I'm going to keep you here until you do."

"I told you I don't know where she is. She could be anywhere."

"Stop lying. Don't make me hurt you," Boogaloo shouted, his tone becoming more threatening.

Brianna lunged for the door, making a futile, desperate effort to get out as Boogaloo grabbed her wrists.

"Stop! You're hurting my wrists," she shrieked. Sensing the futility of struggling, Brianna considered her options. She thought that if she could get out of the house she could escape. She quickly devised a plan.

"Okay, I'll show you where she is if you promise not to hurt me." Boogaloo relaxed his grip.

"I never wanted to hurt you or Betty in the first place. I just want to talk to her and see my kids."

She watched him carefully as he went around the small living room collecting some of his personal items. Her heart nearly stopped as she saw him reach under the couch cushion, pull out a shiny silver gun, and place it into a bag.

"What the hell is that for?" She asked, not bothering to disguise her fear.

"Oh this? I just like to have a little reassurance in case things get out of hand," he said, looking at the pistol admiringly. "I'm going to lead you to the car; please don't try to do anything stupid. Don't try to signal the neighbors or run. If you do, I'm gonna hurt you. All I want to do is see Betty and my kids."

He went to the front door, cracking it slightly and looking up and down the block to see if the neighbors were out. They were. He nudged Brianna. "Let's go and don't do anything stupid."

As they went out the front door, he tightened the pressure on her arm. "Wave at the neighbors. Just look normal like nothing is going on. Now get in the car."

As Brianna got in on the passenger side, he hurried around to the driver's side and quickly got behind the wheel. He started the car and slowly pulled out of the parking lot.

"So where are we going?" She asked, not wanting him to see her fear.

"Why are you looking so scared? You tell me where we're going. You know where Betty is."

"Just take a left and get on the Jeffries Freeway going west," Brianna replied, contemplating all of her options. She wanted to buy some time to figure out how she could escape. She did not intend to lead Bobby to her friend.

She wasn't sure what Bobby was capable of doing. He had a gun. The only thing she knew was she had to get away and get help.

As they approached an upcoming light, Boogaloo slowed the car, preparing to stop. Brianna took a bold chance. In one smooth motion, she undid her seatbelt, opened the door, and jumped. She didn't have the chance to calculate speed and distance. This might be her only chance to escape, and she took it.

She felt her ankle give as she tumbled and rolled scraping her body and face on the pavement. When she stopped rolling, she tried to get up but collapsed in horrible pain. Her ankle and the left side of her body were in excruciating pain. She tried to crawl. Traffic around her came to screeching stops. She could see Bobby slam on the brakes, stopping suddenly. She could see the backup lights as he reversed the car and sped back toward her. She had to get up if she was going to get away, and she tried, but her leg and ankle collapsed at a sickly twisted angle. She lost consciousness, as she lay on the pavement in a crumpled ball.

Boogaloo was out of the car almost before it stopped, and was beside Brianna scooping her up in his arms. "Shit! Get out of my way!" He hissed to the quickly gathering crowd of motorists and pedestrians. "I have to get her to the hospital."

"What happened?" A voice in the crowd asked as Bobby ignored them and gently loaded Brianna into the car. He had to hurry. He knew they would notify the police who would show up shortly. He was not in the mood to explain.

He got back in the car, sped to Detroit Receiving Hospital, and screeched up to the emergency room door. Brianna remained unconscious beside him.

He screamed for an emergency attendant as he searched frantically for hospital personnel or a wheelchair. Unable to find any hospital staff he found a wheelchair, loaded Brianna into the seat, and rushed her into the emergency room. He handed her over to the hospital staff.

"Sir, what happened? What type of injuries does she have?" The hospital staff was bombarding him with questions, and there was another gathering crowd of hospital personnel fast approaching. It was all happening so fast. Bobby surveyed the situation. He knew he would have to act fast. The hospital staff would call the police and he would have to answer questions and explain the circumstances of Brianna's injuries.

He made a decision to leave; and quickly and quietly exited the hospital.

Chapter 2

"STOP IT! JUST STOP IT! CAN'T you for once just let it go?" He chided himself, yelling to hear himself over the blare of the stereo.

Joshua Jericho Battle was doing it again. He just couldn't help himself. "Relax!" He told himself, as he guided the Lincoln down I-94, away from the morning commuter traffic and toward his morning tee time. He was a man with issues. He just couldn't escape this feeling of fear. Whether it was fear of failure or fear of success, he was afraid. He just couldn't quite figure life out. When things were going well, he worried they wouldn't last. When they were going bad, he worried they wouldn't end. Today, he was worried that the good times would not last. He couldn't help it.

He knew he was fortunate; he set his own hours, worked pretty much when he pleased, but he still didn't trust his blessing. Trouble was like a triple bogey; it was always lurking on the next hole. You couldn't predict when it was going to happen, but you knew eventually that it would.

It was 10:00 in the morning at the St. Clair Shores Country Club on the eastern outskirts of Detroit. It was late fall and a chill of the upcoming winter was in the air. This was one of the last days of the golfing season and he wanted an early start but not so early that he ran into the old timers and retirees that dominated the early tee times. He would just check into the clubhouse, get a cart and take off. If he was lucky, he could get in twenty-seven holes, and if he was extremely lucky, he could get in thirty-six. Either way, it would be a good way to wrap up the golf season.

"Good morning, Mr. Battle. I see you're taking advantage of our fine weather today." It was Charley, the course marshal, clubhouse pro, and utility person. Charley did it all at the course.

"You're right, Charley. I thought I'd get in a round before the weather changes. There aren't too many good days left this year."

"Good idea. I heard you're hitting them pretty good these days."

"Not up to your standards, Charley. Too many bogeys and not enough birdies," he said, paying homage to the old pro. Charley, who was well in his seventies, could still beat anybody who showed up. There was talk around the course that Charley had played a few Pro tournaments and did pretty well in his day. Charley never talked about those days, always maintaining a deliberate silence and a far away stare as if he were measuring distance to the pin.

"The course is clear except for a couple of loud lawyer slicksters on the putting green. They might be friends of yours."

"Damn!" The last thing he wanted was a distraction and to be forced to engage in small talk and banter. He knew that golf was supposed to be a social game, but he played it for the game - not for the socializing.

He laced up his shoes, readied his gear, and headed for the first tee. He wondered who the two lawyers were. He hoped that he didn't know them.

"JOSHUA JERICHO BATTLE, world famous litigator. What an honor."

"Damn!" He was disappointed when he turned to see the huge Cuban cigar protruding from the dark and shiny mug of Randy Connors and his law partner Victor Wright. Old Charley was right; he did know these two clowns. They were two of the richest lawyers in town and former law school classmates. Victor and Randy were exact opposites, and people wondered how they made their practice work so well. Randy was short, stocky and dark. Coming from the east side of Detroit, people expected Randy to be tough and resourceful, but nobody expected his legal brilliance. He had a knack for seeing through the most complex issues and fashioning creative solutions. He was a class act and always had been. Their paths had always seemed to cross, but they never met until the first day of law school. Randy was two years behind JJ, and they attended the same grade school, middle school, high school and even under-grad at the U of M, and both were from the east side of Detroit. While not close, they enjoyed a mutual respect and always provided homeboy support throughout law school.

Victor, on the other hand was a rich kid from Bloomfield Hills; he came from money, privilege, and a family of lawyers. He was tall and handsome with creamy beige skin. He had the look and confidence that money and good bloodlines provide. His grandfather, James Wright, was Judge of the United States Sixth Circuit Court of Appeals, who happened to be one of the bright-est legal minds around. His father, former U.S. Congressman Bill Wright, was a partner in the prestigious Detroit firm of Booth, Johnson, and Wolinsky. His mother, Beth Adams Wright, was a judge for the 36th District Court in Detroit. Victor Wright had powerful connections, and he needed them, because intel-ligence was not his forte. He was dumb as a rock. Nevertheless, what he was good at was developing relationships, and he and Randy had forged some of the most powerful alliances in the Midwest. They were ambitious and focused. Victor and JJ were law school rivals. In addition, Victor resented JJ's charm and success with women. He could not get over how everyone continually hero-worshipped JJ's past athletic exploits.

Further, Victor resented the fact that JJ and Victor's wife, Carlena, were study partners and more in law school. It was the *more* that Victor resented. Carlena, like JJ, was from Detroit and was a fun loving girl who knew what she wanted. JJ and Carlena's attraction developed slowly. They started as part of a Black Law Students study group, with about twenty other members. They quickly saw how inefficient and unproductive the group was, and formed their own two-person study group. The closeness and the stimulation of intense legal education were too much. JJ didn't know whether it was the mix of inten-sity, fear, or their frequent togetherness, but whatever the cause, their desire for each other was insatiable. They were like rabbits, having sex any time and anywhere. It was between classes, at her apartment or a quickie and lunch be-fore Warner's one o'clock contracts lecture. They also tried the men's bathroom in the basement of the law library. It was the only bathroom on campus where the outside doors could be locked, allowing them some much needed privacy.

They both agreed and understood the parameters of their relationship; it was not about love or romance; it was about satisfying a mutual need, and incredible sex. That was the problem. The sex had become so good and satisfying that they were missing class, studying less and neither was able to say no to the other. Their torrid and lustful liaison was remarkable in one major distinction; they managed to keep their relationship secret from the entire nosy and inquisitive law school class.

They were not sure how long they could sustain this clandestine affair, but neither was willing to stop. It continued for fifteen incredible, life-sustaining weeks of the school term. Who knows where it might have led had fate not intervened to drop the proverbial ice cube down the pants of lust and love. Finals were one week away, and they had literally screwed the semester away. They decided to meet on Saturday night to discuss their dilemma; how they were going to cram sixteen weeks of law into one week. Curiously enough, they found their inspiration in each other's arms after post-orgasmic bliss. They would end it cold turkey and kick each other's habit for the sake of their legal careers. They agreed to a week of all nighters without sex, filled completely with only legal education. It was a tortuous and grueling week. After they successfully completed exams, they met to discuss their futures.

Like recovering addicts, they agreed to meet in a public place, free of the temptation that an intimate meeting might create. They agreed that as good as the sex and intimacy was between them, the reality was that they were no longer good for each other. They were like two flames that, when combined, became an inferno that burned out of control. They recognized that neither had the power to say no to the other, and rather than being a good thing, in this case it allowed the relationship to wander out of control. They both had lost their focus, which was getting a legal education. When it was finally over, they parted with a special bond and friendship that would last forever. They had shared an intense, honest, and open relationship that explored some of the deepest human emotions between a man and a woman. Because of that, they would always have something special.

Victor, however, had never quite gotten over JJ and Carlena's relationship. Victor loved to gloat about the different paths his and JJ's careers had taken, but JJ was comfortable with the choices he made. While not fond of Victor and Randy socially, JJ did have a grudging respect for what they had accomplished professionally.

"Gentlemen, the honor is truly mine," he replied, with a graciousness he did not feel. He smiled, concealing the resentment of having his morning round ruined.

"I see this is how the independently wealthy spend their leisure time," Victor replied with just a hint of sarcasm in his tone.

"Not quite. If I were truly independently wealthy, I would belong to Oakland Hills Country Club, the way you guys do. This is just where the regular folks play."

"Touché, JJ, I hope your golf game is as sharp as your quips." Victor countered.

"What brings you two big time lawyers slumming at a small time course like St. Clair Shores? We don't have all of the amenities that you're used to."

"We just wanted a game and this is one of the nicest courses around. It was just a coincidence that we met you here," Randy interjected, sensing some rising hostility between Victor and JJ.

Randy and Victor never left anything to chance. They were always thorough. That's how they founded the largest minority firm in the country. They were sharp, bright and connected. They were the new breed of lawyers that were primarily dealmakers. They couldn't bother to get their hands dirty with routine legal matters. They only handled big money clients, and companies anxious to do business in the City.

Their firm handled municipal bonds, financing, bankruptcy, major transactional work, and real estate. The firm also handled all of the bond work for the City and handled the transactional work for the new Ford Field, home of the Detroit Lions, and Comerica Park, home of the Detroit Tigers. Both of those were huge multimillion-dollar deals, and their firm was at the forefront.

They tried to lure JJ to the firm, but he convinced them that he was just a humble advocate from the eastside of Detroit and was unworthy to practice in the higher echelons of the profession. They didn't buy it, but gradually they stopped pursuing him. JJ remembered when they first got started.

"Mind if we tag along?" Randy asked in a conciliatory tone.

"Why not? The more the merrier," JJ said, as if he had a choice. He had envisioned a nice quiet, leisurely round, but now that was ruined. He would just have to make the best of it.

"What do you usually play for?" Victor asked, just a bit too eager, as if he were setting JJ up. It was uncharacteristic of Victor's normally shrewd negotiating.

"Two dollars a hole. Five Dollars Pars, Ten Dollars Birdies, Twenty Dollars Eagles. Sound fair to you guys?" At those rates, he knew it would take about four or five under to beat him. He was playing well and he welcomed the challenge.

"Well, that sounds fair to me. The tee box is all yours," Victor said motioning to the first tee. JJ stepped up, smashed his first drive long, and down the middle of the fairway to approving oohs and aahs from Victor and Randy.

It was painfully clear from the first hole that Randy and Victor were better lawyers than golfers. Victor had obviously taken lessons, but that could not negate his obvious lack of athleticism. Randy had an unorthodox self-taught swing that was not pleasant to watch. They were all over the course, swinging wildly, swearing, and cursing whenever they hit an errant shot, which was often. They played as if they had more money than talent, which they did.

After the first nine holes, JJ knew that there was no way Randy and Victor could win, and he eased up and intentionally missed a few shots to keep the margin close. He had to give them credit- they never gave up, and they made some miraculous recovery shots. He still cleared close to one hundred dollars each from the free-swinging lawyers. However, in the end, it was not pretty. A golfer's true character usually surfaces during a round. Randy and Victor were no exception.

Because the weather had turned cold and windy, he abandoned his plans for any more golf that day, and invited the boys for drinks. In the locker room, they were loud and boisterous, recalling the afternoon's great shots. He had to admit they were gracious losers.

JJ showered quickly, dressed, and headed for the pro shop to have his clubs regripped. He left his clubs with Charley just in case he headed to Florida for some winter golf. He eased into the clubhouse, found a table overlooking the lake, and waited for the guys. He stared out over the lake and reflected on how good life felt.

Randy and Victor emerged, golf chic and slid into the booth next to JJ.

"That was some round of golf. We're going to have to get you up to Oakland Hills to return the favor," Victor said.

"That would be nice." JJ said with false enthusiasm.

JJ ordered drinks for everyone.

"Hey listen JJ, we know that you don't practice criminal law anymore. But Victor and I were thinking about this criminal case our client picked up that needs some special attention. We were hoping to retain you for the case." Randy queried, reaching for his glass of Grey Goose.

"Thanks for the offer guys, but I'm officially out of that line of work."

"Because of the nature of the case, we're prepared to pay a hefty retainer and expenses," Victor chimed in.

"Why me? There are any number of good defense attorneys in the city that can handle a case like the one you describe."

"Like we said, this case requires not just skill but discretion. This is a special client and there are special circumstances," added Victor, with just a touch of impatience.

"No thanks. I'll pass. Drink up guys, you've earned it."

For the rest of the evening they talked about sports, women, politics, and about JJ's college exploits and the unfortunate knee injury that ended his career. After a few rounds, JJ excused himself and left the laughing lawyers to themselves.

Chapter 3

LEAVING THE CLUB, JJ FELT THE warmth of a whiskey buzz as he slid the big Lincoln onto the freeway heading downtown. He had to admit that he enjoyed the round of golf with Randy and Victor, especially the cash he extracted from their wallets. It was nice to see his old law school classmates doing so well. He headed westbound on I-94, and the freeway traffic was lighter than usual. He made a mental note to head to the gym tomorrow. The years since law school had not been kind to either Randy or Victor, physically speaking. Both added some extra weight and had receding hairlines. JJ was proud of how he had managed to keep himself in shape. While he was about twenty pounds over his playing weight, it was all still pretty much muscle, the product of that year of intense bodybuilding with that psycho personal trainer, Cynthia. Whatever, it had given him a healthier appearance and a little more discipline. He had always thought he was too thin, so his new physique made him look and feel healthier and more confident.

As he arrived at the entrance of his downtown office, he looked out over the skyline, thinking how much he loved this city. It was a unique city, with heart and soul. It was a city built by entrepreneurs and hustlers, men with big ideas and big dreams and the courage to make them come true. Detroit had at one time been one of the centers of the industrialized world. It was home to Ford, General Motors, and Chrysler Corporation. Now, it had a different spirit- a tired defeated city, looking for the next new thing. Many thought that the casinos would help reinvigorate a dying economy and infrastructure. Surprisingly, things had begun to turn around and he could see signs of revitalization. There were new major construction projects all over, restoring a newer, more modern look and feel to the city and, more importantly, creating new jobs.

As he entered the lobby, he spotted Sam, the security guard, at his post as he had been for the last thirty years. Sam knew every tenant in the building and could tell you about the history of all the rich and famous that had ever entered the confines of the prestigious Ford Building. JJ made sure that he took care of Sam at Christmas and his birthday, and was always careful to ask about his wife.

"Good evening Mr. Battle, working late I see."

"Yeah Sam" I haven't been in the office lately and I wanted to catch up on some things. By the way, how's Mrs. Sam these days? How is she recovering from her surgery?"

"Just fine. She's still raving about the two dozen roses you sent. She was the envy of all of her church friends. We can never thank you enough for picking up the tab for a nurse coming to the house to help. It really made a difference."

"Sam, it was nothing. It was the least I could do."

"By the way, this package came by courier for you after Marsha left. I thought I would hold it in case you came in."

"Thanks Sam."

He took the package and headed up on the elevator to the 17th floor. He had been a tenant in this building for the past ten years. He could have afforded a more prestigious office, but this was where he opened his first law office, and the building was special to him. He had twice moved to a larger space, as his practice had grown, and now this was like his second home. There was no reason to move now.

He turned on the light and walked around the office, quickly looking at the mail Marsha had stacked on his desk. He went to the refrigerator and grabbed a bottle of water. Marsha was the glue that held this place together.

He reflected on how he met her. She had come in as a divorce client unable to pay her legal bill. Those were desperate times for her, and she bartered his fee against her providing secretarial services. The problem was that she didn't have any secretarial skills. However, what she had, she had in abundance. She was a little fireplug of a woman, with street smarts and ample assets to match. It took months before she got the message that she could not seduce him, but that did not stop her from trying. She was tremendous with the clients, knowing when to get tough, or when to lend a sympathetic ear. As the months went on, she became indispensable, becoming the unofficial office manager. As her role in the office increased, JJ began relying on her more and more. When he decided to give up criminal law, Marsha recruited and developed a small real estate closing practice.

She was also responsible for helping him pull his personal life together in the aftermath of the Young Killers of America debacle, providing support, and comfort. He smiled as he reflected on all that she meant to him as a friend and confidant, and he was thankful that he had the good judgment to give her a chance that first day.

Marsha had gone through his mail, had taken out the important things and handled those, leaving him a stack of things needing his attention. He cleared away the stack that Marsha had left him, when he remembered the package from the courier. He grabbed the envelope and looked for a return address, but there was none. That was odd. He opened the package and saw that it was from the law firm of Connors and Wright. Inside there was a check for One Hundred Thousand Dollars, made out to Joshua Jericho Battle, for legal services. He knew that Randy and Victor were up to something, but he never imagined this. Included in the package were police reports and other discovery information pertaining to Robert Bennett. As he read the file, he could hear the wind howling outside, and he felt a shudder as he contemplated his next move.

To whom much is given, much is required, he thought. This was a rule he consistently lived by. He was thankful for his athletic gifts, that had provided him with a first rate education, and his gifts as an attorney. Nevertheless, he was always mindful that these gifts came with a price. He began to question whether being a criminal defense attorney was an appropriate use for his skills. Now faced with the dilemma of whether to represent Robert Bennett, he had to ask himself if this was what he was destined to do. He had always seen himself as a champion of the underdog, because he viewed himself as an underdog.

He wondered if he should allow himself to be pulled back into the deep dark hole of criminal defense. After all, there were still demons that he had not yet exorcised. There were wounds that were still raw. He had vowed never to practice criminal law again-yet here he was contemplating another plunge into the abyss.

He remembered the Bible stories his mother used to tell him about his namesake, Joshua, and what a mighty warrior he was, and the famous battle of Jericho. He saw himself as a warrior and a man of faith. Although he did not regularly attend church, he still held strong spiritual beliefs. Recent events had tested his faith, but he still persevered. He was someone who had beaten the odds when circumstances suggested he should fail. He was at a moral crossroads. He questioned whether there were more noble, worthwhile pursuits for his talents rather than the pursuit of large retainers and defending society's dregs.

He could not help but believe that by continuing to represent social deviants, he was somehow compromising the very things he believed in the most-defending people who truly deserved quality representation. Nevertheless, here he was again, contemplating a large retainer for an unworthy client. He laughed, chiding himself for making a premature judgment about a client he had not met. He agreed to reserve judgment, fighting off the cynicism of the jaded. He knew he would have to make a decision soon, but before he did, he had one important task to complete; burying the ghost of his former client, Kareem Abdul Boozer. Until he was able to put those events in their proper perspective, they would haunt him forever.

Chapter 4

KATHERINE DEVLIN WAS THE SMARTEST, MOST resourceful woman that JJ knew. She was also one of the most beautiful. It wasn't her beauty alone, or her intelligence that made Katherine exceptional. Some sort of cosmic mix set her apart from other women. In most women, those characteristics might be intimidating. But not Katherine. She had an unerring sense of who she was and a determination to live life on her own terms. She had a joyous nature and a practical understanding of life that was contagious.

JJ needed to discuss his newest client, Bobby Bennett and the largest retainer he had ever received, and Katherine was someone whose judgment he trusted. They had been friends since they met while studying for the bar exam. She immediately impressed him with her intelligence and intensity. She was a no-nonsense woman who knew what she wanted. He was even more impressed when she initially rejected his advances. From that mutual respect, they developed a deep and lasting friendship.

Like most men, JJ liked beautiful women. However, he also knew that beautiful women sometimes possessed considerable baggage. These days, he preferred sexy over beautiful, since you get all of the pleasure and less of the baggage. Katherine was that rare combination of woman; beauty and brains without being self-absorbed. Their friendship gradually evolved into intimacy, and from there into love. Yet, both were comfortable with the pace of things and neither felt the need to formalize things at this point. She could be that woman of a lifetime, but not just yet. He still had some issues to resolve before he could fully commit. He was as they say, "a work in progress." He hoped that patience was one of her many virtues.

He dialed Katherine's number, hoping she would be there to pick up the phone. "Hello, this is JJ," he said, smiling at the sound of her voice. "Is the kitchen open?" He asked, referring to her excellent culinary skills. Being from Jamaica, she was always preparing some exotic Caribbean dish.

"As a matter of fact, I just finished some curried chicken and some rice and peas. I'm going to take a shower. Use your key and let yourself in."

He was pleased at her receptiveness, since it had been a week or so since they had seen each other. Still she treated him as if he was always welcome; it was part of her charm.

He pulled into the parking garage of the Riverside Condominiums and found an available parking space. He took the elevator to the twenty-fifth floor. He let himself in and took a moment to absorb the beauty and luxury of the condo. It was elegantly decorated, and had a three hundred and sixty degree view of the city and of Windsor. It was breathtaking.

He could smell the exotic aromas from Katherine's cooking which stimulated his taste buds. He went to the refrigerator, got a bottle of wine, and poured himself a glass. He sat down and listened to Cassandra Wilson on the CD player, and tried to collect his thoughts about all that he had learned about Bobby Bennett and the developing conspiracy of One Detroit, Inc. He was wondering how much he should tell Katherine, when she appeared fresh from the shower, her long hair wet and glistening in the condominium light.

"I see you haven't lost your touch. The food smells wonderful," he said, moving toward her for a long-awaited embrace. She looked lovely. She was wearing one of his shirts he had left there on a previous stay over. He imagined what she was wearing underneath, if anything. They did not speak as they embraced and held each other tightly. He didn't want to let go. He could feel the warmth and softness of her body as she pressed against him. He smelled the freshness and sensuousness of her soap, with some intoxicating fragrance he could not quite identify. He breathed it all in. He didn't want to end the embrace and lose the power of the moment. He could feel his heart and breathing quickening, as he remembered how good it felt to be with her. He had a weakness for sexy women, and Katherine had sexiness in abundance. Finally, she roused them from their embrace with a final squeeze and a kiss on the cheek.

"Hey, you're not getting all sentimental on me are you?" She asked, holding him at arms length and looking deep into his eyes.

"Who me? I was just admiring the wonderfulness of West Indian genetics. How's your mom anyway?"

"She's fine. You know she always asks about you. If she were a little younger, she would give me a run for my money."

"I hate to tell you, but she already does." They laughed sharing a pleasant memory from the past.

They shared a loving relationship. He even begun to think that it might lead to marriage soon. That was before he had given up on life for a while and couldn't see his future, much less their future together. Beyond that, there were their careers, other people, and the everyday confusion of life that keeps people apart. Still, he could feel the unmistakable passion between them. Theirs was an easy, comfortable love that enabled them to remain more than friends.

"So let's sit down and eat, and you can explain to me why you decided to call me after all this time. It must be something or someone very important."

"Maybe. Or maybe I just missed that West Indian accent and your good cooking." He replied sarcastically.

"If that were the case, you could have gone to the local Caribbean restaurant and ordered carryout."

"Very funny. You always were a smart-ass. But that's one of your more endearing qualities."

They sat down to a quiet candlelit dinner with the wine flowing. JJ told her his theory of the case, and all of the complexities about Bobby Bennett. The meal and conversation lasted two hours and through two bottles of wine.

Katherine was a brilliant lawyer with instincts to match, yet she was reserved in her opinions about the case. She prodded JJ and asked the right questions, helping him to reach a different perspective about the case. Her specialties were real estate, land acquisitions, and public finance. She agreed to have one of her associates research the property acquisitions in the Corktown area of Detroit that Bobby had fraudulently acquired. They agreed they would withhold judgment about the reliability of Bobby's information until they could review any information her associate might uncover.

After the meal, and after all of the dishes and food had been cleared away, they sat down on the couch and reminisced about the past. It was late, and neither wanted the evening to end. Even though so much had happened between them, there was still an awkward uneasiness to the evening. JJ allowed the wine and the comfort of the evening to release the stress of recent events. He looked longingly over at Katherine, who was deeply in her own thoughts.

She leaned over, placing her glass on the table. He could see her shirt-tail open revealing smooth, athletic, golden brown thighs. The view of those thighs made him remember how close he and Katherine had been and what she meant to him. He could feel his excitement building. He wanted her so badly. He breathed deeply, not wanting to be presumptuous and make the first move. It surprised him that as close as they were, he still feared rejection. She noticed his hesitation and moved forward, gently grasping his face in her hands while kissing him. Her kisses had the sweet taste of wine. The kiss turned into an embrace. He responded, enjoying the taste of her and the warmth and closeness of her body pressed against him.

She was so soft, and he loved the feel of this woman in his arms. He felt a sense of urgency, as if he had to have her now, but, he also knew he wanted this feeling to last. They were together now, standing and squeezing each other tightly, as if to make up for lost time. His hands were all over her, and he was hungry for her. He impatiently sought his favorite places on her body. Slowly he undid her shirt, pleased to find her unrestrained breasts firm and receptive to his touch. With his other hand, he reached behind her and gently squeezed her, enjoying her warmth and softness. She rocked slowly in his arms, as if dancing a dance of forgotten love. She moaned softly in his ear, signaling her rising passion. He could feel their combined excitement rising as she arched her body, tightening their embrace. "I missed you so much," he whispered, taking the pillows off the couch and throwing them on the floor.

Slowly, and delicately, he laid her down on the pillows and lay next to her. They said nothing. They both gave in to the moment and the feeling. He could see her body silhouetted against the nighttime sky rising in slow, measured breaths. His mouth was all over her body, tasting the sweetness of flowers and fruit. She responded by unbuttoning his shirt and undoing the belt on his pants.

He could hear the music in the background and the hurried sounds of their breathing. He could feel her excitement, and he hurried to take off his remaining clothes. She pulled him on top of her, guiding him to her. The feeling was new yet familiar, and soon they settled into a rhythm of passion and need. Katherine squeezed him tighter as her movements became more purposeful. Slowly, she let herself go, giving in to unrestrained pleasure. She knew what her body needed and there was purpose in her movements. She shuddered involuntarily in climax and rolled JJ over onto his back. She began to move slowly and methodically to her own rhythm as she straddled him. She was like a virtuoso, playing a wild solo, yet still part of the band. With her head thrown back and eyes closed, she firmly grasped JJ's shoulders, giving into her rising passion. She moaned a deep and sensual moan, punctuating the stillness of the condo. Her body, silhouetted in the moonlight, swayed to her own earthy rhythm. This is how it was supposed to be, he thought, releasing himself to her. He was lost in the depths of this woman and began to meet her movements with his own rising pleasure. He could feel the softness of her inner thighs pressing against him. He squeezed tighter, thrusting harder, his breathing measured and controlled. He matched her every movement as the music, wine, and their own lust fueled their passion. All was lost as he remembered whispering her name, or perhaps he yelled it. They collapsed into spasms of pleasure, as he pulled her on top of him. He loved feeling her weight on him and he vowed to himself to keep her forever.

These times of unspoken, yet undeniable love, bound them. They lay in a passionate, satisfied embrace, naked and vulnerable to the world; oblivious to the fate that waited.

Chapter 5

JJ AWOKE EARLY; HE WAS HUNG over yet satisfied. His contentment was the result of the intimacy, passion and love he and Katherine shared. He glanced over, admiring Katherine's beauty. He hoped she would awake, so that they could repeat their spirited lovemaking of last night. While he waited, he began to think about his new client, Bobby Bennett. He knew this case was about more than just Bobby Bennett. It could potentially involve some of the city's most influential people at the highest levels.

He didn't know who Bobby's story might implicate, so he needed to be very discreet with whom he shared information. He had to decide if he was willing to take on the challenge of dealing with what he might uncover.

JJ was no stranger to battles. Growing up on the east side of Detroit, he fought many battles, and had survived them all. His experiences with the YKA, Young Killers of America, still haunted him, though. His thoughts went back to that case, as they often did, and he felt a shudder as he remembered what happened.

The YKA was an organization of murder-for-hire hit men who used juveniles as assassins. They were dangerous, ruthless, and deadly. These young assassins received military training from former soldiers recruited by Kareem, and they were taught the nuances of killing. Since they were juveniles, they escaped maximum penalties for their crimes.

Many of their crimes went unpunished since witnesses were reluctant to testify for fear of reprisals. The YKA dealt harshly with anyone who informed on them. Consequently, no one ever did.

They killed for a price with cold-blooded indifference. The community lived in fear, and the police were frustrated because of the number of unsolved homicides. These unsolved homicides were a testament to the YKA's skill and ability to avoid detection.

The YKA flourished as the drug trade became more lucrative. Dealers seeking to enlarge their territory enlisted the services of the YKA to eliminate competition. It became a very profitable enterprise. The YKA protected itself through a culture of retributive violence.

It had been the perfect case for JJ. In many ways, this case had defined his legal career. Win and you established yourself as a local legend able to make miracles happen for your clients; because losing was usually never fatal to the defense attorney. The justice system usually worked, guilty people were usually convicted.

Trying a case with the right sense of drama, skill, and passion endeared you to Detroiters because they loved a good show. It was an attorney's duty not to lose sight of that well-known fact.

Kareem Abdul Boozer was the founder of YKA and his case had all of the elements that a defense attorney considers when he taking on a high-profile client - a hefty upfront retainer, an unsympathetic victim to share blame, or another equally despised entity to blame, like the Detroit Police Department. In this case, he had all of those elements. He had nothing to lose.

Kareem Boozer had made an industry of murder and violence. His enterprise stood on the premise that life had value only as a commodity. Some commodities had more value than others. The reality was that all human beings were perishable and their existence temporary. This approach was a practical business decision made without emotion. It was the fundamental consideration when he recruited members to join his organization; they had to possess the ability to see human life in its most basic form.

The success of his organization depended on two very important considerations; a loyal and well-trained crew and information. He was adept at acquiring both. It was essential for success.

Kareem chose his employees much like a CEO would staff an organization. He liked them young and ruthless. They came from extreme circumstances and most were loners and were isolated from their families. Kareem paid them well. They went through a series of training exercises, including extensive weapons training and self-defense. Members worked in teams for efficiency and security. They were taught to be responsible for their partner.

In Kareem's case, he had been on trial for double homicide. He was one of the most notorious criminals in Detroit history. His exploits rivaled those of legendary mafia figures of the fifties and sixties. Kareem was a dangerous man, he was cold, calculating, and fearless. He was feared on the streets because of both his reputation and his deeds. The fact that they had never arrested Kareem was sheer luck. His reputed killings were many.

The prosecution's theory of the case was that these were contract killings and the victims were killed in cold-blooded premeditated murder. At the time, the case created tremendous media frenzy, having all of the elements necessary to excite the public's interest.

JJ had been very careful to make sure that he selected a jury that would understand all of the dynamics of urban life. He fashioned a theory he felt sure the jury could understand - the world of drugs, violence and retribution. He painted the police as incompetent public servants, incapable or unwilling to conduct professional or impartial investigations. The truth of the matter was that it was a popular sentiment of many of the citizens of Detroit. If that was not enough to convince the jury, he threw in a self-defense motive for Kareem.

JJ had carefully painted a picture of the victims as drug dealers who misappropriated the profits of their drug-dealing employers. This was an unsettling and unpleasant fact in urban America. JJ was certain every juror understood this reality. Wayne County jurors were nationally renowned for being anti-establishment and for awarding the largest damage awards to plaintiffs of any jurisdiction in the country.

The victims, Rafael Ferguson and Larry Street, had previous convictions for drug dealing and violence. This made them more hated than Kareem. They were outcasts of their community, and the neighbors desperately wanted them out. Death was also an alternative. Jurors shared those sentiments. It was just a matter of whether their hatred for the victims outweighed their fear and loathing of the defendant.

JJ's closing argument to a packed courtroom heavily attended by the media was passionate and eloquent. It was more than his sociopathic client deserved. It was one of his best. When the jury came back with a not guilty verdict on all counts, the courtroom erupted in equal amounts of excitement and fury. Kareem's family and fellow YKA members were openly celebratory. The victim's family and friends were outraged. The judge, Miles Lane, a veteran Recorder's court jurist, was beside himself with disgust at the verdict. In fact, he had each juror polled forcing them to announce their verdict publicly. It did not change the outcome.

JJ accepted the verdict with subdued resignation. He knew he had done his job well, but secretly worried that he had unleashed a killer back into society. JJ loved the law, but sometimes hated the clients the law protected. Afterwards, in post-trial interviews and sound bites, JJ maintained the professionalism and ethics the situation required. He spoke about how justice prevailed and how the justice system usually got it right. He said all of the right words, but in his heart, he had difficulty justifying the outcome. He doubted that Kareem Abdul Boozer deserved the justice he received that day.

He exited the courtroom to a media frenzy, hungrily waiting for additional sound bites for the six o'clock news telecasts. He obliged.

"Attorney Battle, what do you think about your victory today?"

"First let me say that in a trial of this nature, there are no winners or losers, only survivors of a great American tragedy. Let's remember that two young men lost their lives, and although the jury found my client not guilty, he is far from a winner. We all must live with the consequences of our actions. We must find a way to end the senseless violence that plagues our community and prematurely and unnaturally ends the lives of so many young African American men. It has to stop."

JJ hoped that his words would not be lost or diminished in the aftermath of this real life drama. He knew the media would twist the meaning of this human tragedy; it was the nature of their business. His suspicions were immediately confirmed when he noticed Kareem Abdul Boozer at the bottom of the courthouse steps, his freedom barely minutes old, holding court.

"I knew I was gonna' beat this case, they didn't have nothin' on me. I was just protectin' my right to be a man. This is a hard life, and a man's got to protect what's his, that's all I'm talkin' about. Respect and protect. Hey, there's my lawyer, JJ Battle, the best lawyer in town." Kareem shouted, giving JJ an unwanted testimonial. The cameras shifted to JJ as he reluctantly acknowledged his client. At that moment, he felt an extreme case of sadness. He despised Kareem's lack of remorse at a time when he should have expressed sincere appreciation for his freedom. It was Kareem's boldness and his disdain for the value of human life that had JJ questioning his own role in this case.

JJ hurried to the parking lot with an uneasy sense of foreboding. He wanted to get out of the courthouse scene as quickly as possible. He wanted to unwind and analyze the day's events. He needed to put as much distance as he could between himself and Kareem Abdul Boozer. It would be a while before he tried another murder case. They had become too physically and emotionally draining.

He would call Katherine to see if she was free for dinner and some celebrating. After all, this was one of his biggest victories. He told himself, "this isn't about Kareem; it's about great lawyering and a sympathetic jury." What started out as a slam-dunk for the prosecution, ended in an overwhelming victory for JJ. He beat the odds. He had won freedom for his client when both the evidence and the eyewitnesses suggested the outcome should have been different.

He allowed himself a moment of lawyer's pride and savored the victory. It was a long, hard emotional case. He deserved some time off that was befitting his new anointed title of Best Lawyer in the City. He smiled at that, as both he and his client strode off toward their separate destinies.

He remembered that day as if it was yesterday. Those events and Kareem's subsequent arrest on new murder charges had an incredible impact on JJ.

It had been weeks since Kareem's acquittal, JJ had cancelled all of his appointments and court appearances. He needed the time to readjust and unwind. He spent the time either playing golf or just doing nothing, or sharing some quality time with Katherine.

Today, he was in his doing nothing mode. It was noon and he had not showered or shaven when the phone rang unexpectedly. He instinctively looked at the caller ID that read Shapiro, Lipstein, and Devlin. He picked it up excited to hear Katherine's voice. He hoped she had a late lunch in mind. Before he could answer, Katherine's voice tumbled out, her words running together in a West Indian rush, "have you seen the twelve o'clock news?"

"Hello to you too," JJ responded, wondering about her sense of urgency.

"Turn on Channel 7."

"OK, OK," JJ responded, becoming a little impatient with Katherine's tone.

On the screen, the reporter was doing a live report from some neighborhood on the east side. The scene was complete bedlam. The police and swat units had cordoned off the area and forced all of the residents behind barricades. The officers were in full riot gear and were breaking down the door and storming a single-family house. JJ was amazed that this was taking place on live television. The house, unlike the others in the neighborhood, appeared slightly more prosperous. It was a neatly painted bungalow with a recently trimmed, manicured lawn. JJ half expected the police to drag out some elderly grandmother and grandfather kicking and screaming. He turned up the volume as he marveled at the audacity of a live police arrest. JJ was still holding the phone when he heard Katherine's voice on the line bringing him back to reality, "can you believe it?"

"Yeah, it's amazing what the news media can capture live," he said oblivious to the impact of the unfolding events.

"You really don't know do you?" Katherine asked with just a hint of sympathy.

JJ no longer heard Katherine's voice as he intently listened for the details of the events he was watching.

"As you are witnessing live, the police are about to make an imminent arrest." The announcer whispered in hushed tones as if he were at a golf tournament. "This is the culmination of an investigation into the triple homicide that occurred yesterday about three blocks from here."

JJ was momentarily confused as footage of he and Kareem Abdul Boozer was rolling on the screen. It was recent footage as they were leaving Recorder's court following Kareem's acquittal on the double homicide, He wondered "why were they showing that footage now." He stared at the television set in fear and amazement?

"Holed up inside this residence is the suspected shooter, Kareem Abdul Boozer, who only two weeks ago was acquitted on double homicide charges. He is the prime suspect in yesterday's execution-style murder of three yet unidentified victims."

JJ could feel his knees weakening as he dizzily stumbled to the couch, dazed by the irony of what he was witnessing.

"I'll call you back," he managed to mumble as his heart pounded and he waited for more information. "Damn!" He shouted. While he waited and watched like the rest of the city and perhaps the nation. The footage of a defiant Kareem delivering his courthouse soliloquy was flashing over the screen as JJ watched in stunned horror. "This could not be happening," he whispered, afraid of the consequences if it were true.

Finally, the camera panned to the front door of the house, and there, in all of his gangster and thuggish bravado, was his client Kareem Abdul Boozer. Acquitted killer. Nevertheless, Kareem Abdul Boozer was a killer. He was freed by the great JJ Battle to kill again. The sight of Kareem so full of himself even in this reprehensible circumstance repulsed JJ. He could not help but feel responsible. He watched as they led Kareem out in handcuffs by what looked like a battalion of officers led by homicide detective Harvey Stone.

The reporter edged closer to get some audio. "Kareem, what do you have to say about your arrest?" The reporter shouted over the voices of other reporters and police officials.

"They got nothin. I beat the last case. I'm gonna beat this case, too. Call my lawyer, JJ Battle. Let him know they arrested me, so he can get me out of here. This is bogus," Kareem shouted into the camera, with a surprising air of sincerity.

"Tell it to the judge," Stone grumbled, guiding Kareem into the car, intentionally bumping Kareem's head on the door jam, forcing him into the back seat of the patrol car.

"There you have it folks, the live capture of suspected murderer Kareem Abdul Boozer, wanted for the deaths of three people in an execution-style shooting on Detroit's east side yesterday. "This is David Lewis, Channel 7 action news live," the reporter ended, pleased with himself for capturing the story. "Surely, this would lead to a promotion or at least a raise," he told himself.

JJ turned off the television, feeling sick to his stomach. He rushed to the bathroom barely making it before the vomit and bile overcame him.

JJ remembered those moments as if it were yesterday. He was haunted by his role in this tragedy. It was as if by his hand he had provided Kareem the opportunity to commit these atrocities. He knew that if he wanted to get on with his life, he would have to clear his conscience. But absolution, he knew, would not come easily.

Chapter 6

EVA ANN MOODY LIVED HER LIFE by one simple rule: maintain control at all costs. It was a rule that she always followed. It began in the small western Michigan town of Idelwild, a small resort town that was once famous as a getaway for the Black elite. Situated just across Lake Michigan from Chicago, it was a hotspot of the rich and famous Blacks in the fifties and sixties. Idelwild fell on hard times in the seventies, as more exotic and exciting travel destinations became available. It took less time to get to the Caribbean from Chicago than it did to get to Idelwild. Gradually the tourist industry dried up, and many of the resorts and hotel properties were abandoned and bankrupt. Eva's family had operated the Flamingo Motel, a bright and colorful little motel that featured a spectacular stretch of beach, and dazzling sunsets. It was a family enterprise, with Eva's grandmother doing the cooking and helping with the laundry and other domestic needs. Her mother and father managed the facility, handling the administrative duties and all of the guest needs. It was a great life until the tourist industry died. At first, the Moodys continued to rely on guests coming over from Detroit, along with a few other holdouts from Chicago; however, as the patronage dwindled, they were forced to find jobs.

Neither parent had a high school education, nor were there local job opportunities in Idelwild. Jim Moody, Eva's father, decided to move to Detroit to go to work in the auto industry. That worked out well in the beginning, since the Detroit auto industry was still booming during that period. Jim would send large checks home for the family in Idelwild. He would make the three and a half hour drive back to Idelwild on the weekends he did not have to work overtime. This seemed to work for a while; however as time went by, his visits became less frequent. Eva's mother begin drinking to endure the loneliness and the financial hardship. Finally, Jim stopped coming home at all and his phone calls stopped. Eva's mother continued her drinking followed by long periods of depression and crying. Eva didn't understand what was happening to her family, but she could always count on her grandmother to make her feel better.

As her mother continued to get worse, Eva overheard her grandmother and some of the churchwomen talking about something called cancer. She didn't know what it was but it was making her mother very sick. One day when Eva got home from her kindergarten class, she saw her grandmother crying and singing one of her old sad church songs. When Eva asked about her mother, her grandmother said something about her going to be with the Lord.

Eva remembered asking her grandmother what was going to happen to her and her Grandmother replying, "God will make a way." Granny was right. God did provide a way. Instead of Eva feeling sorry for herself, she made a plan to work hard to get out of that town. She wanted to be like those Black women she saw on television, the ones with the pretty hair and clothes. Although Eva missed her mother and rarely heard from her father, she was happy with Granny and her life in Idelwild.

As she grew older, Eva became a gifted and driven student. She was at the top of her class, getting all A's throughout her school career. When Eva graduated from high school as class valedictorian, everyone thought she would go to Ferris State University in nearby Big Rapids; however, Eva had bigger dreams. She wanted to go to the University of Michigan in Ann Arbor. Although Eva had a scholarship, it didn't cover the cost of tuition, room and board for the U of M. She had no idea where she would get the money. It was Granny who surprised her by taking out a second mortgage on the motel to help pay for Eva's college.

Eva had grown into a beautiful young woman, with long silky hair, and honey- colored skin. She wore her hair pulled into a tight ponytail or rolled into a bun and hidden under a baseball hat. She hid her blossoming figure under oversized men's shirts and baggy jeans. She ignored advances from admirers, refusing to be distracted.

Throughout her undergrad career, a number of students laughed and ridiculed her because she didn't date or socialize for four years. Eva didn't care because she was on a mission. If she was ever going to achieve her dream and create the kind of lifestyle where she would never be poor, she had to work hard, and she did.

When Eva entered college, she had her sights set on law school and she was determined to get there. She graduated summa cum laude with a 4.0 grade point average and had scholarship offers from all of the top ten laws schools. She chose The University of Michigan so she could be close to Granny.

Law school was more of the same, except she enjoyed the hard work and studying. By now, she had opened up and at least allowed herself an occasional friendship. Her life was perfectly on track, proceeding precisely as she had planned. She refused to allow her dream to be derailed.

She remembered one disturbing encounter in law school with her contracts professor, a black Englishman from London. All of the female students were foolishly in love with Professor Stevenson. She could tell when it was time for her contracts class, because all of the female students showed up in short skirts and tight tops, vying for the professor's attention. Not Eva; she couldn't allow herself to be distracted or to lose focus. She remembered making an appointment to see the professor about her confusion about the legal theory of promissory estoppel. She thought it was strange that he set an evening appointment but she kept it anyway. As she entered his office, the professor addressed her in his characteristic British accent. His eyes lingered over her shapely body.

"How are you this evening, Ms. Moody," he said in his most charming accent.

"Fine, Professor Stevenson. Thanks for seeing me. I'm really having difficulty understanding this theory of promissory estoppel."

"Well, pull up a chair and let's discuss it. But before we get into the mundane legal discussion, do you mind if I ask you a personal question?"

"Professor, I don't mean any disrespect, but I don't see how personal questions about me are going to help my understanding of legal concepts." She answered frostily, feeling her anger rise. She could sense that the professor had other things on his mind besides the law.

"Eva, knowing a little bit more about you helps me put the information in the proper context," the professor continued, ignoring Eva's protests.

"The only context in which promissory estoppel is *proper* is the legal context. Nothing about me personally helps make this concept more real or not. Professor, either you are here to teach me law or to harass me. If it is the latter, that will conclude this meeting and I'll speak with the Dean in the morning," she said curtly. Stevenson quickly got the message, as did other individuals whose intentions were improper.

Eva made two promises to herself. First, she would never be poor. She remembered when she was a child, the ridicule she received from the other kids in school who teased her about her clothes. She had three dresses that she alternated every three days. Although they were always clean and starched, they were still the same. Granny would mend them when they needed it and let out the hem when she kept growing. She continually hoped for new ones. She vowed that when she was older she would have all of the finest clothes that money could buy. It always made her study just a little harder.

The second promise that Eva made to herself was never to lose control. She hated weakness. As a little girl she refused to cry, even at her mother's funeral. She saw the sadness and grief her mother lived with, and she promised herself she would never be like that. Whenever the kids teased her, she would toughen up and always have a quick comeback. If that failed, there was that Moody temper that put fear in everybody. She would fight a rock if she had to, win, lose, or draw, she didn't care. All of the kids knew just how far to go with Eva. Nobody wanted to feel her wrath. She had her own little world filled with her own private dreams. She didn't know how she was going to achieve all of her dreams, but she knew that one day she would.

Chapter 7

JOHN "RAT" RATSKELLER HAD ONLY TWO things going for him in his life; he loved his job, and he was virtually invisible. In most professions, invisibility would be a detriment, but not for Rat, it was a benefit. All of his life he had struggled to fit in, to become part of the human landscape and to survive. However, life was not so simple for Rat. He had always had to overcome obstacles just to survive, and like his namesake, he was very adaptable.

He remembered when he was in school and kids teased him unmercifully, and he vowed silent revenge. They called him all types of names, but Rat stuck, partly because of his last name and partly because when he was angry or upset, he looked like a rodent. He was thin and wiry with protruding teeth and an overbite that made him look just like a rat. After the fourth grade he stopped going to school, not because his parents made him stop, they just didn't make him go. His mother would occasionally try to teach him what she knew, but she had only gone to fourth grade herself. Rat didn't mind not going to school; in fact, he enjoyed it. It gave him more time in the woods to hunt. He preferred the animals to people anyway.

As he got older his features softened, and he didn't look like a rat anymore, but the name still stuck. Rat's only distinguishing feature besides his overbite was that he had no distinguishing features. This made him ordinary in an invisible kind of way. He couldn't count the times people ignored him, bumped into him, or moved in front of him in lines. It was always the same, "I'm sorry sir, I didn't see you standing there." He was completely forgettable. He was ok with this, since it made his job easier. Now, people had to take notice of him, even if they didn't know why. He couldn't count the number of personal histories of others he had rewritten by his invisible acts. He couldn't be ignored now.

He took a deep breath and held it, like his daddy taught him to do in the back woods of Goshen, West Virginia. In those days hunting wasn't for sport, it was for survival. If you didn't hunt, you didn't eat. He remembered the time he had been hunting with his father on a cold wintry day in the West Virginia mountains. His hands and feet were frozen to the bone. He was slow to pull the trigger, and he missed his kill shot. His daddy, unwilling to let the prize buck escape, fired a perfect shot, dropping the buck after a few steps. His daddy's disgust was obvious, as he remembered him saying, "You don't hunt, you don't eat." He could still remember the rumbling in his stomach as he went to bed hungry that night. As harsh as that lesson was, Rat never forgot it. That lesson shaped him and had a profound impact on him. It made him an expert in his chosen profession, assassin.

Those lessons helped prepare him for his current assignment. He was providing surveillance on a subject. This process could take up to a week to complete, depending on the target. This target was predictable; same route to work, same restaurant for lunch, same parking spot. Most people were creatures of habit, assuming that a consistent routine eliminated many mundane decisions and simplified one's life. It also made a person an easy target.

Slowly he exhaled, squeezing off a round and bracing against the recoil. He laughed to himself; this assignment went against all of his professional ethics. When you squeezed the trigger, it was to hit your target. Daddy taught him that you didn't miss. That was for amateurs. He didn't believe in intentionally missing the target. Still, he executed the assignment like any other, carefully, professionally, and patiently stalking the target, recording habits and patterns. Today he was only supposed to scare the target, and send a message. He would do it, with the same precision as if he were executing a kill.

He scattered the shots into the door of the Lincoln and near the vehicle, careful not to hit the target. These were message shots. He was certain the subject got the message. This was an unusual assignment, but he was a soldier and didn't question an order. He squeezed off a few more rounds and watched the target speed out of the garage. The Rat gathered all of his equipment and the spent shells, and exited the garage. The subject might not realize just how close he came to death.

As an assassin, it didn't matter to Rat what a target's habits were:; everyone was vulnerable. It was just a matter of time before the right opportunity presented itself, and Rat never missed. He knew hundreds of ways to kill a man, and he enjoyed his profession. He was proud that he never let a target escape. Failure had consequences in his line of work, but Rat never accepted failure as an option.

He learned his craft in the mountains of West Virginia, and perfected it courtesy of the United States Armed Forces. He was identified early in his military career as an expert sharpshooter, and he joined Special Forces and later Delta Forces as a sniper. Two tours of duty in Viet Nam and the Mekong Delta, enhanced by Ranger, Special Forces and elite Delta training, made him a human killing machine. He could kill from long range, short range, with a rifle, handgun, hand-to-hand, explosives, or poison. They sought him out for the toughest, most dangerous missions because he was so good at his craft. He was a survivor. He had killed men in every conceivable way, and some ways even he had not conceived. There was a period where death and killing had consumed him. He had seen so much death and destruction of his fellow troops and of the enemy, that it no longer seemed real. In fact, death became his new reality. The only way he managed to stay alive was by killing. It transformed his world forever.

The army had been the perfect place for him. He could earn a living and do what he did best- kill people in the name of the United States Government. He killed, he reasoned, so that others could live. At least that was what he told himself. It didn't matter anyway, as it was sanctioned by the government. He figured that most people had committed some sin worthy of death in their lives, but had just not been punished. He reasoned it was his job to provide that punishment.

He remembered the time he separated from his Delta Group in the Viet Nam jungle for two months with no food, water, or radio contact. Alarmed, the army sent out search parties for two weeks straight without success. He saw units off in the distance and heard the helicopters overhead. He made a decision. He decided to remain in the jungle forever. It would be his new home. It reminded him of the West Virginia hills except for the stifling heat and humidity. He survived on plants, animals, and occasional raids on small Viet Cong patrols. He would wait for night to come and then silently, secretly attack the small Viet Cong raid parties. He would leave no survivors. He would take weapons, food, and other necessary staples. The jungle, much like his West Virginia home had given him everything he needed, including opium. His discovery of the drug captivated his life so much that he continuously smoked it. In his hallucinogenic state, he decided he was never leaving the jungle. He probably would have succeeded had a U.S. Army Patrol not inadvertently discovered him.

When they found him, he had lost forty pounds was deep in the throes of drug addiction and delirium. The Army mistakenly believed that his condition was the result of having spent two months alone, surviving in the jungle. Unsure of whether to decorate him or court martial him for desertion, the Army decided to give him an honorable discharge. He accepted, and began to build a life for himself back in West Virginia. Surviving on both a generous pension and the land, life was good; however, something was missing. He missed the killing. Coincidentally, that's when the calls began, requesting his special services at substantial fees.

He never knew whom the calls were from, nor did he care. He just accepted his assignment and did his job, just as he had done in the military. Although he didn't know for sure, he thought his bosses were CIA or some other covert government operation. The orders would generally come once a month by special courier with specific instructions to go to a particular city. They gave him plane tickets and hotel reservations and they always paid in cash, and up-front. When Rat arrived in the particular city, they gave him a number to call, and they delivered all of the documents to his hotel room by courier. Included in the package would be the target and any contact information he might need, in case an assignment went wrong. He would be supplied with weapons of his choosing. He had never yet had an assignment go wrong. He knew that no target was untouchable. His only obstacle was time. He didn't like to rush. That's when mistakes were made. In his profession, mistakes lead to death. He couldn't afford that luxury. The Rat was a formidable enemy, a killer without a conscience.

Chapter 8

THIRTEEN HUNDRED BEAUBIEN WAS AN OLD, decrepit building destined for demolition. It was unworthy of being the main headquarters for the Detroit Police Department. In its heyday, it had been the envy of other major metropolitan police facilities. In its present state, it was symbolic of a tarnished department and decaying city-old, outdated, and behind the times, much like the Detroit Police Department. The department had recently come under fire by community groups and even by the Justice Department. The Justice Department launched an investigation of the tactics of the force. There had been frequent incidents of police brutality and charges of excessive violence and deadly shootings by police officers. The image of the department was tarnished. The citizens it was paid to protect disrespected the department. The department was number one in the country in the number of shootings of citizens by police. It was a dubious honor. This created an acrimonious and adversarial relationship between the public and the police. This uneasy relationship made it dangerous to be either a citizen or a police officer of the City of Detroit.

Valerie Worthy was the first female African-American mayor for the City of Detroit. She was the unwitting recipient of the department's political mess. She had been unable to improve police morale or restore citizen confidence in the department. She had changed police chiefs twice in the past year in an effort to stabilize the department. It didn't help that, once again, the department was operating at a deficit, and layoffs were imminent.

JJ had been here many times, always as an attorney, and never as a victim. For a moment, he was unsure of how to proceed. A desk sergeant, sensing his confusion, intervened, "Can I help you sir?"

"Uh, yes. I want to report a crime."

"OK, step over here and fill out the forms, and someone will be with you shortly."

JJ, feeling a momentary sense of frustration, wondered whether it was worth it. He hesitated, doubting the reliability of the department to find whoever was responsible for the shooting attack. While contemplating his options, he heard a booming voice from behind him.

"Well, well, well, if it's not Detroit's cover boy, Joshua Battle, the defender of the guilty, mouthpiece for the criminally inclined. What brings you down here this time of night?" JJ recognized the voice immediately.

"Damn!" he thought, frozen in indecision. He quickly turned, facing Lieutenant Harvey Stone.

"Hello Lieutenant, what a surprise. Congratulations on your promotion."

"I would thank you, but I never believe anything lawyers say! They have a tendency to distort the truth."

"Well, you earned it Lieutenant Stone. Nobody puts up arrest numbers like you," Joshua replied, cursing his luck at having to deal with Lieutenant Harvey Stone. They had had some memorable clashes. Most of them ended in JJ's favor, much to the dismay and misfortune of Stone. JJ knew Stone was a man who held a grudge and would not forget the past.

The first encounter between them occurred when Stone was a member of the anti-drug task force. At the time, that unit was racking up incredible overtime hours and arrest numbers. There were repeated allegations of Stone being a dirty cop and planting evidence, although nothing was ever proven. The reports were usually made by angry, disgruntled drug dealers lacking the credibility to make the charges stick. The department's answer to those allegations was to promote Stone, elevating him to the homicide division, where his army of street informants provided valuable leads to solving many of the city's unsolved homicides. He was a rising star in a department that only cared about results and not about methods.

The first thing you noticed about Lieutenant Harvey Stone was the size of his hands. They were large and meaty, and appeared swollen like some oversized boxing gloves. They were heavy hands and were probably no stranger to physical contact. JJ imagined those hands balled up in fists or fitted around the necks of uncooperative suspects, forcing involuntary confessions. Stone was short and round with a large barrel chest straining the buttons of his cheap sports jacket. He had huge forearms and biceps, which he liked to display by rolling up his sleeves past the elbow. His demeanor, like his name, suggested a hard man with little, if any sense of humor. He was not adverse to inflicting pain if the situation called for it.

Their relationship had always been professional, exhibiting a grudging respect, until the YKA case. Then it became personal. Stone resented being the scapegoat for the prosecution losing that case, and he blamed JJ and others for making him look bad.

Everyone assumed the case was a slam-dunk for the prosecution. They had overwhelming evidence, including eyewitnesses and a ton of physical evidence. They refused to offer a reasonable plea bargain, believing they had a sure win. The prosecution left JJ without options, forcing him to go to trial, in spite of the overwhelming evidence against his client. The evidence forced JJ to focus on the police department's investigation practices and treatment of witnesses. He focused unwanted attention on a department that had already been the subject of numerous unflattering news editorials and government investigations. The homicide department, acting as rogue cops terrorizing the community in the name of law enforcement, was a well-played theme in the City of Detroit, because it had an element of truth. Truth was a prerequisite for any effective strategy; it had to be believable. It had proven a successful strategy-so successful in fact, that the Department of Justice had begun a federal investigation into the department's practices. It also helped enhance JJ's reputation as a trial lawyer. JJ felt a twinge of regret as he remembered how much adverse publicity the department suffered, particularly Stone.

"So what criminal psychopath are you here to bail out tonight, Battle?" Stone asked with his usual tone of disgust.

"He's not here to bail anybody out, Lieutenant. He's here to file a crime report," the duty sergeant volunteered, a little too cheerfully.

"How ironic, the famous defense attorney is now himself a victim of a crime." JJ could see the satisfaction in Stone's attitude. He was enjoying JJ's misfortune.

"Wouldn't it be poetic justice if the perp responsible for this was one of the social deviants you got off on a technicality?" Stone smirked, warming to his subject. "Now you want us to protect and serve."

"I just want you to do your job," JJ answered, a bit too defensively.

"Yeah, yeah. What does he have, Sarge? Did someone steal his hubcaps or some other serious crime?"

"He claims he was shot at in the Griswold Street parking garage. He says it was a sniper."

"A sniper? You must be kidding." Stone was truly enjoying himself at JJ's expense. "More than likely it was a client upset about the exorbitant fees you charged him. I'm amazed at you, Battle. You are an expert on the law, and you're an expert on police investigations as well. Next, you'll tell us how to do our jobs. Anyway, we'll get someone on it right away. By the way, did you get a description or a look at your sniper?"

"No I didn't," JJ hissed, feeling his anger increase as Stone continued to amuse himself at his expense.

"How do you know it wasn't a car jacket?" Stone asked derisively.

"I don't. But if it was, he never came after the car." JJ, sensing the futility of the questioning, decided to appeal to Stone's vanity. "Look, I know how you feel about me personally, but I've never questioned your investigative skill. I'll leave my car for the evidence techs. Do what you can."

JJ left wondering why he had bothered. Judging by the department's arrest record, there was almost no possibility of them apprehending the shooter. Second, he didn't like being the object of Stone's humor and ridicule. He knew that the lieutenant was having fun at his expense. Because JJ couldn't be sure if this was a random act or not, it made tonight's shooting attack even more unsettling. After a lifetime of criminal defense work, JJ had his share of enemies just like anybody else. But who would go to these lengths. He couldn't figure it out. He immediately eliminated the YKA as suspects, since they were never known for their subtlety. They preferred making a statement, letting the world know of their exploits. No, these perpetrators were purposeful and knew the job. If their intention was to send a message, they had succeeded.

JJ left the department knowing that he was on his own. Stone would not help.

As JJ left headquarters, Stone entered his office and closed the door, dialing a familiar number. He spoke in hushed and whispered tones. There was no mistaking the urgency in his voice. Stone knew that his strategy was risky and could backfire, but he had gone ahead with it anyway. JJ Battle was no fool; they would have to watch him and deal with him eventually.

Chapter 9

THE LOUD METAL CLANK AND THE pneumatic whoosh of the jail doors had the unmistakable sound of incarceration and finality. When you entered these walls, there was always the unsettling feeling that maybe you wouldn't be allowed to leave, but the adaptability of the inmates always fascinated JJ. They seemed to adjust to their surroundings and some even thrived in jail. For some it was forced detoxification from alcohol or some other chemical dependence. For others, it was a time of self-reflection and an opportunity to analyze their own situation. JJ hated visiting the Wayne County Jail. He always harbored the chilling feeling that during his visit the guards might make some mistake and forget he was there. He knew the improbability of that happening, but he thought about it anyway.

Today he was there visiting his client, Bobby Boogaloo Bennett to begin developing Boogaloo's defense. The elevator slowly and mechanically ground to a stop on the fourth floor. He exited and headed down a long glass enclosed corridor. When he reached the end of the corridor, he was facing a Plexiglas enclosed cubicle staffed by a beefy Wayne County Deputy Sheriff. Inside the cube were closed circuit monitors and buttons controlling the electronic doors for each of the four cellblocks that made up the fourth floor, north south, east, and west. The walls and doors of the cells were all painted a dull institutional beige. It was as if the state received a discount on beige paint. It was a depressing color, and you could almost feel the sense of hopelessness that these walls contained.

He slid his pass through the appropriate slot and yelled through the intercom system, which never seemed to work properly, "attorney visit," he said, loudly enough for the deputy behind the glass to hear him. This alerted the guards to provide a private conference room for the attorney-client visit to protect the confidentiality of the visit. After a brief delay and a check on the computer terminal, the guard responded, "he's already got visitors in conference room one. You're welcome to join them, or you can wait until they're done." He waited for the door to open and wondered who was visiting his client. It could be anyone from a social worker, to someone from the bond office checking on Boogaloo's eligibility for bail. It could even be a pastor from a local church. It was part of prison lore that inmates routinely found God while incarcerated.

When he turned the corner, approaching conference room one, he was unprepared for what he saw. Huddled together in deep and conspiratorial conversation was his client and Lieutenant Harvey Stone. JJ stopped abruptly, gathering himself while attempting to control his anger. He entered the room, not bothering to knock or engage in conversational niceties. "You better have a damn good explanation for talking to my client without my permission!"

"Attorney Battle, hello to you too," Stone replied, unaffected by JJ's obvious anger.

"You know you're not allowed to talk to my client once he's retained counsel."

"That's probably true in most instances but this is about a separate matter, and your client called me."

"I don't care. You have no right to talk to my client at any time during this case without my permission or my being present. Is that clear?"

"Save the eloquence for the courtroom, I was leaving anyway," Stone replied, amused by JJ's reaction.

"We'll see what Judge Moody has to say about your illegal visit." JJ saw Stone's demeanor harden imperceptibly at the mention of Judge Moody, and then break into a grin. "Do what you have to do, Counselor. I'll see you next time Bobby," Stone said as he rose to leave, managing to bump JJ slightly as he left the conference room.

"What the hell was that about?" JJ seethed, not bothering to hide his anger. "You do realize that anything that you say to Stone can be used against you in court?"

"Relax attorney Battle, I know what I'm doing."

"The hell you do. The penitentiary is full of people who thought they knew what they were doing. As long as I represent you, you do not speak to anyone without my permission. Especially Lieutenant Stone."

"OK, OK, I got it," Bobby replied feeling slightly chastised.

JJ gave himself a moment to calm down. He remembered the reason for his visit.

"Bobby, tell me a little about yourself, what were you doing before you got arrested?"

"Well, I was in-between jobs mostly, but I had begun to do some work for this company that specializes in real estate. But mostly, I just hustle to make ends meet. I used to work for the auto industry before they started laying off. I haven't had a steady job since."

"Are you married or do you have family in the area? All of this will help me try to get your bond reduced by the judge."

"I understand. No. I have never been married but I got three kids, by two different women. I am originally from Louisiana; that's where my family mostly lives. I've lived in Detroit since I was grown. This is my home now."

"Tell me a little bit about your girlfriend, Betty, I've heard stories that you two weren't getting along too well."

"That's not true, attorney Battle. Sure, we had our ups and downs, just like everybody else, but we loved each other. We were just going through a rough spell. The problem with us is that Betty got too many meddling friends. They just can't stay out of our business."

"Is that what happened with Brianna? Did she interfere in your business?" JJ asked, attempting to get an understanding of his client's thinking.

"That was all just a misunderstanding. She was supposed to be showing me where Betty was, and then she just jumped out of the car. I didn't do nothing to make that girl jump out of a movin' car. She did that on her own. I swear to God." Bobby said with sincerity.

"The preliminary police report says that you had a gun and that you threatened her. Is that true?"

"I did have a gun but I didn't threaten her with it. I was just takin' it from Betty's house when she saw it. I did not intend to use it on Brianna. I don't need a gun to persuade a woman."

"So I heard. You have quite a reputation as a ladies' man. That is not going to help you in your case. In fact, that kind of publicity can hurt you with the jury. Here is what I want you to do. From today forward, as long as I represent you, you are not to make any statements to anyone without my permission. This includes the media and Stone or any other police personnel. You know the expression-anything you say may be used against you-well its true. Whatever you say can come back to haunt you. Now tell me a little bit more about the work you were doing for that real estate company, because you have fraud charges pending in that case as well."

Over the next two hours, Bobby told a story of greed and political corruption that reached the highest levels of city government. He had names, dates, transactions, and amounts of payoffs and land deals that would not just rock city hall, but could land some key power brokers in federal prison if it was true.

JJ was uncertain whether to believe Bobby. But he knew he needed some corroboration before he could proceed on Bobby's information. A lot of what Bobby said made sense; there was his unlikely connection to Victor and Randy and the large retainer they paid for such a low-level hustler. Why was the chief homicide detective visiting Bobby? What else was there about the case that he didn't know? He started to get the feeling there was more going on with Bobby Bennett than he knew. JJ seemed to be the last to know all of the details. He hated not having all of the facts.

"So what do we do next, Attorney Battle?" Bobby asked as if they were a team. JJ started to like this chubby lothario; he was very different from some of his past clients, particularly those clients from the Young Killers of America.

"Well, there is a preliminary hearing scheduled for Wednesday in 36th District court. It's a hearing where the prosecution presents evidence to determine if there is enough evidence to show that you committed a crime. It is a very basic hearing. In your case, I intend to waive your hearing. That way, the prosecution cannot produce any evidence on the record about the facts of the case. Therefore, if for some reason a witness fails to appear or a police officer is unavailable, there is no official transcript of the hearing entered into the record. It helps if Brianna changes her mind and does not want to testify.

I also have to get all of the discovery information that the prosecution has on your case so that I can plan your defense." "Well, I'm glad you're on my case, I heard you're the best lawyer in town. I was sorry to hear about what happened after you got those boys off on that murder case. It was all over the news for weeks after. I couldn't believe they went out and killed all of those people after you worked so hard to get them off. That was wrong," Bobby said with real conviction. JJ winced at Bobby's recollection of something that he worked so hard to forget. It was surprising to see that even criminals had a code of right and wrong.

As JJ left the jail, he began to wonder if the large retainer was worth it. He had never shied away from tough cases before, and he would not start now. He wondered whether the dark underside of criminal law with the death, hopelessness, and despair would pull him back in. He made a mental note to start being just a little bit more cautious.

As he pulled out of the parking lot of the Wayne County Jail, the One Detroit, Inc. conspirators were concluding a conference call. The call, unbeknownst to JJ, would have dire consequences for both he and his client. The call concluded with each party making the same resolution, to be more cautious.

Chapter 10

IF IT'S TRUE THAT ABSENCE MAKES the heart grow fonder, then JJ Battle had a newfound love for the law. He had been away from it for two years and could not believe how much he had missed the law. That wasn't quite true; he hadn't actually been away from the law, just away from criminal defense. But it still felt like it. True, he still had the real estate practice and some other non-adversarial matters that he handled, but it just was not the same as trial work. The two-year sabbatical almost made him forget about the circumstances that made him walk away from a lucrative law practice. But, that was all behind him now.

He was excited with the prospect of getting back into the arena. The adrenaline was pumping; he was looking forward to the drama of trial work where you match wits with a worthy adversary, and you literally have the defendant's future in your hands. Skill and expertise would help determine if your client walked out of court free, or suffered the indignity of taking that shackled walk to prison. This case was exactly the type of case he loved. High stakes, high visibility, and a chance to test his talents. The tougher the case, the better he enjoyed it. This excitement was fueled by the reality that whatever transpired in the case, he would be going home at the end of the day. His client might not be so fortunate; however, that was the nature of the game.

This was his kind of case. For once, he was not representing a murderer or those sociopaths of YKA, whose murder-for- hire activities almost destroyed him both professionally and psychologically. He struggled to put that infamous chapter behind him. It had taken two years and some intense alcohol abuse to overcome those episodes. Now he was back, doing what he loved. That had never been an issue. He loved being a lawyer; that wasn't the problem. The problem started when the line between his moral values and ethical considerations began to blur. Clients had become more dangerous, the crimes more heinous, and he began to question whether he was using his skills in the most appropriate way. He had convinced himself that to be the best, he had to take the toughest cases and win. He knew those cases were risky to both his professional and personal reputation, but they helped catapult him into the elite group of criminal defense attorneys in Detroit. The upside of his strategy was the large retainers clients paid for his services. Defending the bad people had it risks, but it also had some huge rewards.

"Never mind," he told himself. That was then; he was a different person now. He had a more realistic approach. He would choose only the cases that were interesting to him, rather than look just at the size of the retainer. The pursuit of money had been a big part of his downfall. It had obscured his judgment and as a result, he represented some unsavory characters, unworthy of his talents. All great lawyers started this way he reasoned, and he was no different. You paid your dues and developed your reputation. But who knew that greatness would cost such a high price.

"All Rise. This Honorable Recorder's Court for the State of Michigan, County of Wayne, is now in session, The Honorable Eva Ann Moody is present and presiding, God Save this Honorable Court. Please be seated." The bailiff, mindful of the captive audience, delivered his opening with Broadway flair. Just like an actor entering the stage from the wings, Judge Moody dramatically strode to the bench, black hair and robes flowing as she surveyed her domain. She scanned the crowd, demanding total silence and commanding everyone's full attention.

"You are in a court of law. The lives of individuals and their personal affairs are at stake. These are serious matters. You are to govern yourselves accordingly. If you display the bad judgment of disrupting this court, I will have you summarily removed. That includes everyone." Judge Moody's opening soliloquy varied only slightly, depending on how heavy the day's court docket was. Judging by the brevity of her opening, she was all about business. She would not tolerate interruptions. She liked to work at a frenetic pace, frustrating her court staff that had to keep up with her killer pace.

"Mr. Clerk, please call the first ca…"she abruptly stopped, as the court doors flew open and a television news crew noisily entered.

"Who gave you permission to interrupt my court?"

"No one, your Honor, I'm just here to cover a story." The reporter and crew came to an abrupt stop, awaiting orders from the Judge.

"Mr. Parker." she hissed, placing her hand over the microphone and addressing her chief clerk.

"Why wasn't I informed that we had a special defendant today?"

"Judge, I didn't see anything special on the docket. There was no notice from the Court Administrator's office." The clerk said defensively.

"RECESS! My chambers." Abruptly she stormed off the bench much to the displeasure of the courtroom audience, many of whom were already late for work.

"Steven, you know this is a political year, and this court is under intense scrutiny. We cannot afford to have the media appearing unannounced in this courtroom. "I will not have it!"

"I know Judge," Steven replied, bristling at the Judge's chastisement.

He hated her tirades even though he usually understood them. He quickly shuffled through the day's docket, searching for the offending case.

"Who is the defendant?"

"Robert Bennett" one count kidnapping and false imprisonment, one count attempted murder, one count assault with a deadly weapon, and one count felony firearm."

"Who is the defense attorney?"

"JJ Battle."

"You have got to be kidding me. I don't need this right now." She shifted uncomfortably behind her desk and tried to contain the warmth she felt. She did not want the staff to know anything about her personal life. She usually overreacted by openly expressing her disdain for defense attorneys, especially the select few she shared an intimate attachment.

"Mr. Battle better not come in here with his custom made suits trying to charm this court. We follow the same protocol as we do with any other case. No deviations for any reason." She said this with much more assurance than she felt. She had always had a difficult time saying no to JJ, but that was a long time ago.

"I'll set a pretrial conference with the DA and Mr. Battle for two weeks."

"Fine. But I want to see Mr. Battle in my chambers immediately. I'm not allowing him to turn these proceedings into his own media circus."

"I'll go find him right away, Judge." Steve was amused. He rarely, if ever, saw the judge flustered, but if one person could do it, it was JJ Battle.

Joshua Jericho Battle was a courthouse favorite. He was a legend, and he had always been there for Steve, like the time JJ gave him a car after he had months of car problems. He did it without fanfare or expecting anything in return. He just drove it over to Steve's house one Sunday after church. JJ asked him if he could keep it in his garage, and, "by the way, here were the keys and the title. " They admired him not just for his legal ability and courtroom triumphs, but because he was a local boy who made it.

He grew up on the eastside of Detroit, and was an all-city and all-state basketball and football player. He went to the University of Michigan on a football scholarship and had a remarkable career. He was the team MVP and captain. He was destined for a pro career, until that career-ending knee injury. Instead of wallowing in self-pity and feeling sorry for himself, he went to law school. The rest, they say is history.

He tried cases the same way he played the game: intensely, passionately, and with an unmistakable flair. On the field, he challenged everyone. He was a ferocious and fearless competitor. He was the same in the courtroom. But what really endeared him to his friends was that he was a just a neighborhood guy. He played in the local rec leagues, spoke to inner city schools, and always remembered the staff on birthdays and Christmas. He was a great guy. He had been missed around the courthouse.

"Joshua Jericho Battle. There must be some real big dollars floating around the courthouse to bring you out of retirement," Steve joked, displaying the good-natured banter that characterized their friendship.

"Just doing my duty. Fighting for truth, justice, and economic freedom. It's good being back. I needed to get back to some gainful employment, JJ countered, reaching for a friendly embrace.

"The queen is seething on the throne, so be prepared. She might set the trial date for next week. A camera crew had the bad judgment to come into court unannounced."

"What's her beef? She loves the publicity. Besides, it's an election year. She can use the publicity."

"Trial services forgot to give her the heads-up about your celebrated client. She's pissed, and on top of that, the defense attorney is none other than the debonair JJ Battle. That alone was enough to raise her blood pressure to stroke level. You better really turn on the charm."

"Steve, there's not enough charm in the world to melt that iceberg." He knew it was going to be difficult to manage this case as long as Judge Moody was presiding, old wounds never healed. The case was not off to a good start. These cases were already difficult to try, having an unfriendly judge against you was an obstacle he didn't need.

Judge Eva Ann Moody, Chief Judge of Recorder's Court, was a law school classmate. Part of what they affectionately called the 'talented tenth' based on WEB Dubois' characterization of the black elite. The University of Michigan's experimental policy of allowing a ten percent enrollment of minority students in its law school for the first time had produced some brilliant lawyers, and Eva was one of the brightest. But, in spite of her brilliance, she was still nicknamed "Evil and Moody" for her frequent temper tantrums on and off the bench.

Only JJ had been close enough to melt that icy exterior on occasion.

There was heavy emphasis on the "Moody." Occasionally, a chastised defense attorney returned from an appearance in front of the judge, with a disheartened, "She's evil and moody today." She had a reputation as a tough, unrelenting jurist who had no patience for incompetence. Her outbursts from the bench were legendary, and if not for her brilliance as an attorney and a judge, it would be easy to dismiss Judge Moody as just another female control freak. But she needed every ounce of her strength, courage, and brilliance to run one of the busiest criminal courts in the country. Without equal, the Wayne County Recorder's court was the best run criminal court in the Country. With the handling of over 60,000 felony cases a year, it was the model for criminal courts throughout the country.

JJ discreetly knocked on the judge's door.

"Yes" she answered coldly.

"Your honor, it's JJ Battle," he said, in his most ingratiating tone.

"Come in, Mr. Battle"

"Your Honorrrr," he stammered, quickly closing the door behind him. He was unprepared for the sight before him - The Chief Judge of the Wayne County Recorder's Court standing before him completely naked!

Chapter 11

"JUDGE, DID I CATCH YOU AT a bad time?" JJ asked, stifling a laugh. It was not often he found Eva Moody out of her element. Although JJ was unprepared for the judge's nakedness, he nevertheless appreciated her level of fitness. The years and a disciplined lifestyle had allowed the judge to maintain a rather remarkable figure. She stood there confident, uninhibited, and unyielding. JJ knew he was facing a dilemma; if he rebuffed the Judge, it could create all sorts of lasting repercussions, both personally and professionally. Yet, if he gave into the judge's advances, it would create a different set of circumstances.

"Eva," he said in a soft pleading tone. "I don't think this is the time or the place for this. Let's think about this for a moment."

"I have. You know I'm not a woman who is prone to impetuous acts, but I couldn't resist." She said, slowly and seductively approaching JJ, still planted at the door.

"Eva, this is inappropriate for the chief judge; it has bad consequences written all over it. Let's rethink and get together in a more private setting."

"What is more private than the chief judge's chambers," she whispered, sauntering over to lock the door.

JJ sensed the futility of resisting, but fired off one last defensive volley. "Eva, you know how I feel about you, let's not spoil it with something we both will regret."

Eva, undeterred, opened her arms for an awkward embrace. "I don't have time for small talk. I have to be back on the bench in fifteen minutes."

"But Eva, you can't keep a whole courtroom waiting like this."

"Watch me." She said as she undid his belt and zipper.

JJ could feel his desire betraying him. Eva's aggressive manner both excited and annoyed him. He could feel things spiraling out of control. JJ wrapped his arms around the judge and squeezed her tight to him, hoping to calm her furious advance.

"Eva, I promise you we'll finish what we've started, but just not right now," he whispered in a reassuring tone. He felt her body relax and she looked up at him and kissed him in a loving, gentle way. He responded accordingly and they held each other a while longer.

Eva managed to regain her composure and once again, she was in control. Slowly and sensually, she walked over to her desk to retrieve her clothing. JJ backed away, preparing to leave the Judge's office.

"No, wait. I still need to speak with you. I'll just be a second," she said disappearing into her private bathroom.

JJ waited in uncomfortable silence, unsure of what to expect next from the judge. He cursed under his breath, angry with Eva for putting him in such an awkward situation. When she returned, she was all business. "Have a seat; we have some details to work out about your case." JJ could still feel the sexual tension in the office and smiled to himself at how quickly Eva was able to compose herself after her earlier escapades.

She sat down at her desk, once again the picture of judicial virtue. She pressed the intercom and asked her clerk, Steven, to have the assistant prosecutor come to her office immediately.

JJ again waited in silence as the judge thumbed through the file. JJ began to wonder if this case was worth it. Every aspect of Bobby Bennett's case seemed to create a new controversy. He wondered where it would end.

He looked over at the judge, intently studying the case file, and once again composed and in complete control.

There was a knock on the judge's door and after a moment, the judge invited the guest into her chambers. It was assistant prosecutor, Anne Moroski.

She was a staunch women's rights proponent and a tough relentless prosecutor. She didn't believe in plea bargains or negotiating. As head of the prosecutor's domestic violence unit, she was responsible for trying the high-level domestic violence cases. Although JJ had never tried a case against her, he knew she was an emotional and passionate victim's advocate. He knew he would either have to match her passion and emotion, or neutralize it. Either way, he had a tough battle ahead of him.

"All right folks, here's the situation. Because of the backlog of cases on the trial docket, I have agreed to hear this case. I'm scheduling trial for two weeks from today, and I will hear pretrial dispositive motions a week from today. I'll hear any discovery issues at that time as well. Due to the nature of the case and the parties involved, may I assume that there will be no early resolution of this case?" The judge asked, referring to Anne's policy of no plea-bargaining.

Both JJ and Anne looked at each other and both replied, "that's a fair assumption Judge."

"Judge, it's the prosecution's contention that we have an eyewitness and motive, and all of the elements of the case are provable at trial." Anne stated in that confident, superior, matter-of-fact tone. "From the state's perspective it's an open and shut case. If the defense wants to plead straight up - guilty as charged- we'll be happy to accommodate them."

"That's very generous of the assistant prosecutor, but on behalf of my client, I must respectfully decline. I think the assistant prosecutor is going to have problems proving the intent element of the crime, so we'll take our chances with the jury," JJ said, starting to believe and embrace the theory of his case.

"Just as I thought. As you know, I do the voir dire of the jurors; if you have questions you would like me to ask the prospective jurors, have them to me by a week from today. Are there any other questions?" The judge waited for responses from JJ and the assistant prosecutor. When none was forthcoming, she politely adjourned the meeting.

As they were leaving, she called to JJ to remain. "Mr. Battle, I need to speak to you on an unrelated matter."

"Yes, your honor." JJ dutifully replied, wondering what the judge would say.

"Mr. Battle, the fact that I'm now hearing this case does not change what we discussed on a personal level. I expect an invitation from you within the week."

JJ did not know whether to feel flattered or intimidated. He couldn't think about how unethical this proposed meeting was. One thing he knew for sure, Judge Eva Ann Moody was not a woman who tolerated disappointment easily. He remembered their past together. Eva was a different kind of woman. She knew what she wanted, and she exhibited a determination to achieve it. Eva was a passionate woman who did not believe in romance. She had very real expectations when it came to relationships. She approached dates as if they were a business meeting, complete with everything but an agenda. She was a relentless and athletic lover, demanding from her partner an intense commitment. Lovemaking for Eva was more sport than romance, more physical therapy that physical intimacy. Either you were a willing participant, or the fire of Eva Ann Moody consumed you. Either way, it was an unforgettable experience.

JJ turned to leave; he couldn't help but remember a naked judge Moody sitting atop her desk. He wondered if he were prepared for Eva's fire. "It will be my pleasure, your honor," He replied, as he quickly left the judge's chambers.

Chapter 12

IT WAS 11:00 P.M. IN THE executive conference room on the twenty-fifth floor of the Renaissance Center and Law Offices of Connors and Wright. The staff had left hours before, and the room contained an unlikely assortment of individuals. Like most criminal enterprises and conspiracies, it was taking place at night.

Assembled in the room were partners Randy Connors and Victor Wright, along with homicide detective, Harvey Stone, and Deputy Mayor Rahsheed Truman. It was an unlikely gathering of individuals with seemingly diverse interests. They were united however, on one fundamental principle - greed. Each had something very personal to gain.

Victor, who was an expert at building coalitions, was coordinating the meeting. He had become very wealthy from a successful legal practice and needed to finalize this deal to offset some anticipated hits to his personal wealth. There were rumblings that there was marital discord in the Wright household and rumors of a mistress in the wings. Whatever the reason, Victor felt more pressure than ever to close this deal.

"We have to make sure that everything is in place in the next two weeks, we can't afford any delays," Victor said, scanning the faces to make sure they understood the importance of the timing. "We need to have all of the deeds transferred and signed. We begin negotiations with the developer next week, and we need the remaining properties to complete the Corktown parcels."

"The mayor's office is squarely behind the project," Truman added. "She needs some positive publicity to counter the beating she's taking in the media." Truman said, referring to Mayor Valerie Worthy.

Largely the same political machine that had elected her predecessor of the previous two terms, Kerry Fitzgerald, was also responsible for getting Mayor Worthy elected. Mayor Worthy was a former classmate of Fitzgerald's and was his former chief of staff. Her duties had included overseeing major city departments including police, fire, and health. There were persistent rumors that the two were romantically involved, and those rumors persisted even after Fitzgerald left office. Worthy was single, attractive, and appealed to a younger constituency. She was a fixture at all of the important parties and functions, and was constantly working to overcome her sagging public image. Her administration had been characterized by record unemployment, scandals, and uninspired leadership. She was in serious need of some public relations victories.

The Corktown project was the Mayor's first opportunity to distinguish her leadership. It would show that she could develop powerful coalitions outside her political network to make things happen for the city. She had given her city department heads permission to green light this project and to give the developers what they needed to complete the project on time. She would deal with the developing citizen backlash after Corktown was completed and the Super Bowl was a success.

Truman, the deputy mayor, was tired of being in the shadow of the first African-American female mayor. He had political aspirations of his own, and he needed a project like Corktown to establish his ability to deliver for the city. For him, the success of this project would firmly establish him as a future viable mayoral candidate.

"Well, the developers need the remaining parcels to complete the hotel and commercial projects before the Super Bowl," added Randy, who was in charge of coordinating the project with the developers. Feeling the pressure of his recent gambling losses, he was aggressively pushing the developers, the recorder of deeds office and anyone else standing in the way of completion of the project. He was relentless in coordinating his end of the project.

"How's the case going with Bobby Bennett? When is it scheduled for trial?" asked Victor. "The case is moving through the system pretty quickly," Stone chimed in. "It's a win-win situation. If JJ Battle wins the case, Bennett goes free and remains a part of the team. If he loses, Bennett will receive a substantial sentence, and he won't be a problem."

"Good, make sure he keeps his mouth shut until this is over," Randy icily replied.

"Continue to monitor that situation and if things get out of hand, take some remedial measures to clean it up," Victor said decisively. He didn't have to tell Stone twice. He already had alternate plans in motion. Whatever developed, he had a contingency plan to cover any eventuality. He was prepared. This was his only opportunity for a big money deal, and he wasn't going to let anything or anyone circumvent the plan.

It was apparent that the enterprise was very well planned. It was a bold yet ingenious plan, and one in which the principals stood to make millions. It was simple. The NFL awarded the Super Bowl to the City. This would be a much-needed economic bonanza for the city. However, the city lacked adequate luxury accommodations to handle the influx of visitors for the game. There was virtually no available space for such a development, except Corktown. Corktown, one of the oldest neighborhoods in the city, was home to an elderly, entrenched community that had spent a great deal of their lives in the same homes.

Over five hundred homeowners were unwilling to sell. Many were longtime residents who refused to give up their homes. The city would have to go to court to force the homeowners to sell by exercising its right of eminent domain. Publicly this would be an extremely unpopular political move, particularly for an administration already plagued by public relations blunders. The city hoped to rely on collaboration with private entities to acquire the property, and then sell to the developers. From a political standpoint, the latter strategy was by far a more effective strategy. The city would achieve its objectives - the development of Corktown in time for the super bowl and all of the worldwide acclaim the city would receive for its new progressive development. It would be a much-needed win for the mayor and the city. That was where the law firm of Connors and Wright came in and the corporation, One Detroit, Inc. was formed. Its strategy was to acquire the property free of the risk of adverse publicity that the city government faced. Its plan was working perfectly, until Bobby Bennett was arrested. This put the project in jeopardy. Bobby was the last remaining lose end that would have to be tied up quickly. Bobby was a loose cannon. They could not afford to have him disrupting the development. It was up to JJ Battle to deliver an acquittal for Bobby and protect the development's timetable, or else.

Chapter 13

IT WAS TWO WEEKS BEFORE BOBBY Bennett's trial. JJ was in full pre-trial preparation mode. This meant no office appointments, telephone calls, or other distractions or disruptions. He had already developed a basic trial strategy, one he believed he could sell to the jury. It was a risky strategy and he needed Bobby's cooperation to pull it off. His trial strategy would require JJ to paint the victim, Brianna Tuller, as a meddling, nosy, overbearing friend. She was a friend whose overzealousness came between Betty and Bobby, he would tell the jury. It was a story that everyone was familiar with and JJ would rely on sympathetic jurors to make it work.

He would have to minimize the seriousness of Brianna's injuries. The prosecution would hammer home that point. JJ would counter with the argument that her injuries were essentially self-inflicted and that there was never a threat of harm or injury had she just remained in the car.

JJ had gone over Brianna's statement numerous times. In her statement, she never mentioned any actual threat of harm from Bobby, it was all implied. That lack of an admission was something that JJ could exploit; however, to do so, JJ would have to take the risk of putting Bobby on the stand.

Putting your client on the stand was one of the most difficult decisions a defense attorney faced. Sometimes the facts of the case dictated your strategy and forced you to put your client on the stand. This strategy was particularly

necessary in self-defense cases in which jurors needed to determine for themselves the sincerity of the defendant's need to use violence to defend himself.
Juries were usually very good at getting to the truth. Only the best defendants
could pull it off.

It was an area where a good defense attorney earned his fee. JJ would
spend countless hours preparing Bobby to testify, repeatedly going over
the facts of the case and his expected testimony, but more importantly,
going over anticipated questions of the prosecution. JJ would instruct his
clients on which facts the prosecution was most likely to focus on in their
effort to confuse them, and he would tell them how they needed to respond. But even after all of the practice and preparation, putting your client on the stand was still a risky maneuver. If the jury didn't believe your
client, no amount of preparation was enough. It came down to who the
jury liked better, the victim or the defendant. Whomever the jury caught
lying first, lost.

So JJ had his work cut out for himself with Bobby Bennett. He would have
to humanize him and portray him as the loving concerned father whose only
interest was in seeing his children. It was a challenge. When he visited Bobby
to discuss his testimony, he was unsure what he would find.

The guards quickly processed JJ through the jail procedures and sent him
up to visit his client.

"Damn!" JJ spat, upset at the sight of Homicide detective Harvey Stone
again visiting his client.

"I'm sick of you meeting with my client without my permission and in
violation of the judge's order." JJ hissed at Stone.

"Don't get too sick counselor, people sometimes die from too much ill-
ness," Stone countered.

"What is that supposed to mean?" JJ asked, wondering if there was an
implied threat behind Stone's sarcasm.

"Don't get your briefs in a knot, I was visiting your client on an unrelated
matter," Stone replied, amused with himself at his play on words.

"What is it you don't understand about not visiting my client without my
permission?"

"I understand perfectly what it means counselor, it's just that you don't call the shots for me, I do." Stone replied, standing face-to-face with JJ, amused at his anger.

"It's apparent you didn't learn anything from our last encounter, detective?"

"I learned that you're not the only one who can teach lessons." I suggest you ease off the threats. It's unbecoming of a lawyer of your stature," Stone replied, easing past JJ. He could see Stone's stocky and squat frame as he passed him. JJ could also see the ominous bulge under Stone's cheap, tight fitting sport coat. For a moment, JJ wondered if he had gone too far. It didn't matter. He continued with the bravado, adopting his toughest east side demeanor.

"We'll see," JJ replied, seething at the exchange.

"What's happening attorney Battle?" Bobby asked in that upbeat optimistic way of his.

"I'm not in the mood tonight Bobby, let's just get down to business."

JJ settled in to his visit with Bobby, trying to put the conversation with Stone in perspective. He wondered what he meant by the words that JJ wasn't the only one who could teach lessons. JJ knew that Stone was very capable of carrying out his threats. He made a mental note to be a lot more cautious.

JJ could swear that Bobby had gained weight since his last visit. It was rare for a prisoner to gain weight from the sorry jail food provided by the Wayne County Jail. The jail didn't want the prisoners getting too comfortable with the accommodations; they might not want to leave.

JJ was surprised at Bobby's upbeat demeanor. He had been in jail for over a month, yet he was still very pleasant.

"Bobby, I told you how important it was not to speak with anybody from law enforcement before your trial. They are not going to help your case; it's their job to put you in the penitentiary."

"I know. But there's some other stuff I'm involved in that has nothing to do with this case. That's what I'm talking to Stone about."

"Since you mentioned your little hustle, fill me in on some of the details."

"JJ you already know a lot of the details. By the way, I don't have to tell you that this stuff is extremely confidential. If my people knew I was talking to you about this, I'd be in serious trouble," Bobby said in a surprisingly serious tone.

"I get the picture. Remember, I'm on your team. I'm your last line of defense between you and the penitentiary."

"OK. Anyway, One Detroit, Inc. hired me to acquire all of the remaining titles to property in the Corktown area. It was sort of like the Malcolm X philosophy: by any means necessary.

"What the hell did that mean?"

"Just what I said. If I could acquire the property by legal means paying a preset amount, that's what I did."

"What if you couldn't acquire the deeds legally, what would you do then?"

"Whatever I had to do. Usually that meant using some scam or trickery, depending on who the homeowner was."

"Did that work?" JJ asked incredulously.

"I don't mean to brag, but I'm pretty persuasive when I have to be."

"Don't tell me, save it for the jury," JJ countered somewhat facetiously.

"I would tell them I was from the register of deeds or some other official city department, and tell them that the city was going to condemn this area and only pay them one-half of the state-equalized value of their property, or less. They could hold out for that amount, which might become lower, or I could arrange for a cash settlement for twenty percent more."

"And that was a successful scam?"

"You have to remember who we were dealing with. But in extreme cases, I simply had the deeds fraudulently signed over to me, and filed with the register of deeds. They lost their property before they knew it. Most of the people were elderly and uniformed and didn't even know what happened."

"Who was providing the money to fund this little real estate scam?'

"All I know is that the checks were from One Detroit, Inc. and signed by Victor Wright."

"Did you deal with Victor directly or did you deal with somebody else?"

There was a long pause before Bobby answered, and JJ could see a look of uncertainty on his face. Finally, after a long sigh he answered, "Harvey Stone."

"HARVEY STONE?" JJ repeated in amazement. How did he get involved in this?"

"Detective Stone and I go way back together. When he was in vice, he got rid of a couple of low-level felonies for me. We've been tight ever since. I help him out whenever I can. Whether it's information, or some other personal favors."

"Such as?" JJ probed, wanting to have as much intelligence on Stone as possible, just as a precaution, if things got rough somewhere down the line.

"You know my reputation in the projects, right?"

"Everybody who can read a newspaper knows your reputation, Bobby. So?"

"Well, Stone has this appreciation for young, somewhat needy, ladies."

"How young?" JJ wanted to know the depths of Stone's depravity. It always helped knowing the limits of the enemy.

"Not that young. All of them were of legal age. I just arranged the introductions, the rest was between consenting adults. But I can tell you that Stone's car was a fixture in the neighborhood and it wasn't official police business."

"Is this Corktown project the reason you picked up that fraud case," JJ asked, trying to put all of the pieces together.

"Yeah, that was where that feisty old man went to the police complaining that I scammed him out of his property."

"What ever happened to that case?"

"The old geezer died before the case ever went to trial."

"How convenient," JJ replied, recognizing the developing hurricane with Bobby Bennett at the eye of the storm. "Just out of curiosity, what was the cause of death?" JJ asked suspecting that whatever the cause, it was unnatural.

"I'm not sure," Bobby replied. "I think they said it was natural causes. He died in his sleep."

JJ wondered how many other residents of Corktown had recently died of natural causes.

Chapter 14

JJ BATTLE WAS RUNNING OUT OF time. He hated the feeling of being rushed; preparation was everything. But here he was, less than two weeks before the trial and there were still too many unanswered questions about Bobby Bennett and his kidnapping trial. The other problem was uncovering the ever-increasing web of the developing Corktown entanglements. Who knew where it would all end.

"There is nothing more attractive than a handsome man deep into his own thoughts. I didn't know if I should interrupt or not?" JJ looked up, momentarily distracted. He was sitting at a table in the corner of Sweet Georgia Brown's, an upscale eatery in downtown, frequented by the court and political crowd. He smiled, happy to see his guest as he rose and embraced Katherine, kissing her on the cheek.

"Nothing is more attractive than St. John Knit on a woman with a figure to do it justice," he teased, admiring Katherine in her business suit that was very flattering. He pulled out her chair so she could sit down, and noticed the approving stares of both men and women in the restaurant. "Why haven't I married this woman?" He asked himself, allowing his senses to take her all in.

"I hope I'm not late, I just got out of court arguing motions before old man Harper, and I could swear that he was sleeping during arguments. But, as always, he usually gets it right in the end. Either he's doing his homework, or his law clerks are getting smarter," Katherine replied with mock exasperation.

"I suspect it's a little bit of both. Isn't he getting close to mandatory retirement age? I remember when he was still handling cases on the criminal docket, and he fell asleep in the middle of a trial. He woke up suddenly and yelled, "Overruled" when there wasn't an objection before the court. Everyone had to contain their laughter, because you know he would have tried to find the whole courtroom in contempt. He was just that ornery." They laughed aloud, ignoring the other diners' glances, savoring this intimate moment together.

"Have you ordered? I'm starving. I might just order one of everything," Katherine joked.

"You always did have a big appetite." JJ teased, surprised, and amused at an embarrassed blush from Katherine.

They ordered drinks and waited for the food to arrive. JJ filled her in on the developments of Bobby Bennett's case and the surprising twists and turns of the Corktown development. After they had eaten and the lunch crowd had thinned out, Katherine pulled out a folder and they discussed what her associate had found on Corktown. They continued eating as Katherine explained what she had learned about One Detroit, Inc.

Katherine began her explanation by asking JJ one simple question, "are you sure you want to continue investigating this?"

JJ could hear something in her voice that he was unaccustomed to hearing from Katherine, fear and trepidation.

"I have to see where this leads. I've been shot at and who knows what else I'm being subjected to. I'm beginning to see a pattern developing and I don't like what I see."

"You could walk away now and that would be the end of it," Katherine said in a fearful tone.

"What would I be walking away from? Besides, you know I like a good battle." JJ added, trying to inject a bit of levity into a conversation that was becoming a bit too serious.

"Well, anyway, why don't you come over tonight and I'll fill you in on all of the sordid and incestuous details of One Detroit, Inc." She said with a coy smile.

"Am I sensing a bit of extortion counselor?"

"I can assure you that you will feel something, but it won't be extortion" she replied as she got up from the table leaning over to kiss him. "I'll be home after six, anytime you get there is fine with me. Think about what I said," he heard her say as she glided past him in a perfumed exit.

Seated nearby in a booth but unseen by JJ, sat John Ratskeller. He was sitting at a booth near the end of the bar, partially hidden by potted plants and a restaurant pillar. He had a perfect view of the restaurant while remaining unseen. He nursed his diet Coke and maintained surveillance on the subjects. He was there for all of the two-hour lunch. He immediately recognized Katherine Devlin from the photograph he had been given. She was even prettier than her photograph. He quickly tucked the photograph inside his jacket pocket and left the restaurant unobtrusively. JJ waited for the waiter to bring the check. He turned to watch Katherine leave, but she was already out the door. He saw the revolving door turn but no one was there. The Rat was on Katherine's trail.

Chapter 15

HARVEY STONE HUNG UP THE PHONE and sat staring out of the window of his office at 1300 Beaubien, police headquarters for the city of Detroit. He was a man who maintained no illusions about himself, the world, or his place in it. He survived in a brutal world of killers, rapists and other assorted degenerates by adhering to one uncompromising philosophy: do the next logical thing. There was no need to romanticize life or circumstances into some Darwinian theory of evolutionary survival. You just did the next right thing. By reducing life to this simple formula, it reduced the number of choices you had to make, thereby increasing the likelihood you that you would make the right choice. This attitude had gotten him where he was today, Chief of the Homicide unit of a large metropolitan police department, and he didn't even have a college degree. He knew his rise to power infuriated his more educated brethren, but he didn't care, because none of them would dare cross him. They knew there would be consequences if they did.

Stone, a Viet Nam vet, still saw himself as a soldier, still taking orders. As a result, he maintained an appreciation and respect for loyalty and duty. No duty had been higher than defending his country, and now, nothing was more important than protecting the citizens of Detroit. He believed in the necessity of a cause. For most of his life, he had pursued the causes of others. But now, late in his career, he found a cause to love for himself. He was so close to making it all happen. He needed to finalize the next details with unmistakable skill and finesse. One mistake and he could lose it all.

When faced with delicate assignments such as these, he could not rely on department personnel to carry out his orders. He needed a detached and focused professional. A professional knew that there was no such outcome as failure. In the event the mission had an unfortunate outcome, the professional assumed all responsibility. That was implicit in the job description and fee. Only a select few could successfully operate under those conditions. He had just such a person. Stone was terse and to the point, "this is Sergeant Major Stone, meet me at the corner of Woodward and Congress at 0800."

At precisely 8:00 a.m., Stone pulled up at the intersection of Woodward and Congress. Waiting on the corner was an average-looking man who almost eluded Stone's view. The two men did not talk. In fact, there was no acknowl-edgement from either man as the man got into the car. Stone smoothly pulled his unmarked squad car onto the freeway and headed out of the city.

After they had been riding for twenty minutes, Stone exited the freeway and pulled into a mall parking lot. Stone handed the man a brief case and a thick envelope containing a letter and a photograph. Stone did all of the talking, and the man listened with a dispassionate stare. When Stone finished talking, he returned to downtown Detroit. Throughout the return ride, the man never said a word. He exited the car with the briefcase in his hand and in a moment, he had disappeared into the crowd.

Chapter 16

JJ COULD FEEL THE EXCITEMENT DEVELOPING as Bobby's trial date grew nearer. A criminal trial was the closest feeling he ever had to the exhilaration of athletic competition. In some ways, it was more exciting because the stakes were higher. He had done all of the prep work for the case, including his opening and closing statements. He liked to keep his opening loose and unstructured so he could adjust to the jury's reactions to his presentation. Conceptually, this was an easy case; the issue was whether or not, the jury believed Bobby had the intent to hold Brianna against her will and to transport her. Since he had lived and breathed this case for the past month, it was easy to identify all of the issues, both on the defense side and the prosecution side. He was ready but he needed to unwind. That was where his weekend with Katherine would be a pleasant diversion. He had to acknowledge that he was starting to feel something more for Katherine than he had wanted to admit. He had even begun to start imaging their lives together.

It was after five o'clock. on Friday, afternoon, and JJ had sent Marsha and the rest of the office staff home early for the weekend. He decided he would get a head start on the weekend and head over to Katherine's for their six o'clock rendezvous. He would arrive early and relax.

It was 6:00 pm when Katherine opened the door. He briefly thought about answering the door naked but thought better of it; instead opting for a pair of shorts and a University of Michigan t--shirt. He was lounging on the couch when she entered, hands full of assorted bags of carryout and other food items. He smiled as he saw the look of surprise and then happiness on her face as she saw him sitting there. He knew that she also felt the warmth and the tug of their love and bond together. He rushed over to help her with the bags, and at once knew this felt right. This was where he belonged and she was the one who could help him to forget the pain of the past. They placed the bags down and embraced. It was as if they had not seen each other for a long while.

"You know, I could get used to this," JJ said, expressing the depths of what he felt in those few words. In those words, he was attempting to show her all that she meant to him. He had never said it, although he had often felt that they were right together. He couldn't describe why it was right this time, but he just knew that it was. He wanted to say so many things to this woman that he had been unable to say before, to let her know of his intentions and commitment to her.

"Sshh," she said, placing a soft manicured finger over his lips. "Please don't say another word. I need to decompress from today's events and give you my undivided best. Can you grant me this one wish my king?"

He looked at her and saw a woman who had the power to reach inside of him like no other woman. "You need only ask, my queen," he responded, giving in to her mood.

She was gone, headed off to the shower in a trail of orders and instructions. He put up the groceries, opened the Chinese carryout, placed the food on plates, opened a bottle of wine, and lit candles. It was a familiar scene, yet he could sense a different mood. He had begun to think about his future and even more important, his future with Katherine. He had been at this point before, but always allowed himself a way out. Now, he couldn't find a reason not to share the rest of his life with Katherine.

"Hey honey," she yelled. "Put some music on, I'm starting to get my energy back. I have so much to tell you."

"Do you have a preference?"

"No, just something romantic. We have the whole weekend together, that is if you can fit it into your schedule." She came out of the room in a short silky nightgown dancing to the tune of Anita Baker. Seeing her so full of life made his life seem more complete. He wanted to grab her and tell her just what she meant to him, and all of the other things he should have already said but had not. Instead, he just held her and tried to show her what she meant to him by the strength of his embrace.

"Katherine, I love you," he said, surprised, not at the words, but at the power those words possessed. He had not said them to anyone in such a long time, nor had he allowed himself to feel love. He felt an incredible lightness, as if he had freed himself from some tremendous weight.

"I know, and I love you too, she softly said, not willing to leave his arms. They remained this way for some time, and he could feel the wetness of her tears on his arm as he held and rubbed her wet hair. He could smell her freshness as they kissed tenderly, then passionately.

She held him at arm's length, staring deeply into his eyes. "You don't know how long I have waited to hear those words from you. There were times I doubted that I would ever hear them. But thank God, I'm a patient woman."

"You do know that even though I didn't say it, I still felt it." He said, meeting her gaze.

"Yeah, yeah, I know. However, it's nice to hear it and know for sure," she said with a coy, yet knowing, smile.

"Where do we go from here?" he asked, trying to put things into perspective.

"I don't know about you, but I'm going to the dinner table to eat."

"But what about us?" He asked, somewhat bewildered by her response.

"We will be just fine. Whatever you want to do, at whatever pace you want to go, I'm with you. There's no pressure. I have always loved you and I always will."

He sat down at the table relieved, but at the same time convinced that he had made the right choice. She knew him well enough to know that she couldn't rush him, and that it had to be something he believed was his idea. He was like one of those young thoroughbreds that needed to be walked slowly, because they were skittish and easily spooked. She let him arrive at the idea on his own. She made the decision a long time ago that he was the one. She didn't put her life on hold waiting for him. She developed her career, traveled, saw other men, and made a life for herself. She knew that when he was ready, she would be ready. She wanted to let the weekend develop from a simmer to a boil. Everything was falling into place.

After they had eaten, they left the table and moved to the couch. Before things moved too quickly, she wanted to tell him all of the information she had gathered on One Detroit, Inc.

"Now that you have sufficiently dined, are you ready for tonight's entertainment? It's a tale of greed and avarice," Katherine said coyly as if she were talking about a good novel.

"Oh, I thought tonight's entertainment was a lap dance or something along those lines," JJ replied with feigned disappointment.

"That comes later if you are a good boy and pay close attention to everything that Katherine has to say."

"You have my undivided attention."

"Where should I start," Katherine asked, taking a sip of wine and warming to her task. "One Detroit, Inc. was founded by some of the most notable figures in the city, the real crème de la crème. For starters, there are the usual suspects, Victor Wright and Randy Connors from the legal community are the majority shareholders, Rahsheed Truman from the Mayor's office, Harvey Stone from the Detroit Police Department, and last but not least, a JJ Battle favorite, Judge Eva Ann Moody. How's that for a cast of characters," Katherine replied incredulously.

"You have got to be kidding. Haven't they heard of conflicts of interest? They better get some jail cells ready; I smell a federal investigation on the way." JJ was still deep in thought piecing together Katherine's revelations along with the information he had gathered during his investigation of Bobby Bennett. It was starting to appear that Corktown might be getting ready to blow. JJ wondered how deep this was going to get and what role he might play in all of this.

"It gets better. One Detroit, Inc., on behalf of its owners and shareholders, now hold ninety percent of the deeds to property in the Corktown area. They are the single largest landowner in the city of Detroit. They accomplished this in 180 days. They couldn't have accomplished this in this short amount of time if they didn't have the cooperation of a lot of city officials."

"What scares me is that you have some people who should know better, abandoning their better judgment and ethics to be a part of this." JJ was having a hard time believing all of the revelations that Katherine was telling him.

"That's what happens when there is this kind of money involved. People lose their perspective, and their greed gets in the way of their judgment." Katherine suggested with her usual accurate assessment of human nature.

"How much money are we talking about here?" JJ asked, trying to measure the risks these people were taking with what they stood to make.

"At last projections, the Corktown project was valued at five billion dollars and climbing."

"Yeah, but what good is the money if you're in federal prison? I'm pretty sure you can't take it with you."

"I can understand the rest of the people, but not Eva. This seems so out of character for her. But you know her better than I do, JJ." Katherine kidded him while moving closer and sitting on his lap. "Now you said something about a lap dance?" She whispered naughtily, as JJ was immediately transported from the complexities of Corktown to the reality of a beautiful sexy woman sitting in his lap clothed only in a silky nightgown. The nightgown, like JJ's thoughts, quickly fell away.

Sleep did not come easily for JJ that night. He tossed, turned, and dreamed of being pulled into deep water by an undertow. He awoke, sweating profusely and feeling disoriented. It took him a moment to remember that he was at Katherine's place. She was peacefully sleeping next to him, deep into her own dreams. JJ, however, could not shake his sense of uneasiness and the feeling they were being watched.

Chapter 17

JJ WAS UP EARLY, UNSETTLED BY his dreams. He decided to cook breakfast for Katherine as a treat for last night. He knew she liked waffles, scrambled eggs, and bacon, so he fixed all of her favorite things and served her in bed. They were feeling so comfortable together when JJ started to wonder if this feeling could last. She assured him it could and proceeded to make love to him so passionately that he quickly forgot his doubts.

"Listen, I have to run some errands today and I'll be back around 5:00 and we can go out for dinner. Is that OK with you?" JJ was surprised at his tone or even that he asked for her permission, but he had to admit that he liked knowing that she cared. He didn't mind that he would be sharing his life with Katherine. In fact, he was starting to see many promising possibilities when he popped the question. This would almost be like a merger. They would have to decide where they would live, if they would have children and all of those other life decisions. He loved this woman and he knew the best was yet to come.

"Wow, I'm impressed, JJ Battle asking me if it's OK to leave for a couple of hours. I don't know what's gotten in to you, but I hope it remains."

"I can tell you precisely what's gotten into me" JJ replied with mock seriousness. "It's called good lovin', didn't your mother tell you that's the way to a man's heart," he said as he leaned over and kissed her. Make reservations for Opus 1 at six o'clock. I'm feeling somewhat special.

"You know this is more than a girl can stand at one time, don't you. How about if I tag along with you today? I don't want to let you out of my sight."

"I thought about that, but I have some errands that I have to run that would probably bore you to death. How about going to the beauty parlor and getting beautiful for me."

"If you insist, my king," she said, sensing that resisting would be futile. "But before you leave, come over here. There's something I forgot to tell you earlier" as she pulled him back to bed.

After a short nap and shower, JJ headed downtown. He made the decision to ask Katherine to marry him, and he needed a ring. He wanted it to be something special, because Katherine deserved the best. She had waited patiently for JJ to come to the realization of what she had known for a long time; they were perfect for each other.

JJ drove to his favorite jewelry store. He already knew what he wanted, something around two carats, single-stone solitaire. He wanted something she could be proud of and that would unquestionably show his love and affection for her. He quickly found what he was looking for and had them wrap it in an elaborate box for their dinner tonight.

He arrived home and went through the mail, realizing he had about three hours before his dinner with Katherine. He had time to watch the Michigan football game. For once, he trusted himself to know he was making the right decision. Just as he was settling down to watch the game, the doorbell rang. He smiled, thinking Katherine had come over to spend time with him. He opened the door and replied, "You just couldn't stay away could you?" He said, expecting to see Katherine's smiling face. He was shocked when it wasn't Katherine, but Eva Ann Moody.

"Were you expecting someone else, JJ?" She asked with characteristic sarcasm, sensing JJ's obvious disappointment.

"Eva, what are you doing here? You know this is inappropriate, with the trial just a week away."

"I told you I wanted to see you, and I'm not a woman who can be ignored."

"That's obvious because you're here. I think it would be more appropriate if we continued this after the trial."

"JJ, I am not going to let my life be dictated by some criminal trial. I'm entitled to a life you know. Just because I'm a judge doesn't mean that I don't have needs. I'm tired of having my life dictated by judicial robes."

"I understand that Eva, but there's a lot at stake, and this meeting could be misconstrued as an improper ex-parte communication. We could both be sanctioned by the Bar," he said, attempting to circumvent Eva's aggressiveness.

"If we promise not to talk about the case, I don't think we'll be violating any rules," she huskily whispered while softening her tone. JJ feeling pressured didn't know what to say. Eva was very persuasive and knew how to get her way. He was unsuccessful in fending off Eva's efforts, and moved aside and let her enter.

"I have an appointment downtown in a little while," he said, remembering his date with Katherine and experiencing a slight twinge of guilt. He swore under his breath and invited Eva back to the den.

"You've really improved this place since the last time I was here; it looks like a woman's touch is present."

"I don't know whether to take that as a compliment or an insult. Would you like something to drink," he asked. He wondered if he would tell Katherine about this weird meeting. He was surprised at how quickly he had started to integrate Katherine into his life and thinking. He found himself considering her in everything he did. He was actually starting to like the feeling of having to consider someone else in his life's plan.

"Can I get that drink sometime today or is a girl going to have to die of thirst?" She yelled, jolting him back into reality. JJ was debating on how he was going to handle Eva. He was compromising his better judgment. He knew Eva could be a handful. When he entered the room with Eva's diet Coke, she had answered the question for him. She was standing in the middle of the den completely naked.

"What is it with you Eva? Every time I see you, you're taking off your clothes. Is this some new form of expression you've adopted? If it is I'm flattered, but you really don't have to." Although he did not intend to indulge Eva in her misguided attempt to seduce him, he had to admit there was something powerful about an attractive naked woman standing in front of you. He had to admit it appealed to his animal instinct and evaporated his resistance and judgment.

"To be perfectly honest JJ, I'm after a lot more from you than flattery. The last time we were together, I recall you saying that we would get together soon, well, here we are. I'm not taking no for an answer," she replied, with conviction and ample breasts. JJ could feel himself weakening, but decided that he wouldn't make the first move. He reasoned that things would go better if he had to explain himself later. It had to be the lawyer in him, already creating a defense for his actions. It wasn't too late, he told himself. He hadn't done anything wrong yet. He could still walk away with his dignity intact, and save himself a lot of embarrassment somewhere down the road. But whom was he kidding. He wanted to say no. But could he? Again, Eva took the liberty of answering for him by coming toward him and taking the drink out of his hand. JJ didn't resist. He was amazed at how easily sexual desire wore down one's will to resist. He wasn't sure at what point he became less of a victim and more of a participant, but he knew he didn't want to stop. Neither his better judgment nor his love of Katherine kept him from this woman. When it was over, he was disgusted with himself for his weakness and lack of commitment to Katherine. He knew he would have to make it right somehow, but he didn't know how. He cursed himself, got up from the couch, and went to the bathroom for a towel. He stayed long enough to compose himself and to come up with a solution.

Eva, still on the couch in the aftermath of sexual bliss, lay there utterly vulnerable. He had seldom seen her that way since she had become a judge. He remembered her from law school as a tough and determined woman, but he knew that deep inside she was lonely and in need of love. Surprisingly, instead of being angry with her, he felt a great deal of sadness for her. She was reduced to these kamikaze-styled rendezvous for fulfillment, instead of a loving and lasting relationship. Earlier he had thought about unceremoniously asking her to leave, without the benefit of conversation or explanation. But seeing her this way, made him remember how much they had shared together and how much they had once meant to each other.

"Hey, wake up sleepy head, I need to talk to you," he said. His voice soft and soothing.

"Listen, I know that we agreed not to talk about the case, but there's one aspect of the case that's troubling me, that involves you." Eva sat up on the couch and pulled the blanket around her, reaching for her watered down diet coke.

"What is it about me and this case that troubles you, JJ?"

"I know you're familiar with the Corktown project and One Detroit, Inc.'s involvement, but how much do you really know about what's going on?" JJ asked in a serious and conspiratorial tone.

"Not very much. Victor and Randy asked me to invest a couple of years ago, which I did. I have pretty much been a silent partner ever since. I think I attended one board meeting. Because they were so successful in the Comerica Park and Ford Field projects, I thought this was a perfect investment. The city needed the development, and I needed some additional retirement income. It sounded like a perfect investment opportunity. What's the problem?" She asked, in an uncharacteristically naïve way that made JJ believe she was telling the truth. She had never lied to him before, and he hoped that she wouldn't begin now.

"First, One Detroit, Inc. has engaged in some shady land acquisitions for the Corktown project, including over 500 deed acquisitions in an extremely short period of time. Many of these acquisitions could not have been accomplished so quickly without some inside help. Some of the acquisitions resulted in fraud charges against my client, Bobby Bennett. Those charges were dismissed when the key prosecution witness conveniently died under mysterious circumstances. Many of those deeds were obtained through fraud and deceit. How many I don't know. But enough to raise suspicion. It appears that your partners are utilizing some unsavory characters and means to complete this project. In addition, there appear to be some serious conflicts of interest with individuals in the mayor's office. That's all that I know now."

"Who do you think is behind all of this?" Eva asked with concern.

"I guarantee Victor and Randy are the masterminds, and Harvey Stone is the muscle, and Rahsheed Truman is supplying the intelligence from city hall. It's a nice, neat operation, except that it's violating a number of federal and state laws."

"What do you think I should do, JJ, withdraw from the Board and get my investment back?" Eva looked at him the way she did when they were in law school when she relied on him for counsel and guidance.

"Don't do anything yet. Let me gather more information before you do anything. Perhaps underneath the obvious fraudulent dealings there's a legitimate basis for all of this"

"Thanks JJ. I can always count on you."

"Listen, there's something else that I need to tell you. I wanted to tell you before you heard it from somewhere else. I'm going to ask Katherine to marry me."

"Is that all? You were so dramatic; I thought you were going to tell me you only had six months to live. I'm happy for you both. She's a great lady. You should have married her years ago." JJ could see that her words were betraying her feelings. Eva attempted to smile through her sadness.

Although there had never been anything definite between them, she still sometimes thought of the possibility of JJ and her being together. She now knew that wasn't possible. She had to maintain her dignity and not let JJ she her pain.

"Yeah, I know. Thanks. It means a lot to me," JJ said and hugged Eva. There was more conversation and sincere questions about his plans, and then she quickly showered, dressed, and left. JJ was glad that it was over. He called Katherine to confirm whether she was on schedule but got no answer.

"She's probably at the beauty parlor getting beautiful for me," he thought to himself.

Eva was busy completing a call herself. Her party did not answer, but Eva left a message nevertheless. "It's worse than we thought," was all she said.

Chapter 18

IT HAD BEEN A BUSY AND hectic day for Katherine. She had so much to do, and time had just flown by. Although she was busy and rushed, she felt good that she accomplished everything. She had gotten her hair, nails pedicure, and a facial for good measure, but the highlight of the day was the black dress she bought at Bloomingdale's for tonight. She had to admit that it was stunning; it showed her figure off perfectly, in a tasteful and elegant way. It was just what she needed to make tonight with JJ perfect. She could feel the excitement building as she thought about what tonight might mean. She didn't want to jump to conclusions, but she had a good idea that JJ was going to propose. It wasn't something she had planned on after all of these years, but she always hoped it would happen. She had been in love with JJ from the beginning, waiting for him to find himself and overcome his setbacks. , He had recently suffered a number of personal setbacks that made him distant and unreachable. Rather than smother him with demands, she let him find his way, and thankfully, it led to her. Now, she had to hurry upstairs, take a quick shower, and wait for JJ to arrive. As she arrived at the front door, she was surprised to see that the doorman wasn't on duty. She was hoping she could get some help with her packages. It was Saturday, and he probably was helping someone else with their packages. No matter, she wouldn't let anything spoil her mood.

She let herself into the condo and dropped her packages on the couch. She was careful to take her dress and hang it in the closet so that not even a wrinkle could spoil its perfection. She turned on the shower as she searched her closet for just the right pumps to complete her ensemble. Next, she needed the right jewelry to accentuate the outfit. She chose a gold necklace and bracelet set. Consciously, she didn't choose any rings for tonight; she wanted her fingers free, just in case they would receive an adornment of their own. She giggled to herself like a schoolgirl going on her first date, amazed at how the prospect of love had her laughing and singing to herself. She turned on the stereo, singing and dancing to the beat of the music as she undressed. She thought she heard a noise in the foyer, and called out JJ's name expectantly, wondering if he had arrived early. She had to laugh, when there was no response.

"Just settle down, he'll be here soon enough," she told herself. She wrapped a towel around herself and searched for her sexiest underwear. She wanted to look her best.

As Katherine patiently went about her ritual of finding just the right items for tonight, the Rat quickly jimmied the lock and silently entered Katherine's condo. He closed the door, being careful not to make a sound and waited breathlessly for any sounds or movement. He heard the shower running, the stereo playing, and the sound of drawers opening and closing in the bedroom. He waited for thirty more seconds, listening for any unexpected sounds. He heard none. Slowly he crept across the marble foyer floor, his rubber soled shoes slid noiselessly across the tile. He approached the slightly opened bedroom door, alert for any sudden movement. He used all of his senses as he silently eased his way into the bedroom doorway. The carpeted room muffled his footsteps and he was careful to hold his breath as he edged closer inside the room. He saw her, hunched over a dresser drawer, her attention riveted on her underwear selection. He stealthily slid into the room with quick and efficient movements. He approached her from the rear; she was still unaware of his presence. He was behind her now, enveloping her with one powerful arm. There was a momentary look of surprise on Katherine's face as the Rat, with a swift and practiced twist, killed her in an instant. Her neck, broken in an inelegant angle, made her appear as if she were sleeping. The Rat gently laid her on the floor, careful not to disturb anything in the room. He surveyed his handiwork and prepared to leave.

JJ was a little perturbed; he had been trying to reach Katherine for the last fifteen minutes. She wasn't answering her cell or the home phone. He was hoping she was at least in the shower and not still going through her beauty ritual. Whatever, he would get there early and surprise her. He was feeling especially good today and the excitement of proposing to Katherine had him in a great mood. He couldn't wait to see her face when he gave her the two-carat ring and proposed to her. After all is wasn't every day that JJ Battle proposed to a woman; in fact, it wasn't any day, because he had never taken this step before. He laughed thinking about how nervous he was, and what he would say.

"Good evening, Mr. Battle how are you this afternoon?" Michael, the doorman asked with a decided air of formality.

"I'm fine, Michael, and you?"

"I'm doing well, thank you for asking, Mr. Battle."

"Michael, have you seen Ms. Devlin today, I see her car in the lot, but she's not answering her phone," JJ asked.

"No, I haven't, but on Saturdays I'm usually helping the residents carry packages in, so I might have missed her. Do you want me to phone her to let her know you're on your way up?" Michael asked in a professional manner.

"No, I'll go up and surprise her. Thanks anyway."

JJ entered the elevator and rode it all the way to the top floor, whistling some silly tune he couldn't get out of his head. He exited the elevator, approaching Katherine's door. He had a moment of apprehension as he inserted the key into the lock. He could see the remnants of her afternoon shopping as the bags were strewn all over the couch. He could hear the stereo playing and the shower running. He thought about recreating Hitchcock's "Psycho" shower scene, but he thought better of it, and called her name instead. He entered the bathroom when she didn't answer. He could see steam coming from the shower as if it had been running for a while. He was surprised when she was not in the shower, and he turned to head for the bedroom.

"Katherine, my love, where are you?" He playfully called. "We have dinner reservations at si….. He abruptly stopped. Confused by what he saw.

"Katherine," he softly called. Her towel-wrapped body stretched out on the bedroom floor. Her long legs slightly folded and her head was at a strange, unnatural angle. His first thought was that she's going to have one sore neck when she wakes up from her nap. He was puzzled by her stillness and the oddity of her, on the floor, like this unmoving. He knew it was illogical. There had to be an explanation. He instantly became alarmed when he saw a thin trickle of blood on her lips. His heart pounded furiously when she did not respond. He leaned over to wake her or comfort her when he felt a tremendous blow. It was as if someone quickly turned on a blast of heat. A bright flash followed that blurred his vision. He collapsed, not knowing if he had fallen or was pushed. He had a hard time focusing. He could see in the distance through the fog, Katherine trying to warn him about something, but he just couldn't make it out. He struggled to get to his feet, but his legs were wobbly and unsteady. He could feel warm liquid running down his face and he couldn't decide if this was real or a dream. He struggled to think what could incapacitate both Katherine and him like this. He collapsed on top of Katherine and started to dream a deep, happy dream. The dream had Katherine in a wedding gown, walking down the aisle. He could see himself smiling as she approached him. That image of Katherine was his last waking thought as he tumbled into unconsciousness.

The Rat, unable to leave the apartment before JJ arrived, hid behind the bedroom door. He did not hesitate. As JJ entered the room, he removed a weighted leather sap from his back pocket, the kind police officers used to subdue unruly suspects. He swung the sap in a sharp, descending practiced blow to the occipital region of JJ's skull. It landed with a sickening thud, and he watched as JJ lost control of his motor functions as messages from his brain were scrambled. The Rat watched in fascination as JJ fought to regain his balance. It was much like the chickens he tortured back home in West Virginia as a boy. He would cut off their heads and laugh as they stumbled around on reflex and instinct. It was a sick image that both amused and fascinated him. He thought about striking JJ again, but quickly saw it was unnecessary, as JJ collapsed in a bloody heap.

The Rat carefully wiped the blood from the sap onto Katherine's towel. He quickly dialed the phone to get further instructions. He wasn't sure if he needed to finish off JJ Battle, or leave the situation as a painful lesson.

"Sarge, I completed the first mission, but there were complications," the Rat relayed dispassionately.

"What kind of complications?"

"Our secondary target entered as I was in the cleanup phase. I temporarily incapacitated him, and I am awaiting further orders."

"Perhaps we can use this to our advantage," the voice on the other end of the line whispered.

"Are you sure you want to let that situation continue? A hurt and wounded animal is the most dangerous. If we complete this exercise, that's one important detail we don't have to worry about."

"Soldier, I don't pay you to think, I pay you to execute. Now do your job." There was a coldness and finality in the voice on the other end of the phone. It left no doubt who was in charge. The Rat did as he was ordered, and slipped out of the building undetected.

JJ finally regained consciousness, but was groggy and disoriented. He grabbed his head in response to the terrible throbbing. He wondered who or what had hit him. He rolled over, recalling the last thing he remembered before the blow. "Katherine," he yelled, crawling over to her still body, cradling her in his arms. "No," he pleaded, hoping against hope that she would stir in his arms. He smoothed her hair and gently rocked her, hoping to rock some life into her. He sat there holding her, trying to figure who would do this to Katherine. He felt both pain and emptiness. Tears rolled down his face, as he called her name in vain. He had no answers, only suspicions, and they all led to Bobby Bennett. He could feel the anger rising up in him, followed by a seething rage. He had never felt this rage before. He would have to call the police, but first he needed time to figure things out. Whoever was responsible for Katherine's death would have to pay, that much he was sure. He kept coming back to the one question he couldn't answer, "who would do this unthinkable deed and why?"

He thought about the likely suspects, but he couldn't figure out who was behind this. He thought about Bobby Bennett, Victor, Randy, Eva, and Lieutenant Stone. Individually, he couldn't see any connection between them and Katherine. Their only connection to Katherine was through him. This made JJ even angrier; to think that someone would harm Katherine to get to him was unthinkable. What puzzled him even further was the fact that they left him alive. Was Katherine's killing a mistake, or were they trying to send him a message? Whatever the killer's reasoning, he knew he needed some answers, and fast.

He looked around the condo for clues and found nothing. There was nothing out of the ordinary, except the steam coming from the shower. He turned off the shower and thought about cleaning the wound on his head. He thought better of it, remembering that the police still had to come and investigate.

"Hello, 911 operator," said a bored voice on the other end of the phone.

JJ took a deep breath and replied, "I want to report a murder at the Riverfront Condominiums on Jefferson."

"What is the condo number sir?"

"Penthouse."

"Is anyone else hurt or injured, sir?" The operator asked in her practiced scripted voice.

"No," JJ replied, feeling as if this couldn't be real. He could hear the operator typing all of the details and forwarding the information to the nearest available units. They would be there in ten minutes, he thought, knowing DPD's response time.

"Who am I speaking to sir?" The operator asked, trying to solicit as much information from JJ as she could.

JJ, saddened and tired, hung up the phone and waited for the inevitable onslaught of police and media. He was bloodied and in pain, but all he could think about was Katherine and what he would do to the people who had done this to her.

This was the ultimate injustice; the life of a remarkable woman cut short. It made no sense. This woman stood for something, and she deserved to continue living a life of greatness. JJ reflected on other women he had known;

many were troubled, insecure and with their share of problems. But Katherine was different; she didn't play silly female games, or use her sexuality as a weapon. She was always able to remain above that level of gamesmanship. Now she was gone forever. He was feeling the pangs of loss and regret, reflecting on what could have been, but now would never be. He knew he would have to deal with the guilt of Katherine's death for a lifetime. He had squandered so many opportunities with her. She was the only woman JJ had truly loved. Now she was gone, forever.

The irony of his life overwhelmed him. Just as he was about to realize true happiness, life again denied him. He couldn't help but think how fragile and elusive life is; one minute you are happy and planning your future with the woman you loved, and the next minute you are answering questions from the police about her death. How could this have happened he wondered?

"Who? Who could have done this?" He kept coming back to that question. He knew the answer to that question would have consequences. This attack was personal and his response would be personal. He vowed with his life, to avenge Katherine's death.

Murder was such an ignominious act. It was like someone using a huge eraser; erasing someone off the face of the earth. The victim no longer existed in this world except for the memories and legacy that lived after they were gone. But JJ felt the huge void Katherine's death had caused. He knew that so many people would feel her loss forever. Her death would be ruled a homicide, and JJ had studied the criminal code enough to know legally what it meant-the killing of one human being by the act or omission of another. Somehow, that definition was so inadequate to explain what happened to Katherine. It was more than just an act; it was an intentional, willful, and deliberate act. He had used those words so often in the past in the defense of others, now just thinking those words in relation to Katherine created something so revolting and indefensible that JJ could barely control himself.

JJ didn't have long to wait. He could hear the commotion and police radios in the hallway. He slowly got off the couch and took one last look back at Katherine who, even in death, was beautiful and elegant. The first face JJ saw when he opened the door was Lieutenant Harvey Stone. JJ could have sworn he saw a slight smirk on Stone's face as he entered the condo.

"What happened here, Battle?" Stone asked with an accusatory tone.

"I wish I knew, Lieutenant." JJ responded sadly.

"Judging by the blood on your shirt, I hope you have some answers."

"If I had some answers you would be the first to know."

"I didn't know you knew Ms. Devlin," Stone said, surprised by the discovery.

"We've known each other for the past fifteen years. We studied for the bar exam together." JJ wondered how much he should tell the detective. He went quickly from victim to defense attorney under Stone's questioning. He decided to provide only the most basic information. He knew the more information he supplied, the less likely the police would be to pursue other suspects aggressively. Besides, JJ wanted to provide only enough information to keep Stone from somehow implicating him in Katherine's death. He wanted to avoid that implication. But, JJ could see Stone's demeanor as he conferred with the detectives and evidence techs analyzing Katherine's apartment like a swarm of ants. JJ would tell Stone enough information to deflect suspicion from himself and to point Stone and the department in the right direction. JJ would begin his own investigation, because he couldn't trust or rely on the department to find Katherine's killer. That was his duty, and he would carry it out with his life.

"Don't leave Battle; I have more questions for you. But first I need to talk to my detectives."

JJ could see Stone conferring with his men and shooting occasional glances at JJ.

JJ watched as the medical examiner carefully examined Katherine and motioned to his assistant with resignation. The assistant moved in and JJ stared in horror as the assistant placed Katherine's body in a black body bag. It was all so clinical and so final, yet JJ felt confused. You couldn't just merely put a person's life so neatly in a bag. There was so much more to Katherine. He felt a twinge of regret, feeling responsible for getting Katherine involved in this case and ultimately for her death. He knew eventually he would have to call her parents and inform them of their child's death, which added to his pain. It was amazing how her death now made him responsible for so many things; notifying her family and co-workers, and most importantly, avenging her death. He had been prepared to pledge his undying love, and to protect her in sickness and in health, until death. He failed to do that in her life, but by God, he would protect her memory in death.

Stone returned to where JJ was standing and eyed JJ suspiciously. "So Battle, tell me what really happened here."

"I told you all of this before. Look, I told you everything I know. I need to get some medical attention." JJ said with exasperation, as he felt his self-control slipping away.

Stone smiled to himself. He would make the best of this situation. The press would be all over the story. He had to spin it to deflect attention from One Detroit, Inc. He was reasonably confident after his questioning of JJ Battle that, even though he had some information about the group's activities, he still could not piece it all together; at least not yet. Stone started to second-guess himself about what role JJ Battle might play in the future activities, and whether he was still useful to the group. The consensus among the group was that he was still an integral part of the proceedings, and therefore not yet expendable. That was the only reason he was still alive. But Stone had vigorously questioned that logic, since JJ and Katherine were the only two people who were even remotely close to piecing things together. The feeling was that if too many dead bodies started appearing, it would raise more suspicion for the project. As chief of homicide, Stone believed that he could control the investigation. He knew that in a city like Detroit, another couple of dead bodies wouldn't make a difference.

Stone's strategy in ordering the hit on Katherine Devlin was simple; he knew that her death would create widespread attention from the media and the community, deflecting attention from the Corktown project. That would buy them enough time to close the deal and make everyone rich. It was a huge price to pay, but it would be worth it in the end. The media would be preoccupied with the scandal and murder of a high profile citizen, and their attention would be diverted from the project. He would clandestinely feed the media the name of JJ Battle as an unofficial suspect, further fueling the media frenzy.

Stone loved the irony of the situation: one of the foremost criminal defense attorneys, JJ Battle, suspected in a murder investigation and likely in need of counsel himself. The opportunity to torment Battle was an unintended benefit of his strategy, but Stone would take it nevertheless. He hated those pretty boy attorneys in their expensive suits, trying to make him and his fellow officers look bad. This was a lesson for Battle and Stone was happy to be the teacher. The great JJ Battle needed to know that in this arena he could never go where Stone had been, because JJ just wasn't willing to risk it all. Very few men could do what Stone had done and survive. Stone would see whether JJ Battle was one of those men.

Chapter 19

RANDY CONNORS WAS FEARLESS. HE HAD possessed this characteristic since birth. Having courage was essential to survival for a child growing up on the eastside of Detroit. It protected him from the predatory older kids in the neighborhood. The older kids stayed away from Randy, with the frequent admonition, "leave that kid alone, he's crazy." Randy's courage was born of necessity. As an only child of a single parent, he had to fend for himself at an early age. His mother, a heavy drinker, had little patience for weakness. Whenever she disciplined Randy, she marveled at his ability to accept physical punishment without crying. No matter how brutal her beatings, young Randy refused to cry. Finally, his mother stopped the beatings when she realized they had no effect. He became a feared fighter in the neighborhood, because he had a philosophy that he was willing to do whatever it took to win. If that meant fighting dirty, he was willing to do that if it meant he would win.

His neighborhood legend was fashioned through one particularly brutal neighborhood fight. Randy and his friends were playing basketball at the neighborhood park on Concord and Strong on the eastside of town. Billy Taylor, then nineteen years old, and known as the neighborhood bully, decided to disrupt Randy's game. He would soon regret that decision. No amount of persuasion would stop Billy from interrupting their game. Randy, tired of Billy's interruption, challenged Billy to a fight by asking him one very simple question. "If I kick your ass, will you leave us alone?"

Billy was stunned, as the crowd jeered and cheered Randy's brazen challenge. Billy had two choices, he could accept the challenge and fight a younger opponent, or refuse and suffer the ridicule of the park's crowd. It was a bold and aggressive maneuver. It put Billy in an unpopular position; his reputation was on the line. He had nothing to gain and everything to lose. In order to win, he would need to pummel the fifteen-year old kid, but if he lost, he was supposed to beat the fifteen year old. They would destroy his reputation and he would be defending himself from challengers forever, if he lost.

Billy, in sizing up the kid, realized that Randy was no ordinary fifteen year old. He was stocky and muscled and was not afraid. It made Billy look at his adversary with newfound respect.

"Be careful what you wish for young boy, that ass beating might be closer than you think." Billy replied attempting to reestablish his dominance over his domain.

"I didn't stutter and I ain't backing down, if that's what you're hoping. You can forget that. You came up here looking for a fight, well you got one." Randy spoke those words with a chilling confidence.

The crowd, in typical city fight-style, formed a circle around the combatants, to prevent either fighter from having second thoughts and fleeing. Billy, about six inches taller than Randy, got into a classic boxer's pose, left hand held at chest level and right hand protecting the chin. Randy, considerably shorter, had an unorthodox stance where both hands were at chest level, his head lowered, and his chin tucked against his chest. From that position, he could throw punches and could protect his face from being hit. The only target for a wary headshot would be the top of Randy's skull.

"I'm going to give you one more chance to back down and walk away with your little butt in one piece," Billy said, trying to send one last discouraging message to Randy. Randy's response was to begin circling Billy with his fists raised, egged on by his younger cohorts.

Billy landed the first blow, a smooth jab to the top of Randy's head. It was quick and sharp like a boxer's punch. He followed that with a crunching body shot to Randy's side. Billy, brimming with confidence after his initial volleys found their targets, continued peppering Randy with combinations. The crowd, sensing destruction yelled encouragement to Randy to fight back. Randy continued patiently circling waiting for an opening. It came as Billy, confident and cocky, was now dancing on his toes like a boxer and throwing jabs. He got a little careless and got too close to Randy. Randy turned with all of his power and landed a punch to Billy's unprotected ribs. Randy's first punch stunned Billy as he gasped for air. Randy followed that up by ramming his head into Billy's stomach and driving him backwards. They grabbed each other and wrestled to the ground.

The crowd, entertained by the spectacle of a fight, was cheering wildly. Randy, extremely strong for his age, managed to get his hands free, placing a well-aimed punch at Billy's face. He heard Billy wince as he felt his nose cave in, and blood gush all over the two of them. Randy again followed with a swift, brutal knee to the groin that left Billy vulnerable. Randy continued to press his advantage, taking Billy's head and repeatedly banging it against the asphalt. He quickly grasped his hands around Billy's neck, as he straddled him with all of his weight and choked him as hard as his hands could squeeze. Randy was oblivious to the sounds of the crowd or Billy's desperate gasping for air. He was determined to squeeze the life out of Billy, and he would have succeeded if they had not pulled him off Billy. He could hear the voices of the older boys attempting to calm him down by saying, "he's not worth it, and you proved your point."

Randy was a protected person from that day forward. He was respected and protected, which meant he was allowed to do special favors for the gamblers and drug dealers. The errands were nothing serious, but they always paid well, because they knew they could trust him with their most important details. He would provide protection for the couriers who made deliveries or the numbers runners who made pickups. He carried a 9mm pistol for insurance, which he never had to use. These endeavors were lucrative and helped Randy provide some needed income for his mother. It was life in the ghetto, and Randy learned to play by the rules to win. He had taken those early lessons and transformed that knowledge into successful strategies for his ensuing career in the legal field.

Randy Connors was feeling lucky tonight. It was Friday night and he needed a little diversion. Victor and the staff had gone for the night and he was alone in the office. He needed to unwind and release the stress from the day's events. Everything was progressing as planned and there were only a few remaining details that needed to be coordinated to complete the Corktown deal. He needed some excitement and he knew the perfect way to achieve it. He walked to the elevator and headed to the parking garage. He grabbed the keys to his Mercedes SL 600 and got inside, enjoying the rich smell of the leather and the sound of the powerful engine. It wasn't bad for a poor boy from the eastside of Detroit. He was a partner in the largest minority firm in the Midwest, owned a luxury home in the suburbs, drove a luxury car, and was well respected in legal circles.

He had come a long way, but to Randy it wasn't quite far enough. He still felt like the poor kid from the eastside. He was not like Victor, who had breeding, money, and the prestige associated with being a member of a powerful family. Victor had the connections; Victor had the trophy wife, and Victor had everyone fooled. Randy was the brains of the firm, not Victor. However, in spite of all he had done to build the firm, Victor still received the credit. Randy was tired of all the empty deals; he needed more to feel alive. The only place he knew that could provide him with that satisfaction was the casino. It was like life, and you had to risk big to win big. It took courage to risk so much on the whimsical turn of a card, but Randy loved the excitement. Tonight he felt that something special was about to happen. When he had that feeling, he couldn't lose.

Tonight he chose the Greektown casino. He usually had the best luck there. It was the best of Detroit's three casinos, the Motor City and MGM being the other two. He could also go across the river to Windsor, Canada to the casinos there, but not tonight. Greektown felt right. It wasn't Las Vegas, but it still provided the type of diversion he liked. It was after midnight, and the casino was already packed with the Friday night crowd of slot players and small time gamblers, desperately wagering their week's earnings. In the casino, there was always a feeling of excitement and desperation. He could hear it in the clangs and bells of the slots, in the roulette wheel, and in the occasional yell of a big winner. There was something pitiful yet hopeful in the expressions of gamblers there. It was the chance they pursued, the opportunity to win. It was all that anybody could ask for, the opportunity to win, even if the odds were heavily in favor of the house. That was why he chose poker. It required skill and luck. You could control a part of your own destiny. It didn't all depend on just luck.

He made his way to the fourth floor, to the VIP section of the casino. Suited sentries were very adept at protecting the privacy and identities of the patrons. There were three big money tables in play tonight, and Randy was careful to watch the playing style, skill, and demeanor of the players. He also closely watched the dealers to get a feel of how they controlled the game. He wanted every contingency covered to minimize the risk of mistakes. He went to the cage and cashed a check for ten thousand dollars. He told himself he would play until the money runs out or the sun comes up, which ever occurred first. He smiled to himself, knowing that his coming and going would be controlled by his luck and nothing else.

He fingered his chips while deciding which table he would play. He concentrated on table two because of the players and the dealer. He would not play if the dealer was too attractive, as it created too much of a distraction for the table. He noticed there were some serious players at table two; a white executive who was likely visiting on business, and an Arab man who was playing as if the family fortune was limitless. He was recklessly lucky, a recipe for disaster. Randy sat down next to the out of town executive, reasoning that his style was more predictable. He was less likely to upset the flow of Randy's cards by undisciplined play.

Randy quickly settled into the game, growing his chips to fifty thousand dollars within three hours. Normally it would be a good place to stop, since he had a considerable amount of the house's money; however, he remembered that recently he had suffered a number of heavy losses; this was an opportunity to get that money back and create a nice cushion for himself. He signaled the crew chief to inquire about increasing the table limits. The crew chief whispered Randy's request into his radio and quickly came back with an approval. Randy would wait for the next good hand to play without table limits. It was pure gambling. He could win or lose as much as he desired to spend. He liked to live life at full throttle.

It wasn't long before he got the hand he was looking for, a pair of pocket aces. He wagered conservatively, not wanting to scare off the other players. He checked the initial bet of the white executive, and the Arab player followed. His strategy worked; everybody remained in the game. On the next round of betting, he sweetened the pot a little by raising twenty thousand. It was apparent that both the executive and the Arab were holding a pair. He continued to bump the pot, and the other two players followed. There was a buzz around the table as the crowd could sense a big hand developing. The flop didn't reveal any apparent help for any of the players. The game was coming down to the river card, the card that would determine each of their fates. Randy put all of his chips in and requested a fifty-thousand dollar marker, which the crew chief quickly granted. This made his bet reach one hundred thousand dollars. When the players turned over their hole cards, each of the players had a pair. Randy had the two aces, the executive had a pair of nines, and the Arab had a pair of tens. The only way Randy could lose is if the other players drew a nine or a ten. If they failed, Randy would automatically win. The noise around the table was hushed. Randy waited, not in fear but in anticipation. This was life and he accepted the outcome, whatever it would be. The dealer turned over the river card and it was a nine. There was a collective groan and a corresponding yell and the reality of the outcome of the hand sunk in for each player. The executive said something to Randy about how fickle cards can be, but Randy barely heard him. His mind was far away, calculating how he might have to liquidate his equity portion of the firm to pay off his marker. He had to accelerate the Corktown project or else.

Chapter 20

THE RAT COULD NOT BELIEVE HOW poorly constructed the project homes were. He got into Brianna Tuller's apartment faster than if he had a key. The trick was not so much getting in; it was getting in without arousing the suspicions of the nosy neighbors. Since it was broad daylight, it required an even greater amount of skill and deception. For these types of jobs, he used a plain white van that would not arouse suspicion and a pair of plain white overalls. He did not dare put a sign on the van, because surely some neighbor would come over requesting his services. "Could you please come over and fix my cable while you're here?" To avoid that possibility he stuck to the nondescript white van. It usually worked. He had a toolbox with him to create the illusion that he belonged there.

He had been watching the house for the previous three days, and knew Brianna's every move. She kept a consistent schedule. She took the kids to school in the morning and then came home and watched television or talked on the telephone. Betty, or one of her other girlfriends, usually came around lunchtime so they could watch soap operas together. He was in the house now to do some reconnaissance before Brianna returned. He wanted to make sure he covered any contingency. He was surprised at how neat and clean she kept the small apartment. There were numerous pictures of the kids at various ages. It was sparsely furnished with kids' toys placed neatly in boxes in each of the

children's rooms. The few clothes that the family possessed were hung up in clos-
ets or neatly folded in drawers. The dishes were all washed and were ready to be
put away. The refrigerator was nearly full, with real food like chicken and pork
chops. There were no fast food containers or pizza boxes. She appeared to be a
loving, and attentive mother. There were no signs of men's clothing or personal
items in the apartment. The bathroom was spotless and there were three tooth-
brushes in the holders; one adult and two children's. She was a woman who put
her children first, which would make the offer he was proposing more appealing
to her. He placed a listening device on the phone for added insurance to monitor
her telephone conversations. After he had gone through the apartment checking
windows, doors and exits, he headed back to the truck to wait for Brianna.

He did not have to wait long. She pulled into the parking lot of the apartment in an old model Ford Taurus. It was clean, but rusting on the rear quarter
panel. He could hear the start of some early engine problems, and the muffler
was just a bit noisy. She got out of the car with a bag of groceries and her purse.
She was a petite woman dressed in a cotton jogging suit and boots. She had her
jacket zipped all of the way up to guard against the cold November morning.
She was still walking with a slight limp, and he could see some sadness in her
expression.

The Rat watched as she opened the door and entered the apartment.
He imagined that she hung up her coat, put the groceries away, and perhaps
turned on the television. He gave her a few minutes to get settled before he left
the truck. He grabbed the toolbox, and a black vinyl briefcase, and surveyed
the neighborhood. He approached the house and rang the doorbell. The Rat
always had an advantage in these encounters, because people always underes-
timated him.

They saw a small, meek rodent-looking man and dismissed him as insig-
nificant. That disrespect usually meant their demise. He would not hesitate to
kill Brianna if it was necessary. He let nothing interfere with his mission, not
people and certainly not emotions. He had long since overcome any feelings
of remorse or the need for love. He compartmentalized his life into one cate-
gory - survival. He let nothing interfere with that mission. He rang the doorbell, careful to adopt his meekest persona.

"Hello, Ms. Tuller?" The superintendent has me going to all of the apartments in the complex, making sure there are no radon leaks. You know radon is a deadly killer."

"He didn't tell me about any radon checks, but I guess it's ok."

He entered the apartment and set down his briefcase. He pulled out some gauges and went through the motions of taking some readings. He saw Brianna out of the corner of his eye and attempted to start a conversation.

"I see the pictures of your kids, they are very cute," he said trying to make her feel comfortable while he tried to steer the conversation around to the offer.

"Thanks." They are my pride and joy; I would do anything for my kids." She said.

"It must be tough raising them as a single parent."

"I didn't say I was a single parent,' Brianna replied, with concern in her voice. How do you know I'm a single parent?"

"Relax, the super told me, plus this is public housing and I know you have to be unmarried to live here," he replied, attempting to reassure Brianna.

"Oh yeah, I'm sorry. I didn't mean to get angry, it's just you can't take too many chances these days if you know what I mean," Brianna replied, relaxing her guard a little.

"Listen, I have to compliment you on your housekeeping. I think this is the cleanest apartment I've come across since I've been doing these inspections."

"Oh, that's nice of you to notice. I have to have a clean house. That's just the way I am," she replied, the pride obvious in her voice.

"Wouldn't it be nice to one day be able to have a nice house all of your own for you and your kids. Somewhere they could grow up safe and near good schools."

"You got that right. I pray for that every day. I want the best for my kids."

"They deserve it," the Rat said, warming to his task. "Kids are our future; they are the most important thing we have. Parents should do everything they can to improve their lives."

"I agree. As soon as I get a job, I'm moving my kids out of the ghetto. She said with real conviction.

"I like to hear people talk like that, about getting ahead. I think I can help you."

"Are they hiring at your job?" She asked with real excitement and enthusiasm.

"No. I have a better offer than that. It doesn't require any work on your part."

"Look Mister, I don't do anything illegal." She replied, eyeing him warily.

"You don't have to do anything illegal. Just make the right decision and the money is yours."

"What decision is that?" He could see there was some skepticism in her face, but he could tell she was interested.

"Here's all you have to do. In the upcoming Bobby Bennett trial, just refuse to testify. Just tell the prosecutor that, after talking to Betty and remembering what happened that day, you're not so sure it was all Bobby's fault. He repeated it just as he had been instructed, and he could see Brianna recoil in fear. He tried to reassure her.

"They can't force you to go to trial against your will. Before you decide, just look in this case." As he opened the case, Brianna gasped.

"I've never seen that much money at one time. How much is it?" She asked, interested yet frightened.

"It's fifty thousand dollars cash and it will all be yours once you agree not to testify."

"I'm not sure. That Bobby Bennett is crazy. I don't want him coming after me or my family."

"You don't have to worry about Bobby. I guarantee it. Besides, you'll have enough money to start a new life, far away from Bobby."

"What happens if I don't take the money and I go ahead with the trial?" she asked with a look of concern on her face.

"The people I work for will be very disappointed, and you don't want to disappoint them, I assure you. Your best choice is to take the money. Do it for your kids."

"I don't know what to do!" Brianna said, sincerely confused. She wanted the money but she wanted to testify as well.

"Well, let me help you decide. Take your time in making a decision. A wrong decision could be costly. If you talk to anyone about this, I will make sure you lose something that you love very much. Do I make myself clear? Don't talk to anyone and that includes Betty."

The Rat was out the door with briefcase and toolbox in hand. As he left, a cold burst of November wind entered the small project apartment. Brianna sat down on the couch and contemplated her family's future.

Chapter 21

JJ NEEDED TO MAKE TWO PHONE calls. The first of which was to Katherine's parents. He was unprepared for this moment. He knew it had to be done, so he just dialed the number. He didn't know what he would say, but he hoped he would find the right words.

"Hello, Mrs. Devlin. This is JJ." He said, searching his soul to find the right words, as if words could comfort this mother's pain.

"JJ, why are you being so formal, you know you and I are on a first-name basis. Has that daughter of mine been treating you right?" There was characteristic playfulness in her mood. In other times, he enjoyed her heavy West Indian accent. He could hear the joy in her voice as he imagined her sitting in her living room, with the warm Caribbean breezes blowing through her open windows. She was probably watching television with her husband, Jasper, nearby, quietly attending her needs. He thought of these things because he knew they were significant not in any life-changing way, but because they would always remember this moment for the cruelness of their loss. For them, they would mark the time that Katherine no longer belonged to them or of this earth and they would mourn and never see life the same again. It was after all, against the natural order of things; a parent suffering the loss of a child and having to bury that which you gave life. It was wrong and no amount of explanation or understanding could change that reality. JJ knew this, and he struggled with his words, wondering if he was worthy to convey the magnitude of what had transpired. He himself was still numb from Katherine's death and had not resolved in his own mind how this tragedy had happened, but he knew he had to be the one to explain things to her parents rather than some indifferent bureaucrat who lacked compassion and sensitivity. There was no other way than to just say it. He had to be the messenger of doom.

There was, he thought, some twisted irony in his having to be bearer of the news, since in some yet undetermined way, he was responsible for her death. He could hear her rattling on in her singsong happy Jamaican voice, suggestive and playful. He wondered if he had the right to take it all away from her, to change her life forever. He had no choice he concluded. It was as much his fault as anyone, and it was therefore his duty. He heard her say, "You call me Nina, boy, how many times I have to tell you that?" "Jasper it's JJ on the phone," he heard her say to her husband, he must have some news about Katherine."

"Mrs. Devlin, I mean Nina," he stammered, wanting to tell her everything in a torrent of words. "There's been a terrible tragedy. Katherine's dead." He said it, and he just let the words float through the phone lines and across the ocean, to settle like nuclear waste, unseen yet deadly. The impact not immediate, but still lethal. He waited, like all men wait who are the bearers of bad tidings. He was helpless and hopeless, feeling like a traitor. He waited for a sign, for some acknowledgement that his words had registered. He knew his words were wreaking havoc on this family. He waited, silently, like Judas must have waited at Gethsemane. Waiting for what would come next after his treachery. He waited, silent and still, quiet, not daring to breathe or utter a sound. He waited until he thought he could wait no longer. He expected her to ask him to repeat what he had just said, to explain himself to her again, but more slowly this time. But, she did not, and so he waited, contemplating the measure of this family's loss and pain. He wondered how he could make it up to them. He wondered if through some divine redemptive process, he could restore their daughter back to them. He knew he could not, but he waited for a sign. After what seemed an eternity, but in reality were just minutes. The telephone receiver dropped to the tile floor with a cracking sound, and he heard the depth of her pain as she screamed the scream of immeasurable loss. It was more a shriek than a scream. It was a hopeless, helpless sound full of pain and grief. It was a sound terrifying in the completeness of its emotion. It was like a crazy symphony of music without the words. It was a tragic jazz sound, a dirge so sorrowful that JJ pulled back from the phone. He pulled back not because of the volume of the sound, but because of the hurt, pain, and anguish the scream signified. It was the pain of a mother's loss. JJ could hear Katherine's father, Jasper in the background, rushing to comfort his wife. Jasper could not have known the cause of his wife's pain, but somewhere inside his paternal instinct must have alerted him of catastrophe. JJ could only imagine their heartbreak now at the realization that their daughter, so alive and brilliant, was no longer among the living.

Finally, after much time had passed, JJ heard the voice of J.D. Devlin on the other end of the phone. The voice that JJ had enjoyed hearing so often in the past was now heavy with sorrow. JJ waited for the words from this grieving father, and he knew that this man would not rest until the people responsible for his child's death were found and dealt with.

"JJ," he said. His voice was surprisingly calm and controlled. "What happened to my baby?"

"JD, the police are still investigating, but it looks like someone broke into her condo and strangled her." JJ uttered these words in a monotone of sorrow. He could hear the words of a father trying to comprehend the incomprehensible.

"Why would anyone do that? She didn't have an enemy in the world."

"I'm not sure, but I guarantee you I'm going find out who did this and deal with them." JJ didn't want to alert J.D. of his suspicions until he was completely able to confirm them. JD, I'll make the arrangements here and contact you in a few days."

"JJ, I still have some contacts in the States that can handle anything that might come up and they are very discreet. I do mean anything. If you feel any pressure or have any concerns about your safety, I have some people who are old friends who can help you. JJ, I want you to send my baby's body home, and make sure they do it right."

"JD, I know this might not be the right time, but you know how I felt about Katherine; in fact, I was going to ask her to marry me on the day this happened. But what I want to tell you is that Katherine, had many friends in the States, and many of them will want to pay their last respects. I was wondering if you would allow me to plan a memorial service in Detroit for her friends and co-workers. I will take care of all of the arrangements and details. I just want to do right by Katherine." JJ knew that money wasn't an object with JD but he wanted him to know how much this ceremony would mean to her local friends.

JJ could hear fatigue in J.D.'s voice as well as gratitude as he gave his consent for the ceremony.

"J.D., let me know when you make the arrangements so that I can be there. Give my love to Nina, and let her know I'm thinking of her." JJ had no other words to say to this family. He thought about how everything seemed to be connected, from his grief, to the Devlins' grief. He owed them a tremendous debt, since he was the person who set these events in motion.

He thought of Bobby Bennett and all of the other characters who were part of this tragedy. He vowed revenge. But before he could avenge Katherine's death, he had to find the guilty parties first.

JJ made his second call of the day to a surprised and unsuspecting person, his Aunt Ruth.

Aunt Ruth was his mother's older sister. Since they were the only children, they had been extremely close. After his mother's death, Aunt Ruth's health had started to decline. They had either talked or visited each other every day. When JJ was younger, he and his cousins were very close, but as they grew older, they each went their separate ways.

"Aunt Ruth, this is your nephew, JJ. How have you been doing? I've been meaning to come by and visit you, but I've been thinking about you anyway."

"Joshua Jericho Battle I haven't heard from you in a month of Sundays, how you been doing, son?" She said, using his full name, as she always did, just like his mother used to do. He was surprised at how much alike they both sounded. It made him pause, as he thought about how much he missed his mother.

"I'm fine Aunt Ruth," JJ said, straining to be heard over the too-loud volume of the television set. Aunt Ruth, in addition to her other ailments and

aches and pains, was suffering from hearing loss. Her vanity wouldn't allow her
to get a hearing aid like her other senior friends. Instead, she compensated by
turning the volume way up and talking at the top of her voice. She was quick
to chastise if you failed to talk loudly enough for her to hear.

"Where you been son? I miss you." She yelled, competing to be heard
with The Price is Right, blaring from the TV. "When you going to come over
and let me make you some smothered chicken and rice and gravy like you
like?"

"I would like that. I'm going to come over real soon. Aunt Ruth, I was
wondering where I might find Junior these days? I need to get in touch with
him real soon."

"Joshua, you know I have a hard time keeping up with that boy. Last time
I talked to him, he was working security for some club downtown. I think it
was called Nightmares or something like that."

"Do you mean Dreams, down on Congress Street?" He asked, gently cor-
recting his aunt.

"Yeah, that's the one. He spends most of his time there or at that Franklin
Wright Settlement on Charlevoix. You know where that is, don't you? Y'all use
to play ball up there in the summertime."

"Yeah, I remember. If you hear from Junior in the next few days, let him
know I'm trying to get in touch with him. I'll call you in a few days so I can
come by and get some of your good cooking."

"You do that, son. You know your Aunt Ruth is always glad to see you."

After JJ hung up the phone, he looked at his watch. It was 11:00 pm and
the club scene would be in full swing right now. He knew this would be a good
time to catch Junior at the club, and he didn't want to wait any longer to talk to
him. JJ decided he needed to change clothes. Dreams was an upscale nightclub
with a strict dress code that was designed to keep the thugs and hip hoppers
out, but they were only moderately successful. JJ chose a dark sport jacket,
some dark slacks, and some soft-sided Bally boots. He wanted to be classy, yet,
understated. He chose his black leather trench coat to complete his outfit. He
didn't really have a strategy for his meeting with Junior; he knew he needed
someone to talk to whom he could trust.

Elijah Ezekiel Spencer Jr., or Junior as he was affectionately known, was a former green beret who served in the Eighty Second Airborne during the Vietnam War. Besides his stint in the army, he had done some duty on the streets of the city, handling security and other odd jobs. JJ had informally used Junior's services on a few occasions to gather information or to serve subpoenas or locate stubborn witnesses. Junior was nothing if not resourceful. If his resourcefulness was not enough, he could always rely on his huge size to intimidate even the toughest of men. Junior was huge by any standard. . He stood about Six feet, four and weighed about two hundred and forty five pounds of chiseled muscle. He was a physical fitness enthusiast who did a daily regimen of thousand pushups and five hundred sit-ups. He was an imposing figure. He was the type of person you wanted on your side in a time of crisis. He was a good guy who had no problem being bad whenever it was necessary. After his tours of duty in Vietnam, like many Vietnam vets, he struggled to adjust to life back home.

Eventually he found his niche, providing security for local Motown groups whenever they performed locally. He provided service for the Temptations, the Miracles, the Supremes, and the Four Tops. He was well known in all of the entertainment circles, but he still had trouble adjusting to life back in the States. There were very few legal outlets for the anger and aggression locked inside of him. There had been occasional bouts with alcohol and drugs, but he always managed to pull himself from the edge of the abyss with the sheer force of his will, but, when he was using, he was a mean, ornery piece of manhood when messed with. He was skilled in three types of martial arts, along with some forms he developed himself. They were a brutal combination of street fighting and martial arts. There was no honor in his combat, only pain and destruction. JJ had seen his handy work up close on a number of occasions when pseudo-tough guys with too much to drink would challenge Junior to try to impress a woman. The results were usually disastrous for those foolish enough to challenge him. Junior would subdue the victim, sometimes by simply bending the pinky finger of the offending lothario, until he was on his knees screaming in agony. He would be humiliated in front of his friends and other club patrons. These displays usually worked as a perfect deterrent for other customers who wanted to raise a little hell.

Junior was just what JJ needed to help him sort out this Corktown mess and help him solve Katherine's murder. When JJ approached the door of the club, he was surprised at the length of the line waiting to get inside. The temperature was in the teens and he could see the steam coming from the breaths of the expectant patrons who huddled together trying to stay warm. JJ hoped that Junior would be on the door so that he wouldn't have to go through the indignity of begging the doorman to summon Junior. Fortunately, there he was, this hulking mass wearing only a beret and a windbreaker with 'Security' in big yellow letters on the back of his jacket. JJ had not seen him in quite some time, and he could have sworn that either Junior's massive shoulders had gotten bigger, or his head had shrunk. In either event, he was like some cartoon character, larger than life, selectively allowing patrons in. Occasionally, he would consult his VIP list, and some lucky soul would be ushered in out of the cold.

JJ sauntered up to the front of the line while Junior's back was turned and said in his most obnoxious tone, "I'm not waiting in this long line; it's too cold out here. Somebody better let me in this place."

JJ could see an almost imperceptible tightening of Junior's back as he slowly turned around to confront the offending interloper. JJ could also see the crowd shifting slightly, as if expecting a confrontation.

"Excuse me sir," he said turning to face JJ, "but you"… he paused as he fixed his gaze on JJ and approached him. JJ was surprised at Junior's restraint and diplomacy. He stepped back, taking a good long look at JJ. JJ had to make a quick decision. A greeting from Junior could put you on the disabled list. His handshake was a crushing vice-like grip that threatened to grind your hand into dust. Or, there was the hug, which, if he held it long enough, could crush an arm or seriously restrict an airway. JJ opted for the hug. Junior was genuinely happy to see his cousin and was a little more enthusiastic than normal. He lifted JJ off the ground, squeezing him in the process like some small child.

"O.K. cousin, I'm glad to see you too, but I want to continue to have the use of my limbs."

"JJ Battle" he shouted, loud enough for the people in line to hear the lawyer's name. "Man, I haven't seen you in months, how have you been?" He said, now oblivious to the crowd.

"I've been good, things have been going well."

"I can tell. Look at the way you're dressed. You always were a sharp dresser."

"You could be too, if you could find some clothes to fit you," JJ needled him.

"Ouch, that's going to cost you cuz. You'll pay for that."

"How about going inside so we can talk? I have a couple of things that I need to talk to you about."

"This must be serious, JJ Battle tracking me down. Momma didn't put you up to this did she?" He asked, eyeing JJ suspiciously.

"No. But, she is concerned about you. But I convinced her you could take care of yourself." He said.

"That's why you get those big retainers, because you're so smooth."

"Listen, something serious has come up and I need to use your services for a couple of weeks, possibly a month." JJ said.

"Sounds exciting, you know I'm always up for some adventure."

"That's what I hoped for. I have to tell you that I have no idea where this will lead. The only thing that I know for sure is that there's a lot of money involved and the people involved are prepared to do anything."

JJ proceeded to tell Junior about the sniper attack that he believed was meant as a message, and he told him about Katherine's death. JJ could see the concern on Junior's face.

"This sounds like my kind of party. We can play any way they want to do it. If they want to play nice or they want to make it hard, it doesn't matter to me. "But I have to tell you, this sounds a lot like special ops work. If so, somebody has gone through a lot of trouble to bring in the heavy hitters. It's good to know what we're up against. Our edge is that we know what we're dealing with, but they don't know what they're facing."

JJ looked over at his cousin and saw the seriousness of his resolve. He knew that Junior would do whatever it took to protect him and that was good. It gave him a great deal of comfort. JJ needed to know there was somebody he could count on unconditionally. He was determined to do whatever it took to avenge Katherine's death. He knew things might get dirty, and JJ wanted to make sure that if things got out of hand he had the firepower to respond.

JJ reached into his inner pocket, took out an envelope, and slid it across the table to Junior. "There's five thousand dollars in there for your services. Tell your boss you need a leave of absence. If you need more let me know."

"You really don't have to do this JJ you know it's not about the money. I would do this anyway. You're family." Junior slowly slid the envelope off the table and into his pocket as he feigned disappointment at JJ's implication that he needed money to buy his participation. Although he would have willingly provided his services free, the money would definitely help.

The club was now packed with well-dressed men and women on the dance floor or huddled in lover's conspiratorial conversations, intimately leaning closer to be heard above the music. JJ also leaned over making sure that he was heard but not overheard among the noise in the club. He leaned over and said, "I need a gun. It has to be small, deadly, and easy to use. Hopefully with a lot of bullets in the clip in case I have to bring down a battalion."

"What's really going on cuz, this sounds like some serious doodoo. I have just the thing you need." He said, getting up from the table and gesturing for JJ to follow him to the back room. The back room that at one time was probably a storeroom had been smartly converted to offices and security center, complete with television and security monitors. There was a young muscular Latino man in his twenties, who awkwardly stood when Junior entered.

"I'll take over for a while Hector, I'll call you when I need you."

"Yessir, Mr. Simmons. I'll be on the radio if you need me." The young man responded.

"I'm impressed Mr. Simmons," JJ said with mock respect and admiration.

"Well I'm sort of teaching him the business and he's a worthy student." Junior said with surprising modesty.

"I never knew this existed. Who would have imagined your own spy central?"

"Yeah it gives us a head start on identifying trouble. Come on over hear and let me show you my wares." He said, opening a cabinet and removing a chest locked with a combination padlock. He quickly opened the lock and displayed an arsenal of handguns in all shapes, sizes, and textures. "I have a little something here that I think will work just fine. It's something that we removed from one of the thugs that occasionally come in here." He took out a small handgun with a dull finish that was easily concealed in the palm of his hand and handed it to JJ.

"What is this little thing, it looks like a 22 special? I said I might need to bring down a battalion, not a Boy Scout troop."

"What you have here is one of the best and most efficient handguns made. It's a Baretta 380 with nine in the clip and one in the chamber. It's small, light, and easy to handle. It's just what you need to cope in a complex and violent world," he said facetiously. "This weapon is deceptive, its small but it has a helluva kick. The best part about it is that it's easy to conceal. There are no unsightly bulges which might attract unwanted attention."

JJ invited Junior back to his house for a few days until things settled down. Junior, make yourself at home. Here's your room. Junior went on for another hour, explaining the virtues of handguns. After a while, JJ thanked him for his lecture, and then headed off to bed. He had a big day ahead. Tomorrow was Katherine's memorial service, and then he had to fly to Jamaica for her funeral. He knew there were still some unfinished details he had to solve; the Bobby Bennett trial and he had to unravel the Corktown mystery. Although things were still unclear to him, he at least felt more comfortable about the odds with Junior on his side.

Chapter 22

VICTOR WRIGHT SEEMINGLY HAD IT ALL; a million dollar home, a successful law practice and a trophy wife. He looked over at his wife in their custom-made bed deep in sleep and admired the sexiness of her body peeking out beneath the comforter. He knew that he should feel more for this woman, but he just couldn't summon those feelings any longer. He took a deep breath as he felt himself losing control. He was feeling the pressure of everything that was going on in his life – the Corktown deal, his crumbling marriage and the unrealistic expectations of his family. It was not easy being an offspring of greatness. Everyone kept reminding him of his duty and responsibility to carry on the legacy. The specter of the Wright legacy had shown bright in city government and political circles, and they expected Victor to continue the luminescence of their distinguished family.

But, for Victor, it was never enough; no matter how much he accomplished. The Wright name was a looming presence over all of his accomplishments and deeds. He could never escape his birthright. Whatever he accomplished, it would never be enough. It didn't matter that he had founded one of the largest minority firms in the country, or that he spearheaded two of the largest minority controlled projects in the country, Ford Field and Comerica Park. He would still be subjected to the inevitable comparisons between his grandfather, the Honorable Justice, and his father, the statesman. It was never enough.

If that were not enough, he had yet to produce his own progeny to continue the Wright legacy. Although he and Carlena had tried in the early days, oh how they had tried, as he reminisced about their earlier insatiable desire for each other. Now their marriage was more about their indifference than their love for each other.

He couldn't remember the last time they were intimate or shared a warm moment. He told her that there was nothing wrong between them, it was the pressure of the project keeping them apart. They both knew that it was a lie, but neither of them was willing to acknowledge the truth. It was easier to co-exist in deception, than face the reality of what their lives had become. Victor had immersed himself in his work, working late hours and rising early to get to the office in the morning. Carlena busied herself in community projects and volunteer work. It filled her days but it left her life unfulfilled. All of the pressure had taken an even harsher toll on Victor. Lately, he noticed his hair had been coming out in clumps in the shower, and he had to admit that his unwillingness to get close to Carlena was more than just his work schedule. He had been impotent for more than two months. He was afraid to admit to himself, much less to Carlena that there was a problem. He had to acknowledge that he was never the most skillful of lovers, but at least he was able to perform. But lately, not even his wife's most passionate advances could arouse him. He politely and discreetly soothed her by telling Carlena it wasn't her, but his schedule that caused their frustration. If he were truthful with himself, it was so much more than that.

For Victor, it was always about proving himself, and that meant competing and conquering the huge expectations that were his birthright. The pressure from the African American community to be like his father Bill Wright was staggering. He lived everyday with the scrutiny and pressure that expected greatness carried. In law school, it was an effort just to survive. He was on academic probation more than anyone knew, and his effort to pass the bar exam was the most difficult thing he ever accomplished. Then there was Carlena, so different than he was. She came from modest circumstances, but she possessed that indefinable quality that made you know she was a winner. Victor didn't have it but he knew it when he saw it, and Carlena had it. He knew if he were to be successful, he needed a woman like her to help him get to the top. He didn't trust himself to do it alone. She was someone with poise, vision and determination to succeed in spite of the odds. She was never intimidated or frightened and she thrived on a challenge.

It was a common knowledge that JJ and Carlena were completely attracted to each other. It was obvious. When they were in the room together, you could feel the sexual tension between them. It was like electricity. Victor resented the fact that Carlena didn't feel that way about him; their marriage was more of a merger than about passion. He felt that he even had to prove himself to his wife. It was as if she was constantly comparing him to JJ Battle. When they made love, he could never tell if he truly pleased her, or if she was faking. Although she never complained and was always a willing partner, he still had his doubts. In fact, he had started coming home long after she was asleep and leaving early before she awoke. Today was no exception.

It was 5:00 a.m. and he was already dressed and ready. He had on a perfectly tailored Charcoal gray Armani suit, with a custom-made French cuffed white shirt with gray pinstripes. For his tie, he selected a burgundy, gray, and white striped tie that perfectly complimented his outfit. He loved being well dressed, and since he was in an image conscious business he made sure he was always impeccably dressed. He took a last look at his wife and started to leave.

"Victor? What time is it?" Carlena asked. Her voice was husky with sleep.

"It's early, I didn't mean to wake you. Go back to sleep."

"No you didn't wake me. I tried to stay up and wait for you but I fell asleep."

"I got in pretty late and slept in the guest room so that I wouldn't wake you."

"Listen, I really want to talk to you, how about coming back to bed." She pulled the blankets back revealing her nakedness and full generous breasts. Carlena, now a woman of leisure, kept herself in excellent condition. She exercised daily and maintained a strict low fat diet. At forty-three, she still had an incredible sex drive that lately had gone unfulfilled. She got out of bed, walked over to Victor, and pressed her warm body against him.

"Carlena, I don't have time right now, but I promise I'll make some time as soon as this Corktown deal is done."

"There used to be a time when you made time for me. What's changed?" She asked, with a deep sense of foreboding. She wasn't sure if she was prepared for the answer, but she had to ask anyway.

"Nothing has changed; I'm just under a lot of stress lately with this deal." He hated when Carlena put pressure on him.

"Well I have just the solution to relieve your stress," she purred as she reached for him. Carlena was momentarily stunned as Victor moved away from her embrace. She was not used to being rebuffed by her husband. She wondered if there was more to Victor's disinterest than just a busy schedule. She made a mental note to take a more active interest in what was going on with her husband.

"Well Victor, if you don't want to make love to me, at least have the decency to talk to me. There's been a lot going on, and I need to sort it all out."

"What's so important that it can't wait until this evening?"

"I just wanted to get your reaction to Katherine Devlin's murder, it was all so unexpected. Do you think JJ Battle was involved? That's what the media is saying. Did you know they were involved?"

"Carlena I don't have time for gossip. I have no idea what's going on in JJ Battle's personal life." He suppressed a slight feeling of jealousy at Carlena's reference to JJ. He was doubly annoyed at Carlena, first for her questioning him about Katherine's death, and secondly for her obvious interest in the exploits of JJ Battle. Carlena's meddling was the last thing Victor needed. He would stop at nothing to complete the Corktown project. Not even his lovely wife would deter him.

Carlena could swear that she saw Victor flinch involuntarily when she asked about Katherine and JJ. It made her wonder about Victor's most recent business dealings. He had always been very open with her about his deals; but this time he was being secretive, as if there were things he didn't want her to know. Well starting today, she would begin to take an active interest in what was going on in her husband's life. Throughout their fifteen-year marriage, she had trusted Victor implicitly. He had always been an excellent provider and husband, but now Victor was showing uncharacteristic behavior. His aloofness, lack of intimacy and secrecy were all signs that something was missing and she was determined to find the underlying cause. After all, Carlena had a lot to lose; she had sacrificed much to help Victor achieve the things he was able to achieve. The successful law practice, the multi-million dollar deals. She had added her own classy dimension to his success. Whether it was hosting a dinner party for important clients or investors, her charm and graciousness created an atmosphere where people felt comfortable in investing their money in Victor's deals. She was more than just a wife to Victor. She was a true asset. Her intelligence allowed her to interact with the most influential leaders and dignitaries, and skillfully promote her husband and his plans. It was never about her, she never felt the need to promote herself. She and Victor were a team. She was content to remain in the shadows and shine in Victor's reflected glory.

After Victor left, Carlena sat up in bed feeling the stress of uncertainty tightening in her chest. For the first time she was contemplating the prospects of Victor's behavior. She wondered if the stress of his work was affecting his attitude and his relationship with her, or if more ominous signs were on the horizon. She believed that she knew her husband and what he was capable of, but she had never seen him wound so tight. He had negotiated big deals in the past and never reacted in such a strange manner. She was determined to find the underlying cause and she knew just where to start. First thing in the morning she would call an old friend whose counsel she valued-JJ Battle. Surely, he could shed some light on what was going on with Victor. She smiled as she thought of JJ and drifted off to sleep. As she slept, she dreamt of her and JJ making wild and passionate love, just like the law school days. When she awoke, her underwear was moist and she felt refreshed, invigorated, and ready to tackle Victor and everything else that was confronting her.

Chapter 23

JJ AWOKE WITH A SENSE OF dread. He sat up groggily in bed and tried to clear his head. It was 5:30 in the morning and he could hear Junior snoring in the other room. It was still early but JJ knew he had a challenging day ahead. It was the day of Katherine's Memorial service. He had attempted to avoid thinking of her by keeping busy; it didn't help. He had a long day ahead of him. After the memorial service, he had to fly to Jamaica for Katherine's funeral there. It still seemed so unreal that she was no longer alive, and his feeling of guilt for her death still tore at his psyche. He decided to get up and go downstairs to lift weights and have some breakfast. He had a few hours before the service and he needed to put together something to say. So much had happened in such a short period. It had begun with the Bobby Bennett case and spiraled out of control from there. Katherine's death was somehow a part of all this, he just couldn't figure out how. He had some things to sort out and a good workout would help him do that.

JJ began to feel the warmth of blood flowing through his body as he pumped out set after set. He thought about Katherine's memorial service and what he would say and about her funeral in Jamaica tomorrow. He remembered that he had a trial date for Bobby's case that was fast approaching, but mostly he felt the pain and anguish of missing Katherine. He felt both sorrow and a great deal of guilt because he pulled her into this mess. He placed more weight on the bar as he pushed his body and tried to push away the pain. Her killers were still out there, and he knew his life could not have meaning until he made them pay. JJ could feel himself changing. He couldn't believe that he was now contemplating life or death matters. Although he had lived most of his life aware of the violent nature of the city he lived in, he had always managed to remain outside the craziness. While many of his childhood friends had become victims of violence, and a few others had become perpetrators, he had always managed to avoid it. Now he recognized what so many people he had represented probably had always known, that sometimes you were powerless to stop the inevitability of destiny. He was surprised how easily he embraced the fact that he might have to kill or could be killed.

He had grown up on the East Side of Detroit, where violence was common. In fact, the national media was fond of referring to Detroit as the Murder Capital because it led the nation in homicides. It was a dubious honor, but it was what made the city what it was. JJ was fortunate that he was never a victim. He had avoided allowing the city to harden him. He had represented a number of murderers in his career, and he knew he did not have the cold-blooded nature of a natural born killer. There was the Kareem Boozer type of killers, those who had no regard for human life. They killed because they could and because it was economically profitable. However, for JJ his motives were different. In his mind, he claimed the moral high ground of a man seeking revenge, and for this, he was willing to pay any price. They had taken something precious from him, and for that, they had to pay.

JJ finished his workout and showered. Although he was not particularly hungry after his workout, he knew he would need his strength for the long day ahead. He fixed himself a cheese omelet with whole-wheat toast and a bowl of cereal. He skimmed the morning's Detroit Free Press and finished his breakfast.

It was time to leave for Katherine's memorial service. He could hear Junior loudly snoring in the guest room down the hall. He decided to wake Junior to tell him that he was leaving.

"Junior, it's me, I'm leaving to head down to the memorial service." He could hear Junior rustling beneath the covers.

"What time is it?"

"It's about 8:30; I thought I would let you sleep." JJ said apologetically.

"Well you let me sleep long enough. It's time to earn my money." He could hear Junior get out of the bed, and remove what sounded like a chair from against the door.

"I guess old habits are hard to break," JJ kidded him as Junior yawned and scratched himself. "Listen, I'm headed down to the Ford Auditorium for Katherine's memorial service, I thought I'd let you sleep and come by and pick you up later."

"Hell no! If you move, I move. So give me a couple of minutes to take a shower and throw some clothes on. I know what you're thinking; I'm not going to embarrass you."

"That wasn't what I was thinking, but it's nice to know you can't read minds." JJ was surprised at how perceptive Junior was. He was right though, JJ was concerned how Junior would fit in with all of the dignitaries and lawyer types. He need not have worried, when Junior finished with his shower he told JJ of his plan.

"I'll just be your driver for the day, and that way I can remain inconspicuous."

JJ had to admit that he liked the idea. He did not want to be bothered with driving today, so having Junior there would solve that problem and he could serve as a second set of eyes.

The memorial service for Katherine was a surprisingly upbeat affair and for that, JJ was grateful. He had imagined that it would be somber and emotional, but it was not. All of the speakers talked about all of the great things that Katherine had accomplished during her brief but meteoric career. The gathering was an impressive collection of political and business leaders throughout the state. There were representatives from the Governor's office and the Mayor's staff. JJ noted with interest that all of the key members of One Detroit, Inc. were present, Victor, Randy, Eva, Rahsheed Truman and even detective Stone.

The memorial service lasted for two hours and JJ felt obligated to remain after the service had ended. Many people knew of his relationship with Katherine and sought him out to give their personal condolences. It was a day of unbelievable emotions. He missed Katherine more than ever. As people began to leave the service, he thought about his flight to Jamaica and Katherine's funeral there. The crowd had thinned out, and there were only a few remaining people huddled in small groups speaking in hushed tones. JJ surveyed the room one last time as the remaining groups broke up and only a few stragglers remained. He noticed for the first time a short stocky young black women standing patiently along the far wall of the auditorium. She was unremarkable in appearance, dressed in plain black clothes. She had the troubled acned skin of youth, but JJ noticed something more. There was determination in her eyes that was in conflict with the rest of her demeanor. She looked around nervously fidgeting uncomfortably for something in her purse.

JJ waited, staring across the room searching for some recognition from this woman. They were alone now, and JJ walked toward her.

"Can I help you?" He asked, wondering why she was still there. JJ could see a look of fear spread across her face as he approached. Out of the corner of his eye, JJ could see Junior approach, not in a hurried sort of way, but with a purposeful stride. She saw it too, and Junior's hand smoothly and casually went inside his jacket, as if he were reaching for a cell phone. JJ knew better, and apparently so did the girl, as a look of fear appeared on her face.

"Hold up a minute JJ, I need to speak with you," Junior said quickly cutting the distance between them. Expertly he was between JJ and the girl. He had his hand on his waist and his eyes focused on the girl.

"Excuse me. I need to have a quick word with Mr. Battle if you don't mind. "By the way, what's your name?" JJ was surprised and impressed at how adeptly Junior had intervened to take control of the situation. He had to admit that having Junior around was starting to have some benefits.

"I'm Lindsay Cross, I'm, she stammered, I was Ms. Devlin's executive assistant she said in a rush of words and emotion. JJ remembered now, Katherine had spoken often of Lindsay and JJ had even spoken to her on the phone a time or two, but he had never met her.

"Hey Lindsay, I remember you now, Katherine often mentioned you."

"She did," she said, beaming from the compliment. "She was my idol you know. She is soooo great. I mean was. You know what I mean. I really loved and respected her. I just can't believe she's gone." JJ could see tears forming in the corner of her eyes and he reached over to give her a reassuring hug.

"That's why I wanted to talk to you. She talked about you all of the time Mr. Battle, and I thought you guys were the perfect couple. You know two high-powered attorneys and all. It was so cool. Then this happened. I knew I had to speak to you to tell you how sorry I was and all."

"Well that's very sweet of you Lindsay. I really appreciate your support. Thanks for coming." He could see the disappointment on her face as she looked first at JJ and then at Junior who was still lurking nearby.

"You don't understand. It's all my fault!" she blurted as tears streamed down her face.

Both JJ and Junior shifted uncomfortably as they watched this young girl struggling with her grief. It's alright, Lindsay, you have nothing to feel responsible for, it wasn't your fault."

"You don't understand, it really was my fault," she sobbed as her crying became louder.

"Lindsay, trust me it really wasn't your fault." JJ said more emphatically, trying to reassure her.

"But Mr. Battle, if only I hadn't told Ms. Devlin about what I found while I was doing the real estate searches, maybe none of this would have happened."

JJ remembered now. Katherine had told him that she had one of her staff researching the real estate transaction records for the city, which must be what Lindsay meant. JJ still did not see the connection between Lindsay's search and Katherine's death. "Lindsay I know how upset you are at Katherine's death, but how are these two things related?" JJ asked.

"Well, Ms. Devlin had me researching all of these real estate transactions and transfers down at the Register of Deeds. There were an unusual amount of transactions all around the same time, and all involving the same neighborhood, the Corktown neighborhood. The strange thing is that all of the properties were quit claim deeded to one company, One Detroit, Inc."

"Who was the principal listed on the deed?" JJ asked.

"They were all deeded to Robert Bennett." She said.

"I knew he was involved in this. But what has this to do with Ms. Devlin?"

"Well, normally when I run these checks, I use my law firm charge card to charge the fees. But this time, I didn't have my card so I used Ms. Devlin's card to pay for the searches and copies."

"Is that so unusual?" JJ asked, trying to find the connection. Well, not usually, but this time, two men came to the firm asking for Ms. Devlin and asking questions about use of the credit card."

"Why would anyone question the charges?" JJ asked, already knowing the answer. "Were these men from the bank?"

"No. One was from Homicide, from the Detroit Police Department. The other man never said a word."

"Did Katherine speak to these men?" JJ asked feeling a cold chill run down his body.

"No, she was out to lunch with you that day." Lindsay said.

JJ was deep in thought, his mind already piecing together the bits and pieces that Lindsay had told him. None of it made sense. But nothing about the circumstances of her death made sense either. This was the first solid piece of evidence that JJ had, and he was determined to use it to find Katherine's killer.

"Did you happen to get the names of these two men?" JJ asked. But he already thought he knew the answer.

"Well yes and no. Lieutenant Harvey Stone was one. He was the short stocky one with the big meaty hands. I remember because when he shook my hand I was amazed at how big his hands were. He also tried to walk inside Ms. Devlin's office but I didn't let him." She said with a self-satisfied tone. The other man did not give his name but he was very strange looking. He was very pale, like he didn't get enough sunlight, and his facial features resembled a rodent." Today I saw Lieutenant Stone at this ceremony.

"Damn." It was the first words that Junior had spoken since Lindsay began talking. They both turned to Junior to see what prompted his reaction.

"What's the matter Junior?" JJ asked, attempting to gauge Junior's reaction.

"You say this other dude looked like a rodent, sort of like a rat. Was he a skinny pale white guy?"

"Yes, that's exactly what he looked like. A giant rat." All of the time he was here, he never said a word. But I got the sense that he noticed everything. His beady eyes were all over the place." Lindsay shuddered as she thought of the Rat.

"You were right, that dude doesn't miss anything. He's one of a kind." Junior said with a knowing nod.

"You know this guy? Who is he?" JJ asked. He was amazed that there might be a connection.

"Yeah, we go back a long way together. I probably know him as well as anyone. But who ever really gets to know a rat. We go back to Nam. Special Forces, Delta. We were involved in some covert stuff that nobody ever talked about. John Ratskeller was probably the best sniper Special Forces ever had. He had more official recorded kills than anyone did, and that doesn't include the unofficial ones that nobody knew about. Most snipers kill because it's their job; the Rat kills because he loves it. He's one crazy dude. If the Rat is on this case, we had better step up our game; we might need reinforcements.

JJ could see a glimmer in his cousin's eyes and a slight smile on his face, as if the fun and games had just begun.

However, JJ did not see any fun in these events; he was terrified of rats.

Chapter 24

THIS WAS A DAY OF DESTINY for Brianna LaShawn Tuller. She was about to make a decision that would change her life and the lives of her family forever. She had plans and dreams, and now she was on the brink of making them all come true. She had been on cloud nine since yesterday, when she received the call from the nasty rodent looking man. He wanted to meet her so that they could exchange the money that would buy her and her family a fresh start. She had spent the day packing the suitcases for them to take on their trip to Disney World. This would be the first vacation her family would ever have. She could not wait to see the expression on the kid's faces when they saw Mickey and the rest of the Disney characters in person. Just the thought of the warm Florida sun shining on them after suffering through this cold Michigan winter would be great. She also might just decide to stay in Florida permanently. She didn't really have any ties to Michigan anyway. It would give her and the kids a fresh start. She had taken the kids over to Betty's so that they would not interrupt her packing.

It was two days before she was supposed to testify in Bobby's trial, and the thought of being on the stand and testifying made her feel uneasy. The prosecutor Anne Moroski had been calling to make sure she had not changed her mind. All of it was enough to make her scream. When the telephone rang and the voice on the other end told her about receiving Fifty Thousand dollars, she thought it was a miracle. Betty would just have to understand. She would send Betty a letter explaining everything. Besides, she would probably get back with Bobby soon anyway – what was the use. Brianna rubbed the scar on her leg, remembering the circumstances that put her in this position in the first place. If she had been minding her own business, perhaps none of this would have happened. She sighed as she put the last piece of clothing in the suitcase and closed it.

She looked at her watch, it was one fifty. She was meeting the rodent faced man at three o'clock. They were meeting on Belle Isle underneath the bridge. It would take her only thirty minutes to get there but she wanted to get there early to get this business over. She felt a little uneasy about not telling anyone where she was going, but who could she tell. Anyway, she would just pray that everything would work out; it was her only choice.

The Rat sat hunched over the desk in the dirty and dark motel on the eastside of Detroit. He hated these seedy noisy motels, but they were cheap and he could pay by the month and more importantly, he could pay in cash. Because the staff was transient, it was unlikely that the staff would remember him. He could hear the traffic noise from the street along with the conversation and sounds of lovemaking of the other guests. He was not distracted. He was working carefully like a chemist mixing the most important of substances. In reality, that was just what he was doing. For his meeting with Ms. Brianna Tuller, he was preparing a special mixture. The Rat had learned his special brand of chemistry in the jungles of Southeast Asia and perfected it in countries around the world. It was particularly useful in his line of work and it made his job so much easier. He wore rubber gloves and was careful not to spill the elixir, as he did not want any of the concoction on his hands or skin, which might incapacitate him. He completed filling the two syringes and he placed them in a plastic pouch so they would be easily accessible. The first syringe contained a combination of Rohypnol and GHB. Once he administered the drug, she would be incapacitated and then he could manipulate the scene. The rohypnol cocktail would paralyze her central nervous system instantly; she would be unable to fight back. He would still have to be quick and precise in finding the carotid artery, and he always was. In his profession, mistakes were fatal. He finished packing all of the drugs, cleaned the room, and gathered all of his belongings. Although he was paid up for the week, he kept all of his personal belongings with him. Just in case he was unable to return to the room or was incapacitated, there would be no evidence of his presence there. It was all part of his military training and he never forgot. He made one last final check of the room and grabbed the brief case with the $50,000 cash.

He was now ready for his mission. He could feel the adrenaline and excitement as he went over in his mind just what he needed to do. He knew it was a foolproof plan, but he always had a backup plan if necessary. He checked his weapon again, making sure it was fully loaded, and the silencer attached. He next checked his backup weapon strapped to his left ankle, making sure it was secure. He then checked the knife strapped to his right ankle, knowing he had everything he would need. He had timed the drive to Belle Isle twice and knew it was only a ten-minute ride. He wanted to arrive at the park first to observe Brianna and to make sure that she was alone and had not notified the police or been followed. He wanted her to wait, but not so long that she would get spooked and leave, but just enough that her anxiousness and the sight of the money would distract her.

He arrived early enough to select a spot well above the area he had selected for their meeting. Today, there were only a few people in the park like all of the winter afternoon weekdays. Only a few brave souls would brave the icy winds coming off the river. He knew the police seldom if ever made patrols on the Island in the winter. If they did appear, it would look perfectly normal, a couple enjoying the view of the frozen river. He hoped he had thought of everything, he usually did. In the event that something went wrong, he would do what he always did - improvise.

He had been waiting for about fifteen minutes when he saw Brianna's ragged Ford Taurus covered in salt and road grime, chugging to their designated spot. He could see that she was alone. She pulled into a parking spot overlooking the river and looked around anxiously. He waited a couple of minutes checking to see if anyone followed her or was watching her. There was no one in sight. He eased the car down the icy road and parked next to Brianna's old beat up Taurus. He fingered the syringes in his left pocket, and felt his weapon with the silencer on his side. He took a deep breath, and removed all feeling and thoughts from his mind. This was how they trained him. Don't think. Just allow your training and instinct to take over. He opened his door, careful to keep his car running. He grabbed the briefcase and walked over to the passenger side of Brianna's car, careful to wave a good-natured wave as he approached. Brianna looked through her fogged windows, making sure it was him before she unlocked the door. She shuddered when she saw his rodent face, not from the cold, but from a premonition she felt. There was something strange about the way he looked. She couldn't quite figure it out. He slid into the passenger seat carefully placing the brief case on the floor in front of him. He looked over at Brianna and made his best effort at a smile.

"Hello Brianna. I'm glad you came alone as we discussed. As I said before, you must keep all of the details about our transaction in confidence. You cannot tell anyone about our business. Do you understand?" He watched as Brianna nodded her head in understanding.

"I understand." She said the words aloud, but they came out in a whisper. Her eyes never left the brief case on the floor.

"Alright, here is what we agreed upon. Fifty Thousand Dollars. Take your time and count it, it's all yours." The Rat leaned down, picked up the briefcase, and handed it to Brianna. He could smell the freshness of her perfume in the closeness of the car with the heater blasting. She had the radio playing softly in the background. She set the case on her lap and stared at it for a moment. Finally, she took a deep breath and slid the locks of the case open with a metallic click. She gasped as she saw the neatly banded stacks of one hundred dollar bills. Beside her, the Rat quickly and quietly removed the syringe with the rohypnol cocktail as Brianna reached for a packet of the money. Swiftly he turned and pierced her neck, sinking the syringe into her carotid artery. He pushed the plunger all the way into the syringe watching the liquid disappear into her body.

"Ouch! What was that Brianna asked?" instinctively reaching for the syringe. He could see the fear and confusion on her face as her body went rigid.

She tried to speak, but in a matter of seconds, the drug had started to paralyze her central nervous system, quickly speeding to her brain. She was awake
but no longer had control of her motor function. The more she panicked, the
faster her heartbeat, and the faster the drug sped through her body maximiz-
ing its effect.

"Just relax," the Rat said in his most soothing tone. "This won't hurt a bit;
in fact you'll enjoy the feeling."

Brianna struggled to move and realized she could not. She tried to figure out what was happening to her. Things were clear but everything was
in slow motion. She could see the man next to her but she could not touch
him. The briefcase was still in her lap, but she could not touch it either. The
Rat removed the plastic bag from his pocket and took out the remaining syringe and a thick rubber band. He gently grabbed Brianna's right wrist and
wrapped the rubber band around her right forearm. He jabbed the syringe
into the protruding vein and pressed the plunger. Brianna's eyes were wide
with panic. Her heart was racing as she wondered what the Rat was injecting
into her body. It was better that she didn't know that the liquid in her veins
was one hundred percent pure Mexican brown heroin. The Rat estimated
that it would take approximately one hundred and twenty seconds for the
narcotic to enter Brianna's bloodstream and cause a cardiac arrest. It would
not be pretty, but it was effective. He waited, as her body began to convulse.
He could see drool and some sort of white fluid starting to seep out of the
corners of her mouth. He waited, watching Brianna's eyelids close as her chin
dropped to her chest as she lost consciousness. He waited feeling a faint pulse
in her wrist. Then he felt nothing, as her breathing and pulse stopped. He was
careful to wrap Brianna's hand around the syringe, making sure her fingerprints would be easily discovered. He carefully placed a packet of heroin and
the tools to prepare it, the spoon, and a lighter. He made certain, that when
the police arrived, they would come to only one conclusion, drug overdose.
Even the Detroit Police department would have a difficult time misidentify-
ing the cause of death.

A syringe protruding from her right arm would not elude Detroit's finest.
It was unlikely that the police would do a toxicology screen for the rohypnol,

but even if they found traces, it would be difficult to come up with a plausible explanation.

He double checked her pulse and her carotid artery and found no sign of life. He quickly gathered all of his tools and the briefcase with the money. He made a final check of the car making sure that he left nothing that could tie him to the crime. He got out of the vehicle and waved, just in case anyone was watching. He could never be too careful. One mistake could mean detection. He noticed that Brianna had a full tank of gas. It could be hours before the car ran out of gas and they discovered her body. The combination of the warm car and the freezing temperatures would make it more difficult to identify the time of death. The Rat got into his car and surveyed his handiwork. Once again, he was able to subdue his prey.

Chapter 25

JJ BATTLE WAS PREPARED FOR WAR. Every fiber of his being and his senses were tuned to his surroundings. This was his domain and here he was king. He adopted a new persona. Everything he did or said, every move or gesture had a purpose. Each move was choreographed to yield but one result; to convince twelve people that the person he represented was worthy of their consideration. That was all he wanted for his client, the opportunity to present his client's case and have the evidence judged fairly. He didn't possess an unrealistic belief that the jury would always find his client not guilty. That was unrealistic and discounted the intelligence of juries. That could be fatal to his client. All he wanted was that elusive slice of justice. He knew that not all of his clients were worthy of acquittal, and if Kareem Boozer's case taught him anything, it was that the outcome belonged to the jury. Although trials like all competitions was ultimately about winning and losing, he had come to realize after some painful lessons, that the losses were not his, but his clients. It was not personal. JJ knew that at the end of the proceedings he was free to walk away and resume his life, regardless of the outcome. His clients would not always be so fortunate. He always tried to maintain the same perspective; this case was about the evidence, not the client, or the size of the retainer. He reminded himself that this was just another trial, just another performance. He thought of his athletic career, and how all of the important lessons in life, he learned from athletics.

It was almost show time. He had a few moments to compose himself before the clerk opened court and the jury filed in. This is where JJ was at his best, charming the jury. Most attorneys believed that the trial began when the jury walked in, but for JJ it began in the hours of preparation before the trial. People often asked him if he was nervous before the big trials, and he told them that he had no reason to be. The key to overcoming anxiety was preparation. JJ was prepared. His preparation had begun this morning with breakfast, a quick workout, and the selection of today's wardrobe. He knew that first impressions by the jurors would be important. Therefore, he chose his outfit with care. He chose a mid-blue three-button wool suit that had been custom made and tailored to fit perfectly. He chose tailor made clothing for court because it made him feel comfortable and confident. He did not have to keep tugging at an ill-fitting jacket, which might distract the jury. It was a few shades lighter than navy but gave him a serious look while not appearing stuffy. His French cuffed shirt was tailored made and powdered blue with a hint of shadow stripe with a solid blue tie that was perfectly coordinated. His jewelry was impressive but not overstated. His look said elegance and prosperity, something Wayne county juries respected and appreciated. During the voir dire, when all eyes were on him the wardrobe and the attention to details would pay dividends.

He was ready. Psychologically, he had temporarily put the recent events behind him. Katherine's death, the memorial service, and her funeral in Jamaica, had taken their toll both physically and mentally. It had been a week since he had returned from the Caribbean and Judge Moody had granted a two-week continuance for the trial. It was more than enough time for JJ to complete his preparation for the case. He had met with his client and went over what to expect. JJ made sure that his client was appropriately dressed, that was crucial to juries. Their initial opinion of Bobby Bennett would largely depend on his appearance. They would look at him and decide if he committed the crime he was charged with. JJ instructed him on proper decorum at the defense table, making sure he always faced the jury. Juries wanted to make sure your client could look them in the eye and they weren't evading them as if they had something to hide. This was a painful lesson that JJ learned the hard way when he was a new lawyer. He provided his client with all of the material from the case and allowed him to read it during the trial. Throughout the trial, the client's back was to the jury. In most instances, this might not have made a difference, but the prosecutor in the case, a shrewd veteran prosecutor made a nasty issue of it in his closing argument. JJ was certain it was the final blow for conviction. He remembered the prosecutor emphatically telling the jury, "take a good look at the defendant, look at how he's sitting at the defense table, notice that his back is facing you, that is a sign of disrespect, but more importantly, he knows that he is guilty of these crimes and he doesn't have the guts to face you." JJ immediately jumped up to object, but the damage had been done, and he could see a number of jurors nodding in confirmation. It was a painful lesson, and he vowed never to repeat it.

JJ was going to love trying this case. This was his specialty, representing crooked yet somehow redeemable criminals. Bobby Bennett fit the profile perfectly. He was a crook; that much was certain, but his previous transgressions were petty theft and fraud crimes. He was a small time hustler, someone the citizens of Detroit could relate. JJ just had to overcome this nasty business of the alleged kidnapping and attempted murder. When he was finished restoring the soiled reputation of Bobby Bennett, the jury would probably nominate Bobby for father of the year. However, before he got to that point, he had to work out some details, such as picking the right jury. It was crucial in criminal cases. You could have the best case and most lovable client in the world, but if you selected the wrong jury, your client could still go down in flames. JJ hoped to avoid that. He knew just the type of jury he needed, he only hoped the jury pool contained those people.

While JJ waited for the judge and the prosecutor to arrive, he decided to visit his client in the holding cell. He wanted to make sure that Bobby was up for the challenge of testifying. Although it was unlikely that he would testify today, JJ wanted him ready nevertheless. He also wanted to make sure that the suit that he purchased for Bobby's courtroom appearance fit. He wanted his client to look his best. Some clients also needed some handholding and sometimes lost their nerve as trial day arrived. The potential penalties were usually enough to frighten ever the hardest of criminals. Bobby was no exception; under his controlled demeanor was a frightened man. He had good reason to be. If the jury convicted him, he could face up to 20 years in prison. Frankly, Bobby Bennett did not look like the type of man that could do twenty years easily.

JJ entered the holding cell and went through the process of going through the metal detectors once again. Recorder's Court was one of the most secure trial courts in the country. Therefore, JJ didn't mind the inconvenience of the added security. As he went past the last security checkpoint the guard stopped him and asked, "What kind of show are you going to put on today attorney Battle?"

"Just the usual bells and whistles, you know you've seen all of my moves by now, Jesse, careful to address the deputy by his first name. JJ was a favorite at the courthouse and he made a point of addressing each deputy by his or her first name. It was a small thing but the deputies appreciated the kindness, particularly in an environment where almost everyone disrespected them.

"You know I'll be there watching."

"Thanks."

As he entered the holding room, Bobby was already at the table. JJ had to admit that Bobby didn't look half-bad in the suit. He made a respectable looking defendant.

"Hey Bobby, how are you today? This is your big day. You get your day in court."

"I'm doing good, how about you?"

"I wanted to go over a few things before they brought you into the courtroom. First, make sure that you maintain eye contact with the jury, don't stare, but also don't avoid them either. Secondly, make sure to take notes, it will appear that you're interested in your case. Third, never interrupt me when I'm listening to a witness, write me a note if you want to get my attention. It's more important to hear what the witness has to say. Is that clear?"

"Yes sir. Bobby said exhibiting a coolness that impressed JJ.

"Whatever happens make sure that you control your emotions. Don't get too high or too low."

"JJ, one last question, what do you think will happen with my case?"

"Bobby, I'm an attorney and not a magician, but one thing is certain, I'll be fighting for you as hard as I can the moment we walk in that courtroom. But I'm not going to kid you; there is a ton of evidence against you, including Brianna's eyewitness testimony. She's going to make a very sympathetic witness, but we'll have to find a way to overcome that. Let me assure you, when I'm done, they will be wondering who's on trial you or Brianna." JJ shook hands with Bobby and headed back to the Courtroom.

When JJ reentered the courtroom, people had already begun to file in. There was a buzz as the media began setting up their equipment. JJ felt a sudden rush of excitement, much the same way he felt before a big game. He didn't feel nervousness or pressure, only the excitement of a big performance. He was ready.

The deputies were bringing in his client through the administrative entrance to the courtroom. Bobby was in handcuffs and leg irons like all prisoners. In his hands, he had a file folder with all of the information about his trial and his notes. He too was ready. As the deputy was removing the handcuffs and leg irons, the prosecution team entered led by Anne Moroski, looking slightly disheveled. JJ noticed that she had done away with her glasses and had replaced them with new contact lenses. It definitely improved her appearance and she almost looked attractive if not for the mess of hair on her head. Anne, was having a perpetual bad hair day, with her blond locks unruly and undecided if they were going natural or straight. The effect made her look slightly crazy. She would be much better off putting it in a ponytail. Perhaps he would tell her after the trial, after the outcome had been decided and the emotions had normalized.

With her was a young black female assistant DA that JJ had never seen before, and they offered a good contrast, the older white, slightly disheveled experienced DA, and the young attractive polished assistant. It was a nice touch, the jurors, both male and female would appreciate her being there. In a long trial, jurors needed to be entertained. Particularly in domestic assault cases, it helped the prosecution better present their case. Jurors needed someone to relate to. The young DA helped achieve a nice balance. He would introduce himself later before the proceedings began, before she could develop a different opinion of him, one tainted by her perception as he went about the necessities of trial defense.

JJ was going over some last minute details when he saw Stone approach out of the corner of his eye. The squat, tank like appearance of detective Harvey Stone entering the courtroom gave the appearance of a fullback approaching the line of scrimmage. He had a confident slow walk that suggested that you would be wise not to get in his way. He stopped at the prosecution table and greeted Anne and the young assistant DA. He purposely kept his back to JJ and Bobby. JJ watched him as he spoke with Anne, and tried to pick up any hints of conversation. The prosecution table and the defense table were only six feet apart in distance, but more than distance separated them. JJ could feel the anger and distaste he had for Stone rising as he thought about Katherine and the role that Stone had probably played in her death. This was not the time, but he knew that the time was fast approaching. He would have to deal with Stone and his One Detroit, Inc. group, but now was not the time.

"Anything else, attorney Battle?" He heard the words, but for a moment, he couldn't quite focus on them.

"No Bobby. Just remember everything we talked about last night, make sure you control your emotions, no outbursts."

"I understand. So what do you think? Do we have a shot?"

"Absolutely! Let's just hope we have a good jury panel."

JJ could see Anne and Stone engaged in animated conversation at the prosecution table. It wasn't really conversation. Anne was talking and Stone was shrugging his shoulders and looking defensive. It was an interesting display. The deputy brought in the list of the jury panel. It provided the jurors' names and occupations. It was the first glimpse into who would be deciding the case. JJ carefully studied the list. He was looking for any bit of information that might be useful. He might recognize a name or get a sense of a juror's makeup by his occupation. He studied the list, and when he completed a page, he passed it to Bobby for his review. After fifteen minutes, JJ had reviewed the list twice and memorized most of the names of the initial panel. That type of detail might be useful later. The clerk entered, signaling that the Judge was ready to begin. JJ took a deep breath, as he did before each game and told himself it was show time. He shook Bobby's hand and they embraced, both knowing what was at stake. JJ had to admit, that as a criminal client, Bobby was one of the better clients. He did not complain or expect you to be over at the jail every night holding his hand. He did almost everything that JJ asked, and that was all you could expect from a client.

"The judge will see the attorney's in chambers," the clerk Steven Parker said without emotion. He was usually a barometer of Eva's emotional state, but today he wasn't giving anything away. Anyway, it didn't matter, this was a jury trial, and the jury would have the last word, not Eva. If Eva interfered in his case, he would put his objections on the record if necessary, in case an appeal was necessary. The appellate court was sometimes the only thing that kept wayward judges in line, but most attorneys were afraid to use it. JJ was not. He let the judges know it early and often, if necessary. It kept the playing field level from overzealous law and order judges, or ineffective judges who let prosecutor's run their court-rooms. Either way, JJ wouldn't allow Eva or Anne to railroad his client.

As they entered the Judge's chambers, JJ waited and held the door open for the prosecutor. He could see the strain on her face. She was always the nervous type and it usually worked in her favor, as juries sometimes felt sorry for her and gave her the benefit of the doubt in the close cases. JJ made a mental note not let Anne exploit that to her advantage.

"Good morning Anne, remember to be gentle with me today. I'm just a working stiff trying to do my best."

"Save it for the jury JJ. I'm not in the mood for your charm today," she hissed, with uncharacteristic venom.

"Ouch, that really stung Anne, you know I have the utmost respect for you. Let's not let this case cause us to lose sight of the bigger picture, our friendship. I was just trying to keep things light. You know the final courtesy before we engage in all-out war."

"I know, I'm just a little bit on edge. Tyler is going to ream me another rear end."

"Why would he do that?" JJ inquired, wondering why the District Attorney, Tyler Green would have an opinion about this case so early in the proceedings. JJ knew that Tyler had political aspirations and that he was coveting the Mayor's mansion. But JJ was puzzled why Anne was so concerned about Tyler's reaction. She was one of the leading prosecutors and had the highest winning percentage of anyone in the office. He guessed that Anne's pretrial jitters were just normal trial anxiety.

As they entered the judge's chambers, there was Eva in her judge's robe and full judicial demeanor. That meant the proceedings had begun and let there be no doubt who was in charge; the Honorable Eva Ann Moody.

"Good morning counselors, have a seat. You have both been in my courtroom enough to know how I"

"Excuse me your honor," Anne cut her off in mid-sentence.

JJ turned his head toward Anne in mock amazement, wondering what Anne was thinking, interrupting the judge. He waited for Eva's venomous response. He wasn't disappointed.

Ms. Moroski, either you are unintelligent or rude, but either way, you do not interrupt me when I am speaking. Is that clear?"

"Yes your honor. But what I was about to say will have a great effect on the outcome of this trial." Anne said with persistence.

JJ stared at Anne in amusement, waiting for whatever came next. This was an interesting turn of events. Usually JJ created the pretrial fireworks. He was known for coming up with some pretrial motion or objection at the last minute to turn the proceedings upside down. However, today, Anne seemed ready to unleash some thunderbolt even at the risk of receiving the judge's wrath. JJ waited, preparing himself for anything.

"Ms. Moroski, I know you have a tendency to be overly dramatic, but exactly what is it that is causing you such consternation, that you continue to rudely interrupt me."

"Well you honor, it seems that we have a problem with our complaining witness, we are unable to locate her." Anne said almost apologetically.

"In all due respect Ms. Moroski," the judge said, waving an angry hand at Anne. "Why should this interest me? May I remind you, this case is entitled the People of The State of Michigan versus Robert Bennett? I don't see anywhere on this case sheet where a complaining witness name appears. It is your duty to bring this case forward witness or not, do I make myself clear."

JJ moved forward slightly in his chair, ready with the appropriate response should it be needed. Otherwise, he would remain silent. He knew when his fortunes were changing, and this was not a fight he needed to enter just yet.

That was the most difficult choice an attorney had to make, knowing when to keep his mouth closed. He knew where the judge was going but it was not yet his time to guide her there. She was well on the path herself.

"I am aware of the implications of my missing witness your honor Anne replied, her face reddening with embarrassment. I need to request a short continuance to locate her, your honor."

"DENIED!"

"But your honor, the court rules allow…"

"How dare you cite the court rules in my courtroom to cover up your offices malfeasance." Eva spat with her characteristic judicial venom.

"But your honor," Anne managed to blurt before a judicial hand wave of disgust silenced her.

"Ms. Moroski, need I remind you that you joined in this court's motion for a speedy trial when it appeared at the time to be advantageous to the State. Now you come to this Court seeking a continuance when your case develops problems. Live with them like the rest of the lawyers of the world. Make do with what you have or dismiss the case. But you will not receive a continuance."

JJ could feel Anne's discomfort, but he also knew what this meant for his client, victory. Although a missing witness tainted the case, it would still allow his client to go home a free man. JJ knew there were pitfalls to overcome with a dismissal. It could allow the prosecution to refile the case if the Judge dismissed the case without prejudice. It was a technical distinction, but one that had serious implications for his client. If the Judge were inclined to dismiss the case with prejudice, the prosecution could not refile the case. JJ needed to find a way to suggest to Eva that dismissal with prejudice was the proper decision, but he had to be careful, Eva could quickly focus her wrath on him, If Eva was angry enough she would arrive at that result on her own, but JJ couldn't be sure.

"But your honor," Anne protested feebly, "at least give me the opportunity to find out what happened to my witness, there may be a perfectly reasonable explanation for her absence."

JJ sat back quietly observing Anne's deepening dilemma. It was an ironic reversal of roles. Often it was JJ throwing himself on the mercy of the court while the prosecution stood smugly by, already knowing the outcome. So JJ waited while Judge Eva Ann Moody argued more eloquently for dismissal than he could. He didn't question the fortuitous disappearance of Brianna Tuller, but somewhere deep inside he knew it was all related. Katherine's death, the Corktown project and the ominous One Detroit, Inc. He knew he would have to sort out all of this soon, but for now, he had to see Bobby's case through to completion, and find Katherine's killer.

"Ms. Moroski, unless you have some more compelling reasons why this case should not go forward, I am going to call the case and you can make whatever motion you deem appropriate. Keep in mind that I allowed you sufficient time to prepare your case. You indicated that you wanted to fast track this case and I allowed you to do that. Now, you can either voluntarily take the dismissal, or run the risk of jeopardy attaching. In either case, without your complaining witness, you have some proof problems. Are there any other pretrial issues that we need to consider? If not, we will put this on the record."

JJ could see Anne's face twist into a mask of anger as her eyes reddened and tears formed at the corners. She was between the proverbial rock and a hard place. If she did not voluntarily dismiss the case, but opted to begin picking the jury, she would run the risk of double jeopardy attaching once the jury was sworn. If she voluntarily dismissed the case, the judge would dismiss it with prejudice, meaning she could not re file the charges. Either way, Bobby Bennett would be a free man. Anne's only hope would be to appeal Judge Moody's order of dismissal with prejudice. But that avenue was highly unlikely. Anne knew that a judge's decision of whether to designate a dismissal with or without prejudice was discretionary. Therefore, the appeals court was unlikely to overturn the decision unless there was some obvious impropriety. Anne knew that this result was always a possible outcome of criminal prosecution, but it hurt all the same. All of her time and effort meant nothing and a guilty man was going free.

As they filed back into the courtroom, JJ approached the defense table. He could see Stone at the prosecution table staring over at him. JJ ignored him and bent over to whisper in Bobby's ear.

"What I am about to tell you is going to make you extremely happy, but you have to control yourself. The prosecution is going to dismiss this case and it can never be refiled. It means after this short hearing you are going to be a free man."

"Are you serious attorney Battle? Don't play with me."

"I'm serious Bobby. Once this hearing is over, they will release you from the jail. Make sure that you keep a low profile until this all blows over." Bobby quickly embraced JJ and thanked him for all of his help.

JJ was slightly puzzled by the turn of events. The circumstances surrounding the dismissal were too much of a coincidence. Witnesses disappearing, judges making the argument for dismissal with prejudice for him, it was all starting to appear a little too convenient. As the judge went through the procedure of putting the dismissal on record, JJ wondered just who was involved in this conspiracy. He was certain One Detroit, Inc. was behind this. Their involvement included Victor and Randy paying his retainer, the disappearance of the Brianna, and Eva's insistence of the dismissal with prejudice. It was beginning to add up, he thought. There was just one thing he didn't know; he didn't know just how far they would go. Witness tampering, bribery, and murder. The case was now over. The only thing left for JJ was to find Katherine's killer.

Chapter 26

AS JJ LEFT THE COURTROOM, HE could see Harvey Stone, Victor Wright and Randy Connors exchange knowing glances with each other. It disgusted JJ to know they may have conspired to fix this case. It especially disturbed him that Eva would put her career and reputation on the line as well. JJ had no illusions about the criminal justice system of Recorder's court, he knew that there was always a bit of corruption and deceit built into the system, but this result left him feeling that the system was hopelessly broken. He had walked away from the law before and he knew he might have to do so again. However, before he did, One Detroit, Inc. and its principals would have to pay. He resented their smugness and arrogance, yet he resigned himself to the fact that vengeance would be his.

JJ quickly left the courtroom and headed down the back stairs, carefully avoiding the gathering horde of reporters. It was time to take the offensive and find out how dirty One Detroit, Inc. was. He would meet with Junior later and plan their strategy. First, he would pay a visit to an old friend.

He drove north on the Lodge freeway carefully weaving his way around evening rush hour traffic. Although JJ was familiar with this part of town, he didn't frequent this part of the city too often. It was, as some Detroiters would tell you, one of the last remaining jewels of a city in decay. The area was called Palmer Woods and the tree-lined streets housed some of the city's largest mansions. Some had fallen into disrepair, while others still had the character of wealth and opulence. There were manicured lawns and luxury cars parked in driveways and in front of classy homes. The irony of this area was that if these homes had been located in Grosse Pointe or Southfield, or Bloomfield Hills, their values would have doubled. But, that was Detroit's curse; undervalued and unloved.

JJ parked down the street from the distinctive beige stucco mansion and waited, and watched. It might have been a good idea to bring Junior along, but this was something he had to do alone. He waited for thirty minutes noting the cars coming and going and then dialed a number on his cell phone. A familiar female voice answered and JJ asked, "Are you alone?"

"What a pleasant surprise, of course I'm alone," the voice answered.

"I'm down the street I'll be right over."

"I'll leave the door open come right in."

JJ fingered the gun in his waistband and felt reassured at the touch of the cold metal. He wondered if he needed it, and thought better of it. Although he had visited Eva Moody at her home on many occasions, under the circumstances, he thought it wise to be wary of what she might do. She was in deep water and swimming with the sharks. He needed to find out if she was now a shark or merely bait. Either way, she was probably in too deep to save herself. It was her choice, and she would have to live with it. He felt no sympathy for her. He just needed answers.

JJ let himself into the mansion and as always the house overwhelmed him by its' sheer size. It was huge. This was an area where the old money lived. She had remodeled a twenty-room mansion that was over 8,000 square feet. She had done a remarkable job. The house was luxurious, if not a little impersonal. "I'm in the bedroom, fix yourself a drink, and come on upstairs."

A drink was the last thing JJ needed so he ignored her request and proceeded up the long spiral staircase. He entered the master suite, and stopped to take in the surroundings; the room was huge and was exquisitely decorated. Eva, as he suspected, was in bed surrounded by gold silk and satin bed linens. She looked tiny beneath all of the bed linen and was swallowed by the king size bed. JJ knew he would have to keep his wits to avoid Eva's amorous attempts.

He usually felt manipulated by Eva. She was not above a little manipulation when it served her purpose, and tonight her purpose was obvious.

"Have you come over to personally thank me for my judicial benevolence to your client today?" She dropped the blanket revealing her nakedness. JJ had almost grown weary of Eva's unashamed and heavy-handed come ons. He had to admit that Eva was a beautiful woman as he forced himself to remember why he was there. It was going to take every ounce of willpower not to take a flying leap into Eva's arms and just give into her. It would be so easy to do. He had to admit, that he was quite lonely since Katherine's death. Being with Eva would help him ease some of that loneliness, but it would also be a betrayal to Katherine. He could feel the warmth of Eva from across the room and imagined himself beneath the covers in a lustful embrace. But he couldn't, there was too much to do.

"On the contrary, I wanted to know if you have lost your mind or maybe just your ethics." JJ could not tell if this was an act on Eva's part, or if she really didn't care about the magnitude of her courtroom actions today.

"What do you mean? I thought I did you a favor, and this is how you repay me?"

She feigned a pained expression as she looked at JJ apologetically.

"Since when did you allow friendship or anything else for that matter to interfere with your judicial ethics and judgment? By the way, for the record, you didn't do me a favor. You circumvented justice."

"I love it when you're self-righteous. It makes you even sexier. Besides, you know I don't have any patience for prosecutorial incompetence. I just saved you the trouble of making a motion to dismiss the case. The State was about to botch this case just as they do practically every other case they try." She said this as she walked seductively over to JJ. "Now let's just leave the day's events at the courthouse."

"Eva, you know the prosecution is going to appeal, and your actions are going to be reviewed by the Judicial Tenure Commission, and they'll have a field day with you. What were you thinking?"

"I was thinking that I have served the citizens of the City of Detroit, the County of Wayne, and the State of Michigan long enough. Perhaps it's time I leave this thankless public service job."

"What do you mean; you wanted to be a judge all of your career. Why would you throw it away now?" JJ could sense a futility in Eva's spirit that he had not seen before. She would never give up except on her own terms.

As Eva came nearer, JJ could smell her perfume and the odor of alcohol on her breath. He braced himself for her embrace. She was warm. Oh so warm. And she had obviously been drinking. He only had a short amount of time to find out what he needed to know, before she spiraled out of control. Eva was a determined woman and she usually got what she wanted.

Before he could speak, she was all hands and tongue. He could taste the alcohol now, and Eva was being her persuasive best. But this wasn't what he came here for; or was it? He cursed himself for his weakness, but he did not push her away. He began to respond to Eva's advances as he probed her body with his hands. She was firm and soft in just the right way, and her body was responsive to his touch. His clothes were coming off as they fell onto the king sized bed in a passionate heap. Eva was wild in her alcohol-fueled state. JJ was content to follow her lead. He allowed her to do with him as she pleased. Her body was hungry and JJ was surprised at his own insatiable appetite. Gone was his reluctance. It was replaced by desire borne out of loneliness and pain. He closed his eyes, trying to forget everything; Katherine, Bobby, Eva and One Detroit, Inc. He was successful for a while, as the problems of the past rolled away in spasms of pleasure.

It was sometime later, he couldn't recall just how much later. Eva's bedroom was completely dark and she was sound asleep. She was enjoying the sleep of passion and too much alcohol. He quietly got out of bed careful not to wake Eva. He grabbed a towel from the bathroom and wrapped it around his waist. He slipped out of the bedroom not sure what he was looking for. He was unsuccessful in getting Eva to tell him anything. Perhaps there were other clues here. He went over to her study and turned on the light. She was incredibly neat. Everything was organized and in its place. He opened desk drawers, careful not to disturb Eva in the bedroom. He didn't know what he hoped to find, but any clue would be helpful. As he rummaged inside the bottom drawer of her desk, he saw it; it was a plain old file folder. It contents were anything but plain however. It was a wire transfer confirmation from the account of

One Detroit, Inc. to Eva Moody, first installment Two Million Five Hundred Thousand Dollars. It was dated today, and sent to her account at Comerica Bank. Perhaps it was payment for today's dismissal, or perhaps something more. Whatever, it was important and incriminating.

He needed a copy, quickly, before Eva woke up. He eyed the fax machine on the desk and pushed the print button, hoping the machine was fast and quiet. He fed the page and waited for it to print. He quickly grabbed the copy and placed the original back in the folder and into the drawer. He turned around, half expecting Eva to be looking over his shoulder. He breathed a sigh of relief as he looked into the bedroom and saw her still sleeping. He found his clothes, slipped the paper in his pocket, and quickly got dressed. He glanced over at Eva still blissfully asleep. He wondered how she had gone from the innocent little naïve country girl from Idelwild, Michigan, to someone who fixed cases and possibly conspired to commit murder. It was becoming more complicated, and he knew that he had some tough choices ahead. But he swore on Katherine's grave that he would find the killers and deal with them and by God's grace, he would.

Chapter 27

JJ AGAIN AWOKE WITH A SENSE of foreboding. Since Katherine's death, this had been a persistent feeling. It was something he couldn't seem to shake. He had to admit it wasn't an entirely unjustified sensation. If recent events taught him anything, it was to trust his feelings. He wondered what he could expect next. It was still early; he would wait for Junior to wake up so they could plan their next steps. He had cleared his calendar, expecting Bobby's case to last at least two weeks. It would give him an opportunity to pursue Katherine's killer aggressively, and to dig more deeply into the inner workings of One Detroit, Inc. He turned on the local news. He would have a light workout and fix himself breakfast. The television volume was turned down, but he was surprised to see Harvey Stone's face on the screen, so he found the remote to turn up the volume. The scene shifted to Belle Isle, as he watched crime scene investigators swarm around a vehicle like insects. He listened in amazement as the reporter described the scene.

"Early this morning police discovered a body believed to be Brianna Tuller who apparently died of a drug overdose. Police found her body with a hypodermic syringe still in her arm. There was an undetermined amount of what is believed to be heroin also found in the vehicle. The police estimate her time of death at 4:00 p.m. What makes her death especially significant is that she was the primary prosecution witness in the highly publicized case of

Bobby Bennett. Bennett's case was dismissed when Tuller failed to appear for the start of the trial. Judge Eva Moody dismissed the case against Bennett yesterday. Reporting live from Belle Isle, Jerry Miller channel seven-action news."

JJ was stunned. He knew that somehow, One Detroit, Inc. was behind this, but he didn't know just how. He knew who might know and he quickly dialed Eva's number. He waited for her to answer and was disappointed when she did not. He decided against working out, opting for a quick shower. He would head to the courthouse to talk to Eva and get some information on Brianna's death. His sense of foreboding was justified, and he wondered just how far One Detroit, Inc. would go.

JJ quickly finished his shower and knocked on Junior's door. When Junior did not answer, he quietly opened the door. He could hear the loud snoring, and looked on the nightstand and saw the empty Vodka bottle. It would be difficult waking Junior, but he needed him today. He shook him and called his name as Junior aroused himself from his vodka-induced sleep.

"Junior, it's JJ. Time to wake up."

"What?" He stammered, his tongue thick with vodka. "What time is it?"

"It's about six-thirty. We need to get an early start."

"No sweat. Give me about thirty minutes and I'll be ready." He said attempting to rouse himself.

"I'll put on some coffee. You look like you could use some. There are some crazy things happening that we need to deal with. I need you to use your special talents to shake some bushes."

"That's what I was waiting to hear. Now I can earn my money." He jumped out of the bed heading for the shower. "I'll be out in a minute," he yelled over the noise of the shower. JJ knew it was time to take the offensive.

Harvey Stone was having a busy morning. The stumpy homicide detective was in his element. He loved nothing better than a good homicide, except talking to the media about a good homicide. As the television crews were packing their equipment and he had finished barking orders to the uniformed officers and the crime tech, Stone could not help but chuckle to himself about the irony of this death. It was not officially a homicide, not yet anyway. It was just too delicious not to enjoy a moment of personal triumph. Not only did he have some highly coveted airtime on all of the local affiliates, the national networks would pick up the video bites as well. As the chief homicide detective for the city of Detroit, he was the anointed expert on all things homicidal.

This apparent homicide, Brianna Tuller's apparent heroin overdose, managed to tie up some very untidy loose ends. Her death brought finality and closure to Bobby Bennett's case. The discovery of her heroin-laced body meant the DA had no reason to appeal Judge Moody's dismissal. Stone was uneasy about the judge's aggressive move in court, and he could not trust the system to get it right. He didn't wait for approval from his partners; they may not have appreciated the seriousness of the situation. That's why he was on the team, to handle the loose ends so that they wouldn't have to get their hands dirty. He didn't care about his role. The only thing that mattered was his share of the proceeds from the Corktown deal.

He was not surprised when his cell phone rang and the caller ID said the Law Firm of Wright and Connors. He had expected the call earlier. He knew what to expect from these soft lawyer types who invariably got nervous when things got rough. He would handle them and move on to the next project.

"Hey, what's up."

"We need to have a meeting immediately. Meet us in the lower level of the parking structure in fifteen minutes."

The phone went silent in Stone's hand and he stared at it for moments. He could not believe the nerve of those pencil neck pretty boys and their condescending tones. Perhaps they could push around clients and attorneys, but Harvey Stone was another matter. He would have to help them adjust their attitudes. He could feel his anger rising as he got in his car for the ten minute ride downtown to his meeting. The closer he got to the building the angrier he got.

When he arrived at the lower level of the structure, he was seething. All of his life he had been fighting to prove himself. This time was no different. He would show them just who Harvey Stone was. He saw Randy and Victor nervously pacing back and forth. It was not a comforting sign. Before he got out of his car, he checked his weapon to make sure he had a full clip. He checked his backup and his knife just to be sure. Finally, he got out of the car and slowly approached the two lawyers. He did not know what to expect, so he was prepared for anything. As he approached them, he felt the steel of the knife in his pocket. He went over in his mind all of the possible scenarios of engagement, just in case it became necessary. You never knew. Nothing in his thinking prepared him for what came next.

Chapter 28

IT WAS THE NEXT MORNING BEFORE Eva Ann Moody woke. She was surprised and disappointed to see that JJ was not there. Although she was groggy from too much alcohol, JJ's lovemaking more than made up for her slight hangover. She really needed the release. Things had been so tense lately with the trial and the finalizing of the One Detroit, Inc. project; she was wound way too tight. JJ was perfect for soothing whatever ailed her. Although he was angry with her, he rarely said no to her and meant it. She remembered what she had been celebrating when JJ arrived; the $2.5 Million Dollar wire transfer. She was probably the richest woman in Wayne County this morning. She turned on the television set for the morning news, as she looked around the office for the wire transfer confirmation. She just had to see it one more time. As she headed into the study, she saw a local reporter interviewing the familiar figure of Harvey Stone. It was an obvious crime scene and it appeared to be from Belle Isle. Stone was saying the victim is a black female in her early thirties, and that she died from an apparent drug overdose. The reporters were yelling questions at Stone and he was waiting for the best question before he responded.

"Detective Stone, can you confirm the identity of the victim for us?" The reporter asked the obligatory question that always yielded the usual response. This time was no different.

"I'm sorry; we can't provide that information until we notify the next of kin."

Eva, shook her head, these things happened so frequently in Detroit, that the interviews almost seemed scripted. She kept on with her search for the confirmation. She knew she had placed it in the bottom drawer of the desk, where she placed all incoming mail until she could file it. But, the letter was not there. That was odd. The reporter's next question distracted her and a chill overcame her as the reporter asked.

"Can you confirm that this is the missing witness in the Bobby Bennett trial that was dismissed by Judge Moody yesterday?"

Eva's heart was racing as she strained to hear Stone's response. The reporter must have had some idea this was Brianna before he asked the question. Otherwise, to suggest it would be too remote.

"I can neither confirm nor deny that this is the missing witness. As I indicated a moment ago, we have to notify the next of kin, and I would caution you not to speculate on the identity of the victim until we disclose that information."

"Can you at least confirm the possible time of death?'

"The victim has been deceased for at least 24 to 36 hours. It's difficult to tell until we get an autopsy. Because the cold weather delayed the onset of rigor mortis, the body was partially preserved."

Eva set down in the chair, shocked by the breaking developments. She wondered what this meant. Did Brianna die before the trial, or was it a reaction to the dismissal. Was she so distraught with her ruling that she took an overdose of drugs? For one of the few times since Eva had become a judge, she truly felt responsible. Generally, justice was an easy thing to administer. You just followed the law and did your job, no matter how unpleasant. But this time it was different. Maybe it was, as JJ said, wrong for her to circumvent the system, especially to aid her own personal greed. Eva's normally tough resolve was wilting. Did her actions set in motion some irreversible cataclysmic event that might have changed lives for the worse? She began to cry. She didn't know if it was a result of the news she just heard, or just a by-product of too much alcohol last night. She took a moment to compose herself. She tried to remember last evening's events. She remembered the wire; she remembered celebrating, and JJ's visit. After that, things were fuzzy. One thing that was not fuzzy was that the wire confirmation was in her drawer last evening. Only JJ could have removed it. She continued to search lifting papers to locate the wire. Her frustration rising, she was about to give up hope of finding the paper when she saw it underneath a folder. She sighed with relief, not wanting to think about what could happen if JJ knew about the transaction. She sat down at the desk to calm herself. The news about Brianna had shaken her. Throughout her career on the bench, she had never allowed her personal motives to interfere with her judicial ethics. The one time it did, there were tragic results. Maybe it was all starting to unravel. Katherine's murder now Brianna's death. She hoped that would be the end of these matters. She would have to pull herself together for just a little while longer, she told herself. $2.5 million dollars was worth the deception.

She pulled up her blackberry to see what her schedule looked like today; she was contemplating taking the day off. She was starting to get comfortable with the feeling of being independently wealthy. She remembered that she had cancelled all of her docket in expectation of the Bennett trial; now that it was over, she was free for a few days. She would take some much needed time off to reenergize. She would call the court administrator and let him know she wouldn't be in today, and possibly tomorrow. She would go to the spa and pamper herself.

As she turned back to her desk, something unusual caught her eye. It was there in the fax machine- a single white sheet of paper. She could not recall the last time she used the fax machine. In fact, she almost never used it all; she relied on her office machine or she received documents electronically. That's what caught her attention. She took the paper out of the machine, reading it quickly. Her heart was racing as she realized what it meant. The date read last evening. It was a confirmation statement that someone had made a copy. It listed the time. She was furious at JJ. But more importantly, she wondered what he might do.

She cursed, trying to figure out her next step. She considered all of her options and none of them were appealing. She could take the money and run.

But, how long would that last before the authorities pursued her. She could call JJ and try to reason with him. Perhaps the money could persuade him. Immediately she realized the futility of that option. She cursed JJ again and consoled herself with the fact that JJ set this chain of events in motion. He would have to suffer the consequences. Although she knew in her heart this was not true, there was no other alternative. So she did what she had always seen her grandmother do in times of crisis, she prayed. Then she dialed the number.

The conversation with Victor left her with a sense of helplessness. It made her feel that she had no control over what happened next. For a woman who worked all of her life to control her environment, she now realized just how little control she actually had. She could hear it in Victor's voice, the unspoken condemnation, "this is an unnecessary complication, and how could you be so careless? Forget it; I understand, it was the great JJ Battle," he said dismissively. "I'll take care of it." She shuddered in fear as she thought of all the implications. She did something she had not done since she was a child; she went to bed, burrowed beneath the covers, and cried herself to sleep.

Chapter 29

HARVEY STONE WAS GETTING TIRED OF taking orders, especially from these lightweight knuckleheads in the expensive suits. They didn't have a clue about him or what he was capable of, which made his indignation even greater. He had been taking orders all of his life and now he resented it. He had to admit that although it paid very well, he still resented the arrogance of Victor and Randy. This hastily called meeting was an inconvenience; he had scheduled a morning rendezvous with one of his project honeys. They usually shipped the kids off to school and old Sarge came by for a couple of hours of delight. So Stone was particularly surly when he arrived. As he approached, he could see Victor, Randy and Rahsheed Truman all huddled together like nervous schoolboys ready to scatter when the school bully arrived.

He got out of the car as they stared in his direction. They exchanged gruff greetings. Stone wondered why they were meeting here in the cold and the exhaust of the parking garage, but said nothing. These guys were amateurs who had probably watched too much television. In any case, he would go along with their plan as long as it continued to pay.

"I'm sorry about the short notice and the cryptic message, but we might have a developing situation on our hands," Victor explained. "I got a call from Eva this morning and she was getting a little too squeamish for my tastes. She was sounding as if she wanted out of our little business arrangement. And to top it off, she may have allowed JJ Battle to get his hands on a copy of the wire confirmation."

"Yeah, we are too close to completing the project to have her flaking out now. Besides, she has already fulfilled her primary duty- making Bobby's case go away," Randy said with finality. He usually deferred to Victor on most matters but recognized the need for quick and decisive action.

"Well, what do you propose?" Stone asked searching the trio of lawyers and trying to determine just how far they were willing to go. It didn't take long for a response as Rahsheed jumped right in.

"As I see it, there are two issues we have to deal with. First, what will we do with Eva, if anything, and secondly, what about JJ? He could be a real boil on our asses. He's still crazy since Katherine's death. There's no telling what he might do."

Stone was content to let the lawyers sort out the problem themselves. He wanted everyone to have a role in this little conspiracy, whatever the outcome. He knew where this was leading and wondered how long it would take them to come to that realization as well. It didn't take long as Victor said what the others were thinking; Eva had to go. Although it was a drastic solution, it had many residual benefits. It would eliminate some untidy loose ends, and with one less person in the equation, it would increase everyone else's share.

The decision to silence Eva had been a relatively quick decision. They just couldn't trust her judgment. She was panicking and having second thoughts, which jeopardized everyone. The way she handled the dismissal invited too much scrutiny, which could ultimately lead back to One Detroit, Inc. They could not tolerate that kind of scrutiny.

"She's no longer an asset. She could compromise the rest of the deal. I think we know what has to happen next," Victor said.

JJ on the other hand was a more problematic issue. They couldn't be sure what he knew, or if it was worth risking the deal to include him. The sudden discovery of bodies showing up all over the city would be too messy. They all had their reasons for wanting JJ out of the way. Victor's were personal. JJ had been his nemesis since law school, and there was JJ's law school fling with Carlena that he had never forgotten.

Randy's reasons were economic- the sooner the deal was done, the sooner he could receive more proceeds thereby satisfying some of his annoying creditors. He had been chasing money so long he was tired of the chase. It was starting to affect his work.

Rahsheed's motives were political and financial; the sooner the Corktown deal concluded, the sooner his citywide profile for getting things done would improve. Then he could take a run at the Mayor's office for the next election. He would have visibility and power, courtesy of his new alliances.

It was Stone, however, who provided the ultimate solution. It was always that way; while the so-called leaders were figuring out how to lead, he usually came up with a solution. This time was no different. To the lawyers and executive types, the unthinkable was too remote for them. But for Stone, he was trained to look at the hard options and to make tough decisions quickly. He had no problem silencing JJ Battle anyway; he had become a nuisance to Stone.

"How about we go after two birds with one stone, excuse the play on words? It's simple; we do the judge, and frame JJ for the murder." We know he was there at her place, because he made the copy of the wire transfer. This way we eliminate them both. JJ will be so preoccupied defending himself; he won't have time to meddle in One Detroit, Inc.'s business. Since I'll be heading up any potential investigation, I'll make sure it's very uncomfortable for him. You lawyer types can use your PR sources to sensationalize the story, while we discreetly finish the project. By the time JJ gets himself out of this one, we'll all have much larger bank accounts." Stone looked at each of his three partners, checking for any sign of hesitation. He knew that once the wheels were in motion, they couldn't be stopped.

They looked at Stone in both fear and amazement, thinking how brilliant his plan was. They nodded with appreciation seeing him in a new light. Victor had always seen Stone as nothing more than muscle to handle all of the difficult issues and provide a hard edge for the operation. He was proving to be more than just a hit man, Victor thought.

"How soon do you want me to handle this? The sooner the better. It's going to cost you."

"We'll leave that up to you," Victor said, already thinking about the re-percussions. It was nasty business, but so was One Hundred Million Dollars.

Stone got back into his city issued vehicle and turned on the heater full blast. He waited to see if the lawyers would spend any additional time discussing things. They did not, as Victor, Randy went back to their offices, and Rahsheed presumably went back to City Hall. Stone pulled out his cell phone, dialed a number, and waited for the beep. He then entered the numbers 999 followed by 930. He quickly hung up the phone and headed for the Airport Motel. The Rat would know to meet him outside at nine-thirty. He pulled up outside and waited. The Rat came trudging out, pulling on his coat in one motion. He got in, feeling the warmth of the car.

"Hey Sarge. Something urgent?"

"Yeah, got some cleaning that needs to be done today, ASAP. I'll take you there and show you the location. No mistakes and no evidence left behind."

The Rat was disappointed. He never made mistakes. But, he understood. He had worked with the Sarge long enough to know that what he meant was that this is important. He didn't have to tell the Rat twice. You never got a second chance. They were silent as they drove to Palmer Woods. It had started to snow and the roads were slippery. They discreetly pulled down the block and waited. Stone provided the Rat with a photograph of Judge Eva Ann Moody. He studied the face and features and committed them to memory. It was an older home, which had been remodeled with new security windows and doors. It would not be easy, but he would find a way. After they had watched the house in silence for thirty minutes, they headed back to the Rat's Motel. Stone let him out of the car with instructions to report to him when the mission was completed.

Chapter 30

JJ KNEW IF HE WERE TO find Katherine's killers, he would have to take some risks. That meant confronting the killers and exposing himself and Junior to the possibility that they could be killed. He didn't care anymore. With each subsequent deed by One Detroit, Inc., he felt a greater urgency that they had to be stopped. First, it was Katherine and now Brianna. He had decided that Stone was at the center of everything; he would be the one coordinating the murders. He was the logical choice to pursue. JJ had tangled with Stone on many occasions, and he had no illusions of what he was capable of doing. But JJ's advantage was the fact that Stone had no idea of what JJ was capable of.

The logical place to start was to follow Stone in the hope that he would provide them with some concrete evidence implicating him in Katherine's murder. They decided to wait for Stone at headquarters. Thirteen hundred Beaubien was a difficult place to begin surveillance. Logistically, it was a multi-sided building, and there was no public parking. There were numerous marked and unmarked police vehicles parked and double-parked around the building. This made for a permanent bottleneck. When you added the fact that all of the streets around the building were one-way streets, you had cars continually circling the building. Those brave enough or foolish enough to double park would often find their cars ticketed or in some cases towed. It all added to the unpredictable nature of the Detroit Police Department.

JJ and Junior were inconspicuously double-parked across the street from the precinct. They were in Junior's beat up Jeep Cherokee. They spotted Stone's department -issued Chrysler parked near the building. It was easy to spot Stone's vehicle because he had a large Chief of Homicide sign on the dashboard. It was 10:30 in the morning and JJ assumed that Stone would be wrapping up the morning roll call and briefings. He hoped they wouldn't have to wait too long. Junior wasn't the best conversationalist, and the morning had started to drag. It wasn't long before their patience was rewarded, when Stone appeared bounding out the front door with a purposeful step. He was talking on his cell phone as he got into his car. He quickly sped off headed down Gratiot toward the city airport and the East Side.

"Remember to make sure you keep plenty of distance behind Stone," JJ reminded Junior.

"Cousin I told you not to worry, I was tracking Viet Cong in the jungles of Southeast Asia, when you were still trying to figure out how to shoot a jump shot. If I could track those sneaky bastards, I can certainly track Stone."

"You're right. I've heard this story a million times. How you survived in the jungle for six months with no food or water. That's right they were supposed to make a movie about your life story starring Denzel Washington if I recall."

"Damn right. That was before I had that little problem over at the VA. Damn quack doctors, they'll kill you over at that place. But, that's beside the point. I know what I'm doing."

"I know you do. But the point is that I don't want Stone to know what you're doing," JJ laughed good-naturedly.

"I see you've got jokes."

The both rode in silence as Junior kept a one to two block distance between them and Stone. It wasn't long before Stone reached his destination, The Airport Motel on Gratiot. It wasn't one of the city's finer establishments and JJ wondered what Stone was doing there. It wasn't long before they had their answer as the Rat came bouncing out of room number eight.

"I'll be damned. You just can't kill a rat, no matter how hard you try, and they say cats have nine lives. I know one rat that has more lives than a cat. They say that rats are the most adaptable mammals in the world. I guess they were right. I thought that vermin had died in Nam years ago. I guess that's the company line when you get into black ops in the army."

"What are you talking about Junior? Is there something I need to know? Do you know this guy?"

"Yeah, I know him and there's a lot you need to know, but I'm not sure you're ready for the answer. You remember how I said this could get dirty and dangerous, and you had to be prepared for anything, well anything just showed up."

"You remember the guy Lindsay described at Katherine's memorial service? That's him. You see that rodent looking character that just got in the car with Stone, he and I go way back together, back to the jungles of Nam. We were together in Special Forces. Our unit was an elite advance crew. They dropped us in a zone ten miles behind enemy lines. Our job was to train the locals to fight the Viet Cong and help them set up an infrastructure. The Rat as we called him was our sniper. He was the best sniper the army ever had. He wasn't just a sniper; he was a cold-blooded calculating killer. It didn't matter what the situation was, the Rat was going to come out alive. He would do whatever he had to do to survive. That's why we all wanted him on our team. That boy could kill a fly from two hundred yards with a sniper rifle. Nobody knows how many kills he had. We lost count. Stone was his commanding officer before he came into Special Forces, and he talked about Stone like he was his father. If you're looking for Katherine's killer, you found him. He probably did Brianna too. When this guy shows up, the murder rate goes up. It makes sense for Stone to call this guy in for the heavy stuff. That way he don't have to worry about the locals flaking out on him."

"What do you suggest we do?" JJ asked with a look of concern on his face.

"Nothing for now, we just observe. What do you do to catch a Rat? You set a trap. That's what we're going to do. This is going to get nasty, and you might have to get your hands dirty. If you want me too, I can call in some reinforcements to help us get the job done. It's up to you. But, I'll tell you this JJ, we can't leave this guy alive, or nobody will live to tell about it. But for now, let's just see what these guys are up to."

They continued to drive in silence for a while, carefully remaining a discreet distance behind Stone and the Rat. They headed down Gratiot and merged onto the Ford freeway headed westbound. Traffic had just started to get congested. There were a few more cars between them and Stone. Neither JJ nor Junior said anything more about what they might have to do, they both settled into the ride and their own thoughts.

They could see Stone merge onto the Lodge freeway going northbound. It had begun to lightly snow and the roads were becoming wet. Because of the freezing temperatures, the snow had started to freeze. The salt trucks had not yet salted the roads and traffic was beginning to slow. They could still see Stone in the distance as they continued north. Suddenly, the car in front of Junior began to fishtail and lose control of the vehicle as he drifted into the right lane. JJ could not believe what happened next. It was like a weird form of bumper cars, as cars on the crowded freeway tried in vain to stop on the wet pavement. Car after car collided with a sickening crash of metal. Junior fought to maintain control of the vehicle and to avoid the melee in front of them. He was too late. He tried to veer smoothly to his right to pass on the median as he pumped his brakes to keep the car from skidding out of control. But, before he could steer the car in that direction they were rear ended and pushed sideways as another vehicle struck them on the driver's side pushing them forward. Junior quickly regained control of the vehicle, lightly tapping the brakes and gently turning the steering wheel to the right. The car came out of the spin and came to a stop on the right median.

"Are you alright?" JJ asked, since Junior received most of the impact on the driver's side.

"What kind of question is that? Did you see what just happened?" They were distracted as Stone and the Rat were now clearly out of sight. The freeway had come to a complete stop. There was no way they could catch Stone or know where they were headed. They both got out inspecting the damage.

"Damn." Junior said as he surveyed the damage of the multi-car pileup. "These are some no driving folks. I ought to pull out my pistol and shoot every one of these sorry bastards."

"Yeah, I almost feel the same way. The problem is that Stone and the Rat are long gone. They were our only lead." JJ felt the frustration of losing Stone and his henchman. It was the first time since this ordeal began that he had a sense of getting closer to finding Katherine's murderer. If Junior was right, and it was the Rat, at least they knew where he was staying. The next part was finding the evidence implicating him in Katherine and Brianna's deaths. Junior was right again, when this guy showed up the death toll increased. They just needed a plan to catch him.

They got back in the car with the heater turned on high, and waited for the tow truck to arrive. It was over an hour before the tow truck arrived and the snow had continued to fall accumulating to about two inches. They discussed strategy while they waited and decided to go back to the motel and to find out what the Rat was up to. When the tow truck driver finally arrived, they hitched a ride to the dealership as Junior found out how much it was going to cost to get his prized possession repaired. JJ put his mind at ease as he volunteered to pay the repair cost. Junior was reluctant to file a claim, which probably meant he had no insurance. That was the least of their worries but at least it put Junior's mind at ease. JJ called Marsha at the office and asked her to give them a ride home so that they could get the Lincoln and continue the surveillance.

When Marsha arrived, Junior began to flirt with here in the most inept way that JJ had seen in a long time. Marsha, to her credit was amused by the whole process and went along good-naturedly. At least Marsha was keeping Junior's mind off his wrecked car.

"JJ, where have you been keeping this fine specimen of a woman all of my life?" Junior asked with a foolish grin on his face.

"She's been down at the office, like always."

"Why haven't I seen her before, she's a treasure, meant for the world to see."

"Why Cousin Junior, I was thinking the same thing about you, why haven't I seen you before, handsome?" Marsha was obviously enjoying herself. If there was one skill that Marsha possessed, it was the ability to handle men. She managed a seductive glance back at Junior in the back seat, and JJ could almost hear Junior involuntarily catch his breath.

"Both of you just need to stop it, you're both old enough to know better." JJ said.

"JJ you can't stop the laws of nature. Don't player hate because Marsha and me are attracted to each other.

"Marsha, is there anything of interest going on in the office?"

"Just the usual stuff. I continued all of your cases for a month like you told me."

"That's why you're the best in the business." JJ said appreciatively.

"No, it's because I work for the best boss in the business."

"Okay, okay, Junior added, exasperated. You guys are making me sick. I get it. You both are the greatest. Can we leave it at that?" They all laughed heartily.

As they arrived at JJ's house, Junior decided he couldn't resist one last pass at Marsha.

"Marsha, why don't you come inside for a quick drink before you head home?" Junior asked sounding somewhat charming for a change.

"I would love to Junior, but I have to pick up my kids from day care." She smiled to herself knowing that young children were like kryptonite for most men.

"Honey, if you think you're going to scare me away with a few kids, guess again. Uncle Junior has been to Nam and back, and nothing scares me."

"Well maybe I'll have to check my schedule a little closer and check my availability." She said.

"Why don't you do that and let my assistant JJ here know when you're available." He said, warming to the task.

They all broke out in laughter and enjoyed the moment. It was somewhat funny yet a little disconcerting to JJ to see his cousin trying to make a move on Marsha. JJ knew Marsha could handle herself so he didn't feel the need to intervene. He shifted his focus to the Rat and wondered what he would do next. They said their goodbyes and watched Marsha drive away. "She's a heck of a woman," Junior said admiringly.

"Yes she is, but we got more important things to do right now remember?"

"Well I don't know if they are more important but I agree they are important."

"Let's head over to the Airport Motel and see what the Rat's up to. Just for the record, I'm driving this time."

"That hurts JJ. That really hurts." Junior grabbed his heart just like Fred Sanford used to on the old Sanford and Son shows as if he were having the big one.

"I'm just being truthful with you Junior; you are a danger on the roads." They laughed good-naturedly, as they headed over to the Airport motel and their rendezvous with the Rat. They drove around the building and parked out front. They did not see any sign of the Rat or Stone. As they pulled around the front of the building, a white van was already pulling away from the curb. Neither the van nor JJ and Junior saw each other. This would not be the last time their paths would cross. The Rat left undetected on his way to death and destruction.

Chapter 31

THE RAT BEGAN ASSEMBLING HIS GEAR with care and precision. He gathered all of his essential tools. He made sure his two Beretta 380's were loaded with silencers and there were extra clips for each. He packed his burglary tools and made sure he had his syringes filled with Rohypnol and GHB. He liked the combination because it subdued his victim easily. He then dressed carefully in his gray work coveralls that made him look like an ordinary repairman. He prided himself on his deception, the ability to make himself invisible. In his line of work, it was a useful skill. He loaded the van and thought about how he would carry out his mission. He knew from the Sarge's intelligence that the subject was home. That would make getting inside a little more complicated. The drive over was a short one. He parked the van in front of the house and waited. At this time of the day, there wasn't much traffic. He waited and thought about what he might encounter when he entered the house. He became excited as he thought about what could possibly happen. Normally, he would have been able to do some pre surveillance, which might have been helpful. But, all of the uncertainty just fueled his adrenaline. He made a mental checklist of what he had to do once he entered, and now he was ready.

He grabbed his tool belt from the seat of the truck and closed the door. He went around the side of the house with a flashlight searching for gas lines, electrical outlets, phone lines, and alarm systems. If he was discovered, he always had a ready explanation. When he found the phone lines, he pulled the wire cutters and carefully clipped the lines. He recognized the alarm system and quickly de-activated the alarm. He laughed to himself at how simple it was to neutralize an alarm. People thought they were secure behind their elaborate security systems, but the opposite was true. They were more vulnerable because they had that false sense of security. Next, he went to the patio door at the back of the house. The patio was designed for privacy and was hidden in a huge expanse of trees. He worked quickly but not so quickly that he would be noticed. He pulled the small pliers from the tool belt and a thin screwdriver and proceeded to pick the lock. This took skill and patience. Carefully he probed the cylinders of the lock until the tumblers clicked and the lock opened. He gently pushed open the door waiting for an alarm siren. There was none.

He gave his eyes time to acclimate to the darkened basement. He could see the stairs leading up to the main level. He hoped the basement door was not locked or padlocked, because it would cause him to alter his plan. He turned the knob with his left hand while clinching the Beretta in his right. He pushed open the door not knowing what to expect on the other side. He found himself in a modern clean kitchen. He waited for the sound of a dog or cat. A barking dog was his worst enemy. It might alert the owner before he could silence the animal. He waited but did not hear anything. He got his bearings and quickly got a picture of the layout of the house. The bedrooms appeared to be up the far staircase. He proceeded to check all of the rooms downstairs. They were empty. He waited, filled with excitement. He enjoyed the hunt and the surprise of the victim when they knew death was near. It was just like back in West Virginia when he hunted as a kid. He liked to make a game of it. He sometimes killed them slow, enjoying their pain. It all depended on what the mission called for.

He headed for the staircase, and stopped abruptly as he heard a noise coming from upstairs. He listened as he pressed himself against the far wall and gripped the Beretta. At first, he thought it was conversation, but then realized it was coming from the television. He waited, listening for other sounds coming from upstairs. He heard nothing. He slowly made his way up the stairs, taking one stair at a time. When he got to the landing at the top of the stairs, he could see the light flickering from the television in the master suite. He waited, controlling his breathing and excitement. He didn't know what he would find in the room but he was prepared for anything, almost. As he crept forward, now on his knees, careful to stay below the line of sight, he wasn't prepared for what he found. Judge Eva Ann Moody was spread across the bed completely stark naked and sound asleep.

This was going to be easier than he thought. He crawled over to the bed and reached for the syringe with the rohypnol cocktail. He didn't allow himself to be distracted by her nakedness, although he could not remember when he had last been with a woman. He didn't have time for relationships or complicated emotional entanglements. When he had the need for a woman, he paid for the privilege and found a prostitute. It was a perfect business arrangement. There was no commitment. When the act was completed, he politely excused himself and left, or if she were at his room, he politely paid her and asked her to leave. There was no lingering feelings or uncomfortable or awkward post coital cuddling. He liked it that way; there was no confusion or misunderstanding. It was simple yet effective.

He edged closer to the bed. He could hear her breathing and see her breasts rise and fall with each slow breath. What a waste he briefly thought, but forced those thoughts from his mind. He had a job to do, and he would complete it. He was next to the bed and he could smell her perfume as she lay on her side facing the window. He raised the syringe, poised to plunge it deep into her throat, when her eyes abruptly opened. They both stared in disbelief. Neither moved immediately as Eva tried to make sense of what was happening through the fog of sleep. They moved at the same time, Eva scrambling to the other side of the bed with the Rat diving on top of her. She struggled as he landed on top of her pinning her arms back. She managed to scream,

"Please don't hurt me!"

"Shh!" he cautioned, placing his free hand over her mouth to quiet a scream. "I'm going to inject you with this syringe, or we'll do it a more painful way. But I need you calm."

"What do you want from me?" She pleaded, as he again forced his hand over her mouth. "Is it money you want? " She tried to think of what was happening to her and to find a way out. She thought if she could just negotiate with this rodent like man maybe he would be reasonable and spare her life.

The Rat was used to people pleading for their lives and was unmoved. He grabbed both of her wrists with his left hand and plunged the syringe into her throat with his right. He squeezed the plunger until the syringe was empty and removed it from her neck. He could see the shock registering on her face as she struggled to free herself. Slowly the drug took effect as she lost control of her motor function and speech. The Rat lifted himself off Eva and waited. She was completely incapacitated, and it was time for him to complete his assignment.

He watched her as she followed him with her eyes. He picked up a pillow from beside her and placed it over her head. He held it there with his full weight until she was no longer breathing. He waited, thinking how simple it was taking a life. Moments ago, she was a living breathing woman, and now it was as if she didn't matter. He began to clean up and arrange the evidence. He closed her eyes and covered her lifeless body. He took one last look around the room, and felt no remorse. He didn't know this woman nor did he have any feelings for her in death. She may have been an important Judge before, but now she was just another corpse to be buried.

He felt nothing except the satisfaction of knowing that he performed his job well. It was not his place to judge her. That was God's province. All he knew is that one day he too would be judged, and he shivered at the thought. He knew that when that day came judgment would be harsh. The Rat slipped out the patio door as unobtrusively as he had entered, leaving death in his wake.

Chapter 32

THEY WAITED OUTSIDE THE RAT'S MOTEL for another hour hoping that he would surface. He did not return. It was nighttime and they were tired of waiting. They were hungry so they headed over to Green's Barbecue for some ribs and strategy planning. Although it was in the heart of the ghetto on the east side of town, they served some of the best ribs and chicken in the city. It didn't hurt that JJ knew the owner. It guaranteed the best service. As they ate their meal, they also planned their strategy. They now knew or at least suspected that Stone and the Rat were behind the killings of Katherine and Brianna. All they needed to do was to predict who would be next and then either take steps to prevent it or catch the Rat in the act. If they considered the most likely candidates there would probably be three who were either loose ends or who posed a threat to uncovering their conspiracy. Bobby Bennett was a likely candidate, because he knew more than anyone about One Detroit, Inc.'s scheme. Eva Moody was also a likely candidate, because she was the most likely to flake out when things got tough, and then there was JJ Battle, because he was starting to become a nuisance to everyone.

"If we consider Eva as the first and most likely target she might already be in danger. She's already received a huge share of the proceeds. Would they risk having to explain the origin of that much money for a State Court Judge? That might start people asking questions." JJ said as he brainstormed aloud.

Junior marveled at how JJ's mind worked, as he theorized about the possible scenarios.

"That might be the least of Eva's worries. If they started thinking that way, it may already be dangerous for her. Her only hope is to help us or leave town. I'm hoping that her anger at being betrayed by Stone and the One Detroit, Inc. boys will make her want to help us. She'll get a little dirty in the process, but at least she'll survive. Frankly, what choice does she have?" For the first time since this ordeal began, JJ could finally see an ending.

"There's another option. We could let the natural course of things evolve and clean up the mess." Junior said.

"How do you propose we do that?" JJ asked, somewhat unnerved by Junior's suggestion.

"I'm talking about the beauty of videotape. We set up cameras to record the perimeter of Eva's property. It would record everyone entering or leaving her home and the time of day. Of course, we would have to explain how we came upon such a piece of incriminating evidence, or we could anonymously send it to the local media and law enforcement."

JJ was taken aback at the ingenuity of Junior's plan. It would solve many of their problems without personal risk to themselves. It was brilliant except for one important detail; Eva would be sacrificed in the process. Although she had chosen this group of thieves to undertake this criminal enterprise, she didn't contemplate being murdered. JJ didn't know if he was prepared to be a part of this type of outcome. Either plan would be difficult to implement, but it would probably be easier to tail the Rat and then catch him in the act. It might be easier said than done. At least they now had a plan to follow. JJ knew he would have to contact Eva and share his thoughts about her co-conspirators. He was tired and hoped it could wait until morning.

As they finished their meal, Junior was feeling no pain. JJ was thankful that Junior was with him, he was a good man to have around whenever there was trouble. JJ knew that their next moves would have to be careful ones, with Stone running the investigations it would not be out of the realm of possibilities for him to plant evidence implicating JJ. Tomorrow, if they could not pick up the Rat's trail, perhaps they would focus on Stone. He was at the center of all of the recent events for One Detroit, Inc., and perhaps he would lead them to the evidence they needed.

JJ paid the check and helped Junior into the car. It had been a long day and although there was nothing specific that he could point to, he had a gut feeling that they were getting closer to the truth. He would let Junior sleep it off until late morning and try again to shake the truth from these crooks.

It was nine-thirty in the morning and JJ was awaken by the ringing of his cell phone. Who would be calling him on his cell this early in the morning? He looked at the caller ID and recognized Eva's chambers number. He considered not answering but thought better of it. "What do I owe the honor of a personal call from you Judge?" He said with more emotion than he really felt and a tremendous sense of relief. In spite of the recent encounters, he was still very fond of Eva, and he wanted to help her if he could.

"It's me JJ, Steven, the Judge's clerk." JJ sat up in bed, surprised to hear Steven's voice instead of the Eva's; especially if he was calling from her private chambers. He felt a sense of apprehension as he tried to remember the last time Steven called him at home. It had to be over a year ago, when Steven was having some financial difficulties.

"Hey Steve, I was just surprised to hear your voice, I was expecting Eva," he said trying not to betray his rising fear.

"I didn't know who else to call. Judge Moody hasn't been to work in two days, and I can't reach her on her cell phone or at home. She won't respond to e-mails and I don't know what else to do or who to call. The docket is backing up and the court administrator is starting to ask questions." JJ could hear the concern in his voice, and knew this wasn't like Eva.

"Alright Steve let me check on a few things and see what I come up with. I'll give you a call as soon as I hear something. In the meantime, adjourn court until after lunch. That will buy some time until I can find out what's going on with Eva."

"OK JJ, I knew I could count on you. This just isn't like the Judge; she's been acting sort of weird lately anyway. Well let me know what you find."

JJ jumped out of bed throwing on his clothes as he went. He banged on Junior's door yelling, "Junior we've got to move, there's something serious brewing."

JJ was dialing Eva's number as he hurriedly got dressed and brushed his teeth. He got no answer on the home phone or her cell phone. He could feel his stress level rising, as he went down the hall to wake Junior. He didn't need to worry as Junior was already dressed and lacing up his boots. He didn't know if he slept in his clothes or he was merely a fast dresser, but he was thankful for either.

"What's up JJ, what's the emergency? You sound like my former lieutenant; he always got real excited in a crisis. So what's goin on?"

"Its Eva, her clerk hasn't heard from her in a couple of days and she's not answering her phone or e-mails."

"Could be that she doesn't want to be found or could be somebody doesn't want her found, either way, we better find out." Leave it to Junior to put things in perspective.

They were in the car headed on the Ford Freeway westbound as they passed the spot where they had the accident yesterday. "Did you have to go this way and bring back those painful memories? I was just getting over the damage to my baby."

"I know, but it's the fastest way to Eva's house." JJ was reminded that this was also the way they were headed when they were following Stone and the Rat and wound up involved in the fender bender. Soon they were on the Lodge and exiting at Seven Mile. There wasn't much traffic headed away from the city and they were able to make good time. JJ went over in his mind all of the possible scenarios for Eva's absence, and the likelihood there was an innocent explanation. He hoped that it was just a coincidence that Eva was unavailable. That she was not permanently unavailable due to the Rat's efforts.

It was all so unthinkable, that people he loved and cared about were dying for no real reason except greed. First Katherine and now possibly, Eva, he could feel a tremendous anger and sadness building deep within himself. He knew it was illogical, but he wanted to hurt people and make them pay for what they had done. But, he also knew that there might come a time when he would have to sacrifice his principles and strike back, regardless of the consequences. He was quickly approaching that state of mind.

He understood on a practical and professional level why people killed. He knew all of justifications and psychological profiles that killers possessed. But, he also knew that revenge was a powerful emotion that motivated people to kill. It was the purest of motives and existed since biblical times, "an eye for an eye." The law even made provisions for it, in self-defense, defense of others, and justification defenses. On an intellectual level it all made sense, but the state of mind that he was developing went way beyond logic; it was about righting wrongs and punishing people who took something irreplaceable from you. He knew there was no justice that could give him Katherine back, or allow him to feel the warmth of her skin on his again. But, he could cause her perpetrators to lose something that they valued as well; their lives. He was filled with all types of thoughts as they approached Eva's house. She still had not answered either her home phone or her cell. He even text messaged her to no avail. He pressed down on the accelerator, unconcerned about the snow-covered roads. He wanted to get to Eva as quickly as possible and find her safe and alive. In spite of what they had been through, they still shared a special bond. He wanted to protect her if he could.

As they pulled up to the house and parked, there was no activity in the neighborhood. He rang the bell and waited for Eva to come to the door so that he could admonish her for being so irresponsible and not answering her phone. He waited for a response and became concerned when there was no answer. He rang the bell again, this time longer and more insistent. No response. He cursed himself because he didn't have a key. He remembered all of the times that Eva had offered him a key and he refused. He signaled to Junior who had remained in the car, to follow him around the back of the house. He looked in the garage and could see Eva's Mercedes Benz parked there. He tried the back door and it was locked. He walked around to the patio door and it was locked.

"How bad do you want to get in?" Junior asked with a devilish smirk on his face.

" Do you have a way to get in?"

"I do, but I'm going to need you to walk around to the front door. I don't need the great JJ Battle being implicated on a B&E charge."

"I see your point, but I don't think it really matters."

"Well humor me anyway."

JJ waited on the front porch trying to look as inconspicuous as possible. He waited for Junior to find a way into the house. It wasn't long before Junior appeared at the front door with a hand over his mouth. "I hate to say this, but that smell is not a good sign. Either the judge is a poor housekeeper or that's the smell of rotting flesh."

JJ didn't wait for an explanation but sprinted up the stairs to Eva's bedroom taking the stairs two at a time. He knew what to expect, but was still unprepared for what he found. She lay there nude, her body gray, and decaying. She was dead, that was certain. The smell of death was obvious and her skin was a pale lifeless color. He stumbled backwards as much in disbelief as he was repulsed at how unnecessary her death was. He forced himself to touch her as if by some remote implausible chance she might still be alive. He stared at her laying there, an accomplished life of purpose and success, ended because of greed. He vowed to avenge her death, just as he had for Katherine. He had gotten closer to the killer, but that didn't mean he could stop him. As a criminal defense attorney, he had often wondered of his clients just what circumstance or moment propelled them into murderous rages, he could now understand what sent them over the edge. A beautiful talented woman murdered just to preserve some million-dollar deal. He was startled out of his trance by Junior's hand on his shoulder.

"We have to get out of here JJ, Stone might not be far behind. Make sure that you don't touch anything, we don't want to leave any unnecessary clues."

"It's too late for that; my DNA is all over the house and in some very incriminating places. How did I let this happen? I'll be implicated in her murder. With Stone running the investigation, the odds are perfect I'll be the number one suspect. That way he accomplishes two things; he gets rid of Eva and he implicates me in the process."

"Wow. This gets juicier as we go along. You've been a busy man cousin. How do you find the time?"

"It's not what you think. We need to come up with a plan fast. If this guy is as good as you say, either I'm next or I'll be the chump holding the smoking gun."

"Don't worry I've got your back. That's why you pay me the big bucks. I can handle the Rat, but it could get dangerous. You might need to call in some favors from you law enforcement buddies, getting out your side of the story before Stone does."

JJ had to give Junior credit. For once, he made sense. This was no different from what he did for his clients; get their version of the facts out first. He knew he could buy some time before the police found his DNA. That might take a few days. It would be sooner before they found his fingerprints. At best, he had twenty-four hours to get his story out there, but perhaps even less time with the Rat on his trail. As they left Eva's house for the last time and drove back downtown, he made two phone calls and arranged a very important meeting.

Chapter 33

THEY DROVE IN SILENCE FOR A while as they headed to the meeting. Finally, Junior broke the silence.

"Listen JJ, until this thing is over, I'll be so close to you, that when you go to the bathroom, I'll be there to shake it. You understand me. These guys are nothing to play with."

In spite of the circumstances, JJ had to laugh at Junior's crude attempt at humor.

"Although the visual of you with me in the bathroom is scary, I get the point. Thanks for being here with me."

"Hey, where else can an old soldier get this much action?"

They rode in silence a while longer as they approached the Penobscot Building on Fort Street. It was late, so there was plenty of parking in front of the building.

"Drive around the building again," Junior said matter of factly.

JJ looked over at his cousin but said nothing, trusting his judgment. As they pulled up to the building the second time, Junior pointed out a parking spot right in front of the building. He got out first, taking his time, but casually looking around at his surroundings. JJ had for so long looked at his cousin as something of a screw-up, an eccentric career soldier who couldn't do anything else. Now, when JJ needed him, Junior was right there, willing to put his life on the line; JJ now saw his true value. Junior leaned in motioning for JJ to get out of the vehicle. He opened the door for him, allowing JJ to enter the building first.

Although it was evening, there was still a guard stationed in the lobby and each guest had to sign in. JJ signed in and they took the elevator to the twenty-sixth floor. This was one of the older elegant buildings with marble floors and walls, unlike the new buildings with metal and glass. As the elevator silently made its way to Suite Twenty Six Hundred, JJ thought carefully about how he was going to tell this story. Although Saul Mendoza was his best friend in the legal profession, JJ knew that his story was going to be difficult to believe-especially without evidence.

JJ first met Saul on his first day in court. JJ could remember being nervous and unsure of what he was supposed to do next, when this polished well-tailored lawyer took him aside and gave him a crash course in lawyering. They were friends since that moment with Saul serving as his mentor. JJ could not have chosen a better mentor-Saul was the best litigator in the city, smart and tenacious. The prosecution feared and respected him and judges gave him plenty of deference.

Saul himself was an enigma, he was half African American and Puerto Rican and half-Jewish. His father was Black and Puerto Rican and his mother was Jewish. He was equally comfortable in the ghetto or the barrio, at the synagogue, or anywhere else. He spoke Spanish, Arabic, and Yiddish; he was truly a man of the people. When you added his incredible intellect, he was a remarkable man. He was good looking in a refined dark European way, with silvery dark hair, which made it difficult for people to determine his race. He was frequently mistaken for Italian, Middle Eastern, Asian, and Latino, which he accepted good-naturedly. Because of his mixed heritage, he had taken much abuse growing up on the Westside of the City of Detroit. He was wealthy, but money didn't matter, powerful but not driven by power. He was a man who had an unerring sense of who he was and what his purpose was in life. He pursued life passionately, and didn't care where it led him. He didn't measure success by the cases he won but the lives he helped change. He was a man you could count on.

"JJ, I knew this was serious when you chose such an unusual hour for our meeting, and then you insisted we meet at the office. Now, I see you're traveling with your own security, what am I supposed to think?"

"Saul, this is my cousin Junior, he's sort of looking after me. Junior, Saul."

JJ crossed the room and he and Saul embraced. It was evening and the traffic outside was slow. There were just a few stragglers remaining downtown. JJ was impressed with the view from Saul's office, he had floor to ceiling windows and the people and traffic looked like toy figures as they moved twenty-six floors below. Saul motioned for them to take a seat on the couch. Junior stood by the window and stared out below. He was deep in his own thoughts. JJ, never at a loss for words, wondered where to begin. All of the recent events were real to him, but how could he communicate the incredible nature of what had happened and not appear to be suffering from paranoid delusions. He thought about how much he could share with his old friend, since he was afraid of what could happen to Saul if One Detroit, Inc., knew of his involvement. He had already lost two people who were very dear to him, Katherine and now Eva. It seemed that everyone he encountered was a potential target. He couldn't afford for anything to happen to Saul. However, he had nowhere else to turn.

JJ took a long look at Saul, and considered his story and the names of the people he would implicate, Victor Wright and Randy Connors, Judge Eva Moody. It made JJ's story seem even more incredible. JJ knew there was no other way, he needed help, and he needed someone with unimpeachable credibility to tell his story. If things turned as sour as he imagined they might, they could brand him anything from a serial killer to a psychopath. That might not be enough to escape Stone's smear campaign when Stone finds out that JJ's DNA is conspicuously present at the murder scene. He knew they would arrest him. Saul was his only hope, and JJ was thankful he was there.

He decided to tell Saul everything and to start from the beginning, with Bobby Bennett. "Saul, you may not believe what I am about to tell you, I don't really believe it all myself. It all started innocently enough, with a case Katherine and Eva wanted me take. It was a low-level criminal named Bobby

Boogaloo Bennett. He was involved in a domestic dispute with his girlfriend that got out of hand, and ended with him being charged with kidnapping and attempted murder." JJ could feel himself slipping into his defense attorney mode, reciting the facts as if it were a closing argument. He could hear the stillness in the room as Saul listened intently, his eyes never leaving JJ as he paced back and forth over the office.

He continued with his story, being careful not to leave out any facts, even the smallest of details might be something that Saul would need to know. JJ remembered the gunshots in the parking structure where someone shot at him. He described the chance encounter with Victor and Randy at the golf club and the offer of the One hundred thousand dollar retainer. It seemed a coincidence then, but now, after weeks of reflection, he knew Victor, Randy, and Eva had orchestrated it. Unwittingly, Katherine may have even had a part. Her interest in getting JJ back into legal practice may have given the One Detroit, Inc., crew the opportunity to get to him. It all fit so nicely. That was how a well-planned conspiracy worked; the planning helped ensure success for the criminal enterprise.

JJ told Saul about discovering Katherine's lifeless body and about their intended engagement. Then there was the blow to the head knocking him unconscious. He remembered how little progress Stone had made in finding Katherine's killer. A million little details came flooding back to him. There were the conversations with Katherine's assistant, Lindsay Cross, about the suspicious activity of the Corktown land deeds. JJ told Saul everything he could remember. He knew that much of what he was saying amounted to circumstantial evidence at best. However, great lawyers were able to see beyond the circumstances to see the truth. JJ knew Saul would see beyond the speculation to the heart of the conspiracy. All of the sad and painful details were tumbling out of him. So much had happened. He hoped that the facts were obvious to Saul and not just his own paranoid perceptions. Saul listened without expression, while Junior continued staring out the window. JJ could only hear the hum of the heating system and his own voice as he told about confronting Eva and finding the fax confirmation of the wire transfer from One Detroit, Inc. He found himself shaping the facts much as he would to a jury, presenting them in their most persuasive light, hoping that Saul would also see the evil nature of what One Detroit, Inc. had done.

JJ paused in his recitation of his story, searching for just the right words to explain his relationship with Eva. Although Saul could be trusted and everything JJ said to him was attorney-client privileged communications, he still felt uneasy sharing all of the intimate details.

"Eva and I have had a complicated relationship ever since our law school careers. It was more friends and confidants, which sometimes became intimate. We were always there for each other. Which makes what I am about to tell you even more difficult. Today, I found Eva dead in her home. I had been trying to reach her but I was unsuccessful. Then I received a call from Steve Parker, telling me she hadn't been in court for two days and he couldn't reach her either." He paused, collecting himself before he continued. "I had visited her the day before, to speak with her about her conduct in the Bennett case and how I thought she was damaging her career. She had been drinking and was very indifferent. One thing led to another and we had sex. It was an unintended consequence, but it was hard to say no to Eva. Afterward she fell asleep, and I was snooping around when I found the wire transfer from One Detroit, Inc." He could hear the defensiveness in his voice. "I made a copy and quietly left while she was sleeping," he said. The implication that she was still alive hung in the air not needing to be said. "When they perform an autopsy, they'll certainly find my DNA. Stone will have a field day with that. He'll tie it to Katherine's death and maybe Brianna's as well. There's no escaping that fact."

"Those are the essential facts. What I haven't told you is why all of this happened. I know I've been rambling like a witness with too much to say, and not enough facts."

"What you've told me is just fine," Saul said in a soothing, understanding tone. "I know the what, but I don't know the why. I suspect the motive is money and greed, but don't let me put words in your mouth. If I'm going to have to defend you, I need to hear the words from you. So, continue." Saul motioned to JJ with a reassuring nod, coaxing him to continue much as he would a reluctant witness. JJ smiled at how many times he had made that same gesture himself, reassuring a witness. How ironic, the he was now on the other end. It was a surprising revelation that being on the wrong end of a criminal prosecution was such a frightening proposition. Instinctively, as a lawyer he always had some sense of what his clients stood to lose. Now, in contemplating the circumstances of his own legal entanglements, he was paralyzed by what could go wrong in his life. He had cautioned hundreds of defendants with legal niceties and clichés in response to their questions about their case. "Plan for the worst; hope for the best," he remembered saying too many times. He used to utter those shallow, meaningless phrases that trivialized someone else's life. Now his perspective was different. He was fighting for his own life, and there was no time for clichés.

"Katherine and I started to see a pattern with the recording of the deeds for the Corktown properties. Then we found out who was behind the purchases, One Detroit, Inc. It wasn't hard from there finding out who the principals were. Victor Wright, Randy Connors, Eva, Rahsheed Truman, and Harvey Stone. My client, Bobby Bennett, helped fill in the pieces about their plans for the property, and the development of Corktown for the Super Bowl." He paused, remembering all of the things that had happened because of Bobby Bennett. "The development was for hundreds of millions of dollars with the principals each receiving a hefty share. Each of them had a specific role to play.

JJ watched as Saul listened to his explanation about the recent events and Saul continued to make notes while JJ talked. He rarely interrupted except to elicit more detailed information. He had been talking for over two hours and was becoming tired and drained. It was one thing to tell the story, but quite another to live these events. These were serious allegations, and the outcome would mean life or death, or at the least, long-term incarceration. He needed a plan, which would protect him when the allegations, rumors, and innuendos hit the streets. It was all circumstantial he knew, but frequently, that was the most difficult evidence to overcome.

When he had finished telling Saul every detail of what he could remember, he slumped back on the couch, weary and uncertain. Whoever said that confession was good for the soul had probably never been a suspect in a criminal case. He went over in his mind what he already knew; this was his best alternative, having Saul Mendoza as his defense attorney. Secondly, together they could devise a strategy to stay one-step ahead of Stone and his co-conspirators. JJ knew that as the investigation intensified and he became the focus, there would be little time to formulate a strategy; they had to do it now. That way it would not appear as if they were making up things as they went along. Nothing made a suspect appear as guilty as an unprepared, unrehearsed response to a reporter's question. So, he waited. It was as if he was waiting for the doctor to give his diagnosis. What would Saul have to say? He didn't have to wait long.

"We've known each other for too long for me to beat around the bush or mince words, so I'll tell you exactly what I think and what I believe you must do to protect yourself from the possibility of these insidious allegations." Saul did not hesitate; he looked at JJ with neither pity nor fear, but rather an expression that questioned how evil and detestable people could be. JJ knew the answer, but knowing the answer brought no comfort, only the realization that no matter how hard he tried, evil like injustice would always exist. He had managed to stay on the periphery of trouble for most of his life, but now he was unwittingly sucked into the turbulence of One Detroit, Inc.

He thought of the consequences. He waited for Saul's assessment, placing his trust and essentially his life in his hands. JJ had been in that situation many times before as an expectant client waited for words of absolution; oftentimes there were none forthcoming. He waited, feeling the weight of circumstance and fate, conspiring to take him under. It was unfair, but he knew how the game was played, and it was played for real. Saul told him to prepare a brief of all of the allegations with copies for the media outlets and the US Attorney. He was to make provisions for mailing them if he was arrested.

He harbored no illusions; he had assessed his situation before he came to Saul. What he wanted, or more precisely, what he needed was a plan that shifted the circumstantial evidence building against him into concrete, specific evidence that pointed squarely at One Detroit, Inc. He needed time to unravel the facts and to gather evidence of One Detroit, Inc.'s complicity. It would not be easy, and there was precious little time remaining. He could imagine Stone tightening the rope and putting the pieces together to implicate him. They had to make something happen. If Saul could not help him, he and Junior would take matters into their own hands and force Stone, the Rat and the other One Detroit, Inc. conspirators to admit roles in the murders and conspiracy. Deep down he knew that would never happen. The truth would not set him free. He prepared himself for what Saul had to say, but deep down it did not matter, he told himself, because he knew he would have to take matters into his own hands. There were times when you relied on the system to save you and other times when you had to save yourself. This was such a time. He would listen to Saul, and even follow his advice, but that would not be the only remedy. Someone would have to pay, and JJ knew just where he had to begin.

Chapter 34

THE FORTUNES OF ONE DETROIT, INC. had never been more tenuous. They were days from closing the biggest real estate deal in the history of the city of Detroit, yet there were still too many loose ends. Systematically, they had gone about removing each of the obstacles, but one troubling, nagging loose end remained – Joshua Jericho Battle. He was the last remaining person who could derail the deal. The members of the group, those still living, sat huddled around the table. There was a feeling of excitement and trepidation as they decided how to proceed. The jubilation from the distribution of the initial deposit and the anticipation of their full shares had them giddy with excitement. Harvey Stone, who had been responsible for the all of the dirty and objectionable assignments, watched his fellow conspirators with disgust. They would never have made soldiers he surmised, as Victor, Randy and Rahsheed took turns saluting their own brilliance. Stone felt like it was his duty to keep them on task and to help them finalize this mission and then celebrate. He needed to remind them that no matter how brilliant a plan, they still had to execute it, and he was all about execution.

"We don't have a lot of time," he said raising his voice interrupting their boys' club banter. "As we discussed, there is just one loose end, and we all agree that it has to be finalized."

They were silent for a moment, each reflecting on their own individual commitment to the enterprise. They all recognized the unmistakable fact; they could not turn back now, or change the events that had already occurred. Victor expressed what the others were thinking; "Do what you have to do." For Stone, the words didn't necessarily need to be said, but he needed to force these guys to accept their role in the process. Besides, if there ever was an investigation, those statements would be damning. It was sort of a blood oath. They were all in this together, and everybody had blood on their hands. He liked it this way because it kept the weak links from getting a conscience and wanting to break the chain. They didn't know that he was recording their meeting, just in case they wanted to throw him under the bus. Stone had already decided what was needed, and now he had the insurance he needed to keep everyone honest.

It was all coming together nicely for Harvey Stone. He had five hundred thousand dollars in an offshore account in the Cayman Islands, his cut of the proceeds and irrefutable evidence if his partners suddenly became overly ambitious. JJ Battle was the last detail that remained. The Rat was just waiting for a call to unleash his talents. Stone had enough circumstantial evidence to convict JJ from the grave. Katherine's death and Eva's death would be hard for JJ to refute after he was dead. It served the cocky lawyer right, Stone thought, for all the times he tried to make his life miserable. It was the least he could do to return the favor. He wanted him to feel pain and the Rat was just the person to do it. The tape recordings were Stone's insurance against the remaining members of One Detroit, Inc., and he would not hesitate to use them.

JJ awoke from a restless night of sleep. He was feeling the pressure of too many unresolved issues. He knew that at any moment Stone would release details of Eva's death, further implicating him in this mess. Secondly, there was the Rat who he had to contend with and not knowing when or how he might make his presence felt. He was starting to give into the paranoia of suspicion. He expected that every siren from a police vehicle was meant for him. He didn't know whether to make a move or stay put. After they returned from Saul's office, he spent a great deal of the night drafting a document, not unlike a brief, outlining all of the details of what had transpired in the last few weeks. He wanted to make sure that there was at least his version of the facts that would survive, God forbid, even if he didn't. Saul's plan was a great one.

The facts and circumstances seemed so simple and obvious when he thought about them in the abstract. But, when he told Saul what he believed, everything became complex and speculative. It was like a criminal case; there was either circumstantial evidence or direct evidence, or sometimes a combination of the two. However, here many circumstantial pieces that, if viewed alone, made very little sense, but viewed together made a dangerous and murderous conspiracy. He knew who was responsible and how they accomplished it, but he needed proof, and that was going to be difficult to obtain. He was used to using his skill and expertise to help others, now it was necessary to use it to save himself.

He estimated that he had perhaps twenty four-to-forty eight hours more before the details of Eva's death became public. Shortly after that, the autopsy results would reveal the presence of his DNA.

He was running out of time. He needed to shake things up. He needed to make Victor and his crew feel less certain about their plan and its potential to succeed. If he were clever enough, perhaps he could force them into a mistake that he could use to his advantage. It was a long shot but he had to try. He dialed a number that he had not called in a long time. He waited patiently for the person to answer. Finally, he heard the familiar voice on the other end.

"Hello?" The voice said pleasantly and without the least hint of irritation.

"Are you alone?" He asked bracing himself for a negative response.

"Why, is this an obscene phone call?" She answered playfully.

He was relieved that she was alone and able to talk to him. Hearing her voice brought back fond memories, but now was not the time to relive them. "I need to see you right away. Do you remember that restaurant in Southfield we used to go to, The Golden Mushroom? Could you meet me there in an hour?" He wanted to convey the importance of the meeting, but did not want to alarm her over the phone.

"This sounds serious. Should I be worried?" He could hear the rising concern in her voice and he wanted to say the words that would reassure her.

"Nothing we can't resolve over lunch." He shuddered as he said the words. They sounded like the empty words he told clients when he knew they were unprepared for the truth. He never knew which was worse, the tactful lie meant to spare feelings or the cold hard truth delivered without fanfare. He didn't know the answer, but in this case, discretion weighed heavily in favor of waiting.

JJ rounded up Junior for their ride to Southfield as he thought of the best way to tell Carlena Wright that her husband was orchestrating a conspiracy to commit murder and other capital crimes. Although they had shared many intimate moments, none of that would mean anything when he told her what he knew. It would not be easy, but he had made a career of succeeding at difficult and unpopular pursuits. You could not be a criminal defense attorney if you were afraid of being unpopular. It was an occupational hazard, and was like being the referee who makes a tough call against the home team. It might be unpopular, but it is a necessary part of the game.

Junior was quiet on their ride to Southfield and deep in his own thoughts. JJ could see him keeping his eyes and focus on the rear view mirror, making sure they weren't being followed. He didn't know how Carlena would take the news that he was about to unload on her, but that wasn't the point, he reminded himself. His purpose was twofold- to enlighten an old friend about impending disaster, and to force Victor and his people into making a mistake that he could exploit.

As they pulled into the parking lot of the restaurant, he was thankful that the lunch crowd had cleared out and it was not crowded. He could see Carlena had already arrived. She had valet parked the Mercedes and the vanity plates loudly proclaimed 2 WRIGHT 1. He slid Junior a hundred dollar bill and told him to get a table for himself. He looked like a kid at Christmas as he eyed the bill. JJ saw Carlena already seated in the back. He paused, gathering himself and his thoughts. Wow. She was gorgeous. Secretly it made him hate Victor even more. It wasn't envy or jealousy that fueled his anger, it was disgust that Victor did not value her more. But like most women married to rich and powerful men, there were choices to be made. Often those choices involved personal sacrifices. It was the nature of the game. Carlena was no fool. He hoped that she was prepared for the consequences. He had to find a way to tell her that circumstances were about to make her vow of for better or worse, a reality.

He had to admit that she had come a long way. She was nothing like the raw unpolished woman he saw when they first met at law school. The physical beauty was always apparent, but so was the ghetto charm and crudeness. There was something to be said for wealth helping to define a woman. The benefits of a privileged lifestyle were obvious. Carlena was the epitome of beauty and class. No one who saw this woman could ever imagine that this well dressed, well-coiffed woman was born and raised in the harshest of conditions. She was a refined and worldly woman who had found her place in the world. He was about to change all of that.

He had thought long and hard on whether he should tell Carlena about Victor and One Detroit, Inc. He debated whether to allow things to progress normally and let the chips fall where they may. He had almost resigned himself to that strategy, when he remembered their friendship and what they had once meant to each other. Besides, he had another more selfish motive; he wanted to force Victor to have to make a move. He knew Carlena would resort to her street savvy and survival instincts to save herself. That would force Victor to have to react. At this point, anything that made Victor and One Detroit, Inc. deviate from their plan was good. The more distracted they were, the more time JJ had to implement a plan. Right now, he didn't have a plan, but with time he was certain he could develop one. Sometimes the best plan was no plan; this was one of those times.

She greeted him with a mixture of genuine affection followed by deep concern. He could see the strain and uncertainty on her face. They embraced and held each other. She held him for what seemed like minutes but was only seconds. Before he could speak, she spoke first. "It's really great to see you. But, I have to admit I am a bit concerned by how evasive and clandestine you're acting. Is that anyway for old friends to act?"

"Please, sit down," he said calmly, holding her chair for her as she sat. "Lena," he said using his pet nickname for her, "I wouldn't have asked you here under these circumstances if it weren't important. We have always been honest and truthful with each other. I owe it to you to tell you what I know and to let you decide what it means and how you need to respond." Before he could continue, the waiter appeared asking for their drink order. "Whiskey and water," he ordered thankful for the interruption so that he could organize his thoughts. Carlena ordered Stoli on the rocks. She was always a serious drinker. He suspected she wanted to be prepared for anything.

"So, what is it that's so important that you brought me all the way out to Southfield? Bad news goes down just as well in the city." He had to admire her brazenness. Beneath all of the glamour, he could still glimpse that eastside neighborhood girl who wasn't afraid of anything. He wondered if she would still be so brave after she heard all about the exploits of her husband and One Detroit, Inc.

"What I'm about to tell you is going to sound outrageous and perhaps even a little crazy, but I believe it's true, and more importantly, my life depends on its truth. I know this may sound very dramatic, but please hear me out." He held up his hand, gently motioning for her to let him finish speaking. He began telling the story from the beginning.

"You know I hadn't practiced criminal law for over two years, when a number of my friends began to encourage me to get back into criminal defense. At first, I was reluctant, considering my notorious past. However, against my better judgment, I agreed to represent a defendant named Bobby Bennett. By itself, that name probably doesn't mean anything to you. It sure didn't to me. But soon after I took the case, a lot of people started taking an interest in the defendant, most notably the firm of Wright and Connors."

"Why would Victor and Randy be interested in some low level criminal defendant?" She asked.

"That was my initial reaction. They were not only interested in this defendant, but interested to the tune of a One Hundred Thousand Dollar retainer." He could see from her expression that she, too, was contemplating how strange a development this was. Although she wasn't practicing law, she was still extremely bright and blessed with common sense and street smarts. She could see where he was headed.

"Although I hadn't been practicing criminal law, I still had some nice income streams and had managed to save some money from the glory days. Money wasn't an issue, but a retainer that size was difficult to ignore. Still I had some reservations. Shortly thereafter, I was shot at in the parking structure of my office building. Then they killed Katherine. At first, I thought it was random. Then I received information that linked her death to activities of One Detroit, Inc., Victor's company."

"What does One Detroit, Inc. have to do with Katherine's death?" She asked perceptively.

"I'm getting to that. I asked Katherine to investigate some strange land deals involving the Corktown development. My client, Bobby Bennett, was at the center of the acquisition of a number of questionable deed recordings. A number of people were making noises of being swindled out of their property or forced to sign over their deeds at the threat of violence. Katherine surmised that One Detroit, Inc. was behind these deals."

"That isn't necessarily a crime," she said, just a bit too defensively.

"It is when people start dying and there are fraudulent conveyances and One Detroit, Inc. is the beneficiary of a billion dollar land deal involving those fraudulent conveyances." He stopped and took a sip of his drink. He was concentrating on keeping the argument logical and unemotional. He wasn't trying to convince her that what he was saying was true, but rather to let her draw her own conclusions.

"As the coincidences became more and more frequent, other strange things started happening. The Bobby Bennett case was improperly dismissed, and then other people began to die."

"Wait a minute. Who else besides Katherine died? Don't misunderstand. I'm not trying to minimize Katherine's death. But this is the first I heard about multiple deaths."

"Do you remember the death of Brianna Tuller? She was the key witness in Bobby Bennett's trial. She died of a drug overdose on Belle Isle, the day before the trial began."

"Yes, I do remember something about that case. If I recall, it was a drug overdose and not a murder."

"You're partially right. Well, there was never any indication that she was a drug user. I investigated her thoroughly in connection with the trial; if there was any indication of drug use, I would have found it. Plus, the investigating detective is one of the members of One Detroit, Inc., Harvey Stone. In addition to that, the judge who improperly dismissed the case is, Eva Ann Moody, who, not coincidentally, is a member of One Detroit, Inc." He was just getting started, but he could still see a bit of skepticism on Lena's face.

"JJ, like always you make a convincing argument, but like our criminal law professor used to say, it's circumstantial at best."

"I would be inclined to agree with you if I heard the same facts, but there's more. One evening I happened to be at Judge Moody's home, the circumstances are not important," he hurriedly said, heading off Lena's peaked curiosity. I happened to intercept a faxed confirmation of a bank transfer for Two point Five million dollars to Eva from One Detroit, Inc."

"C'mon JJ, a large wire transfer alone doesn't necessarily indicate a crime." Although Lena said it with her trademark bravado, he could see the shock that this revelation had on her. She had no idea of the magnitude of the deal. Clearly, Victor had not been keeping her apprised of his business dealings.

"Once again, you're right. But, it doesn't stop there. The following day, I received a call from Eva's clerk saying she hadn't been in the office for two days and she hadn't called. He had been covering for her, but now the court administrator was putting pressure on him for some answers. I was trying to reach Eva myself to talk some sense into her regarding her dismissal of the case. When I couldn't reach her by phone, I went over there. When I got there I found Eva dead."

"Oh my God!" All the blood drained from her face and gone was the bravado. It was replaced by what JJ saw as an emerging realization that what he had been saying was true. He waited for a response, but she did not respond. She only stared blankly back at him. "My cousin, Junior, who is an army veteran, identified a mercenary named John Rathskeller, who we suspect is doing the dirty work. They were both a part of Delta Force in the last two wars, and he recognizes him and his work." He almost felt sorry for Lena. Hearing all of this must have made her feel helpless as her lifetime dreams were evaporating.

"Now here is the tough part. Victor is the head of all of this. By my count, that's three murders, fraud, and conspiracy. Those are just the crimes we know about. By the time this is over, the Justice Department and the FBI will all want to know a lot more about Victor's business dealings. I'm certain they will find something. I'm telling you all of this because I care about you. I wanted to give you an opportunity to make some decisions. You have to appreciate that when the Feds get involved they cast a very wide net. Everyone is a suspect. I have a strong feeling that in the next forty eight–to-seventy two hours, everything is going to start unraveling. The government is going to freeze all of his and your assets. If you have access to some cash that you can withdraw without being too obvious, you need to do so immediately. Banks, investments, safety deposit boxes, joint accounts will all be frozen and seized. If you have someone you can really trust, that might be a good place to park some funds before the seizure. Look, I'm sorry to have to tell you all of this, but I thought you would rather know than not know."

"I can't believe this is happening. Then again, I can. I could see the signs but ignored them. I knew Victor was capable of a lot of things, but I never thought it would be murder." Her voice was barely a whisper and tears were rolling down her face, streaking her mascara and makeup. He didn't know how she was going to proceed; it was strictly her call. He didn't know if she would confront Victor or just take the money and run. Whatever her decision, her life would never be the same. Sometimes we are victims of our own dreams and ambitions. JJ had done all he could to save her, now it was up to her to chart her own course and to save herself. JJ had some unresolved issues to settle himself. The demise and destruction of One Detroit, Inc. was first on the list.

Their lunch was over. JJ asked the waiter for the check, paid it, and left a generous tip. He leaned over, kissing her on the cheek. He tasted the salt from her tears mixed with mascara. She was unresponsive and buried deep in her thoughts. He quickly turned and left the table, turning for one last glance. She absentmindedly sipped her drink, oblivious to the other people in the restaurant. She is a survivor, he thought. If anyone can survive these events, she will. As he exited the restaurant, Junior joined him. He gave his ticket to the valet and glanced at his watch. He had started things in motion with Lena; he only hoped that he had time to see his plan come to fruition.

Chapter 35

TIME WAS RUNNING OUT ON JJ Battle. He knew that at any moment Stone could have him arrested, so it made each move critically important. They were still no closer to getting hard evidence on Stone or the Rat. All of the evidence that he had now was merely circumstantial and conjecture. It would not be enough to save him from murder charges. He knew that Stone would have to have Eva's body discovered, and that would allow him to implicate JJ in the murder of Katherine and Eva. Perhaps Stone would even throw in Brianna's body as part of a conspiracy theory. In any event, if he didn't act fast, he would be defending himself from a jail cell.

He had one important thing he had to complete; his synopsis of the facts. He had been working on it for the better part of two days. It was in the form of a brief and represented everything he knew about One Detroit, Inc. and its dealings. He completed copies for individuals that he knew would understand the implications of what he was saying and more importantly, would act on the information. He needed a contingency plan. It wasn't that he didn't have total confidence in Saul, but he needed as many options as he could muster. His instincts and training told him that things could easily turn against him. He addressed the envelopes and left a detailed message for Junior and Marsha.

JJ had to acknowledge that he was no further along than when these sordid events started. He believed that he knew a lot more of what One Detroit,

Inc. was up to, but he still didn't have any real facts to support his conclusions. The best plan was often no plan, and he had to admit that he was making it up as he went along. He had begun with Carlena and he knew it would be a matter of time before Victor would have to react. That meant that he had only a few hours before everything came crashing down on him. He had to make something happen now. He woke Junior and told him his plan for today. Junior as always was more than ready for today's events.

"Listen, I have some packages that I may need you to mail for me if things get out of hand."

"You know you can count on me."

"I know. We have to take a set of these down to the office for Marsha as a contingency plan."

"I hear what you are saying, but I don't think it's necessary." Junior said, his voice becoming serious. It was obvious that he understood what JJ had left unsaid; before this was over they could kill either or both of them.

"Look, I'm not sure it's fair to include you in my mess. You didn't sign up for murder and mayhem."

"But I did. All of my life I have been fighting one battle or another, whether it was the military or civilian life. Some of the battles were worthy causes; some were not. I've concluded that's just the way it is. Some people are destined to be fighters; I'm one of those people. If you're asking me if this is a cause I'm willing to die for, the answer is yes. Besides, it's the only thing I'm really good at. Besides sex." Junior said, lightening the mood.

"Spare me those sordid details. That's information I really don't need."

"You don't, but your secretary Marsha might be interested."

"That's between you two. You are both consenting adults"

"That's what I'm talking about. I can't wait to get her consent."

"Be careful what you wish for. Marsha's quite a woman."

"Trust me; I'm equal to the challenge."

"Whatever. What I'm saying is, now is an excellent time to get back to the rest of your life if you know what I mean. You've been invaluable. There are no hard feelings either way if you want out."

"Look. Let's just end this right here. I'm in this to the end, whatever that might be. So let's not speak about this again. Okay?"

"Agreed." He said with a great deal of appreciation for his cousin. He didn't know where this would lead, but he was thankful that Junior would be there to go down that road with him.

They headed downtown to the office with Junior driving. He was cautious as usual, making sure they weren't being followed. When they reached the building, they left the package on Marsha's desk. JJ briefly thumbed through the mail, not seeing anything of particular interest. As he prepared to set the mail down and leave, an official looking envelope drew his gaze. He separated the envelope from the rest. Detroit Mutual Insurance Company the envelope read. He didn't recall any recent cases involving Detroit Mutual. He opened the envelope and stared in disbelief. How could this happen. It was more than fate. He had to admit that the irony was unmistakable.

The letter stated that he was the beneficiary of a life insurance policy that paid him, Joshua Jericho Battle, the sum of One Million Dollars. It further stated that Katherine had designated him the beneficiary and that a representative would contact him regarding instructions for the proceeds once a preliminary investigation was completed.

Here he was holding a letter that made him an instant millionaire, but by the very nature of its contents, he might not be able to collect a penny of the proceeds. The policy that Katherine had so graciously and thoughtfully made him the beneficiary, could help lead to his eventual incarceration. It would give Stone further evidence of motive. He continued staring at the letter until Junior roused him from his trance.

"Is everything alright JJ?"

"Yeah." He said. "It just continues to pile on. It's just that everything that has happened seems to draw me deeper into this mess. It's like quicksand."

"What are you talking about?"

Instead of explaining, he just handed him the letter. He waited as Junior read the letter.

"Why you lucky son of a gun. The rich just get richer. I don't see how this can be a problem. You are now officially a millionaire."

He didn't bother to explain to Junior, it wouldn't change the facts anyway. He felt another tremendous weight had just been added to his already overburdened shoulders. He was also beginning to feel the weight of an ever-increasing pile of mounting circumstantial evidence. Much of it was beyond his control. He knew that under ordinary circumstances, being the beneficiary of a million dollar insurance policy had no downside. But now, this unexpected bequest by Katherine could be his undoing. This was one more bit of circumstantial evidence that Stone would use to make his case against him. Although he was unaware that Katherine had made him her beneficiary, a jury would be less understanding. Besides, the insurance company would conduct their own investigation into Katherine's death. He knew that if Stone arrested him and charged him with her murder, the insurance company would void the policy. At this point, it hardly mattered; money was the least of his worries.

He had no time left. Every conceivable avenue had just about been closed; Katherine, Eva, and now this insurance claim. Even to his trained legal mind, things were looking desperate. He had one last remaining hope, and if he knew Stone and One Detroit, Inc., that option may be fleeting. He made one quick phone call, and searched Marsha's rolodex for an address. He couldn't believe that he had not thought of it earlier, it all made perfect sense. There was one person who could help unravel all of this-Bobby Bennett.

He hurriedly opened the closet door, searching inside for the video recording equipment. He frequently used it to allow witnesses to practice their testimony. It definitely helped them improve their in court testimony. However, today he needed it for another purpose. He needed to get Bobby Bennett's testimony on tape. It might be an important piece of the puzzle. The problem might be that they had to get to Bobby before Stone and the Rat. He rushed out of the door with Junior following close behind.

"Where are we headed in such a hurry?" He asked, running to keep up with JJ.

"We need to pay someone a visit before Stone and the Rat."

"Who might that be?"

"Bobby Bennett. He's the person who started all of this. I can't believe it took me so long to come up with this solution."

"Don't beat yourself up over it." Junior said. "It's better late than never."

"Perhaps. But it wouldn't matter if Bobby wasn't alive to tell his story."

It might be just the corroboration that JJ needed to help prove the conspiracy. As they drove over to the west side of town, he wondered if he was doing enough. Only time and circumstances would tell the story. He was preparing himself for the worst-case scenario-that Stone would arrest him and he would have to try to keep himself out of jail. He hoped that he had put enough pieces in place to deflect attention from himself. He needed to put the blame where it properly belonged-on the members of One Detroit, Inc.

In order to make that happen, Bobby Bennett would be an important piece of that puzzle. He was the one person who could provide the details of the land acquisition scheme of One Detroit, Inc. It would take some convincing, but he believed that he had built up enough of a trust relationship with Bobby that he would cooperate. Besides, it might be the only way to keep Bobby alive. JJ's plan was simple. They would videotape Bobby providing the details of the scheme and enclose the tape in the package that JJ had created. The tape, along with the synopsis of the case, would be given to the Detroit News, the Detroit Free Press, the U.S. Attorney's Office, the Department of Justice, and the Wayne County Prosecutor's Office. That was sure to keep everyone honest. He had provided strict instructions to Junior and Marsha that in the event he was arrested or killed; they were to mail the packages immediately. Just for insurance, he would make sure that he sent a package to Saul as well. It was a good plan. In fact, it was a great plan. There were only two problems- it required either his arrest or his death. In either case, it would save his life, or his reputation. However, he hoped it would never get to that point.

He questioned whether he should contact Bobby to let him know that they were coming, or just show up. He decided not to contact him in advance, opting for the surprise visit so as not to spook him or raise an unnecessary alarm. Bobby was the kind of person that having too much information was dangerous. He couldn't trust him to keep the reason for their meeting confidential. He knew that as soon as he hung up the phone, Bobby would call Stone with the details. That would put either or both of them in danger. It would be a miracle if Stone and the Rat had not already gotten to Bobby. He might be the last remaining link to the conspiracy. Other than the principals, Bobby would be the last person that would have substantive knowledge about the Corktown scheme. Why would they allow him to remain alive, yet kill Katherine, Brianna, and Eva? It didn't make sense. But none of it made sense. They were making up the rules as they went along. They eliminated anyone who was an obstacle.

As they got closer to Bobby's house, he knew that there was only one approach that might work with Bobby- telling him that he had more to lose by not cooperating with him than he stood to gain by remaining loyal to One Detroit, Inc. The logic was simple, unless he put his story on tape, there would be no reason for One Detroit, Inc. to keep him alive. It was as simple as that. But he knew that with Bobby nothing was ever simple. He would do as he always had done, try to play both sides against each other and get the best deal. JJ knew that whatever was said between them could very well be repeated to Stone. Bobby only felt loyalty to himself. JJ knew it was risky, but it was necessary to gather as much evidence of the conspiracy as possible. If nothing else, it would further rattle the cages of One Detroit, Inc. and force them to make a move. Up to this point, he had done as much as he could to protect himself from any charges or allegations that Stone could make. If nothing else, he had a good public relations campaign to help refute the allegations that Stone might make. In the best-case scenario, perhaps they would underestimate his desire to avenge Katherine's death and would not trouble him any further. It might be that he was overreacting, and they didn't have a plan to implicate him. He doubted that this was true, but he wanted to consider the possibility nevertheless. It would not change his strategy.

He was determined to expose this conspiracy and bring down whoever was a part of it, even if he was destroyed in the process. He didn't want to think about that possibility, but he knew he must consider it. That was the essence of his plan. He had to do whatever was required to avenge Katherine, and his own circumstance could not be a consideration.

He looked over at Junior asleep in the passenger seat. He wondered if that was how he approached military battles. Did he rest beforehand, conserving his energy? They were almost at Bobby's house.

His file indicated that he lived close to the old Tiger Stadium, coincidentally right in the heart of Corktown; how ironic. Was this a part of Bobby's spoils for his part in the scheme? It made JJ slightly more determined to get to the truth. He thought about the poor people and the elderly who had been duped out of their homes, all for the sake of greed. It was amazing that a conspiracy of this magnitude affecting so many people and so much property had gone virtually unnoticed.

He reminded himself that that was not his battle. He didn't want to lose his focus. If, because of his efforts to uncover this conspiracy, it made amends to the people who had been wronged, then he would be happy. That was a battle for others.

They were about two blocks from Bobby's house when he woke Junior. He awoke with the practiced ease of a man used to short naps. He quickly oriented himself and checked his weapon. "Let's circle the block and do some recon," he said, as they searched the surroundings for anything suspicious. After they circled the block, he motioned for JJ to park about four houses away. As was their custom in these situations, they waited. It was a quiet residential neighborhood with small houses in various states of repair. They were amazed at what they saw.

The neighborhood was straight out of some urban developer's playbook. On either side of Bobby's block were these neat rows of homes. But, soon, two hulking behemoths of modern architectural wonder, Ford Field and Comerica Park would rise out of the landscape like prehistoric monsters. These structures would be so out of place with the existing neighborhood. It would be a shocking contrast between the old and new urban development. JJ had to admit that the new structures would be impressive, *but at what cost*, he wondered. The city was dying from within because of declining industry and increasing unemployment. Yet the administration's response was new stadiums and casinos. Give the people what they want, he thought sarcastically. There was nothing like a city with its priorities straight. There was very little traffic, not many cars, or people out walking. The weather was still quite cold, in the low teens. After they watched the house for fifteen minutes or so, they walked to the small frame bungalow and stepped on the porch. They could hear music coming from inside, but no voices. They debated if Junior should cover the back door, but they thought better of that idea. Bobby had no reason to fear them and therefore was unlikely to run.

The house was in good shape architecturally, but was in need of repair. The doorbell hung precariously from the wall, the victim of an ill-fated repair attempt. The screen door barely hung on hinges, rusty and missing screws. The door, however, was a steel security door, reinforced to withstand even a police onslaught. The bottom portion of the door had the remnants of scuffmarks, the result no doubt of a non-working doorbell. Overall, it was just what he expected for Bobby Bennett's home. He gave a hard knock on the door and there was no answer. He knocked again and still no answer. He began to wonder if Bobby was home, or worse, if Stone and the Rat had gotten here first. Junior, annoyed by the cold and impatient for a response, gave a heavy kick with the sole of his military boots. JJ, surprised by Junior's action, looked at him with a wry smile. Inside they could hear some rustling and Bobby's voice over the sound of the music. They heard the unlocking of multiple locks, the door swung open, and there stood Bobby Bennett, alive and well.

JJ was relieved at the sight of Bobby, something he never thought he would feel. But, there he was, in baggy sweat pants and no shirt, his belly obscenely hanging over the waist of the pants. "Attorney Battle, what a surprise," he said. "Did they re-open my case?" He asked more out of curiosity than fear. JJ could see the look of surprise on his face. From the backroom they heard an excited female voice, "Boogaloo who is it?"

"Just some friends," he said, with a rather amused look on his face. "I'll be there in a minute. Sorry, I wasn't expecting visitors."

A chubby, well-endowed young woman, clad only in a man's undershirt, stuck her head around the corner, making sure that the friends Bobby spoke of were just that, and not competition.

"Sorry for the interruption," she said, unexpectedly polite, as if she really meant it. "Bobby, I'll be in the room if you need anything."

Bobby said nothing, merely nodding his head as the girl sheepishly retreated to the back room.

"Bobby, I can see you're busy, but I needed to talk to you about something. This is my cousin, Junior. He's helping me on a special project." Junior grunted and nodded in Bobby's direction.

"Whatever it is, I'm willing to help, you know that Attorney Battle. Come on in."

"Thanks, that means a lot. Here's the problem. There have been some serious developments involving the people in One Detroit, Inc. I don't want to go into all of the details, but I'm implicated and you might be as well." JJ waited allowing his words to sink in. He wanted to convey the seriousness of the problem, but didn't want to spook Bobby. "Here are the important things you need to know. A very important friend of mine, Katherine Devlin, was killed because of the Corktown project. Brianna Tuller and Judge Eva Moody were also killed. All of these deaths are directly connected to Corktown. I believe that the people who are responsible for these deaths will try to blame me for them."

"I'm not going to ask why they want to do that. I'm going to assume there's a good reason. I don't doubt you Attorney Battle, but why hasn't this information been in the newspaper or on television yet?"

"Brianna's death was on the news. Judge Moody's will be on soon enough," JJ said.

JJ wasn't surprised at Bobby's ability to grasp the complexities of the situation, but he still needed him to understand the particular nuance that would encourage him to want to help put the final piece of his strategy together. That required JJ convincing Bobby that at this stage, One Detroit, Inc. still had the ability to implicate both him and Bobby in this conspiracy. Bobby's only insurance was to preserve his version of the facts on tape.

"How do you want me to help?"

"Bobby, I want you to know that anybody with any knowledge of this conspiracy is a target. That includes you and me. The only common denominator of the people that I mentioned who are dead is that they all had some connection to the Corktown project. As I see it, Bobby, that makes you and me likely candidates for extinction. Our only protection is to get our story in the hands of people who can make the facts public. We will then have a record of our version of the facts."

"Excuse me for saying. But what good is our version of the facts if I'm dead?"

"Well, you're right to an extent. But, at this point, you are still an asset to them. There's no reason to change that. In the unlikely event that something does happen, your story will be on record."

"Excuse me if I don't jump for joy. If these guys are as dangerous as you say, it could be too late already."

"That's unlikely. I'm going to put this information in the hands of people who can put it to good use."

"What do you need me to do?" Bobby asked. Showing a grudging willingness to cooperate.

"We need to videotape your statement briefly telling about your involvement in Corktown, and what One Detroit, Inc. asked you to do. In a civil case, it would be a deposition. But here we're going to be more informal. I'll just ask you a couple of basic questions and you just tell what you know."

"It sounds simple enough. Attorney Battle, I trust you to do the right thing."

"Bobby, I'm betting my life on it," JJ said, painfully aware of the prophetic nature of his statement.

"I'll get the equipment out of the car," Junior said, speaking for the first time since entering the house. He buttoned his coat against the chill of the winter afternoon. As he left the house and headed for the car, he noticed for the first time, a white panel van parked across the street about four houses down. It had not been there when they arrived. He knew then that someone was watching the house. He immediately became alert. He opened the trunk of the car and leisurely took out the equipment. He was watching the van for any activity. He had choices. He could sense that someone was watching him also. He could empty the clip into the side of the van, thereby solving JJ's problem forever. He instinctively knew the Rat was inside and this was an opportunity to trap him. On the other hand, he could walk back to the house as unobtrusively as possible and not let on that he was aware that the Rat was there. At the least, the Rat would know who he was up against and know that it would not be easy.

Junior quickly decided to choose the latter, and nonchalantly walked back to the house. He would have to alert JJ and Bobby that it wouldn't be safe to remain there. JJ's suspicions were true; Bobby was the next target. Junior could not resist taunting the Rat just a little. As he approached the porch of Bobby's house, he set down the equipment, made a figure of a gun with his hand, pointed it at the van, and pulled the trigger. He was sure he got the Rat's attention.

When he entered the house, he was all business. He closed the curtains in all of the rooms and made sure he locked and closed the windows. He went to the back door and made sure it was locked and secure. He was happy to see that the back door, like the front, was a steel security door. As he went about his elaborate security check, JJ and Bobby looked on in amazement. Junior said nothing but went about the house in an efficient manner.

"Attorney Battle, your cousin is just a little paranoid don't you think?"

"He might be a lot of things but paranoid is not one of them. One thing I've learned is to trust his judgment."

"I think we're ready. Bobby, can you find me an extension cord for the battery pack?" Junior asked.

"Sure," Bobby replied, eyeing Junior warily as he left in search of an extension cord.

"You're getting better," he said. "Your instincts were right. The Rat is in a van across the street. Either he was waiting on Bobby or he followed us here. I don't think he followed us, so Bobby must be next on the hit parade."

"What do you recommend that we do?"

"Well, nothing for now. Let's go ahead and tape Bobby's statement. Then we can decide what to do. I have a couple of suggestions."

"Well, let's hear them. There's no point in saving them."

"We have two choices. We can take Bobby with us and watch him 24/7, or we can let the natural order of things happen."

"That sounds ominous. Are you saying what I think you're saying?"

"Precisely. Bobby Boogaloo Bennett makes a nice chunky piece of cheese. Just the kind of meal a Rat likes." While Bobby searched for the extension cord, Junior explained the details of his plan.

As Bobby entered the room, JJ once again marveled at the beauty and simplicity of Junior's plan. Although there was risk involved, it would be necessary if they were going to catch the Rat. It was deliciously ironic. Bobby Bennett, in so many ways, was at the inception of the case; he could now represent the final piece. JJ was just a bit taken aback; he had begun all of this with a moral code that he thought inviolate. But now, after all that had transpired, he was willing to sacrifice Bobby Bennett's life. For what? Was it merely for the opportunity to expose greater evil and greed? Was he seeking justice and revenge for Katherine's murder? He was beyond a rational distinction for his actions. It no longer mattered what his motives were, it was no longer about him, and there was a larger objective. He had to acknowledge what he had always known- that everyone had a price. Apparently, destroying Victor and One Detroit, Inc. was now his price.

Chapter 36

HARVEY STONE AWOKE FROM HIS DAYDREAM by the persistent ringing of his cell phone. He wanted to ignore the phone but its persistent ringing forced him to pick it up and look at the caller ID. "Yeah," he said, "what is it?" He did not bother to conceal the annoyance in his voice.

"I'm here at the subject's house and he has visitors. JJ Battle and Lieutenant Spencer are here also with an unidentified female. Should I go ahead with the cleaning project and include the others?"

"Damn, I'm sick of Battle interfering in my business. However, don't take any action. I have a plan for him. We'll deal with him another way. This Spencer character is Battle's cousin. Let's send him a message. Don't kill him. But incapacitate him."

"With pleasure," the Rat replied. He was anxious to inflict some pain on an old nemesis. He would just wait for Spencer to appear and then squeeze off a round. First, he would have to change position. Spencer would be looking for the van where the Rat had left it before, so he would have to move it to a location he wouldn't expect. There would be a momentary pause that he knew Spencer would take, relieved that the van was apparently gone. That would be just the time he would need. That was a basic lesson that he learned in sniper school- distract the subject and disorient him. It would have to be a perfect shot. Spencer wouldn't give him much of a target, that much he knew.

However, he didn't need much. When he squeezed the trigger and heard the swoosh of the silencer, he would be long gone before Spencer knew what hit him

Stone knew he couldn't delay his plan any longer. If the Corktown deal was to close on time, he had to silence JJ Battle immediately. If the deal didn't close on time, then the developers couldn't begin to build by their deadline. Not only would the deal fall through, but it could also jeopardize the Super Bowl preparations. There were strict time deadlines to meet. Stone could not risk allowing JJ to prevent the plans going forward. He called his chief homicide Investigator, Mike Russell, and directed him to Judge Eva Anne Moody's residence to investigate her possible disappearance. He told him that he had received a call from a source at the courthouse saying that Judge Moody had been AWOL from court and some of her staff was concerned. He didn't want to arouse suspicion unnecessarily, so he instructed him to investigate on the pretense that he didn't want to send a patrol unit just in case there was something of a sensitive nature. He knew Russell was ambitious and would love to make the discovery. He made a phone call to his contact in the news department of Channel 7 News. Next, he called the Medical Examiner and directed him to the Judge's house. He had just set in motion the events that he hoped would keep JJ Battle out of his hair forever. If not forever, at least until the Corktown deal closed and his money was safely deposited in his off shore account.

After his phone call, the quiet upscale neighborhood of Judge Eva Ann Moody was overrun with police crime crews and local news organizations. It was a chaotic scene, and Stone was orchestrating everything. There was a press conference scheduled in thirty minutes and he would release the details of the suspect in the Judge's death. He wanted to give the news and wire services the time to set up so that they could receive the widest coverage. He knew that the death of a prominent African-American female judge would have wide-ranging implications. He wanted to make sure that he had all of the details covered. He had his best crime techs doing the inside investigations. This would ensure a thorough investigation. In addition to the financial windfall he would receive for the Corktown deal, he was looking forward to the notoriety for the investigations into the recent string of murders. It was like shooting fish in a barrel. Naturally, he would control all of the information and details in the investigation, and would appear to be psychically attuned to the case, since he was directly responsible for the murders. It was like a doctor creating a disease, because he alone had the cure. How could he lose? It was time for the press conference to begin. He stepped to the podium, assured and confident, and addressed the media.

"Ladies and Gentlemen, as you are aware, today we received an anonymous tip informing us of the tragic murder of one of our greatest and most beloved Judges Eva Ann Moody. We confirmed her death. However, today we are prepared to say that there may be a link into three of these recent murders. As you know, recently we have had a number of murders of women. These murders at first appeared to be random. We couldn't find a common thread to link the murders, until today. The recent deaths of Katherine Devlin, Brianna Tuller, and now Eva Ann Moody may have something in common. These deaths may be linked to a single killer. While we currently don't know the identity of the killer, we are seeking an individual of interest in connection with the murders. This individual has a strong connection to each of the victims."

Simultaneously, there were shouts from the media gallery, "who is this person?"

Stone took a long pause and let the enormity of his revelation hang in the air. "Please, ladies and gentlemen, I caution you that this person of interest is not a suspect at this time, however, we believe that he has relevant information regarding these three women."

"Who is it?" They shouted, fueled by the frenzy of an impending scandal.

Stone spoke slowly, choosing his words carefully. "The person we seek is Attorney JJ Battle."

The gallery erupted in unison. Cameras clicked, and reporters spoke in excited voices as live feeds were broadcast across the country. Reporters scurried like ants to file stories and to make deadlines for their live reports. Stone knew that this was just the diversion that would deflect attention away from the Corktown project. It would also get JJ Battle off his back. For once, the cocky attorney would see what it felt like to be a criminal defendant. Let him use his slick lawyer tricks for his own defense. He knew this announcement would create a firestorm of attention but he didn't care. He only wanted to close the deal and get his share of One Hundred Million Dollars from the Corktown deal.

JJ and Junior set up the video camera and began questioning Bobby regarding his involvement with One Detroit, Inc. They were careful to stay away from the windows so as not to give the Rat a clear shot. They decided not to tell Bobby about the Rat until after the taping. They did not want to spook Bobby unnecessarily. Now that they had Bobby's statement on tape, they could reveal the danger he faced. They now had to decide the best way to use Bobby.

At that moment, his cell phone began to ring. He recognized his office number and Marsha's extension. "Attorney Battle, I don't know if you've heard?" He could hear the fear and apprehension in Marsha's voice. Something was obviously wrong. He waited for her to continue.

"What is it, Marsha?" He braced himself for the worst. You couldn't be a criminal defense attorney and not be used to receiving bad news. It was an occupational hazard. You expected the worst and hoped for the best.

"It's on the news. They are saying that you are a person of interest in the murder of three women. What do you want me to do?" There was no mistaking the panic in her voice. She was barely holding it together.

"It's ok, Marsha. I expected it to happen any day now. I was prepared for it. Call Saul and let him know, and ask him to set up a meeting tonight with Stone. Call me back on my cell when he gives you the details. Marsha, don't worry. Everything is going to be alright," he said the words with more conviction than he really felt.

"I hope so. Let me know if there's anything else you need me to do."

As he hung up the phone, he was overcome by a deep sense of sadness. Although he harbored no illusions about his life or his profession, he was still struck by the unfairness of his circumstance. It was more than ironic; it was tragic. Here he was, a man whose job it was to defend the wrongfully accused, and now he was wrongfully accused himself. A more cynical person would say it was karma, he reflected ruefully. It seemed as if the universe was merely exacting revenge for his many transgressions. Whatever forces were responsible, he would now have to rely on a system that he had been all too willing to expose its flaws.

He could recall many times when his clients, faced with similar circumstances, loudly and passionately professed their innocence. He had trained himself not to be swayed into believing or disbelieving their protestations. He believed that the guilt or innocence of the individual should not affect his or her defense. It was the evidence or lack of evidence that should dictate the strategy. Guilt, or the presumption of guilt, got in the way of a good defense, he always told himself. He couldn't allow emotion to interfere with providing the best strategy that the facts would support. But now, faced with similar circumstances, it all felt so shallow and superficial. He now desperately needed someone who mattered to believe him.

They had finished interviewing Bobby and Junior was taking down the equipment and packing it back in the boxes. When Junior was finished, JJ called him over and said, "It's started. Stone just had a press conference. He all but named me as a suspect. He called me a person of interest. This is just his way of saying I'm the suspect, but they just don't have enough evidence to arrest me yet." JJ, said matter of factly.

JJ could not quite read Junior's expression. It was somewhere between excitement and consternation. He looked as if he couldn't wait to get things started. If that were the case, his wish had come true. JJ figured he only had a few hours left before his status of "person of interest" was elevated to suspect. The most important use of that time, he surmised, would be compiling the information that implicated One Detroit, Inc. Additionally, he and Junior needed a way to catch the Rat and Stone in the act of their murderous deeds. If they had targeted Bobby, it was unlikely that they would abandon their plan before completion. That could be just the break they needed. But, they needed a plan, and this is where Junior's expertise would be invaluable. He was a master at strategy. Besides, he probably knew the Rat better than anybody, with the possible exception of Stone.

"JJ, here's what I'm thinking. The Rat already made us. I doubt if he's still out there. He knows I saw him. That doesn't mean that he's abandoned Bobby as a target. On the contrary, now that he knows we're in contact with Bobby, it will probably accelerate his timetable for finishing him. We can do this one of two ways. If you feel an allegiance to Bobby and you want to protect him, we can take him with us and force the Rat to come and get him. The obvious risk with that strategy is that we make ourselves convenient targets as well. We learned early in special ops training that the more targets a sniper has to shoot at, the greater the likelihood he will hit something. I personally don't want to be an unintended victim because of Bobby. You have to decide if Bobby's important enough to take that risk." JJ was fascinated as Junior outlined his strategy and the reasons for and against a particular move. It was carefully thought out with the risks and benefits considered. JJ had a greater appreciation for his cousin's special expertise now than ever before. He continued to listen and mull over each option as Junior went along. He was careful not to interrupt, especially since Bobby was in the other room, unaware that they were deciding his fate.

"Now," he continued, excited about planning the operation. If we take Bobby, we might as well take the girl, she will only complicate things if something unintended happens to Bobby. We are the only people she can identify for the police. She'll say he was talking to his attorney and that handsome cousin of his, and that was the last time I saw Bobby alive. That's not good for us. Either they both go or they both stay."

"What's your other option?" JJ asked, mesmerized by the precision and thoroughness of Junior's planning.

"We leave him in his own mess. He created it-let him clean it up. With one provision; we place hidden cameras around the perimeter of the house just in case the Rat returns to finish the job."

"How long will that take? We don't have much time."

Once I have the equipment, thirty minutes tops. It's real basic equipment. I'll have it wired before they know it."

"When do you propose to do this?" JJ asked. He looked at his watch, concerned about his impending meeting with Stone. He forced himself to stifle the pressure he was feeling. He had always managed to turn the fear he felt into an adrenaline rush. He could now feel the excitement of the plan coming together.

"We can do it now. I know a little shop nearby that has all of the equipment. I have a friend there who owes me a favor. We'll have to come up with a believable story for Bobby as to why we're wiring his house. I'll leave that part to you. You're famous for creative lying." Junior had that characteristic smirk on his face that said, I know you are surprised, but just don't let it show.

"Alright. I'll talk to Bobby. You call your friend and get the equipment lined up."

"Don't go trying to act like an officer, giving orders. This is my operation."

Junior started packing away the gear and as he prepared to go pick up the surveillance equipment, he went around the back of the house making sure the Rat was no longer there. He carefully looked down the street for the white van or other suspicious vehicles and didn't see anything. He was confident the Rat was gone, but he knew he would be back another day soon.

"JJ, I'm leaving to go get the equipment, I checked out front and our friend is gone. But just in case, I wanted to make sure you had your piece."

"It's right here," JJ said touching his waistband where the Beretta was safely tucked. "We'll be fine. I'll call if I need you."

"You do that."

Junior went out the back door with a sense of determination. This was his domain and JJ could see the change in his demeanor. He stared at the street long after Junior had left, wondering how bad things would get. He had many things to do before that question would be answered. He still had a meeting with Stone looming. He looked at his watch, calculating how long it had been since he talked to Marsha. He wondered whether not hearing from Saul had any special significance. Like all good criminal defense attorneys, he thought about all of his options. Like all suspects, he fought that one overpowering urge-the need to flee. He knew that he would solve nothing by running, but it was an instinct that was difficult to suppress.

"Bobby, I need to speak with you." JJ called out to Bobby in the bedroom, putting aside his own troubles for the moment. Bobby came out with his characteristic grin, oblivious to the actions being taken for and against him. If it was true that the Lord protected fools and children, than surely Bobby was being looked after by a higher power.

"Listen," he began with his most soothing voice. "Look, when and if Victor and One Detroit, Inc. find out that you've talked to us, they may be upset and wish to retaliate."

"Attorney Battle, I don't think that's going to happen. Why would they want to harm me? We have too much history together."

JJ shook his head in sympathy. "Bobby, it may be because of your history that they may want to hurt you. But, as a precaution, we want to put some video surveillance equipment around the perimeter of your house. This will alert us if something strange is going on outside and we can notify you right away. The system will be monitored by a friend of Junior's. So, you will be safe. We don't expect anything to happen, but we just want to be sure."

"Attorney Battle, as I said before, I don't think they would do anything to hurt me. They need me." JJ was surprised at how naïve Bobby was being. But then Bobby didn't know all of the things that they had already done. Perhaps it was best that he was unaware of the circumstances so that he didn't panic and do something to alert Stone.

Junior walked back to the car with a purposeful, yet unhurried, step. He attempted to keep the vehicle and the camera equipment between him and a potential shot.

But, he knew he could not completely protect himself. If the Rat wanted to finish him, there was really no defense. He proceeded cautiously to the car. It happened so unexpectedly that at first it did not register. It started as a stinging in his right shoulder. It was as if the weight of the equipment suddenly became unbearable. Instinctively he dropped the equipment and grabbed his shoulder. It burned as if someone had stuck burning metal on his skin. It was with sudden understanding that he saw the blood on his hand and knew. He dived to the ground, rolling in the snow, while reaching with one motion for his gun with his left hand. He continued rolling, looking for the van. He heard it before he saw it, driving away from him. He still managed to squeeze off four rounds before the van skidded out of sight.

He lay in the snow, cursing himself for his carelessness yet thankful that he was still alive. He knew that it was a message shot and not a kill shot. He also knew the target area was selected to incapacitate him. It was a trademark shot by the Rat. It was his signature. It was a message that meant that Junior could not escape him. But, he was wrong. A wounded animal was the most dangerous. All he had to do was survive. He tried to push himself up using his left side. He knew he could not avoid the pain in his shoulder. He rose to his feet, oblivious to the dampness and cold from laying in the snow and the quickening loss of blood. He only had a few feet back to Bobby's house. He pressed his shoulder with his left hand seeking to stem the flow of blood. He made it to the porch and collapsed against the door with a heavy thud. The door opened and he stared up at JJ saying in a gasp, "damn Rat."

JJ looked around, realizing immediately that Junior had been shot. He dragged him to the house. He needed to know how serious it was. He searched for a pulse and found it beating strongly. He yelled for Bobby to bring some clean sheets or rags. He needed to stop the bleeding and to clean the wound. Then he could determine the seriousness of the wound. "Bobby, call 911."

"The hell you will." Junior exclaimed. There's no way I'm going out like that. I don't need a doctor."

"Junior, it's not your call. I'm not going to let you bleed to death."

"That's the least of our worries. Think this thing through. There's no way I can protect myself in the hospital. Besides, they would have to report it to the police, who we know we can't trust. So, the police and doctors are out of the question. I'll have to rely on home remedies."

"Are you sure?" JJ asked, feeling guilty because someone else he cared about was hurt. Where would it end?

"I'm certain. I'll live to fight another day. Some strong antibiotics and I'll be good as new."

"I'll get you home. Bobby, I'm taking him home. Will you be alright?"

"Don't worry about me. I'll be fine."

"Alright. Call me if you have any problems."

"JJ, we need to put the video equipment in the car. I sort of dropped it when I got hit."

"We'll take care of it. You just keep quiet while I get you home."

"Wait here while I go get the car." As JJ left, he removed the Beretta from his waist, holding it at his side as he retrieved the equipment and placed it in the car.

He pulled the car into Bobby's driveway and left the engine running and the passenger door open. Together with Bobby's help, they eased Junior off the porch and gently seated him in the car. JJ drove home quickly, but carefully. He checked his rear view mirror frequently. He dialed his cell phone.

"Marsha, there's been an accident. I need you to meet me at my house right away. Can you get somebody to take care of the kids for the night and possibly tomorrow?

"Are you OK?" She asked. Her voice choked with fear.

"Yeah, I'm fine, but Junior is a little worse for the wear. He might need a little TLC."

"I'll be right there."

They rode in silence the rest of the way. Marsha was in the driveway when they arrived. She opened the door and came back to help Junior into the house. Junior smiled when he saw her.

"I'll be fine. Let's just get this thing bandaged. I have a debt to repay."

"The only debt that you'll be paying is to let me bandage that shoulder and to get a good night's sleep. I have some medication that will make you forget you have a shoulder."

"If you insist, doctor," Junior said, putting up little resistance.

"I have to go to a meeting. I'll call you later." JJ was relieved that Marsha was there. He knew that Junior would be safe and it would free him to do the things he needed to do. He was tired of being manipulated. Since the day he saw Victor and Randy on the golf course he had unknowingly been seduced. First, it was the large retainer. Then when he got a little too close, they started to hurt the people he loved. It all became too much when they tried to frame him for Katherine, Brianna's, and Eva's murders. In their effort to destroy him, they had gone too far. Now he would make them pay and pay dearly.

Chapter 37

HE WAS IN THE CAR HEADED downtown. He knew it might be risky, but it was something he had to do. He called Saul and asked him to delay his meeting with Stone for two hours. He told Saul about Junior being shot, and who was responsible. Saul, like any good defense attorney didn't ask questions. He merely asked JJ if he needed his assistance.

"By the way Saul, is there an outstanding warrant for my arrest?" He knew that if there was, it would severely hamper his plans.

"No. There's nothing pending yet." He relaxed when Saul told him there were no warrants. So, it appeared that Stone only wanted to speak with him about the homicides. He assured him that he would be there and would cooperate. First, he had to tie up some loose ends.

JJ had considered every conceivable way to conclude things. He had tried everything, with disastrous results. Katherine was dead. His career and reputation were in ruins. Eva was dead, and now Junior was wounded. To make matters worse, he did not create these circumstances. He was caught in a tidal wave of circumstances that were pulling him under. But, these circumstances brought him to this solution. He never thought that he would ever feel this type of desperation. All of his life he worked hard to maintain control-control over his environment and circumstances. Now he was contemplating risking it all because he couldn't see any other way out. He hated to admit that he was no different from his clients. At least when they acted out of desperation, self-interest, or survival, they usually had no other choice. He had no excuse, nor did he feel compelled to come up with one. He was doing what he felt he must do-fight back.

He parked his car in a familiar spot beneath the Wayne County Jail. Once again, he was on familiar ground. This was his turf and he felt a heightened sense of purpose. He prepared himself for the inevitable ridicule that the sheriff deputies would inflict. It was necessary if he was to do what had to be done. He took a deep breath before entering the jail and assumed his defense attorney persona; he hardened himself and yet easily adopted the glib, self-assured manner that people expected. He presented his bar card merely as a formality; he was well known here. The deputy on duty, an old veteran of the system, greeted him with surprising compassion.

"Good evening JJ, we don't see you down here much. Sorry to hear about your recent trouble. Hope everything works out."

"Thanks Deac." He said. Everyone called the deputy, Deacon, because of his penchant for quoting scripture and reading the Bible. JJ was grateful that he was on duty tonight. He signed in and took the elevator to the eighth floor. The eighth floor was reserved for prisoners who were the most dangerous. These prisoners were usually awaiting trial on first-degree murder charges or other violent felonies. JJ was no stranger to this floor of the jail. He went through the metal detector and X-ray machine. He always made sure that he never brought a briefcase, to minimize the time it took to get through security. When he cleared security, he headed to the private attorney-client conference rooms. These rooms allowed attorneys to meet with their clients in private. They checked the prisoners for weapons and contraband when they left their cells, and again after their visit. JJ waited for him to bring the prisoner to the room. He knew that this was extremely risky. This was a public place and his name would be recorded in the record along with videotape of his image. It was a calculated risk, but one he felt he must take. He had run out of options. He had been playing their game by their rules and he was losing, and losing badly. It was time to launch the equivalent of a Hail Mary pass. It was what brought him here; re-opening a chapter that he thought he had closed forever.

Kareem Abdul Boozer. He held the key to JJ's plan, as tenuous as it was. It would be no small feat to convince him. It might even require JJ representing him in his pending murder case. It was a desperate place that he found himself, seeking the aid of a murderer. If it failed and things went wrong, everything would be destroyed. Kareem was his only hope.

He waited for them to bring Kareem to the conference room, anticipating his reaction. JJ had not responded when Kareem was arrested and he had refused to represent him. It had been over a year since his arrest, and he had been in jail throughout that time awaiting trial. It was a slow process for the legally disadvantaged. Kareem survived. But, JJ knew his reaction would not be one of reconciliation. Men like Kareem lived by loyalty and demanded as much from his people. JJ's refusal to represent him was betrayal. If JJ had been a member of his organization, there would have been consequences. JJ had to take all of this into consideration when he thought of approaching Kareem. He had to find a way to overcome Kareem's vindictive nature and enlist his cooperation. In doing so, it meant that he would be indebted to Kareem, and that indebtedness could require any number of repayment options.

Kareem came strutting out, the epitome of self-assured bravado. Whether it was an act or true persona, Kareem was someone who commanded attention and respect. He was dangerous because life had no value to him, not even his own. JJ's method of dealing with him was to appeal to his intellect, and not feed his voracious ego. This was the surest way to earn his disrespect.

"Well, well, well. When they said my attorney was here to see me, you were the last person I expected to see. Especially since you don't represent me. I thought we were tighter than that." JJ watched carefully as Kareem adopted equal parts sarcasm and sincerity.

JJ waited. He knew that with Kareem, everything was about power and control. If JJ resorted to a groveling apology, or if he was too hard line, he would lose him. If he lost him, he lost everything. So, he waited and watched, waiting for a telltale sign on how to proceed.

"It was business," he said, waiting for Kareem to take a seat across from him.

"I was going through some personal issues and it was too much at the time."

"Yeah, I heard. I'm sorry about your woman. That was cold-blooded. Word on the street is that there's some kind of serial killer running around."

"That's what I wanted to talk to you about." JJ paused, wondering how much he wanted to tell Kareem. If he provided him with too much information, it might unnecessarily complicate matters. But, he had to give him enough information to allow him to make the connection on how he could fit into all of this. He decided to give him only as much information as was necessary to convince him of his need to participate.

"It started with a client I represented in a criminal case. Because of my representation, I uncovered some information about a multi-million dollar scandal involving some very important people in the city. I shared this information with my fiancé and she was murdered. A witness in the case, along with Judge Moody, was also murdered. The police authorities are implicating me in the murders."

"That's foul. Who are these people?"

"They are a group called One Detroit, Inc., and there are some very influential people who are part of the organization. I uncovered this fraud, and they want to stop me from exposing their deal."

"Why don't you just walk away? He asked, with unexpected concern.

"Because I have too much at stake. They've taken something very valuable from me and it cannot be replaced."

"What do you want from me?" Kareem asked, already certain of the answer.

"I need to know if you're still the man?" The question hung between them, creating momentary discomfort. It had come to this. JJ was gambling that there was nothing to lose. So many times he had sat in these very cells, grinding to salvage the remains of someone else's broken life. Often he had felt their desperation and most times their fear and vulnerability. They wanted what he now wanted-someone committed to his cause. JJ took pride in being that man. He was the one who accepted unpopular causes and fought for the underdog. He did it because beneath the expensive suits and trappings of success, he was just like them. No, in fact, he was them.

He could feel an imperceptible shift. His universe had always spun on a perfect axis; it was about to spin out of orbit. It was as if some cosmic force was pulling him beyond his will. He looked at Kareem sitting across from him and knew he was now a part of the wake that this evil man wrought. They were now collaborators, co-conspirators, yet that thought neither surprised JJ nor repulsed him.

The heating system hummed quietly. In the distance, he could hear inmates' conversations full of bravado, laughter and laced with profanity. It was a place of despair yet these men found some humanity in the midst of their circumstances. Perhaps there was hope yet for these forsaken souls locked in these cages. Perhaps hope was alive. But, JJ was perched on the brink of madness, unable to pull himself back from the precipice. He took that final knowing leap. He knew he might never return, and if he did, he would not be the same. Yet he did it anyway. Anger, revenge, and the pain of a lost love were proving to be emotions he could not conquer, yet he refused to surrender. He leaned forward, waiting; waiting on this monster to provide acknowledgement that he was on board.

"If you mean am I still running things, the answer is yes. If you mean is my organization still operational, the answer is still yes."

"In that case what we need to discuss obviously involves some serious issues of confidentiality. I know we've been through a lot, but I need to know if this is something you can handle."

"Attorney Battle, I'm insulted." He said, feigning pain. "If you mean can you trust me? Let me tell you this. I run an organization where loyalty is essential. We take an oath that our work is secret. Violation of that oath means automatic death. I am old school. It goes to the grave with me. The same for my people. They know the consequences. The work I do for my clients is protected. It's sort of like attorney-client privilege. I do not reveal secrets."

"I believe that. That's why I'm here talking to you. I couldn't trust this to anybody else. But, to ensure that our secrets are safe with each other, we need to have a mutual commitment to each other. I made a decision to get out of this business. But, I was pulled back in. So this is what I am proposing: in exchange for you handling these two matters for me, I'll agree to represent you in your current legal difficulties."

"How do you know I won't refuse your offer?"

"Because you can't afford not to accept my offer. You need the credibility that my representation can bring. It will look better to the court and the jury if your previous attorney believes in you enough to represent you again. Besides, I'm the best attorney for your case. My unique talents are perfect for your situation."

"You make a persuasive argument, counselor. I believe we have a deal."

"I know that between professionals I don't have to emphasize that there can be no mistakes. The timing of what I need must be perfect. There are a number of factors that depend on precise timing."

"It's like you always tell me. Leave the logistics to the professionals. You just tell me the target and the date and I'll handle the rest."

"I need to caution you that based on my visit, it's likely that the police will try to develop a conspiracy theory. That's why I'll have you sign a retainer agreement tonight. That will provide a reason for our visit. Secondly, when this all happens, they will verify your visitor log, phone records, and try to make a connection. You need to be very careful about how you manage this."

"I'm way ahead of you. Just provide me with as much information as you can. I'll arrange to get it to the correct people."

"I purposely didn't tell you who the targets are. I didn't want that to change your mind." JJ said.

"It doesn't matter. Everybody is a target. Everybody is vulnerable. You let me worry about those details."

"The first target is someone we both know quite well. Harvey Stone, Chief of Homicide." JJ waited for Kareem's reaction. All he saw was a wry, knowing smile curl across his lips. He nodded in approval.

"If ever a man was deserving. It's Harvey Stone. That won't be a problem. He has some nasty habits that frequently put him in dangerous situations. He'll be easy to find.

"The next person won't be so easy. This guy is a former Green Beret and Mercenary. He's an expert at killing. They must be very careful. I believe he's responsible for all of the killings that they're trying to blame on me. He's dangerous."

"My guys will see that as a challenge. I'll have to pay top dollar. But it's an easy exchange, considering I won't have to pay the cost of your legal fees."

Kareem laughed, enjoying his brand of negotiation. "It sounds like mutual consent to me," he said.

JJ stared across the table at Kareem as he had done on many previous occasions, but this time he saw something different. He was the same old Kareem full of hip-hop bluster and swagger. But, there was hardness to his character, an evil in his eyes that JJ had not seen before. He didn't know if it was always there and he had just failed to see it. You didn't control a man like Kareem, you handled him. JJ was never intimidated or fearful of Kareem because there were always mutual benefits between them. He was aware that as long as the dynamics of the relationship remained the same, Kareem could be trusted. It had come to this - bartering with a killer for the cost of legal fees.

Today JJ had come to a sad realization; that he wasn't much different from Kareem after all. They were just different sides of the same coin.

"Kareem, I might have to go away while this is going on. I'll be back in plenty of time for your trial. Besides, nobody knows the facts better than I do. But, we'll just have to wait and see. I have definite plans for your defense."

"Attorney Battle, you know I trust you completely. I know that you will do whatever you have to. I know that you will give me your best. Just like always."

JJ felt the sense of loathing returning. He knew that whatever happened, this would be his last criminal case. He finished giving Kareem all of the details about the Rat. He next told him of the timing of when he wanted things to happen. When he was sure that Kareem had all of the information he needed, he left the jail.

It was foolish to trust his future to a man like Kareem, he knew that, but he was out of options. He knew that a man without options was dangerous.

Outside, the temperature had fallen even more. He hurried to the car, keeping a close eye on everything around him. The Rat could be lurking anywhere, even this close to police headquarters. He looked at his watch, it was 7:45, and he had fifteen minutes before he was to meet Saul and Stone at police headquarters. He knew the meeting was a formality but Stone could still be a nuisance. The important thing was to stay out of jail.

Chapter 38

ALTHOUGH JJ HAD BEEN IN POLICE headquarters at Thirteen Hundred Beaubien many times, he had never been there as a suspect. Usually, he entered the building with a great deal of righteous indignation; it was a defense lawyer's best weapon. In Detroit, it was the only way to get things done; otherwise, you encountered a healthy dose of skepticism. But, today, he was happy that Saul was here on his behalf. It freed him up to pay attention to detective Stone. He entered the lobby of the once grand building and looked around for Saul. He was there in a corner of the lobby, completely nonchalant. He was the attorney that important people in trouble sought. He was capable of managing any situation in any court, from district court to federal court. He had a skill and a presence that suggested he was in control. JJ was thankful he was there.

"JJ I have already had some preliminary talks with Stone and this is just a formality. Let me do the talking and handle everything, unless I indicate it's all right to speak. I know that goes against your normal approach. In this instance, you are a suspect, and we still need to protect your right to remain silent. I know I don't have to tell you this, but I just wanted to remind you to let me handle this."

JJ liked the calming effect of Saul's demeanor. It was soothing and allowed JJ to take a deep breath and to control his emotions. He knew he was so close to this being over. He just had to be patient for a few more days and allow everything to sort itself out.

They entered Stone's office and JJ was surprised at the orderliness of the office. Stone, a street detective at heart, spent very little time in the office. He felt more at home on the streets than being an administrator. They sat down in the two chairs in front of Stone's desk and waited while the detective intentionally fumbled with papers on his desk. The desk, unusually large, was not your standard government issue, but was high-end mahogany. The rest of the furniture was equally impressive, catalogue issue. The artwork on the walls was tasteful but inexpensive, selected more for its coordination with the décor than its artistic value. Still it was not what you would expect from Harvey Stone.

Finally, Stone spoke to Saul in a calm, controlled voice. "Thank you for bringing your client in today." He said, looking at Saul while ignoring JJ. He typically used this same strategy with criminal defendants. He designed the strategy to make them feel disrespected, which might force them into blurting out something incriminating. JJ was used to the tactic and had counseled his clients many times to avoid the trap. He waited to see what strategy Stone would choose and he didn't have to wait long.

"Counselor, as you know," he began, adopting an official air. "There have been a number of murders recently and your client has been implicated in at least three of them. We have compelling evidence that links him to each of the three victims. We feel that the evidence is more than circumstantial and we wanted to give your client a chance to give his side of the facts."

Saul studied Stone before he responded. "Lieutenant Stone, thank you for allowing us to meet with you today regarding these unfortunate deaths. I assure you that my client has no information concerning these horrible events. In fact, we were hoping that you could provide us with some information that would help me understand why you think my client might be involved. As you recall, my client himself was a victim of an attempted shooting that he reported to this office. I suspect that the individual responsible for the attack on my client is also the person responsible for these murders."

JJ liked the way that Saul smoothly shifted the burden to Stone to force him to provide information on the crimes. Saul knew this was not the place to try the case. Putting forth theories now would not help JJ. Besides, he didn't want to give Stone ammunition that he might use against him later. Instead, he sparred with Stone, repeatedly forcing him to support his theory. It was text-book defense strategy and JJ had used the strategy many times himself. This time, however, he had a more personal interest in the outcome. It was a subtle strategy that was not without risks. You didn't want to antagonize the police and force their hand. The police could tire of the sparring and decide to get an arrest warrant, in which case the defense looked foolish. Sometimes there was no choice, the police intended to arrest the defendant anyway, and simply didn't want to go through the time and expense of picking up the defendant. However, usually, if there was to be an arrest, they notified the defense attorney first, thereby preserving the civility of the attorney-police relationship. It was a tenuous relationship that relied on mutual trust.

They sparred back and forth for over an hour as JJ sat passively by as Stone continued to talk about him as if he were not there. He watched Stone's demeanor as he spoke, looking for signs of what he intended to do.

"Well, we are still conducting DNA testing of evidence, so that might provide your client with a slight reprieve until we get a final analysis back from the lab."

"In the meantime Lieutenant, I would focus my investigation on suspects other than my client. I am certain that will be more fertile ground," Saul said confidently.

"Well, I would advise your client not to leave the jurisdiction. There may be a warrant any day now."

"If that possibility occurs, I would appreciate the courtesy of being notified first so that I may bring my client in voluntarily."

"It would be my pleasure. I'll deliver the news myself." JJ watched as Stone gloated at having the upper hand. He knew that it was a matter of days before the Corktown deal closed. He merely wanted to inconvenience JJ long enough to allow the deal to close. In a few days he wouldn't care about any of this, he would take the money and run.

JJ found it easier to remain silent than he thought. Stone's effort to antagonize him had failed. Saul had adeptly kept Stone on a professional level, which controlled the usual acrimony between Stone and JJ. JJ knew that in a matter of days it would all change. He felt comfort in the old adage that his mother was fond of quoting, "he who laughs last, laughs best." How prophetic, JJ thought. He was prepared for the final laugh. He wondered if Stone was equally prepared.

Chapter 39

JJ HAD NEVER HEARD KEISHA JAMES' voice before so her gruff, matter-of-fact demeanor was a bit surprising. She was abrasive and blunt. They agreed to meet at the IHOP on Jefferson at 10:30 am. He would let Junior sleep, but he would take the Beretta with him just in case. He had an inkling that the phone call meant that things had gone as planned, but you could never be too sure. This could mean that all of the things that had been happening for the last few weeks were nearly finished.

He pulled into the parking lot of the IHOP and remembered that he didn't know what Keisha looked like. He hoped that she would be able to find him. He didn't have to wait long. He could see her approaching from across the room, and knew it had to be her. He was right. He stood there staring in amazement. Her demeanor was less abrasive but still direct.

"Mr. Battle," she said, extending her hand and grasping his in a firm handshake. "Thanks for joining me. The waitress has our table over here."

JJ followed her to the back of the restaurant to a table in a section that appeared to be closed. They were the only diners in this section. Keisha James was striking. That was an understatement. The first thing JJ noticed was her size. She was a large woman. She was over six feet tall and very solidly built. Not fat, mind you. She was body builder-muscular. Her biceps were large and developed, which made JJ remind himself to get to the gym to workout. She wore a tight lycra top that accentuated her massive arms and breasts. Her waist tapered narrowly to wide and round hips. She was not attractive, nor was she ugly. Her angry demeanor though, dominated her looks. She was not the type of woman with whom a man took liberties. Her height was further exaggerated by 4-inch stiletto heel boots. On top of her size, she wore a long blond wig that hung to her waist. She was the type of woman that commanded attention from both men and women. Not all of the attention was flattering, however. You could not help but stare. Keisha was obviously a woman who didn't care what other people thought. She would not have been JJ's choice for a breakfast companion, but he had no choice in the matter. You could tell that she was used to being in control as she sat down across from him.

"I thought that a public place would be better for our conversation. I'm not a big fan of discussing confidential matters on telephones. Let's just say that I'm a little mistrustful of government involvement."

"That's always a prudent approach." JJ watched her and was content to allow her to direct the tone and direction of the meeting. She obviously was in no hurry to say what she came to say. She was a walking paradox. She was large and had a hard street-looking appearance, but her speech and demeanor suggested she was articulate and well educated. So, JJ waited and listened.

"I want to thank you for representing Kareem in the past; we really appreciate everything you did. It meant a lot. I don't know what you have worked out for this new case, but I hope you represent him again." JJ could hear the sincerity in her voice. He also could see how much she cared for Kareem. He figured that even cold-blooded killers needed love. Although the news that JJ was waiting to hear was vital, he learned long ago never to rush news, whether it was good or bad. It would reveal itself in time. He adopted that philosophy after waiting on countless juries to arrive at a verdict. It didn't make any difference how much you wanted to hear a particular verdict; you couldn't rush the process.

So, JJ went along and ordered breakfast. He loved their buttermilk pancakes and redskin potatoes covered in catsup. He added a side order of fruit so he wouldn't feel so guilty. Keisha ordered the lumberjack special. She had pancakes, eggs, bacon, sausage, and hash browns. She had a healthy appetite. They made small talk while they waited on their food. Mostly they talked about the cold weather. JJ was beginning to like Keisha James. She had the toughness of a street thug, but also possessed an intelligent and educated attitude. She was as comfortable discussing street crime as she was discussing politics and the state of the economy. He was impressed.

They finished eating and were on their second cup of coffee when JJ knew it was time for Keisha to give him the news. He looked over at her searching for what was inside her. He had trusted his life to her in a sense, yet he knew so little about her. The fundamental question was left unanswered between them, could he trust her? After all, she and Kareem lived in a world where human life had little meaning. To them, life was merely currency to fund necessary transactions. What made him think that they would value his life? He didn't know the answer but he remembered the circumstances surrounding his decision. He knew that whatever happened he would have to live with the consequences. But, he also knew he had to balance the odds. If he did not, he might leave himself vulnerable to Kareem's psychopathic whims.

He had to finish this chapter forever and not look back to the past, or allow these events to haunt him. He had to acknowledge that he had given tremendous power to Kareem with the knowledge of these events. Along with that power, Kareem also had the power to misuse this knowledge. JJ had to accept this reality. He could not change these facts. It was a decision he made, knowing the consequences. But, he would try to minimize his exposure.

"Now that we have the pleasantries out of the way, I want to talk ..."

"Excuse me Keisha," he interrupted, gently placing his hand on her arm. "My old criminal defense lawyer instincts keep getting in the way."

"What exactly do you mean?" She countered. A look of rising anger was forming on her face.

"If we discuss what I think we are about to discuss a number of things happen. The first, we lose the confidentiality of attorney-client privilege. For example, let's say hypothetically we were about to discuss some criminal behavior. Ethical rules and such. As Kareem's and your attorney, I am bound by ethical duties to report an ongoing crime. Secondly, some over-zealous law enforcement official might consider our conversation as being in furtherance of the commission of a crime. In other words, it might be viewed as a criminal conspiracy. Lastly, and I'm certain this is not the case, you could perhaps be working as an informant, wearing a wire or a listening device, and what we say may be construed as incriminating or implicating ourselves in a crime. Do you get my point?"

JJ expected an eruption of anger from Keisha. Instead, he got a knowing nod of her head.

"Kareem said you were sharp, now I believe him. What did you have in mind? But just so the record is straight, do I look like the kind of person that would wear a wire, or betray a confidence?"

"The answer is no. But, that's not the point. The fact that the possibility exists makes it a risky proposition. Law enforcement has compromised tougher and more seasoned individuals in the past. Let's not digress into a philosophical discussion about your loyalty. We'll agree it is unquestioned. So, here's what I propose. If there are any unresolved issues regarding our mutual obligations, call my secretary and make an appointment for an office consultation. If I don't hear from you by close of business tomorrow, I'll assume this concludes these matters forever."

"What about Kareem, she asked. Her expression was one of confusion and uncertainty. JJ could see the genuine concern she had for Kareem. She was expecting something in return for their services. It was the first time that he saw any softness in her. It was ironic that even someone like Kareem had someone caring about him. JJ had a plan for Kareem but he didn't want to reveal it to Keisha, not yet anyway. It was all part of the larger plan and he needed additional time to finalize the details. What he didn't want was to feel that Kareem and Keisha were leveraging what they had done as some sort of quid pro quo. He didn't need that sort of pressure. He had to provide her with an answer. He needed to buy time. He was so close to completing everything and he couldn't afford any last minute slipups. He looked at her straight in the eye and said to her what he had said to hundreds of clients; "TRUST ME!"

Chapter 40

HARVEY STONE WAS FEELING POSITIVELY EUPHORIC. His plan was working to perfection. The Corktown deal was nearing closing and he was about to reap his windfall. The thought of having enough money to retire was furthering his excitement. He enjoyed toying with Battle and making him feel the discomfort that he was so good at subjecting others. His intention was to distract Battle and delay him while the Corktown deal was completed. If Battle was busy clearing his own name, he would have less time to meddle in One Detroit, Inc's affairs. It was a personal treat smearing Battle's name and reputation in the media. Now he needed to put all of that aside, because this was his night to unwind and enjoy some of the fruits of his labor. Tonight he had lined up a rendezvous with one of his favorite little dates and he pressed the accelerator as he thought about her tight, young body awaiting him. He dialed her number on his cell phone and waited for it to ring. When the voice answered, Stone said tersely, "meet me downstairs in ten minutes." Stone, feeling the excitement of the upcoming date, turned on his flashing blue lights, forcing slower cars to move out of his way.

Stone selected his dates carefully. He screened them and investigated their backgrounds. They had to be young and could not be drug users. They had to be unattached without boyfriends or lovers interfering. He didn't mind children, but the women had to be available when he called. He worked out the financial arrangements in advance. It simplified his life and eliminated any emotional entanglements. Tonight he was seeing his favorite, Shonda Lewis. She was a sweet girl who was always very accommodating. She was sexy in a shy, young girl way. She was patient and did everything that Stone asked her to do; just the way he liked it.

She was waiting at the door for the lieutenant's car. It was Wednesday, and this was his usual day to visit. She had put the kids to bed early, bathed and put on her best perfume. She hated what she was doing, but it helped pay her bills. She didn't receive child support from her children's father, and these dates helped her make ends meet. She knew that didn't justify it, but she didn't have any other answers. She ran out to the car and quickly got in, escaping the frigid cold temperatures. The lieutenant had the heat on in the car and the windows were already starting to fog. She asked him if he wanted to come upstairs and get out of the cold, but he said no. He had the local jazz station playing softly in the background, and she could sense that he was in a different mood. He seemed happy and a little excited, and she wondered why. This was the hardest part for her, beginning and starting to make conversation. She wanted to hurry up and get it over with so she could get back to her apartment and the kids. But, he liked to take it slow. So, she went along.

He handed her an envelope and she folded it and put it in her coat pocket, remembering to say "thank you." She knew she didn't have to count it and there was always a little something extra there; he was generous in that way. This was the hard part, and she didn't know where to begin. She looked around hoping that no one was watching. Fortunately, because of the weather the streets were completely deserted. She wore a long, silky nightgown without panties. He liked it that way, knowing that she was ready and accessible for him. She gently took his large hand and guided it to her. She heard him catch his breath as he touched the softness and warmth of her thighs. She waited patiently for his clumsy touch. After all of these times she had hoped that he could just once please her. But, that was too much to ask. So, she endured and thought of shopping and the mall. She waited and fantasized about other men as she waited for him to get aroused.

She was not the only person waiting. Across the street in the shadow of a burned out liquor store stood two young assassins, Juanita Isom and Jason Lee, two of YKA's finest. They were specially chosen and trained for this assignment. Unknown to them, there was a backup team dispatched to make sure that they completed their assignment. It was the backup team's job to clean up any loose ends that Juanita and Jason left. Tonight that would not be necessary.

Juanita was a runaway who had been living in and out of foster care since she was twelve. When she got tired of foster care, she lived on the streets and hustled, selling drugs and shoplifting to survive. An uncle had repeatedly molested her until one day she plunged an ink pen in his neck and fled. She hated men ever since. She was tough and ruthless and a favorite of the YKA management because of her toughness. However, she was also recruited because she was Stone's type. She was well endowed and attractive in a rough, streetwise way. Her look encouraged men to take liberties, but they quickly found out how dangerous she could be. In addition to the YKA-issued Berettas she carried, she was incredibly proficient with an ever-present straight razor.

Jason Lee was another story. He had been abandoned by his mother and sent to live with an aunt who already had too many children of her own to raise. Jason ran away and began to live on the street in abandoned homes. When he left, his aunt thought, *one less mouth to feed*. He found other young, abandoned boys and they formed a gang, surviving by selling drugs, theft and robbery. He wound up in the juvenile system after a series of arrests.

He was small and frail and by the time he was twelve, he had been in and out of foster homes and juvenile detention facilities. He had been beaten and raped. Because of his small size, he could not defend himself. One day, fed up with being a victim, he struck back. While his primary tormentor slept, he doused him with a concoction of gasoline and other fluids and set him ablaze. His tormentor suffered severe burns and barely survived, but Jason's reputation quickly spread throughout the juvenile system, and he was never victimized again. That began his fascination with fire, and he was always called, 'Pyro', short for pyromaniac. He continually experimented with fire and flammable compounds and could set fires that were untraceable. His favorite now was a compound that burned hotter than gasoline but was undetectable by smell or sight. You were consumed in flames before you knew you were even burning. These young killers had been dispatched to kill Lieutenant Harvey Stone.

As Pyro and Juanita waited in the shadows, Shonda could feel Stone's excitement. Usually, she had to work much harder for him to be ready to enter her. But, tonight was different. She started to unfasten his belt and unzip his pants. The heat and the closeness of the car was making her warm. She pulled off her coat and gracefully slid over to mount Stone. He obliged, leaning back as she guided him. She could tell he was lost somewhere deep in his own thoughts. She took her time as the clock in her head began to count down the minutes. She was careful. If things happened too fast, she would have to repeat the process again. That would take time. So she slowly moved against him gently and rhythmically rocking, her eyes closed and focused on silk blouses and fine clothes.

This was how she managed. She mentally escaped to more pleasant things. She moaned a soft, gentle moan in his ear, calling his name. She gripped tighter, pulling him closer and increasing her pace slightly. This was her job and she was quite good at it. He was almost there she thought, and soon it would be over. She moaned a practiced moan of fake pleasure that increased Stone's pleasure. He grabbed the softness of her round hips and pulled her closer into him. She thought she saw something move outside the car, but she couldn't be sure. The windows were purposely tinted, and the combination of their heavy breathing had completely fogged the windows. Again, she thought she saw movement on the side of the car. It was too late, for a number of reasons. Stone was beginning an incredible orgasm and was thrusting and grunting and squeezing her tightly. His eyes were tightly closed. She had quickened her pace and thrusts to bring him to climax. It would be his last.

Shonda Lewis was twenty-one years old with two children. She would not live to see her children grow up. They would become orphans. She was a victim of circumstances beyond her control. She had never heard of Corktown or One Detroit, Inc., but she would die because of it. Her dreams and ambitions were meaningless. She was a victim of randomness and irrelevance and would be an inconsequential footnote when the facts were reported. She mattered, but not to Juanita and Pyro.

Juanita and Pyro both approached the car with Berettas equipped with silencers in both hands. They were at a point where there was no turning back. If witnesses appeared, they would become part of the tragedy, victims of fate and circumstance. They had practiced their assignments and now they were ready to complete their mission. Juanita approached from the driver's side and Pyro from the passenger side. They both squeezed off rounds with Juanita aiming first for the head and chest and then for the groin. Pyro's shots caught Shonda just as she realized too late that the movement that she thought she saw was actually real. The bullets entered her brain and killed her instantly. Juanita broke out the glass on the driver's side, and fired a couple of more shots into Stone, making sure he was dead. She then removed the razor and slit his throat. Pyro was also working quickly. He pulled a vial out of his pocket and poured liquid onto the interior of the vehicle. He then placed two tablets into the gas tank. He lit a match and they quickly walked away from the vehicle. When they were a hundred feet away, it exploded in a ball of fire. In seconds, the car was completely engulfed in flames and burning hotter than a normal vehicle fire. Neighbors from the projects were looking out of windows and coming outside to view the flames. Someone called the fire department but it would be too late. As a crowd formed, Pyro and Juanita blended in with the crowd. The fire department arrived while the car continued to burn. The smell of burning flesh hung in the air. Because of the temperature, the firefighters had difficulty putting out the blaze. They could not have known that the accelerant used by Pyro could not be doused by water. The vehicle was quickly destroyed. The bodies were burned beyond recognition. Harvey Stone, Chief Homicide Detective of the Detroit Police Department, was now a homicide victim himself.

Pyro and Juanita wanted to admire their handiwork longer, but decided to head back to the east side. They were going to take the bus but decided to celebrate by taking a cab. When the cab arrived, the driver took one look at them and wondered if he could collect his fare.

As they got in the vehicle, they could see the driver eyeing them suspiciously. "Do you kids have money to pay for the fare?" He asked skeptically.

"Yeah, we got money. Now just drive the cab you pervert and don't try nothin.'" Juanita said, holding up a wad of money.

As they settled into the back seat, Pyro slid closer and looked at Juanita affectionately, thinking; "that's my kind of woman."

Joshua's battle had officially begun.

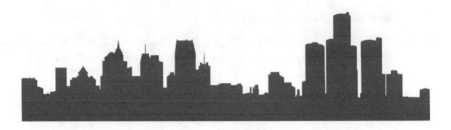

Chapter 41

IT WAS SIX A.M. AND THE city was still in the throes of an arctic cold spell. The day promised more of the same, with the wind chill hovering in the minus numbers. Only a few hearty souls waiting on the perpetually late city buses were on the streets. The restaurants along Gratiot Avenue were full as people opted to take advantage of the heat inside while they waited on buses. Sipping on a warm beverage was preferable to enduring the cold temperatures outside.

"Damn! I almost wish I was back in Mexico City, at least it was warm," said Pepino Chavez to his sister, Mariela. He spoke with a heavy Mexican accent that suggested he had been in the states for only a short time. In reality, it had been three long years. He had come over with his sister and family illegally, escaping poverty, and overcrowding in his hometown. In Mexico, his family barely eked out a living doing whatever they could to survive. They lived in the Cuautepec neighborhood of Mexico City. Over a million people lived there with little or no water or electricity.

His father had come over first and migrated to Michigan where there was a large Latino population and plenty of work, if you were willing to work hard. A year later the rest of the family arrived and settled into a sort of little Mexico, a part of the city on the near west side and favored by Mexican immigrants. It was a tough life for Pepino. He did not speak the language, went to school where they ridiculed and hated him for his thick accent. He quickly dropped out and fell into gang life. He joined the Latin Counts, which ruled the near west side. In spite of his youth, he quickly rose to the highest ranks. He was fearless and ruthless and relied on his boxing skills that he had developed on the streets of Mexico City. Older members of the gang respected him for his ability to defend himself. They still talked about his initiation into the gang, because he fought so valiantly, and ended up knocking a number of gang members unconscious. It was also how he got his gang nickname, Mule, because he hit like a mule.

Mariela Chavez was more than just an illegal immigrant. She was a dangerous immigrant. She did not buy into the American dream. In fact, she was intent on creating her own American dream on her terms. She was 15 when she arrived in Detroit, and now at 18, she was a woman. Like her brother, she did not attend school, and had difficulty speaking the language. She spoke a mix of Mexican and English slang that she learned on the streets. Her life on the west side of Detroit was not much different from life in Mexico City. She had her chicas, which she had formed into a gang and fought for control against the white and the black girls of her neighborhood. She did not bother going to school; she just hung out every day, drank, smoked marijuana, and had sex. Her gang became more and more ruthless with the violence escalating from beatings to knifings and occasional shootings. When Kareem and his lieutenants recruited Mariela and Pepino for YKA, it seemed like a natural progression to them. They were being paid for what they had been doing free, committing murder and mayhem.

"Stop complaining, you puta," she scolded her brother as they walked to their destination. She was freezing as she tugged at the maid's uniform that she borrowed from her cousin for today's job. Pepino had on overalls under his down jacket that gave him the appearance of a typical Mexican worker. The presence of Latinos on the streets of Detroit was a common occurrence now, as Mexican immigrants filled many domestic and day laborer jobs. They had both been working for YKA for about six months, had handled a few cases, and knew what the expectations were. What they did not know was that YKA had hired a backup team to finish the job should they fail. They did not intend to fail.

As they were about a block from the motel, they both stopped to check their weapons. They were both equipped with standard YKA-issued Berettas. They both carried smaller weapons of their own in addition to knives that they were both skilled in using. They had done preliminary reconnaissance to get a feel for the location where the subject's room was located. They had gone over the plan so many times that they knew it by heart. There was a backup plan in place in case the subject was uncooperative or something went wrong. This was the first assignment they worked on together and they were excited about the expected payoff for the job. They walked with purpose as the snow crunched under their feet.

The Rat was slowly waking as the television flashed in the background. He was starting to feel claustrophobic in the small motel room. It was difficult to remember how long he had been in Detroit. He did not care for the weather but overall it was an OK assignment. He had made a nice sum of money; it would be over one hundred thousand when he was finished. It should have been more if they had allowed him to kill JJ Battle and Lieutenant Spencer. He wondered how much longer they would need him.

He heard a knock on the door. Instinctively he grabbed his weapon and quickly headed to the door. Who would be knocking at the door at six a.m.? He had already paid his rent for the month. He left explicit instructions with the manager that he did not want to be disturbed. That included maid service. Who could this be knocking on his door this early?

He peeked out of the peephole and saw a young Latino girl in a maid's uniform holding a set of sheets and towels. "Shit! I don't need any sheets or towels," he said, disgust in his voice. He had left explicit instructions with the manager that he didn't want to be disturbed, and he didn't need maid service. He hated interruptions.

"Si. But my manager told me to bring the sheets and towels to your room to change." She said, with a thick Mexican accent and the gun concealed beneath the sheets and towels.

"Just leave them right there and I'll get them later," he said, trying to discourage the girl. He hated when people didn't follow orders. He also hated contact with people, for a number of reasons, the least of which was that he hated people.

"No senor, I must deliver them to your room. My boss will fire me if I leave them in the snow. It will just take a minute." They had rehearsed this part many times in case the Rat would not open the door. They considered firing through the door but decided against that strategy except as a last resort. Mariela stood patiently waiting while the Rat decided whether to open the door. Pepino stood to his sister's left, his gun casually at his side.

"Please Senor," Mariela pleaded.

The Rat, muttering to himself, slid the chain back and unlocked the door. In one smooth, practiced motion, Mariela tossed the sheets and towels, momentarily distracting the Rat. She wasted no time, squeezing off one round to the forehead and another to the chest. Pepino followed, with shots to the stomach and groin. The Rat fell, and the siblings pounced with multiple shots to his body. The Rat lay dying; his last thoughts were ironic. He had often wondered how his life would end. He knew he would not make it to old age. You live by the gun, you die by the gun, he thought. He had survived wars and the jungles of South East Asia, but now two spic kids finished him. He couldn't believe it.

It was over in seconds. They moved quickly, dragging his lifeless body inside the motel making sure he was dead. He was. They shut the door behind them. They worked quickly. Both of them had assigned duties. This was the critical part of the job. They found his suitcase and placed the package inside. They didn't know what was inside, nor did they care. Pepino took another package out of his pocket and removed it from the plastic baggy. It was a Beretta exactly like the one he and Mariela used. He squeezed the Rat's fingers around the gun making sure the Rat's fingerprints were firmly on it. He placed the gun in the Rat's suitcase along with the gun from the Rat's hand.

They stepped over his lifeless body as if it were a piece of trash. Pepino took a quick glance under the bed and saw the shiny case glistening in the light. He opened it quickly, seeing the neatly bundled bills. It was more money than either of them had ever seen. He closed it quickly, talking rapidly in Spanish.

"Que bueno suerte." They took one last look around, closed the door, and left the motel. They walked back down Gratiot toward the bus stop, exhilarated and giddy. They laughed and joked in Spanish as they waited for the bus. No one would imagine that these two carefree kids were deadly killers, especially not the Rat.

Chapter 42

THE CALL CAME IN ON HIS cell phone at eight forty nine a.m. Although it was expected, it was still surprising. He had been up early watching the morning news. They had discovered Stone's burned city vehicle but they had not made any identifications of the two bodies found inside. They would have to wait for the medical examiner to review dental records and notify next of kin before they could make a positive identification.

The reporter, in his early morning mix of excitement and titillation said, "The vehicle and the occupants were burned beyond recognition." JJ felt neither remorse nor sorrow. He watched as the authorities swarmed around the vehicle like locusts. He suspected that they knew it was Stone's vehicle but they were withholding the official announcement until they had more facts. He turned off the television and went in to check on Junior. He was still asleep. JJ showered and dressed. JJ knew that the next twenty-four to forty-eight hours would be the most important of his life. He looked up at the gray winter sky and could smell wood burning in fireplaces across the city. He knew he might have to answer for his actions. He also knew he would have to explain all of the facts that he had come to know about One Detroit, Inc., Stone, and the Rat. He might also have to explain about their sudden demise. It would have to be a persuasive argument.

As this ordeal was ending, he reflected on how it all started, innocently enough with Bobby Bennett. He was the key to everything: One Detroit, Inc. and their conspiracy; the murders and the fraud. His instincts had told him to walk away from Bobby, Victor, and Randy. But, greed and ego pulled him back in like an ocean tide, inviting yet dangerous. He hated living in fear, being shot at, and having his reputation disparaged by Victor and his henchmen. But, most of all, he hated that he had lost someone he loved. He didn't know whether the outcome of the events he had orchestrated could ever ease the pain of losing Katherine. But, what else was there to do but strike back at those who had taken so much from him. After all that had happened, he didn't want to forget his memory of Katherine.

He had arrived at this point because of One Detroit, Inc., and their evil actions. So many people had been hurt, so many needless murders, and for what? Greed.

He remembered something he had read as a child. It was a book about a child buyer. The essence of the book was that everyone had a price and could be influenced. It was not necessarily money. Nevertheless, everyone had a price. The only thing that remained was the negotiation of that price. Victor and Randy had their price as did Stone and the Rat. JJ had to admit that even he had a price. Only time would tell if the price he paid was worth it. For now, he was willing to pay, even if there were consequences.

As he exited the freeway and headed for home, he still needed a plan to pull everything together. He had done his part by putting everything in motion, arranging all of the pieces until everything fit together like a puzzle. But, like a puzzle, the pieces were not completely assembled. He had to tie everything together. He had to convince the authorities of all that had happened, without them believing that he was the architect. He was the only one with all of the facts.

By now, the district attorney and the US attorney for the Michigan District had received the brief he drafted detailing the One Detroit, Inc. conspiracy. Stone and the Rat's escapades were well documented, including the deaths of Katherine, Eva, and Brianna. What he didn't have was confirmation by the various agencies that they agreed with his theories. Perhaps that would come shortly.

His cell phone rang. The caller ID displayed his home number.

"You finally woke up, I see." He said, needling his cousin for his late afternoon naps. He noticed that Junior was sleeping a lot longer and was not as energetic since the shooting. He would keep a close eye on him for a while. Perhaps he would invite Marsha over to provide some personal attention, he thought.

"JJ, you have some visitors. The unwanted kind. Federal Agents. They're making a lot of noise about wanting to talk to you. They're here for the long haul."

"Alright. Continue to entertain them and I'll be there shortly." JJ hung up the phone, thankful for his cousin and his advance warning. JJ quickly dialed Saul's number as he continued driving and circling the perimeter of his neighborhood. He was relieved when Saul's secretary put him through to Saul.

"Saul, the FBI is at my house waiting to question me," he said with a calmness he didn't feel. He wondered if he should tell Saul about the new developments of Stone and the Rat. He thought better of it, deciding to save those details.

"They must have received your brief on the One Detroit, Inc. crew. I suspect it made some very interesting reading. Particularly Stone's involvement. You know they've had it in for the Police Department for some time. This will give them some ammunition to get Congress' approval to take over the department. But, that's another issue. I'll be right over. Meet me at the Coney Island at Cadieux and Harper. We'll go in together. That way they will be less likely to question you at the house. I'll see you there in thirty minutes." Saul was gone.

JJ was left to contemplate whether he needed to share all of the details with Saul. He could make a case for either. Normally, it was prudent to share all of the information with your attorney. Arguably, it allowed the attorney to make informed decisions on the client's behalf. The danger was that if the attorney knew damaging information, it might compromise their representation. JJ didn't think that would be a problem with Saul. But, he wasn't ready to divulge all of the complex issues just yet. He needed to polish his presentation and he couldn't afford to have Saul judge him quite yet.

His life had come to this. He needed to create his most persuasive performance ever. He needed to have everyone believe his version of the facts
unchallenged. He could not afford too much scrutiny. That could mean that
an inquisitive prosecutor might ask too many questions for which there were
no perfect answers.

His life had descended to proving to authorities that Victor and One
Detroit, Inc. were responsible for all of the things that had happened – the
deaths, conspiracies, and fraud. This had become more than just revenge for
Katherine. He had been threatened and they attempted to kill him. Junior had
been shot. So much had happened in such a short period. He was rationalizing
his actions for the death of two men and the collateral death of Shonda Lewis.
He was questioning whether the ends justified the means. Was he justified in
the killings of Stone and the Rat merely because they were evil? He remembered his Sunday school lessons as a child, "Vengeance is mine saith the Lord."
Had he gone too far and invaded God's province? How would he be judged?
The reality was that for now it didn't matter. He only had to get through the
next few hours. It would not be easy, but he would do it. Then he would con-
centrate on rebuilding the rest of his life. Although he had to admit to himself,
he hadn't envisioned a life without Katherine.

He would never be able to fill the void that her death created. But, knowing
that the people responsible were being punished would be a start. He imagined
that there would be consequences when this was all over- the Corktown project and the fallout from that and its impact on the city. He wondered about the
homeowners who were swindled and displaced by One Detroit, Inc.'s fraud.
What would happen to them? He had more questions than answers.

He pulled down the street to the Coney Island restaurant and waited.
Saul would arrive shortly. The drive from his office would not take more than
twenty minutes. So, he waited. He would have to coordinate things just right,
and beyond that, he would have to have a great deal of luck. It was complicated, and he had to rely on the government's need to create a public image
that showed it was tough on crime. This would provide just such an opportunity. If it went wrong, he would have no one to blame but himself.

He had carefully planned everything, down to the possibility of the U.S. attorney going after One Detroit, Inc. There was just one variable he was not sure about – Kareem Abdul Boozer. JJ had never been good at trusting, not in personal relationships or in business. That's why he was a sole practitioner. He believed in relying on himself. With Kareem, he was risking that Kareem would honor the code that he based his life on-you didn't confess to the police; that you took confidences to the grave. JJ was relying on it. Beyond that, JJ would have to deliver a satisfactory solution for Kareem's legal problems. So much depended on others. He usually only relied on himself. He was deep in thought when he saw Saul's Cadillac Escalade pull up beside him. He could see a look of concern on Saul's face as he got out of the truck.

"This is quite a web you've woven. How do you want this to end?"

"I want to fly off into the sunset and live happily ever after."

"That's noble and even a bit romantic. But you've left a lot of carnage in your wake." JJ didn't like the tone or direction that Saul was taking. Saul's tone was more disapproving than JJ needed from his attorney.

"Saul, you are assuming that these circumstances are my creation. I did what I thought needed to be done. If you recall, the people involved pulled me into this mess. I was happily getting on with my life when they contacted me. Look, if you have second thoughts about being here, I respect that. I assure you it won't affect our friendship." JJ could feel his anger rising. Although he and Saul were close, JJ wouldn't allow Saul's doubt to derail his plan. He would go it alone if necessary. The plan was already in motion, and he could finish it alone.

"Aren't we self-righteous. That's precisely the reason you do need me. Your anger doesn't bother me; I think you know me better than that. What bothers me is that we don't have better control of the situation. I prefer to control these meetings as much as we can. I don't like having to react to the government. It places us at a greater disadvantage. Their strategy is to frighten and intimidate, and what better way than to have you arrested by the FBI. Let me call the US attorney and take you down to their offices on our terms."

"That would be a great plan in normal circumstances Saul, but I don't have that luxury right now. This needs to happen now. There are a lot of moving parts to this that have to connect right now. So if this is how they want to make it happen, I need to accommodate their schedule." JJ stared at his old friend and mentor but did not say what he was thinking. Discretion, he thought, would save a friendship. So, he left the words unsaid.

"It's true that attorneys make the worst clients. They never take your advice. They always think they know best. In this case, I'm going to trust your judgment. But if I see things going sideways, I'm intervening and taking charge." Saul was resolute in his position.

They stared for a long moment and felt the mutual respect that they had for each other. There was no one else that JJ would trust in this situation but Saul. But, he still had to do it his way.

They left the restaurant, with Saul following the two blocks to JJ's home. They could see the unmarked government cars in the driveway and in front of the house. As they approached, Junior opened the door with a look of frustration and anger on his face. "The feds have been here waiting like vultures. I told them it's just a waste of government funding. Why did they have to send so many agents, what are they afraid of?"

"Relax, Junior. Everything is under control. As you can see, I have my attorney with me. So everything will be alright." Junior nodded his head in Saul's direction.

The agents were seated in various rooms. Some lounged comfortably on the couch in the living room and others were seated at the dining room table. There were six agents in all, and all had that serious federal government look. The look said, although I'm a paid civil servant, I'm an important one, and I have the right to take away your freedom.

"Mr. Battle, I'm federal agent Hall and I've been instructed by the US attorney to bring you down to his office for questioning. You are not under arrest. The US Attorney would consider it a personal favor if you would accompany me. I see you have your attorney, Mr. Mendoza, with you. That's fine. If you want to follow us down to the office, that's not a problem."

"Agent Hall, just for argument sake, what would happen if I declined your invitation to accompany you to see the US attorney? JJ asked with mock seriousness.

"I would have to let you speak to US Attorney Grimsley in that case."

" That won't be necessary. We'll just follow you down to the office."

The drive down to the Federal Building was uneventful. Saul went over some basic procedures for handling the meeting. But, for the most part, they were both deep in thought. As they approached the Federal Building, JJ could see the imposing structure. The Federal Building was designed to intimidate and displayed the immense power of the federal government. They followed the agents underneath a special entrance designated for federal personnel. They got out of the cars and silently followed the agents to the elevators.

They took the elevator to the twenty-fifth floor, Office of the US Attorney, Stu Grimsley. Stu Grimsley, known as the "Grim Reaper" in criminal defense circles, was a career prosecutor who always sought the maximum penalties. He didn't believe in plea bargains and was a tough adversary in trial. Since his appointment to US attorney, there were rumblings that soon he would make a run for governor or the US senate. He had become more political, personally prosecuting large high-profile cases himself. He took great delight in huge forfeiture and corruption cases where ill-gotten proceeds were confiscated from the bad guys. He frequently posed for television cameras and media, with bags of money and drugs confiscated from criminals. The conviction rate for his department had never been higher. Powerful people in Washington were starting to take notice. It was only a matter of time. He was aggressively prosecuting terrorists much to the delight of Washington. All of this made JJ believe he would have great interest in the dealings of One Detroit, Inc.

The offices of the US Attorney for the District of Michigan were nice but not overly ostentatious. It was in keeping with the public image of Stu Grimsley. Everything was politically correct, from the composition of his staff, to the décor of the office. He left nothing to chance; every detail was micro-managed down to the office stationary. JJ and Stu had crossed paths many times when Stu was a state prosecutor. JJ remembered his passion and determination. He was a formidable opponent. Back then, his passion and emotion sometimes got the better of him and obscured his judgment. If he lost, it was not for lack of effort; he was always extremely well prepared. The problem with Stu was that his ambition sometimes blinded him. JJ hoped that was the case now. All he needed to do he reminded himself, was to tell the story. Truth was his defense, and that was all he needed.

Stu greeted Saul first and they shook hands. Next, he greeted JJ and ushered them into a conference room. He introduced them to the other people in the room many of whom they already knew. There was the assortment of federal agents and assistant US attorneys and what appeared to be court reporters and secretaries. Included in the group sitting apart from the others was Dan Stevens, Chief Deputy Assistant DA from the Wayne County Prosecutor's Office.

It was meant to be an intimidating collection of the government's finest, all assembled in an effort to achieve justice. For the inexperienced, it might be intimidating, but for JJ, he knew what to expect. He was used to crowds and hostile environments. You usually represented unpopular people and causes. Today, he had the opportunity to right a wrong. If they could ever be made right again, after all you couldn't bring Katherine back, or Eva or Brianna. But, to know that Victor, Randy, and the rest of One Detroit, Inc. would pay for their transgressions would have to be enough.

JJ took a deep breath and prepared himself for what was to come. He would be grilled, prodded, questioned, and challenged, and when it was all over, Stu would make a decision. There would be consequences and people would be held accountable. This was the easy part, he thought. He had already done the hard work. This was like the closing argument at the end of a trial. All that remained was to provide the missing details that would complete the picture. It would not take much since Stu was a receptive audience. He just needed facts to complete the picture. Fortunately, for JJ, he knew what to expect. He would not be intimidated. He merely had to tell his story.

He started at the beginning, with Victor and Randy approaching him at the golf club. He spoke in calm, measured tones, unaware of the other people in the room. He was telling the facts as he remembered them. It was easier telling the truth than remembering a lie. Occasionally as he told the story, Stu or one of his assistants would ask a question and JJ would respond matter of factly.

He told them of Victor and Randy's payment of the retainer and his subsequent representation of Bobby Bennett. He told of how he received the retainer. He spared no details. He could feel himself reliving the events and the circumstances.

The most painful aspect of his story was Katherine's death, which they asked him about in excruciating detail. He told them everything.

"I was planning to propose to her that night," he explained. "I had purchased the ring and we had made reservations for dinner that night. Katherine and her assistant, Lindsay Cross, were the first to uncover the fraudulent deed transfers by One Detroit, Inc. We discussed the transactions but had not concluded anything at that point. She had gone to the hairdresser and had some other errands to run before we were to meet at the condo. I couldn't reach her by phone, so I just went over there. I had my own key so I just let myself in." JJ paused, gathering his thoughts; he could hear the silence in the room. Even Saul was transfixed as JJ spoke. The court reporter silently typed away, recording his every word. He was surprised at how easily the words came. He had lived through this but he had never told anyone all of the details.

"The doorman told me she was upstairs and I took the elevator to her penthouse." He said, again reliving the tragic moments. "I opened the door and went to the bedroom, and saw her lying there, lifeless. As I rushed over to see about her, I was knocked unconscious from a blow to the head. I was only out for a short period, perhaps ten minutes before I awoke and called the police." JJ recalled the facts as if they happened yesterday.

"Did you know at the time who was responsible?" Stu asked.

"No I didn't. A few days before that, someone shot at me in the Griswold parking garage. I didn't connect the two events at the time. I made a report to the DPD, to Lieutenant Stone, but that went nowhere." JJ said the words knowing that they were damaging to Stone. It was Stone who was at the center of the murder and conspiracy, and JJ was determined that Stone's legacy would reflect his deeds.

JJ continued his story, touching on the events surrounding Bobby Bennett's trial, and Eva's dismissal of the case. He wondered about telling Stu of Eva's involvement in One Detroit, Inc. and her possible tampering with the trial. He remembered that they had already investigated her murder and would try to implicate her in the conspiracy. He didn't think it would make a difference, but he would try to clear her name anyway. It wouldn't make a difference in the outcome. It was the least he could do for someone who had a distinguished career that might be tarnished by a single lapse in judgment.

"I talked candidly with Judge Moody prior to her death about One Detroit, Inc. and I don't believe she knew all of the details of their dealings. I'd known Eva for years, and I genuinely believe that she thought they were operating a legitimate enterprise. She would never have risked her career and reputation for money" He said these words more passionately than he believed. It was up to Stu to sort it all out. Eva was gone as was her family; all that remained was protecting her reputation. Stu was more interested in living defendants and JJ hoped he would have respect for the dead. Victor, Randy, and Rahsheed provided enough fodder to satisfy Stu's voracious need for blame notoriety. He had previously provided Stu with his detailed brief about the fraudulent dealings of One Detroit, Inc. He knew that Stu had probably memorized every word.

He had been talking for over two hours without a break and he needed to talk to Saul. So, he suggested to Stu that they take a short break. He got up and motioned for Saul to follow him. They grabbed their coats and headed outside. Neither Saul nor JJ trusted the Federal Building as a place for secure communication. It was part of the criminal defense mentality and was something you couldn't escape. As they arrived outside, neither spoke for a long time. Finally, JJ broke the silence.

"Saul, I've known you since I became an attorney. You were my mentor and I value your friendship and counsel. As you know this has been very difficult for me, losing Katherine and then Eva. I didn't share many of the details of what was going on for a number of reasons; first, I didn't know all of the facts myself; second, it seemed that everyone close to me was winding up dead. I didn't know who to trust. I'm telling you this as my friend and my attorney, there are some things that have happened that have changed me forever. I've done some things that I am not proud of, and I have caused things to happen that only God can forgive. I must deal with that later." He knew the danger of what he was about to say, but he also knew that Saul was the only person that could tell him what he needed to do. He was the only person he could trust, who had both the knowledge to advise him, and the love to protect his best interests, he hoped. He took a deep breath and chose his words carefully.

"Here is the point I need to make; I have information that conclusively proves the One Detroit, Inc. conspiracy beyond what I've shared with Stu. But, if I disclose this information, I could implicate myself in a crime. The risk, however, of not disclosing this information is that I may not have sufficiently convinced Stu of enough of One Detroit, Inc.'s evil deeds for an indictment. They may not arrive at this information on their own in a timely fashion. What should I do?" He asked.

"JJ, I understand your dilemma, and the risks you have taken. I believe you have sufficiently given Stu what he needs to do his job. Your job is not to solve the crime for them, but to help facilitate its solving. I must ask you a question. Is there any other possible means that the evidence would be discovered?"

"Yes. In fact, it is a certainty. The only issue is when."

"You have answered your own question. Let the events proceed naturally. Leave the authorities to their own resources. If you disclose how you came about this information, it may further incriminate you. If you don't tell me, I can never be subpoenaed to testify against you." Saul was giving his best lawyerly advice. JJ already knew he couldn't and shouldn't divulge all of the things that had recently happened, but confession was good for the soul or so they said.

"There is one other matter that I need your help with. It's going to require some creative lawyering and the assistance of the county prosecutor." He waited for Saul's response. Although he had not revealed to Saul the nature of all that had happened, it would be easy for him to figure everything out from his next statement. JJ had no other choice. It was the final piece of the puzzle. It would allow him to walk away for the last time, relatively unscathed. But, it would not be easy. The demons would haunt him forever.

"I can only imagine what it might be. It's not like you to be so clandestine."

"It's the nature of a criminal defense attorney; you can never be too sure. Things could get complicated from here."

"I guess you're right." Saul said, for the first time looking weary and concerned. "What is it you want me to do?"

"I need you to use all of your skill and influence to convince Stu to accept a deal I need to propose. It's unconventional and risky, but something I need to make happen. You can say no, at which point, I'll pitch the deal myself. There won't be any hard feelings."

"I can't wait to hear what the deal is, I'm intrigued." JJ could see that Saul was questioning himself on just how far he would go. He was willing to help a friend, but he was unsure where this would take him.

"As you know, I represented Kareem Boozer on his previous murder case."

"Yes, and you successfully defended him as you usually do. But how does that tie into what's going on in this case?" Saul asked, searching for a link.

"Shortly after Kareem's acquittal, the prosecuting witness and his family were murdered. They arrested and charged Kareem. The police are alleging that Kareem and his organization are responsible."

"Yes, but I'm still waiting on the connection."

"Well, my theory of the case is that Kareem is not responsible, nor is his organization. I believe it was Stone and his mercenary that were responsible. I'm not certain of their motives, but this looks like their handiwork. It could have been payback for Kareem's acquittal, or some other sinister motive. They may have been attempting to implicate Kareem in the second murder. We just don't know."

"You want me to sell this to Stu, is that what you're asking? If it is, it's extremely weak." Saul seemed unconvinced.

"It's going to be easier than you think. Stu isn't interested in murderers, he's after bigger fish. Besides, this gives him more leverage to promote his law and order platform. You know the spiel; corrupt cops and shady lawyers; that will play very big in Washington. It will help further his career. He doesn't care who pays; all that matters is that it makes big headlines. We give him that. I want Kareem to walk out of jail a free man. I believe that you will see a changed man in the future."

"Why are you doing this for Kareem?" Saul asked, already suspecting that he knew the answer. "He doesn't deserve it. You realize don't you, that once you go down this road, there is no turning back. You can't put the genie back into the bottle."

"I know that. I'm not doing this for Kareem. He's only part of the puzzle. There are a number of reasons. What I realize from all of this is that nothing will ever be the same. We will never be the same. Everything is constantly changing, and we have to change with it whether we like it or not. We don't control change; we can only control the degree to which we change as individuals. I'm tired of being a helpless victim, continually reacting to my environment; I'm going to initiate the change myself, on my terms." JJ was surprised at the passion of his response.

"That sounds very philosophical and intellectual, but are you creating change or creating chaos? Be careful JJ, that you are certain of your motives, and that you are clear where you want all of this to end."

"That's the one thing I am clear about. I know where I want this all to end- on a Caribbean Golf course at some plush resort. I just want to restore some normalcy to my life again. That's all. I don't want to have to look over my shoulder and wonder if someone means me harm. I just want to be able to trust people again." He said.

"I hope it's that simple, my friend. In any event, I can help you." Saul smiled as he watched his friend sigh with relief. JJ was correct; Stu was a sucker for a good conspiracy; the more complex the conspiracy, the better. JJ had provided him with the nexus of a good theory. He would now weave it into something that both Stu and the county prosecutor could accept. He would not make a value judgment about JJ's actions or motives; that was not his job. He would do what he had always done- be a persuasive and powerful advocate for his client.

As they entered the room, Saul Mendoza stood and adjusted his tie. It was now his turn to tie up any loose ends and to complete the conspiracy between Stone and the Rat. He knew that in the coming days, there would be questions, but he was certain that he could provide the answers for JJ. He had to admit that it was brazen and risky, but JJ had pulled it off. Katherine's killers were identified, as well as Eva's and Brianna's. They would soon indict Victor, Randy, and the other members of One Detroit, Inc. Kareem Boozer would walk out of jail a free man. JJ would be a million dollars richer. Stu Grimsley would have a platform to run for US senator or governor, or whatever else he aspired. It could not have ended better for JJ. Although he had lost someone dear to him in Katherine, he gained something precious in return, **CONTROL.**

Saul knew it would not be easy for JJ going forward, but he was confident he would survive.

Epilogue

THE FLIGHT ATTENDANT WAS CALLING FOR the first class passengers to board the plane. He had his carry-on bag in one hand and a copy of the Detroit Free Press in the other. He had avoided reading the front page of the paper although the headlines screamed back at him. "Prominent attorneys have been indicted," it displayed in bold headlines. But, he ignored the headlines because he wanted to savor every bit of the juicy news at thirty thousand feet. Besides, he wanted to know that there was no turning back.

This was his escape. He had chosen the Caribbean Island of Nevis, because of its beauty and obscurity. He wanted to get away to a place where he could be anonymous. Nevis, sister island to St. Kitts, was known for its perfect weather, white sand beaches, luxury accommodations and excellent golf. It had everything he could want. He booked his stay for one month, but he would extend it for longer if necessary. He was prepared to leave his old life behind. He would eventually take the time to plan his future, but right now, he just needed to unwind and decompress. He had many things he needed to forget, and Nevis would help him do that.

He settled in his seat in first class, a luxury he had earned. Although he had the benefit of Katherine's generous life insurance policy, he did not consider himself rich. The money would not change him, he vowed. On this trip he would golf, over eat, and relax by the pool and the ocean as therapy. It would help him heal his wounds. He hoped that he would not be seated next to some talkative passenger who wanted to share their life story. He was rewarded as the flight attendants closed the cabin doors and prepared the plane for takeoff. The seat next to him remained empty. It was a good sign.

As the plane taxied down the runway, he pulled out the sports section and began reading the paper. He was not quite ready for the hard news just yet. Somewhere over the southern United States at thirty thousand feet, he pulled out the front page of the Detroit Free Press and read about what he already knew. Victor, Randy and the rest of One Detroit, Inc. were going down hard. Stu, the Grim Reaper, was not just throwing the book at them; he was throwing the whole library. In addition to the fraud and conspiracy charges, there were the nasty murder charges as well.

It was a scandal of immense proportion and everyone in the city had an opinion. In addition, the national media was also feasting on the juicy details of the scandal. Stone and the Rat were linked to the killings and the conspiracy allegations. Victor, Randy, and Rahsheed, the only surviving members of One Detroit, Inc., were then linked to Stone and the Rat's murder. How convenient, he thought. It had all come together just as he planned. There was also the mention that Stone and the Rat were linked to other murders in the city, including the family who had testified in the highly publicized Kareem Boozer trial. This was priceless. Saul had worked his magic. Stu had bought the whole story, as JJ knew he would. For an ambitious civil servant, this case was too good to pass up. It was a slam-dunk and JJ Battle delivered the lob pass. Katherine would be proud he thought.

Stu would probably be in the senate or the attorney general before this case ever went to trial. It was a career defining case, and JJ had wrapped it up and placed it in his lap. He was feeling the euphoria of his good fortune and rang the bell for the flight attendant for an early afternoon cocktail. There was nothing like a drink to celebrate good news. He could feel the stress and the pressure of the last few weeks slowly easing away. He had no plans for the future and that suited him just fine. The past was in the past. He had tied up all of the loose ends back home and at the office. He gave Marsha two months off with pay and a healthy bonus. Junior was house sitting and he too, had a hefty bonus to help him recover from his wounds. He was allowing himself to relax and could almost feel the warmth of the Caribbean. Life was good. But, could he really trust it? He would have to start over, and starting over meant dealing with the uncertainty of the future.

He was jolted out of his daydream by the sweet smell of roses and the southern drawl of an angel. The words were so simple, yet he felt electricity. "Here you are, Mr. Battle," she said. The words were like magic. They floated from her lips to his heart. He knew at that moment that he didn't want her to stop speaking. He wanted to know her. He knew it was silly. Yet, the feeling was there anyway. There is a moment, perhaps a split second, when your life changes. It could be a subtle change or a defining moment. Sometimes fate and God intervene on your behalf, and all you have to do is recognize it. It could be a word, a glance, a touch, or something as simple as the sound of a voice. This moment happened to JJ. However, like all great moments, you have to act upon them or lose them forever. He didn't want to lose this moment. He was sure of that. There was he felt, some connection, as their eyes met and locked and she smiled the obligatory smile of the service professional, or so he thought. "Thank you," he said, feeling as if the moment might be lost forever.

"What is the matter with you?" He chided himself, feeling like a shy schoolboy when the prettiest girl in class notices you. He didn't know if it was his loneliness or his need that was making him feel this way. He couldn't determine if he was simply overreacting or imagining this moment of chemistry. Was it karma or insanity? Whatever there was between them, real or imagined, JJ decided to ignore it. Perhaps it wasn't worth the risk, he had lost so much already. He wasn't emotionally prepared to take a risk.

I'm losing it, he thought, settling in his first class seat as he sipped on his whiskey and water. I've been out of the dating scene too long he reasoned, feeling the calming effects of the alcohol. He went back to his newspaper, but the thoughts of the flight attendant did not stop. It felt as if he had received a subliminal message that he could not ignore.

He found himself watching her as she went about her duties, watching as she interacted with other passengers, watching her to see if he were imagining things. *STOP IT, you stalker,* a voice in his head yelled. *Leave that woman alone. She was just doing her job. Being nice to passengers is part of the job description. It is not an invitation or a come on.* Wow, he had been without companionship for too long, and he was starting to lose it. The fantasy was taking shape in spite of his better judgment. But, he had to admit, the creamy skin, and the rustle of her dress as she walked down the aisles moved him. He watched those legs, shapely and well defined, in a slow and unhurried step. Her hair was neatly pulled back and bouncing playfully as she walked. He was transfixed. He knew he was on the brink of doing something stupid. He hoped there was no air marshal on the plane watching him. Surely, he would be arrested and taken into custody as soon as the plane landed. He was sure that stalking a flight attendant was a federal offense. But, he couldn't help himself. He tried to appear nonchalant and conceal his interest. She was gorgeous, in an unpretentious and natural way. It was like money. Either you had it or you didn't. If you had it, you didn't need to flaunt it. She didn't need to flaunt it. His mind was racing with all of the possibilities and permutations. What should he do next?

He was imagining a romantic dinner in Nevis, followed by a walk on the beach, when he was jolted back to reality. There it was staring him right in the face. He knew it was too good to be true. The wedding ring. He didn't know how he didn't see it before. It was displayed on her left hand like a small trophy. It was gleaming and gold, a tasteful yet powerful testament to the world of her unavailability. How naïve and immature. He couldn't believe he had given in to a schoolboy crush. Well, at least there was no public humiliation, only his pride had been damaged. He went back to his newspaper, determined to just enjoy himself and experience what Nevis had to offer.

But, fate would not leave him alone, tempting him at her every move. "Here she was again, Little Miss Married flight attendant, coming over to serve him again," he thought sarcastically.

"Can I get you anything else, Mr. Battle," she asked, in that syrupy-sweet southern voice. He wanted to resist and even attempted to reply with coolness that he didn't feel. "No thank you," was what he said, betrayed by an uncooperative heart. "I'm fine." The words came tumbling out along with his most charming smile. He couldn't believe himself. He was not a flirt, and especially not with married women. They were totally off limits.

"Maybe it wasn't flirting, maybe it was just his need for a woman's company." He told himself. Whatever his motives, he waited, holding his breath, unsure of exactly what he was waiting for. The seconds passed as she observed him with what appeared to be amusement. Then she spoke.

"I see you're traveling alone. Would you mind…," she asked. The pause lasted for what seemed liked minutes. He could not imagine what she would say next…

"If I join you? I get a short break in a few minutes and I would love to get off my feet. Meet me at the galley in five minutes. Is that Okay?"

"Of course," he mumbled, shocked at his good fortune. He didn't know what would happen next, but he was excited about the possibilities. Maybe his fortunes were changing. There was, he thought, nothing like a beautiful woman to make you forget your problems. He forced himself to relax as he waited, feeling like an adolescent getting ready for his first date. It was just a conversation; he reminded himself. "Don't get ahead of yourself." He thought of Katherine and a pang of guilt entered his brain, sobering him. He saw the flight attendant pass by and thought, he didn't even know her name. So what. She knew his, wasn't that enough? He waited for her to summon him. He busied himself by studying the newspaper, but it was all an act. He was really studying her. It wasn't long before she summoned him. It was subtle, two seductive fingers and the nod of her angelic head. It had him out of his seat and heading to the galley. He searched for his lawyer cool and bravado and found it halfway to the galley. Stomach tucked in and serious, yet sincere expression on his face. It was his jury demeanor, which said, I am in control but I'm also a very nice person. He hoped it worked.

She motioned for him to sit down in the galley seat across from her and he quickly obliged.

"Hi, I'm Grace Courville," she said, extending a soft manicured hand. It was warm and electric with possibilities. "I'm not usually this formal or this forward, but you seem like such an interesting person. I just wanted to meet you and talk to you."

"I'm glad you did. For the record, I'm JJ Battle. Pleased to meet you."

"So tell me, why is an attractive man like yourself, traveling to an exotic, romantic place like Nevis, by yourself?" JJ could feel himself blush under the scrutiny of her directness. She laughed, seeing his obvious discomfort.

"That's a great question. To be honest, I just needed to get away for some rest and relaxation. Besides, Detroit winters can be long and brutal. What about you? Although this is work, is your husband joining you for a mini vacation?" JJ couldn't resist. Although he knew the answer might crush him, he had to hear it anyway.

"I'm not married," she said, responding with a knowing nod. "You mean the wedding ring," she said, holding up the offending hand. "I wear this to keep the wolves at bay. You have no idea. Many men think flight attendant really means something else. The ring discourages most advances."

"Well, it worked." JJ breathed an encouraging sigh of relief. "By the way, where is that accent from? It's definitely Southern, but from there I don't have a clue."

"New Orleans, Louisiana. That's where I'm from. I'm just a country girl at heart. I'm living in Atlanta now since that's Delta's hub. What about you?"

"I'm a city boy. Born and raised in Detroit. Lived there all my life. I'm an east sider. There's sort of a badge of courage being from the east side." He was pleased that she was so easy to talk to. The ease of their conversation made him feel as if they had known each other forever. He was disappointed when her break was over and it was time for her to go back to work.

"By the way, what does JJ stand for?" She asked with a mischievous grin.

"Joshua Jericho," he said unashamedly. My mother was a Bible-toting Baptist."

"Well, it suits you. When the plane lands, don't get off, I want to talk with you some more. Unless you have to." He could hear the apology in her tone.

"I'd be delighted to wait. Besides, I have a few probing questions I need to ask you as well," he said, not bothering to conceal the smile. It was, he thought, an enjoyable conversation and an auspicious beginning. Besides, what did he have to lose? He was going to be here for a month, and Grace was a great way to kick off a vacation.

The rest of the flight was uneventful. Grace made sure that she kept his drink refilled and that he had an adequate supply of snacks. Whenever she passed, she managed to make some funny comment about a passenger or another crewmember. He already appreciated the subtlety of her humor. He looked forward to getting to know her better.

The plane landed and the other passengers were scurrying for the exits, anxious to partake of the fabulous Caribbean weather. JJ waited and watched as Grace said goodbye to the departing passengers. Finally, they had all left the plane and she came over and plopped down in the seat next to him.

"So where are you staying while you're here?" She asked nonchalantly. He felt that her directness was refreshing. He hated the coy little games that men and women usually engage in.

"The Four Seasons Resort, I think. I can check my itinerary for sure. But that sounds right," he said.

"Very impressive. Most people generally stay at the Carlyle. Well, great. The crew is staying at the Four Seasons as well. You can hitch a ride over with the crew. Unless, you have other arrangements. It will be fun. I'm sure there will be some good-natured ribbing. But, who cares. This is Nevis."

"I'll get my luggage and meet you at ground transportation. Don't leave without me," he teased. "I need a tour guide to show me the sights." Grace had an energy and enthusiasm that was contagious. He couldn't help but get caught in her wake, he thought.

As he exited the plane, he was surprised by the smallness of the airport. It was quaint to say the least. He had gone ahead of Grace as she and the crew finished their post-flight duties. It didn't take long for him to get his luggage and his golf clubs. Frankly, he was always more concerned about his clubs than his luggage. He could replace his clothes, but a good set of clubs was irreplaceable. He gathered his gear and headed to ground transportation. Outside, he was almost overcome by the heat and humidity. He reminded himself that he had gone from zero degrees to ninety degrees, and his body would need some time to adjust. Besides, he was still carrying his jacket that he knew he would never need here. As he looked outside, he was in love with Nevis already. He could see the ocean in the distance, and felt the unmistakable warmth of the tropical breeze. He had taken out his sunglasses and was quickly decompressing and soaking in the rhythm of the island. He unbuttoned his shirt a couple of buttons and rolled up his sleeves. He smiled at the patois of the natives as they asked him if he needed a taxi. Every second that he stood there made him feel like this is where he belonged. He was going to enjoy every minute of his stay.

He turned in time to see Grace and the crew sauntering out of the airport sharing laughter and jokes. They were feeling the intoxication of Nevis as well. This had to be a coveted route for the airline crew. Grace hurried over and quickly made the introductions. JJ could feel the scrutiny of her crewmembers as he shook hands with them. "JJ is going to catch a ride with us to the Four Seasons," she said, not waiting for challenges. JJ didn't know whether his riding with the crew was a breach of protocol or not, but no one seemed to mind. They all piled in the van and were loud and boisterous on the ride to the resort. Grace and JJ sat in the back, and JJ felt the closeness as they squeezed in for the ride.

JJ waited for the obligatory questions and he wasn't disappointed. "So, JJ, what do you do for a living back in the states," the captain asked in an official tone. "You don't have to answer," Grace chimed in, coming to his defense.

"I don't mind at all," JJ said good-naturedly. " I'm with the FAA," he said in a serious tone, waiting for a response. The van suddenly grew quiet, waiting for what might come next. "Really, I'm just kidding," he said. I'm an attorney, but I once thought about working for the FAA."

"Great," one of the crew members responded, because I violated about ten rules on that flight." The crew all broke out in hearty laughter. He saw Grace out of the corner of his eye watching him with a pleased and approving look. This led to a whole series of lawyer jokes and legal questions that lasted until they arrived at the resort. The laughter and the camaraderie was so good that they agreed to meet for dinner and drinks later that evening. As they unloaded the van and got their luggage, he managed to pull Grace aside. "How about meeting me for lunch when you get settled?" He asked.

"I thought you'd never ask. Just give me a couple of minutes to check in and to freshen up and shower and I'll meet you in the lobby." She said this with warmth that held promise.

He settled into his suite and quickly showered and searched for something to wear. His wardrobe was limited, since tropical clothing was not a seasonal item in Detroit in November. It was just lunch, he reminded himself. But, he was at a crossroads. He dressed, and headed to the lobby. While he waited, he talked to the concierge about setting a tee time for tomorrow. As he waited, he spotted Grace stepping off the elevator. Her airline uniform did not do her justice. She was gorgeous. She was wearing a simple flowered sundress that fit her to perfection. Her long hair hung down her back and with sunglasses on, she was a vision. JJ had to make sure that he didn't have some stupid look on his face, which said, I'm way out of my league. Instead, he sauntered over with all of the cool he could muster. Music was playing softly in the lobby. When he got there, he did something so unexpected, that it surprised them both. He hugged her and whispered softly in her ear.

"I have been waiting for you," he whispered.

"I'm sorry I took so long," she replied apologetically, while still in his embrace.

"I'm not finished," he said. "**FOR A LIFETIME.**"

In that moment, Joshua Jericho Battle knew that his battle was over. He knew he had conquered all of his demons of the past. He knew that he was where he was meant to be. With the woman he was meant to share his life with. She, too, felt the power of the moment and gave in to the moment as well. "I am here to fight all of your battles with you," she said. In their embrace, they felt the power of God's perfect match.